Elizabeth Fytton Gawsworth

C000121558

Revised Edition
Incorporating The Master of Littlecote Manor

LIZ HOWARD

When Elizabeth Fytton fell in love with her cousin William she could have had little idea what the Fates had in store for them both. At the age of fourteen, her unswerving passion brought her into disgrace and after the birth of her daughter she was banished from the family home, Gawsworth Hall. Although incarcerated in a Convent at Chester and whilst William enjoyed all the pleasures of the Court of King Henry, Elizabeth's faith in him never wavered. She had her own beliefs, and her own Gods, and with their help she knew that she would one day be by his side in London Town. Sadly, her trust was largely based on the ignorance of youth and when William did ask her to join him, he had no intention of marrying her. Through his influence she became a maid to the young Anne Boleyn only to find herself caught up in the tragic affair of the King's second marriage. Tragic for Elizabeth Fytton because her cousin, her lover, was William Brereton.

Also by the same author:
The Squire of Holdenby
Isabel the Girl
Isabel the Woman

(Cover from a tapestry by Gillian Sayers-Howard)

Elizabeth Fytton
of Gawsworth Hall

Revised Edition
Incorporating The Master of Littlecote Manor

First published by Robert Hale, London, 1985.
Reprinted 1986, First Paperback edition 1991

ISBN
978-0-949001-64-1

C.C.PUBLISHING, MARTINS LANE,
HARGRAVE, CHESTER, CH3 7RX
TEL: 01829 741651. EMAIL: editor@cc-publishing.co.uk
WEBSITE: http://www.cc-publishing.co.uk

Dedicated to the memory of
My Mother
Elizabeth Fitton
1922 – 1973

Introduction

Liz Howard had a dream. Not a nightmare. Not even a recurring dream. Just a dream.

She was standing outside an ancient manor house, looking in through closed iron gates at an upper window. A girl stared out at her. Who was she?

Liz was in two places at the same time. She was looking at the girl, but at the same time she was that girl, looking down at herself beside the gate. Outside the house, people dressed in Tudor costume were strolling about in the spring sunshine. She was in another place in another time. Then the dream ended.

Almost one year later Liz and her family accepted an invitation to visit friends living in Southampton. Driving down from Cheshire on the Easter weekend, and, seeing a sign for a tourist venue they stopped for refreshment. The driveway eventually took them past an old manor house, and set in the estate wall were closed iron gates. It was the house of the dream! But the window where the girl had been was not there. Something was different, but even so Liz was shaken and told the family that she had seen the house before. In a dream.

Making their way to the café they discussed the coincidence of a dream that had apparently come true. Almost. The window where the girl had been looking out wasn't there, but Liz became convinced that something terrible had happened in the missing room. Something that terrified her.

Out of curiosity the family decided to join a conducted tour of the house, expecting to find that there was no substance to Liz's strange reaction to the place.

Approaching the Manor from the café Liz was amazed to see a crowd of people dressed in Tudor costume strolling about the lawn, just as in the dream. It was uncanny, and very disturbing. How could a dream become reality?

The tour eventually took them to the first floor, through a private chapel and onto a square landing containing a huge fireplace with a door each side leading to two rooms.

Liz panicked. This was the room! Something dreadful had happened here. She had a sensation of a storm outside. Heavy rain on the windows. Yet in reality the sun was still shining. She was almost overcome with fear, yet if this was the room where the girl had been in the dream, why couldn't it be seen from the gate?

Examining the plan of Littlecote Manor in the booklet they had bought they could see why. A later extension covered it from view but in Tudor times the window would certainly have been visible from the front of the house.

The tour guide, a lady, again dressed in Tudor costume, stood beside the fireplace.

"In 1575 something terrible happened in this house. A midwife was brought blindfold from a distant village, in the middle of the night with a great storm raging, to attend a woman about to give birth in that bedroom." She indicated the room on the right of the fireplace. "The woman was masked so that the midwife didn't know who she was. Nor did she know which house she was in. When the baby was born, a boy, the midwife carried it out to the master of the house, William Darrell. He took the child and threw it onto the fire where it burned to death. To this day, no one knows who the woman was, or why the child was so cruelly murdered."

Liz Howard could not believe what had happened. How could she have known about this house? Known of some horror in a room she felt she had been in centuries before?

This shouldn't happen to a down-to-earth mother of three teenage boys, working in Biological Research at ICI and not given to fanciful ideas. There had to be a sensible answer. Was it possible that others had experienced this kind of phenomenon?

Investigations led to Joe Keeton, a hypnotists working in, among other things, pain control clinics, and the relief of phobias. Could Liz have read about Littlecote, or seen a documentary? Perhaps someone had told her of the mysterious woman giving birth and the fate of the child.

Joe Keeton took Liz back, under hypnosis, in easy stages through her life hoping to uncover the moment when she first recognised the manor house. There was nothing. No memories at all.

"Can I regress you? Take you back to times before you were born?"

To Liz Howard, as a scientist, such an idea was ludicrous. There could be no memories when there was nothing to hold those memories. However, out of curiosity she agreed to be "regressed".

Two years of hypnosis saw Liz Howard ostensibly speaking through her alter ego Elizabeth Fytton. This eventually resulted in the book "Elizabeth Fytton of Gawsworth Hall" telling how the girl moved from Cheshire to the Court of King Henry VIII, and ultimately giving an explanation to the mystery surrounding the horrific murder at Littlecote Manor in Wiltshire in 1575.

Liz does not believe that this is proof of reincarnation, although the detail given under hypnosis was remarkable, but is it possible that memories can be inherited and passed down through the generations? There is much about the human brain yet to be uncovered.

Those who do believe in reincarnation will be interested to know that the family tree at Gawsworth Hall proves that ELIZABETH FYTTON was born to JOHN and Ellen Fytton in 1503, the year King Henry VIII's mother Elizabeth died.

Among her siblings were a brother EDWARD and a sister ELLEN.

Coincidentally, Liz Howard's maiden name was ELIZABETH FITTON.

Her father is JOHN FITTON, her brother is EDWARD FITTON and her sister is HELEN FITTON

Further research into details given under hypnosis revealed that all characters named had existed in that place and time with the exception of Megan ap Y.

One

INSIDE the squat little house with its unevenly tiled gables and flaking walls, the baby started to cry again. To the scrawny wraith of a girl, her dainty, piquant face swamped by a mass of auburn hair as she sat uncluttered as a peasant on the door-step, the nerve-jangling sound was irritating. It scratched away like dust trapped underneath an eyelid, too small and feeble a thing to grasp but a great source of annoyance until it had been jiggled into a more comfortable position. It wasn't a day for comforting wet and fractious infants. It was a day for running free, for talking to the summer breeze, for feeling the hot dust slip like silk between her toes and chewing the sweet, green juices from the meadow grass. Flitting from one patch of shade to the next, Elizabeth Fytton made good her escape. It only worked if you held your breath until you were out of sight. Sigh too soon and you would be caught. Cicely's spiteful voice would wind itself around your ankles and trip you, and then she would have to look after the baby.

She was nearly bursting with the effort by the time she reached the safety of the park, but it had worked! She knew it would. Cicely never caught her if she held her breath until she reached the park. The wide green eyes shone with exhilaration. To the river! A twisted tangle of uncombed curls spiralled carelessly down almost to her hips, which could already twitch and sway with the instinctive lure of the female animal, although nothing was further from her mind. Her senses had not yet been aroused by the fascinating scent of the male. It was all to come. Unless of course you counted her cousin William. Sometimes, like today, Elizabeth thought about William. He was different. Remember the occasion when she visited Malpas?

Will Brereton had been the only one to bother with her. His brothers were too old to even notice a little girl. But Will had taken her by the hand

7

and guided her stealthily into the kitchen. Pulling her close behind the chimney wall and covering her mouth with his fingers they had waited for a chance to steal a new-baked tart. She'd been frightened of Matilda catching them, but somehow safe with Will holding her. And then later, when only the crumbs were left to show what they had been up to, her brother Edward and Will's younger brother Rian had found them. What a fuss they had made at being left out of the feast. When they set about Will, calling him a greedy pig, her big, strong cousin had only laughed and held them both off single-handed. That had all happened some time ago, while mother was birthing the latest baby, but she had a secret, and Elizabeth loved secrets. She had drawn a picture of Will. Well, two to be honest, but one was a much better likeness than the other. Sometimes things worked out better than others when she tried to draw them. It was hidden with her other special things. The stone with shiny bits in it; the silver tassel which had once adorned some great lady's gown, a four-leaf clover, pressed flat and a lucky golden-yellow feather which she found in Yates's Spinney.

Her eyelids, pale, almost translucent, drooped slowly in the heat of the afternoon. Only inches away from her feet the foaming currents of the Dane swirled by to unknown lands, places she could only dream about, peopled with princes and kings in velvets and pearls, where castles, not little houses, were the order of the day. Elizabeth closed out the mundane buildings of Congleton, with its bake house and mill, its weaving sheds and tumbledown church.

Somewhere, out there in the mysterious, unknown world, a world of fantasy and fun, was another way of life. One day she was going out to find it. But not today. Today she would go to visit Old Megan and sample the peas from her big, black iron cooking-pot. *They* could say what they liked. *They* could scold and frown at her all they wanted and warn her that children who went to see Megan were never heard of again. *They* could call Megan a witch if they had to, but Elizabeth would still visit her friend. The Fyttons were always suspicious of anything Welsh. That was the real reason she had been forbidden to cross the river into Dog Lane.

Megan ap Y was at home to visitors. Not so Dai, her great lumbering ox of a son. Gone out looking for straw, Elizabeth was told on enquiring after him. To make his dogs with. Dai, poor soul was a simpleton. Harmless, but not very clever or worldly. He spent most of his time making twists of straw into miniature models of animals. The pair would have been hard put to it to live on Dai's meagre earnings, but fortunately his mother had tricks up her sleeve. Herbs and cures and potions for every affliction were her business and she had perfected her uncanny skill to such an extent that the people of Congleton credited her with the ability to revive all but the dead. If ever there was illness, who was it they crept to see? Certainly not the physician who killed more than he cured and charged a fortune into the bargain. There was a Welsh remedy for everything! Absolutely everything!

Superstition kept Megan and Dai isolated from their neighbours. Wisdom from the mouths of the uneducated poor was unnatural, so for the most part the Welsh witch and her familiar were left in peace.

The respectable citizens of the town did not know what Elizabeth knew. Megan had taken a strong liking to the child and finding her to be intelligent and interested had taught her many of the simpler skills already, and with every visit now the lessons were becoming more intricate, the reasons more obscure. Not only the names of roots and herbs and berries were repeated rote, but other words, to be muttered over the brews and chanted into the night to add more potency to the mixtures. Strange foreign sounding words. Nerthu, Cryfder, Twyll and sometimes, at those very secret times which no one else was aware of. Marw, Llad.

Elizabeth learnt it all. Megan ap Y understood everything. Everything in the world, and Elizabeth wanted to be the same. Then she could show her brother Edward who had the more power. Then it would make no difference that she was only a girl. Megan was teaching her how it was done. Everything. Even the strongest magic of all, though that could only happen at special times of consummate hate. As it had once happened to Megan herself.

Elizabeth hadn't been sure what consummate hate was, being placid by nature and too young to have felt the passions of strong emotions, but Old Megan had explained. It was impossible to believe that this ancient crone had once been a pretty, dark-haired beauty of the valleys. Now she stayed inside these cracked mud walls, as mentally immersed in the mystic chants and words as she was physically immersed in the pungent atmosphere. How different it all was from the cosy little cottage beside the silvery sparkling waterfall. It had been heaven on earth for the young wife of that God-fearing man Dafydd. Until the night the brigands came.

Their oaths and blasphemies disturbed the awesome loneliness of the craggy Welsh mountains from east to west and north to south but on the night they discovered the cottage of Dafydd ap Y, snuggled into the hillside beside the stream, their steps were muffled by the autumn fogs and the crackle of the blazing logs in the hearth. The door had splintered like tinder beneath the onslaught and Megan had watched her husband's brave efforts to defend his family brushed aside as though he had the strength of a child. At the first hint of trouble, Megan had pushed her small son out of sight behind the wool-sacks in the corner and stood beside Dafydd to protect their few possessions. She had watched with horror as a huge hairy man, more beast than human being, had crashed her husband to the ground. His head had struck the hearth-stone with a sickening crack and his wife had been unable to tear her eyes away from the dark, sticky trickle of blood which ran like a small river across the uneven stones of the floor before forming a still, black pool beside his chair.

Bellowing with insane laughter the three vile creatures had turned their attention to the terrified young woman. It was obvious to anyone that she was heavy with child but men who murder simply for the pleasure of it will stop at nothing. An enormous hairy hand grasped the wool of her dress and in one sudden movement ripped it down from neck to thigh. Knocked to her knees by a massive blow, her brain seemed to rattle inside her head and her senses were revolted by the overpowering stench, evidence of previous corrupt excesses. They showed her no mercy, and neither, she thought afterwards, did God. Defiled by the callous brutes in every perversion they could think of her mind remained clear and her eyes fixed on the delicate pinkness of her husband's spilled brains. How long it went on for she had no way of knowing but it seemed like an eternity before they finally pounded her poor abused body into oblivion. Consciousness had not returned until the fierce contractions of her belly had dragged her back to face cruel reality. The child was coming, a month before its time. In the silence of the chill half-light, without help or comfort, Megan's daughter was born dead.

Digging the soft, mossy earth with her bare hands had rimed her nails black with earth, symbolic of her mourning, and there she laid her Dafydd to his final rest, his only daughter against his heart. Cold flesh against cold flesh. No prayers were said for the repose of their souls. There was no one to pray to. The ancient ways of her forefathers were the only ways and they would be adhered to from now on. Megan ap Y had felt no sorrow. Only consummate hate. She cursed those men into a hell so eternally damning that it defied description, every fibre of her being reaching out to seek and torment them no matter where they tried to hide. The total concentration of her mind was given over to revenge for hours and days at a time until she felt that she had succeeded in her aim. She knew that they were dead.

Turning her back on the past she had taken Dai by the hand and led him through the mountain passes into England. It was then, as they carefully trod a path beside a steep ravine, that she had witnessed the results of her mutterings. There they lay, at the bottom of a jagged crevice. All three of them. She had the power and Megan believed.

Their journey had ended at Congleton and there all the insults and brickbats of mistrust from the local population were less than pin-pricks to a woman who had to live forever with those indelible memories of degenerate lust. In his mind, Dai never grew past the age of four, firmly closing a door on those atrocities he had been forced to witness and refusing to enter the brutal world of adulthood.

Wrenched from the light to the dark side of religion Megan had studied her chosen way with all the fervour of a fanatic. As she grew older she also grew more determined that all the things she had discovered should not die with her, and her hopes centred around the waif-like figure of Elizabeth Fytton. The child had an aptitude for the work and was quick to learn.

'Beware the priests and their lies. They try to trap you into being good. For their sakes, not your own. They will tell you to give, for the sake of your soul, but they are the ones who take. They never give. Only take. God is not good. God only helps those who help themselves. So always help yourself, child, for if you don't, no one else will help you. Shun the Church and its hypocrisy. Shun the buildings and the people in them or they will take you and mould you like clay. They will make you into one of their living dead.'

The thought of being one of the living dead was not a prospect which conjured up an appetising picture in Elizabeth's mind. And Megan was right about the priests. They were either drunk, or much too sober, and they were always trying mightily to 'save your soul'. Besides, Megan's chants did at least have meaning. Megan had explained it all. Whereas with the priests' rantings, Elizabeth could not make out a single word. Cicely said it was Latin, whatever that was. Megan knew everything and Elizabeth decided that she didn't like the Church. Like Megan ap Y, she believed, and her greatest wish was to please her teacher by learning and understanding. For one who hated being indoors and who was already fully conversant with the wonders of the natural world it was no penance.

***

Gawsworth Church was packed to its doors with the well-wrapped bodies of the mourners, their steamy breath hovering before their faces in the cold air at each response. Some had come for the feasting, some for the spectacle, and some, Elizabeth supposed, had come out of respect for her grandfather. She shuddered, and not on account of the weather. The moment she had been dreading had come. The children went forward one at a time, Edward first and Cicely next, the eldest of the girls. Oh, how Elizabeth wished she could run away. Hide from the probing eyes of the priests and shut out the weight of the sonorous dirges from her ears. Stop them entering her brain and turning her into one of the living dead. She felt like the living dead. A frightening tightness in her throat was slowly creeping downwards into her chest as she almost stumbled. What if she fell in? Right into the coffin? It felt as though every eye in the church was on her. Staring at her. The staring empty sockets of the living dead.

His face felt cold to her lips. And he didn't smell very nice. Elizabeth had the sickening sensation of the sweat on her face suddenly turning to ice

12

as death filled her nostrils. He moved! She was sure of it. Just as she lifted her head. He moved! Were they all really the living dead? It was just like Megan said. Don't listen to them! Fear and claustrophobia closed in on her. To the consternation of her mother and the disgust of her father, the eight-year-old girl crumpled on the floor in a dead faint.

The icy fingers of the February winds tore at her clothes and prodded her into consciousness as Elizabeth sat uncomfortably against the awkward angle of an ancient tombstone. Shivering violently, it took her some seconds to get her bearings but at last she focused on the worried face of Alice peering down at her.

'Lord have mercy!' Alice exclaimed as she saw signs of life returning to the child. 'What on earth persuaded you to go and do a thing like that? Threw the whole family into a right confusion, you did. Come on now. Let's get you into the warmth before you catch your death.' A pair of well-worn, capable hands helped Elizabeth up and supported the still wobbly girl along the church path and across to Baguley's Glebe. Sitting by the roaring fire in the rectory kitchen, the colour soon returned to her cheeks.

'Whatever ailed you, child?' Alice continued to chatter non-stop as she bustled about the business of the kitchen. 'A healthy young woman like you shouldn't go putting the fear of God into us all like that. And in the middle of your grandfather's requiem! Whatever will the good Lord think of you?'

Elizabeth dreaded to think. She wasn't going inside a church ever again, if she could help it. She wanted to stay alive and free. Like the birds in the forest, and the glorious River Dane.

Alice gave her a honey cake to nibble on. 'And how do you like living at Gawsworth Hall? I expect they will soon turn you into a great lady now that your father has come into his estates.' The housekeeper paused in her work to study the girl. It was hard to imagine this delicate waif as any kind of lady, never mind a great one. She didn't seem to fit in with the arrogant Fyttons at all. One could almost believe that she was a foundling child, spirited in when no one was looking.

An enormous pair of dreamy green eyes gazed imperturbably over the rim of the goblet at Alice. Elizabeth shook her head. 'If ever I become a lady, I hope it will not be here. I would like to see other places and the wonders of the world. Mountains as high as the sky, and bottomless seas, and pirates, and mermaids and strange plants and animals.'

For the first time Alice glimpsed the agile mind which normally hid behind the quiet, restrained exterior.

'Still waters run deep,' she thought to herself. Aloud she said, 'And who has been filling your head with this nonsense? I've never heard of such things. Bottomless seas, indeed! Mermaids!'

'Mister Christopher told me, so it must be true. Mister Christopher has been everywhere and done everything and one day I shall too.'

Alice nodded her head knowingly. Christopher Savage was a romantic through and through and had charmed women a sight older than this one with his fancy ideas. In fact, rumour had travelled before the Fyttons from Congleton to Gawsworth and there had been many a wink and a nod about John Fytton's blind eye. Christopher Savage had taken quite a shine to Ellen Fytton, who had been Ellen Brereton before her marriage. A regular visitor he was and not above keeping the young ladies of the house amused with his tales by the sound of things. Elizabeth here was just the right age to be swept off her feet by the fascinating notions which the happy-go-lucky Mister Savage could provide. It wasn't right, filling a young girl's head with such stuff. Who knew where it would lead? Alice would have been appalled to know the lessons Elizabeth had learnt at Old Megan's knee. At least Mister Christopher's stories were whimsical rather than mystical and gave the child the idea that some things ended happy ever after rather than the reverse. For the time being it helped to balance out the stark reality that life always ended in death and that death was invoked by the priests to fill the churches. Megan had shown her the remedies for health and strength but she had also shown her that sometimes the only way to fight fire was with fire. These things Elizabeth knew and she believed, but these were things which were never spoken of except to the initiated. Alice would not have understood.

Not so with the house itself. It was silent, never speaking but it heard and stored every remark made in its rooms and gardens and watched the comings and goings of a succession of occupants with a cynical eye. What were its thoughts on the new Master of the Hall who, since his arrival, had celebrated his change of fortune by an increased daily intake of good ales and wines? And what of the new Mistress?

Elizabeth loved the place. When the sun shone on the house, it smiled and she could see the twinkle in the mullioned eyes. Three storeys high, the proud building looked over a deep green slice of Cheshire countryside. Bordering its cobbled court was the long, low apple store and there, one day, Elizabeth discovered another secret which the house already knew, along with half the population thereabouts. Truth to tell, she had been keeping out of Cicely's way again, trying to avoid her sister's interpretation of 'useful employment.' It was more fun outdoors, without the silly chatter of the girls and Edward's obnoxious pomposity. An ever-widening crack in one wall of the store had caused Father to place the building out of bounds to the children. He had plans, when he got round to them, to have it repaired. Or rebuilt. Or demolished. John Fytton hadn't quite made up his mind. In the meantime, no one would think of looking for Elizabeth in there, would they?

Chaff had gathered in one corner where the wind had blown in through the ill-fitting door. Sitting down, hidden from view by a screen of seldom-used farm implements, Elizabeth let her mind meander from one favourite day-dream to another. The murmur of voices startled her, catapulting her guiltily into the present.

'You shouldn't take such risks.' The whispered words were accompanied by a girlish giggle. 'It is in a terrible worn state and the roof is in danger of collapsing.'

'When the Lord provides, 'tis a sin not to partake.'

Mister Christopher! And Mother!

'Then the whole thing must be renewed if it isn't to fall on your head and bury you alive.' Mother's voice was soft and caressing, as though her mind was being distracted by something. The words were followed by a strange tremulous sigh which was almost a moan. By the sound of it, things other than the roof were in danger of collapsing.

Fortunately for Elizabeth, she had become expert at disappearing, as her sister Cicely had discovered. Mother was too completely taken by her visitor to notice a silent shadow flit across the far wall and she herself was careful to stay hidden by the cunningly concealed door between the angle of the old beams.

Lifting up her skirts as she ran Elizabeth didn't even look where she was going. Her mind was in a daze. Gawsworth Hall knew all the secrets and some it had given up to her. She told the house her secret dreams and in return it had provided her with a safe harbour. That was where she went to now. Agile as a monkey, the young girl hoisted herself out of sight and into the little windowless room. The air was stale and dusty but that didn't matter. It had its own special smell. Why the room was there, Elizabeth didn't know. She only knew that it was her room. No one else ever went there. That's why it was special. It was there, as she thought about the things she had heard, that Elizabeth began to grow up. Were things ever what they seemed? She liked Mister Christopher. And she loved Mother. As for Father? Well, he was Father and that was all there was to it. All the more reason for keeping this secret to herself! She wouldn't like anything bad to happen to Mister Christopher!

Despite such profound thoughts, her father's words, only a few days later, came as a shock. He was in a merry mood. On being beckoned to his side, Elizabeth expected to be sent to refill his jug from the barrel, so she was surprised when he held out his hands and lifted her on to his knees.

'Hair the colour of chestnuts.' He smoothed a soft, silk circle of her crowning glory between his finger and thumb. 'Enough to pleasure a lord.' Bellowing loudly he jiggled her playfully.

What plan was the ale fermenting this time? Was he serious, or was he merely dreaming his great dreams? Elizabeth knew that John Fytton was intent upon being the envy of his neighbours and even more, the envy of his relatives. How many times in the last year had he told them how he was going to build on these mighty foundations until Gawsworth Hall was talked of countrywide?

'I'll make you into a fine lady, Bessy Love. You wait and see.'

A fine lady, was it? That must mean as wife to some fine gentleman, or she was very much mistaken. Elizabeth too had her dreams. He had golden

16

hair and violet eyes. Oh, such all-encompassing eyes. And he was strong and handsome and brave. And his name was William Brereton.

'So if he is older, it is all to the good,' Father was continuing. 'And the waiting will be no hardship. Thomas will make a fine husband.'

'Thomas?'

'Thomas Davenport, daughter.' John Fytton chucked her under the chin. 'A goodly match for a pretty girl, eh? All he asks are plenty of sons to fill his forests.' He laughed at the thought until Elizabeth thought he would choke.

Plenty of sons? With Thomas Davenport? Never! For Will she would have babies by the hundred, no matter what the suffering to bring them into the world. But Thomas Davenport? The very idea of it made her shudder. Marriage could hold pains a-plenty when made to one who was handsome. Look at poor Queen Katharine. How many times had she endured the rigours of childbirth and still nothing to show for it? Her baby Prince Henry died after only so few weeks. How much worse must it be to endure such anguish without the man of your choice at your side?

Ellen Fytton was uncomfortably aware of a pair of cool green eyes following her every move as she skimmed the milk in the big, flat pans. Bessy had always been the quiet one but lately her solitary silence had been somehow eerie. As though she had some superior knowledge which she was withholding. About what, though? That was the question Ellen would like answering. It was almost as though the child knew more than she ought! But no! She was too young to understand such things. Wasn't she? It was just that she had that odd look about her, as though she could see through all the tricks and subterfuges.

'Why so solemn, child? Are you ill?'

Elizabeth shook her head. 'Not yet. But I shall be if I have to wed Thomas Davenport.'

Ah! So that was it! Frightened of the marriage bed, was she? Unconsciously, Ellen sighed with relief. The girl was worrying about her own problems, not those of her elders. She tutted cheerfully. 'Don't you bother your pretty little head about it, Love. You won't be leaving us yet a while and I'm sure when the time comes you will see the advantages of the match. You'll hardly want for a thing.'

Except the one I love! Elizabeth was prudent enough to keep that thought to herself.

'I wish to choose for myself.'

Those eyes! They seemed to see right through her and Ellen, feeling a tell-tale flush warm her cheeks, became annoyed at losing her composure. What was the child hinting at now?

'Your father knows best in these matters,' she pronounced somewhat abruptly. 'It appears that you have had your own way too long, mistress, and it is time that I put a stop to it. In fact the matter is in hand. There will be no more disappearing without trace when you are called for, and no more solitary rambles far afield. You are growing fast and should show more decorum, especially when you are betrothed to Mister Davenport. He will not want his bride to sully her reputation by foolhardiness. And neither will your father!'

'Betrothed I may be, but wed I'll not.' The words were not said with anger, but with certainty.

The impudent madam! Ellen would have clipped her round the ear but for the fact that she was still unsure about how much the girl knew. It wasn't what she had said. It was more the way she had said it.

'I thought you would understand.' Elizabeth's steady gaze never faltered.

So, she did know. Or at least, she suspected. Ellen Fytton held her ground. The child wouldn't tell her father, would she? And if she did, she wouldn't be believed. Ellen knew she could get around John. Especially when he had been at his wines!

'Careful, before you go too far. I have told you that you have no need to worry for some time yet, but I also have news for you of other changes which are afoot.'

Elizabeth stuck her bottom lip out stubbornly. 'What changes?' She didn't like the sound of this.

'A young girl is to be placed with us and she is to be your charge, being the same age. Your Aunt Eleanor Brereton is sending her over from Malpas where at present she resides with a relative. Her family have left for other parts in the south. You will have to lose those silly solitary ways and be a sight more sociable.'

Elizabeth's heart skipped a beat at the mention of Malpas and Will's mother, her Aunt Eleanor. A girl? Coming from Malpas? Perhaps she knew Will and could be persuaded to talk of him; to tell of his likes and dislikes, his skills and his achievements. Oh, just to be able to mention his name to someone would be heaven!

'What girl? What is her name?'

The ploy seemed to have worked. It was strange really, but Ellen was too relieved to have turned her daughter's mind from other things to question the sudden interest.

'Her name is Cicely Bulkley, but she is always known as Cissy to her family and friends.'

Elizabeth's excitement scarcely showed, but inwardly she was bubbling over. So much so that she didn't even look up when Mister Christopher arrived unexpectedly for lunch.

***

The world was a lovely place. All the way to Chester Elizabeth and Cissy had exchanged secret looks and now, as the city walls rose in splendour before them, their knuckles showed white as they strove to behave like young ladies.

Inside the gateway a lattice of narrow streets waited to confuse them, while the colourful kaleidoscope of humanity swamped their senses with its constant motion, like rivers and streams, merging and diverging, and its squawking, squealing, joking, cursing sounds. There were carters carting and merchants parading, and while good-wives went about their business, vagabonds went about theirs. The place had a smell which always hung about the towns.

Elizabeth nudged Cissy as a woman in an elegant gown which had seen better days swung past, her expression haughty under the faded silk of her cap. The chalk-white face and red-spot cheeks gave her game away. Some rich man's doxy, fallen on hard times! There was a beggar, with no arms, feeding himself with a crust of bread held between his toes; and there a priest, rolling drunk, by the looks of him. And somewhere amongst all this, somewhere in this higgledy-piggledy city of Chester was the young man of her dreams.

John Fytton led his family through the chaos to the house of John and Margaret Talbot. His wife didn't realise that the route closely followed the locations of the ale-houses, from the Bull to the Bluebell. Mister Fytton had passed this way before.

The City was full almost to overflowing. It was always the same in the summer months when the guilds performed their plays, especially now in the year 1513 with the King about to leave for France, leaving Queen Katherine in charge despite the fact that she was once more expecting a child. Some thought she might do better to put more of her energy into producing an heir and leave the men to worry about the safety of the land.

Space was at a premium and every inch of the Talbots' residence was taken up by visitors. The children were all to share an upper room and Elizabeth and Cissy were shown the way by Mary Talbot, the daughter of the house. Not that this was their only home, the girl was quick to point out. Oh, no! The Talbots had connections in high places and her bed-mates would do well to remember it. The two girls exchanged glances behind Mary's back. Little Miss Hoity-Toity this one! Not a one to share their secrets!

That day Elizabeth fell in love all over again, but not with a boy this time. The object of her adoration was the baby daughter of another visitor to the house. Mistress Parr was on her way to her husband's estates in the north and travelling with her was her daughter of less than twelve months. Katherine Parr had a dimpled smile which revealed two tiny pearls protruding from her lower gum. She wobbled rather than walked on her fat little legs and would brighten the gloomiest day. Elizabeth Fytton was lost. Everywhere she went she took the baby with her and of course she came in for some teasing from Cissy.

'Pretending she is yours? Yours and . . .?' There was nothing Cissy Bulkley didn't know about those secret dreams of hers.

Elizabeth blushed furiously at Cissy's insinuations, the more so as they were true. She knew he was there, in the same city and that they were bound to meet. Her Uncle, Randle Brereton, held office in the city and though he himself was at the King's side in France, he had left his sons to make up for the deficiency. Not that Will would be taking any part in the meetings. He was too young, much to his disgust. Elizabeth didn't care. She had her fantasies and Katherine Parr was part of them.

At the back of Mister Talbot's house the ground was laid out with paths and flower beds, herbs and trees. Brilliant butterflies flickered through the shrubs and big fat bumbly bees invaded every flower in their search for nectar. Elizabeth didn't notice. Will Brereton tumbled somersaults across the grass and the rest of the world could have disappeared for all she cared. Katherine Parr squirmed on her knee, wanting to join him and it took all Elizabeth's ingenuity to control her without once taking her eyes from the performance of that confident young extrovert. Panting a little, he finally sprang over to them and sat at Elizabeth's feet, grinning, a big yellow daisy in his hand. It hadn't taken William more than a couple of seconds to become aware of Elizabeth's admiring glances and he enjoyed nothing more than playing to a susceptible crowd.

'For my lady.' He held out the flower, mockingly.

Elizabeth could see that he was laughing at her, but it didn't matter. She put Katherine on the ground and took the bloom from him, unable to free herself from the total fascination of his nearness. Violet eyes framed by black, silky lashes. Gilded curls lay damp and glistening on his brow, while the flush of his cheeks gave his features an angelic quality which completely hid his mischievous nature.

Briefly, his fingers touched her hand and she had the most peculiar feeling that he had burnt her. The feeling flashed from hand to arm before spreading and tightening right through to her stomach. Taking her hand in his he deliberately turned her whole world topsy-turvy.

'One day,' he said softly, 'we shall sit like this, master and mistress of our own home and with just such a child as Kate to keep us laughing.'

She could have drowned in his limpid gaze, locked in the wonderful moment, except that she had a feeling that he was teasing her. Her face flamed red and these strange new experiences were making her feel sick. It was she who shattered the illusion by turning away to hide her embarrassment and, picking up the cooing baby she fled into the cool depths of Mistress Talbot's house. Had he been only teasing? Whether he had or not, one thing was certain. Never could Elizabeth Fytton consent to marry Thomas Davenport.

That magic time passed in a blur of sun-drenched afternoons and balmy, romantic evenings under a star-spangled sky. Cissy couldn't believe the effect a blatant show-off could have on a quiet, unassuming girl like Elizabeth Fytton. There was no denying he was handsome, with smooth pink-and-white skin and tousled hair more fitting to a street urchin. Apart from which, Will always seemed to be in trouble. To Cissy's mind he would not make a very steady husband. It was obvious that he was enjoying the adulation of her friend and playing on it, but that he really felt anything for Elizabeth, Cissy doubted very much. It was too late to do anything about it now, though. Elizabeth was wearing her heart on her sleeve for the whole world to see, if they had a mind to.

Mister Christopher offered to take the boys across to see the ships. Somehow Elizabeth wheedled her way round him to have the girls invited too. Even Mary Talbot, though in her case Fate intervened and eliminated her from the outing. That deity appeared in the form of little Gilly Talbot who truth to tell, was rather too young to have stayed the distance anyway. The party hadn't even got as far as the city walls when the infant landed himself in the mire. Pausing at the edge of the street runnel to piss into the accumulated garbage, as little boys do everywhere, the unfortunate Gilly slipped on the foetid slime. With a predictable squelch, he landed yelling in the stinking slutch. Having to take the boy home covered in slops rather dented Mary's dignity and the sight of her humiliation had Elizabeth and Cissy doubled up in fits of laughter. So much for Her Ladyship!

It was during that innocent ramble that Christopher Savage became aware of Elizabeth's feeling for her cousin Will. It would have been difficult not to see it. And Will was making the most of it too!

'That's the way, boy,' Mister Savage thought to himself. 'Take them while they're eager. Better than chasing them when they're not.'

If the girl was half as eager as her mother, Will Brereton couldn't go far wrong. Not that there was any harm in it. They were only children, after all. Still, it amused the older man to encourage the budding friendship as he told tales of the sea and storms and shipwrecks; tales frightening enough to have a young girl clutching at the arm of her real-life flesh and blood hero. Christopher Savage had no way of knowing that his casual interest in Ellen's daughter was to have far-reaching consequences which would eventually thread themselves into the very fabric of the history of England.

Will needed no encouragement to set him off on the trail of new mischief. He'd heard his brothers talking about their exploits with the fairer sex and wanted nothing more than to try it for himself. If only he was old enough! If only Elizabeth would let him! His chance to test her out came on the day of the parade. The men were all away to talk of defending England from the daggers of the Scots. Except Mister Christopher Savage. He declared he would not miss the charming company of the ladies even if the barbarians were knocking at his front door. Will listened to the smooth speech and watched the effect it had on the women, even his own mother, but especially Mistress Fytton. Flatter them. That was the beginning. He already knew the way Elizabeth blushed whenever he went near her. She was hooked to the end of his line. All he needed to know now was how to land the catch!

There it was. The tell-tale flush of her cheeks. Elizabeth felt the familiar shiver down her back. Delicious! He didn't have to do anything. He just had to be there.

The great sword was carried high before the long procession, opening the way for Mayor Dutton, dignified and official in his magnificent cloak of office. The men of the guilds filed by, their grand performances yet to come.

There was, no doubt, some nail biting and last-minute alterations going on amongst the ranks. Not so with the tumblers in their garish clothes showing off their rude antics to a willing crowd. Somewhere beyond the delighted crowd's earthy responses to the hilarious ad-libbing could be heard the tinkling music of the players with their pipes, cymbals and drums setting toes a-tapping and hands a-clapping. The whole atmosphere was one of gay abandon.

But where was he? Oh, where was he? The lofts of the city were closed to accommodate the crowds milling through the streets, and the trestles were all battened down as the throng lined the upper boards and the lower, noisy roadway. Finding him amongst that heaving mass was like looking for a needle in a haystack, even from the vantage point which Mister Christopher had been astute enough to find for them.

A warm hand settled on her back, just above the waist. Elizabeth's flesh began to tingle uncontrollably as it slid smoothly round to hold her. She didn't need to turn her head. She knew who it was. Was it possible, she wondered, to die of happiness? Will was whispering something to Cissy, and before Elizabeth realised what was happening Katherine Parr was taken from her arms and she felt herself being tugged backwards into the crush of people. Apart from Cissy, only Christopher Savage noticed them go.

The darkened, inviting chink of a narrow covered passageway attracted Will's attention and in the dim seclusion it afforded, as Elizabeth's eyes were still trying to adjust to the lack of light, he kissed her. It wasn't a father's or a brother's kiss, but as Elizabeth was to realise later, it was not the experienced kiss of a lover either. His soft lips found hers, and then hesitated as though unsure what to do next. She felt them press more firmly against her mouth and then relax again. It was nice. But not enough. Putting her arms round him and pressing herself against him, her instincts taking over completely from her head, she kissed him back. Elizabeth moved her mouth on his, tasting him for the first time.

So this was what his brothers had meant! Will was beginning to enjoy the subtleties of the performance. What strange, exciting feelings it aroused! With a look of studied concentration he began to practise, kissing her brow, her cheeks, her eyes, and then, with much more feeling than before, her succulent lips, full and red from their first attempts at this new art. And this was only the beginning, he realised. William Brereton knew there and then that he was going to enjoy growing up.

Elizabeth was in heaven. The strong emotional sensations coursing through her young body threatened to choke her. This was Love. And this was the boy she would one day marry. The only one she would ever even consider marrying. He felt the same. She knew he did. She just knew. The sweet tenderness of the moment, and the sickening thought of Thomas Davenport lurking somewhere at the back of her mind, brought tears to her eyes. She blinked them away. Crying was not the answer. Hadn't Megan always said that crying was a waste of valuable energy? And hadn't she taught Elizabeth the way to make things happen? Concentration. Determination. And the philtres and the brews. And those special, secret words! One day he would be hers. Hers alone!

Cissy was all of a giggle over these goings on. 'You know your father won't allow it. Not marriage. But what did it feel like? Tell me!' She was whispering very quietly into Elizabeth's ear, careful not to waken Mary Talbot who lay snoring and sweating in the bed beside them. Mary was oblivious to the heat but it was keeping the other two girls wide awake. That, or the excitement.

'He will allow it. He'll have to! You'll see.'

'Have to? What do you mean, have to? You've not ...?' 'You didn't ...?' Cissy was incredulous.

'Idiot! Of course not. But you just wait. One day I shall, and it will not be with Thomas Davenport. I shall either be Mistress Brereton or no man's wife. I believe! And so should you.'

Elizabeth sounded so certain. 'I'll attend you on your wedding day then and when I get married you can attend me and we shall both have lots of babies and elegant homes and entertain each other royally. And always be the best of friends.' Cissy yawned. It was a lovely dream. Wondering who her own lover would be her mind began to drift away. Tall? Short? Dark? Fair?

Somewhere he was waiting for her. Sleep closed in at last.

The visions which Cissy's words had conjured up for her friend had their darker side. Flickering lights of altar candles threw grotesque shadows around the claustrophobic interior of the church. The hollow eyes of the living dead pierced her with a thousand hot needles as she waited for Will to repeat the vows. His mouth opened but no words came out. He stared at her silently, his mouth still wide and black and then, to her horror, blood began to gush from it, splashing down her gown and on to the cold stone of the church. Elizabeth tried to scream. Silence. She tried and tried but not a single sound could she utter. And still the hot blood poured over her. The church began to spin, just like a top. Faster and faster. Faster and faster. The force of it tore Will from her side and as the fury of the church came between them she could hear her father laughing. Crazy, cruel laughter. Her father? It was her father, wasn't it? It had to be. He was behind her, allowing the church to take Will away. Laughing! The building became a storm-tossed vessel, drowning in the great waves the monstrous man had caused. And then nothing. A suffocating silence covered everything and Elizabeth was quite alone.

She jerked awake from the nightmare, drenched in a sweat of fear, stunned by the realism of the dream and overwhelmed by its sinister implications. Megan had told her that she had the sight, but if that was a vision of the future what hope was there for them? The horror of it fired her vivid imagination and made sleep then, and for several nights after, impossible.

***

No words could comfort such raw suffering. Elizabeth watched silently as her mother's shoulders rose and fell, propelled into motion by the convulsive sobs which threatened to shake her whole body to pieces. It was strange that the same news which had caused this grief had set Father celebrating well into his cups. Or maybe it was not so strange! Mister Christopher Savage was dead. But then, so were all the Scots, including the tyrant, King James. His stinking offal had been ripped apart and trampled unceremoniously into the mud of Flodden if first reports were to be believed. Not that the news was any consolation to Ellen Fytton. Elizabeth remembered how those heavy-lidded eyes spoke his thanks aplenty for Mother's kind services on many an occasion. And the tales he used to tell. And the things he had seen. All gone. It seemed that Megan was right. There were no happy endings for her mother because her mother had not believed. Her mother had become one of the living dead.

'Damnation to the Scottish bastards!'

Elizabeth applauded silently as Ellen's grief turned into hate. That was the way to stay alive; to avoid the haunting emptiness!

The young girl left the laughing, crying household for the timeless beauty of the forest, where the leaves were already turning gold, saluting England's victory, Placidly she set about gathering the herbs she would need to calm her mother into sleep when her fury had run its course and left her exhausted.

Two

AT first it seemed that nothing was going right. To Elizabeth's dismay, Uncle Randle procured a place at Court for his son William. At Court! No doubt it was done in Will's best interests but to Elizabeth it was like the end of the world. There was no hope of her being allowed to join him there, and very little chance of anyone being in a position to plead her cause. Then, when she calmed down and thought about it, she remembered. Determination! And patience!

Now, after two years of constant, urgent invocation, on this, the Feast of St. Philip and St. James, her hopes were about to be realised and her dreams fulfilled. Wasn't May Day the time for the tying of lover's knots? And wasn't Will to visit Gawsworth Hall with his family? Would he have changed? Would he still want to kiss her? Would he even remember her? How many other maids had he kissed at King Henry's Court?

Cissy became increasingly impatient with her. 'Your mother will notice your flushed face and keep you a-bed,' she warned. 'Then you can't go a-Maying with your sweetheart and I shall be forced to take your place.' Skipping well out of reach she began to giggle. 'Bessy's got a sweetheart, Bessy's got a sweetheart,' she sang, teasing.

Elizabeth decided to rise above such taunts. 'Jealous, are you?' she asked, doing her best to appear cool. Calmly she began polishing the length of her hair with a soft linen, trying to prevent the inner panic which she felt from showing. What would he think of her now? She was no longer the child she had been at Chester. Smoothing the bodice of her gown she felt the pleasing curves of her newly developed breasts and tiny waist. How did she compare with fashionable London girls? Perhaps he wouldn't notice her at all!

Cissy was no fool. She could see all the doubts written on her friend's face. 'Don't worry. Neither I nor anyone else would stand a chance when he sets eyes on you.' She spoke without a trace of malice, knowing that Elizabeth's strange aloof beauty owed as much to her modesty as to her actual features. It was no use trying to tell her though. Fussing with her hair and searching every other minute for blemishes of the skin Elizabeth waited for the arrival of her cousin in a mixture of impatience and dread.

When at last the moment came it seemed that all her fears were well founded. He hardly looked at her. His first greeting was no warmer than that which he gave to her sisters, nor Cissy. He wasn't the same. He had changed. For one thing, he was much taller than she remembered him. She had grown, but he had outstripped her by inches. In the dusk, his hair, though still fair and curling to his collar, was a shade or two darker than those golden memories had kept it. And he looked older; more sophisticated! He was a courtier from that dream world of hers; a world of princes in pearls and velvets, living in palaces and castles in a style which she had imagined since she was old enough to listen to the stories of Mister Christopher. Elizabeth spent a wretched night, tossing and turning and wondering what had gone wrong.

Morning dawned bright and cheerful, with a light breeze to refresh them as they made the ride to Congleton. Elizabeth's eyes never left William Brereton. Not one stitch of his clothing nor a hair of his head escaped her attention. The cut of his doublet was in the new fashion and the deep red suited him handsomely. And what a fine leg he had. No one could have had a better. The soft leather boots set them off to perfection. What beautiful craftsmanship. But his face! So manly! So adult! It was no wonder such a fine courtier had no time for her. He must be inundated with offers from every maid at Court who had eyes in her head. The more she saw of him and admired him the more despondent she became. He had so much confidence and elegance! Why should he bother about a mousy little country cousin like her?

Her soulful gaze made the back of his neck prickle. Turning, he gave her the benefit of a dazzling smile whilst he assessed her best features. A trim little figure, the newly sprouting breasts pushed temptingly into two creamy soft cushions by the tightness of her deep green gown. It was just a shade darker than the largest pair of sorrowful eyes he had ever seen on a human being. And the long auburn hair. The morning sun had invaded the wayward curls and turned them into a fiery halo.

Who was she? Some hazy memory suddenly took on a more substantial form. It was his cousin Elizabeth! Little Bessy! But hadn't she grown! It all came rushing back to him. Those first childish kisses! That was it. But that was a million years ago. Will Brereton had learnt a lot since those days, but by the looks of the girl she would be willing to repeat the games they used to play. At Court Will knew himself to be amongst the lowest order of things. But here the younger ones at least looked up to him and thought he held a position of great importance. Compared to them, he did, so why spoil the illusion. William loved to be admired, especially by the ladies, and he meant to make the most of the situation while he could. He'd be back in his role of underling soon enough. Yes, Bessy would be a welcome distraction from family affairs during his leave in Cheshire, and what better opportunity to make her closer acquaintance than at Congleton Fair on the first day of May?

Elizabeth couldn't believe her luck. If it was luck, of course. How many charms had she made so that he would not forget her? She had recited the words over and over again to prevent him falling in love with any other girl, and to bring him back to her side. It had taken a long, long time but the waiting was worth it.

Will's mother, Aunt Eleanor, was expecting yet another child and the journey to Gawsworth had tired her. It would be her twelfth baby, and, God willing, her last. Neither she nor Mother had made the journey to the fair with the rest of the family, and without those two pairs of eyes to restrain them the young ones could look forward to rather more freedom during the outing than was usual. As they expected, the older men of the party wasted little time in making their way to where the gentlemen of the town were congratulating each other on the quality of their ales.

May Day was the day for lovers, and all the young girls were hoping to catch the eye of some personable young man. And all the young men were similarly occupied in which girl looked to have the most amenable disposition. Will flashed Elizabeth a lop-sided grin accompanied by a wink which had an unmistakable meaning. If she was willing to leave the rest of them to their own devices, then so was he. Cissy's sharp elbow poked her unnecessarily hard in the ribs in case she had missed the invitation and though Elizabeth's heart was in her mouth and she desperately wanted to run to him she somehow managed to keep hold of some dignity. Clutching Cissy by the arm so that her friend was forced to keep pace with her she made her way casually towards him across the grass. At last they stood face to face. Conscious of his responsibilities for keeping up appearances he bowed to them both courteously and engaged the two of them in conversation. Elizabeth was overawed. He was so close. Cissy had a perfect gauge of her friend's nervousness in the bruising pressure of the grip on her arm.

'May I?' Will held out an arm to Elizabeth, devilment shining in his eyes. 'I would not be accused of taking more than my share of today's beauties so with your leave, Mistress,' he turned to Cissy, 'I have asked Edward to accompany us to watch the tumblers and the cock-fight.'

Cissy's features dimpled her approval, though Elizabeth could not understand why. The last thing she wanted was to be saddled with her brother. It didn't take long, however, before it became clear that Will had invited the other two merely to prevent eyebrows from being raised and comments made about her virtue by her sisters. They hadn't even got as far as the tinkers before the two couples went their separate ways by silent, mutual consent.

The pulse at the base of Elizabeth's throat throbbed visibly. Lately, when she was alone or almost falling asleep at night, her body had surprised her with strange sensations and yearnings, and the most unladylike thoughts had filled her mind. Thoughts that she wouldn't dare share, even with Cissy. It was almost as though she was two separate people. One was the quiet, modest young woman who believed herself in full control of all her faculties and, with the knowledge she had gained from Megan, in control of a good deal more. The other was a wild abandoned wench of easy virtue who in her fantasies did all the things respectable girls would never consider. She had sometimes wondered whether she was sick.

Elizabeth realised that she was no longer in control of anything. Will was leading her by the hand through the crowds of merrymakers without speaking and she was following without question, along the narrow pathways, through the shrubs and into Yates's Spinney beyond the park. In the pale green silence of a sheltered clearing he finally stopped and nervously she lifted her face to look up at him.

'You've grown so tall.' Elizabeth was frightened and excited at the same time. Perhaps she shouldn't have come. But she had wanted to so much. How could she have missed the chance and had him thinking she didn't care? And now that she was here she couldn't make a fool of herself by making excuses and running back to safety. What would happen if she stayed? What would he expect of her? But if she left? She knew that if she went now she would never have another chance. Will was so handsome that he could have any girl he wanted, she was sure, and he would never wait until a stupid, frightened child had conquered her nervousness. He would be away to more convivial company.

Will was pleased with himself. He had thought she looked innocent. She had that air about her, and she was scared. Scared but willing to be persuaded, if he read the signs aright. Considering the dearth of such girls to be found around the King's Court, a close acquaintance with Cousin Bessy could prove to be quite a novelty. For both of them! It would make an interesting change from the expertise of those ladies of the Court who took it upon themselves to initiate every new arrival in the much-flaunted art of love. Cautiously, so that she wouldn't take to her heels, he slipped one arm round her waist and raised the other carefully to rest his fingers gently on small but perfect mounds of virgin flesh.

Somehow Elizabeth held her ground, her gaze unflinching. She desperately wanted to be a woman in his arms. How many nights had she imagined this scene; longed for it and gone over and over it again and again in her mind? And now it was happening. So why was she afraid? He hadn't said a word, but his eyes were asking, and she knew the answer she wanted to give.

Try her. It was the only way. Will brought his lips down on hers, caressing her mouth with a soft and sensuous rhythm, and any doubts she might have had vanished. Those feelings he aroused seemed to acquire an uncontrollable urgency which had her body crying out to be touched, and left her gasping with the force of previously unknown emotion. Then her arms were round him; holding him; clinging to him. Oh, never let this wonderful moment end. He loves me!

Will pulled away, disappointed. He had been sure she was an inexperienced country girl. Damn whoever had taken her first. It was just like they always said: mount guard on her cradle if you'd mount a pure maiden. It wasn't what he'd hoped for, but even so! Will was not the one to turn his back on any offer and bending, quickly scooped her legs from under her and laid her down on the grass. Elizabeth was surprised at the sudden change in him. He didn't seem to be seeing her anymore. It could have been anyone. Just anyone! Without preamble Will had lifted her skirts, and then everything seemed to happen at once. His hand was moving smoothly from calf to knee to thigh as Elizabeth fought a furious battle between instinct and desire.

'Oh-ho, oh-ho! Go to it, lad!'

The silence and their privacy was shattered as a rowdy group of merrymakers burst through the trees waving branches and garlands, dancing and laughing and playing chase-me-kiss-me through the undergrowth. Ribald comments came thick and fast, and as all the jokes were at her expense, Elizabeth didn't dare to look in case she saw anyone she knew. It was an age before the vulgarity became no more than an echo through the birdsong.

With a wry grin and a shrug Will was about to begin where he had left off when he noticed a faint tremble of her body as he held her.

'Bessy?' He moved away slightly so that he could see her face. As he thought. Tears! 'What's wrong? They were only having fun and meant no harm by it. Come on, sweetheart. I thought you wanted me.' He paused as two big, silent tears dripped from her lashes. What was wrong with the girl? She had been as hot as fire only moments ago. And now it looked as though those idiots had ruined his chance. He was sure that he would never understand women. He'd have to start all over again. Resignedly Will started to kiss her wet face. Gently. Tenderly. 'Tell me, Bess. Don't you want me?'

At first Elizabeth couldn't bring herself to speak in case she made an even bigger fool of herself so she just nodded. Swallowing hard, and after much hesitation she told him.

'I love you.'

What on earth was she talking about? Love was pining for the unattainable and writing pretty verses, not a tumble in the grass. Then it dawned on him. She loved him. The silly goose loved him. He had been right the first time when he thought her a novice at such games and her passion was brought on by her feelings for him and him alone. A virgin! He'd really found himself a virgin!

'And I love you, sweet cousin.' That was what she wanted to hear. And it worked. The tears disappeared as if by magic. Cautiously his hand fumbled at her skirts, but as he had feared, she would have none of it.

'Not here.' Seeing the look on his face she hurried on, 'Can't we wait until we are private? I want you to love me. Truly I do, but here I would not be able to . . .' Her voice trailed off as she saw his expression of disbelief.

'This may be the only chance we have. There will be many people around us at Gawsworth and how can I be sure that you will not be away with another as soon as my back is turned?'

That hurt. It was like a slap in the face for Elizabeth. How could he even consider such things? Had she ever thought of anyone else? Hadn't she sworn she would never marry Thomas Davenport? And why? Because she loved William Brereton. 'There will never, never be anyone else for me as long as I live. That I swear!'

He believed her. But where? When? After today he would wager that they'd not be left in peace for a second. Those sisters of hers would be round him like flies and not one of them a patch on Bessy. Better somewhere else. That's it! Better if she came to Malpas!

'Accompany your mother when she journeys to our home in Malpas for my mother's lying in! Would she let you? Do you think you can persuade her?' Will raised himself on to one elbow, waiting for an answer. 'On my own ground I can find a place where we'll not be disturbed.' The wait would only add spice to the event, and even that could be turned to his advantage.

'Won't that prove to you how much I love you. Say you'll come, Bessy. Don't torture me with doubts.'

How sweetly she offered her lips to be kissed. And how passionately he took advantage of the offer. Without overstepping the mark, mind. Enough to arouse her desires without frightening her again. Play the game her way, for now.

'I'll come. I know how to get round Mother.' As Megan had always observed, secrets can be valuable, if you know how to use them.

The pact was made; the plans were laid, there under the swaying birches of Yates's Spinney. Sealed with a kiss. Or two. Eventually, as they made their way back along the winding paths to the open park Will presented her with a gift. Casually, he hung the little silver bluebell around her neck. It was one of several trinkets which he carried in case he should find some small token payment necessary but Elizabeth was overwhelmed by his thoughtfulness.

He had bought it just for her! She looked up into those honest, deep violet eyes and thought she would die of happiness.

'Perhaps it will suffice to keep me in your mind. At least until I am wealthy enough to buy you jewels to match your worth.' Will kissed her one last time.

Elizabeth couldn't believe that anything would ever mean more to her than that tiny silver bell.

***

Elizabeth was sure that she was going to faint. Just like the time she had disgraced herself at Grandfather's funeral. Oh, how she hated churches. Wait for him outside after the christening, he had said. It was a hot June day, but inside the ancient stone of the building Elizabeth could feel nothing but a cold, clammy sweat as the priest droned on, putting one more youthful life into bondage. Chaining it; caging it. Removing all its freedom in life to possess its soul in death. Under her breath, Elizabeth recited her own powerful words to counteract the churchman's edicts, to prevent them from entering her mind and weakening her strength. Surely the ordeal must end soon?

As the family filed out through the doorway into streaming sunlight Will caught her eye and winked. It would not be long now. It wasn't difficult to avoid Mother's watchful glance in the crush of villagers who had been invited to the celebration, first to the church and then to the ale afterwards. Before the hour was up they would all be too merry to notice that she was missing, and if what Will said was true, the priest would be the first to slide under the table. Feeling sick with both religious abhorrence and excitement Elizabeth gathered up her skirts and ran along the dusty footpath to the steep rise behind the building where a cluster of trees waited with shade and shelter. There, with her hot cheek resting against the pitted bark of a gnarled old oak, she peeped back to be sure that no one had followed her. Her heart was banging like a sledge-hammer and her head felt strangely light and empty. She knew that she had to go through with it this time.

'They've gone.'

Startled, she nearly jumped out of her skin. Will had walked some way down the hill with the others before doubling back to make sure that everyone had left, and that there were no stragglers.

'Come on.' He hesitated as she held back. 'You haven't changed your mind again? Don't worry that we shall be seen this time. No one will come back to the church for hours with all that wine and ale flowing at the house.'

'The church? You mean in the church?' For a moment Elizabeth couldn't believe it. They couldn't, could they? Then the comedy of the situation struck her and she began to giggle. Why not? Megan would have approved heartily of such desecration. What better way was there to show her reverence to Will, her God, and her contempt for their Deity in the House they had built for Him?

Will appreciated her sense of humour. God willing, he was about to initiate her in the finer points of what she so touchingly called love and she was laughing. What a thrill it would be to be the first for her, to show her, to teach her.

'Come then, Bess. 'Tis time we were wed and warm.' Grasping her hand he ran with her down the slope and together they entered the echoing silence of the now darkened church. The black interior halted them in their tracks until their eyes had become accustomed to the change and Will wondered just how best to proceed.

Promises? Girls liked promises. Declarations of love? Naturally. Marriage? Well, that kind of talk was perhaps taking things a little too far. Still, in for a penny !

'Bessy sweet,' he turned the full force of his boyish charms on her. 'I wouldn't want you to think that I'm only taking advantage of your youth and innocence. You know I have to return to Court soon and we may not meet again for some time, but so that you'll not think I've abandoned you I would like to make you a pledge before God.'

'Marry me?' God meant nothing to Elizabeth but Will's pledge would be to her as binding as any marriage vows. 'And then consummate the promise on the altar.' Still giggling cheekily Elizabeth pulled him across the paved floor toward the front of the church.

Will was amazed by her profanity. It was as though the idea of violating anything holy excited her in the same way as her purity excited him. It was that odd, wicked streak coming out in her again. Something so different could add to the fascination. Who would ever have thought that so modest and virtuous a maid would be transformed into a wanton, blasphemous whore by his suggestion?

Kneeling, they faced each other, and delight danced in her eyes as he took both her hands in his. The statue of Our Lady smiled down on them serenely.

'I, William Brereton, do swear before God and the Virgin Mary that we shall be joined for the rest of our days and ask their blessing on this our union.'

'And by the power and strength we shall so remain until death. Nerthu Cryfder Marw.' Her words faded to a whisper.

There it was again. That eerie way she had of saying things. As though she knew something more. More secret even than the face of God Himself. But the moment he raised her to her feet to kiss her and search with his fingers for the ties of her bodice she was laughing and giggling like a child again. An ordinary warm and human child. Squirming from his grasp she ran chuckling down the church towards the staircase by the door, which led to the old priest's room above. He had no difficulty catching her and, with her skirts flying, he half carried her up the steep flight into the cramped, untidy recess which housed an apology for a bed.

The room smelt of the sweat and incense of years and Elizabeth wrinkled her nose as she almost fell in through the door.

'Not the most gracious of wedding beds,' she grinned. 'It stinks overmuch of righteousness.'

'We'll soon level it to its station and show it hotter passions than the priest's solitary offerings. Are you disappointed?'

By the look of her she couldn't have been happier in a gilded bed with velvet hangings. 'One day, My Lady, you shall have feather pillows and fine linen sheets, and I shall dress you in silks and furs to make you the envy of the Court.'

The Court! Elizabeth hadn't thought of that. She would have to go to Court to be with him, she supposed. He saw the question on her face.

'Don't worry. I'll send for you when I've made my way. It won't happen overnight, and you must be patient, but one day I will send for you.'

They were only words. And soon forgotten he thought. She'd be married before long, if her father had any sense. But first, this was the moment he had been waiting for.

The shock of his warm, naked flesh against hers brought her back to the reality of the situation. What? How? She found it impossible to move as he nuzzled against her. She was frightened and Elizabeth felt herself torn apart at his sudden hard thrust, and used, as though he had no thought of her in his frantic rutting. Hot tears stung her with their disappointment as she tried to understand why all the passion had evaporated, leaving her lost and lonely in his arms. Bitter frustration spilled out with the tears as Will slid his body from hers to leave nothing but an overwhelming sense of emptiness. She had felt nothing but pain. Nothing!

Will had expected this. Tenderly he rocked her in his arms like a baby, kissing her face and murmuring soothing noises at her to show that he understood.

'Bessy, my sweet, I didn't want to hurt you, but there was no other way. Hush now and I'll make it better.' He kissed her mouth and she could taste the salt of her own tears on his lips. Carefully he let go of her and knelt before her. She was beautiful. There was not a blemish anywhere on that soft, white body, slim and straight except for the firm undulations where her little breasts tilted proudly upward. With surprising gentleness, after his earlier forceful attack, he wiped the smears of blood from her thighs with a rag. Watching the measured concentration for a moment, she allowed her gaze to slip from his ruffled hair down to his smooth shoulders with their newly forming muscles. They were broad compared to his narrow hips and as she watched Elizabeth saw the sinews of his belly tighten. He leaned forward to kiss the downy red curls between her legs. A sharp, unreal excitement shot through her as his fingers began their soft, inquisitive probing, stroking her deftly to awareness. This time his approach was gently and controlled, progressing slowly, and only when he felt that she was ready. He heightened her desire until she moaned softly, wanting him. Her gasp of astonishment as she felt him grow and swell within her was exhilarating. She was his and his alone as he brought her to complete fulfilment.

Elizabeth writhed against him, raising her knees to press them tight against his ribs as the whole world threatened to explode. And as it did, she clung to him in a paroxysm of ecstasy which made all thought obsolete and irreversibly bound those two young people together for life.

Will looked down at her with a certain smug satisfaction. It had definitely been worth the wait. It was a rare female who could appear so demure and quiet as Bessy could and then change in seconds into a willing and eager-to-please wanton. He knew he had possessed her completely. What William Brereton couldn't have known at that moment was that she too now had a hold on him, and that he would not be able to let her go until the day he died.

***

Cissy's comely face was red and blotchy and her little nose dripped uncontrollably. There was no comforting her at all.

'Oh, Elizabeth, what will happen to you? Where will they send you?'

Certain events surrounding Elizabeth Fytton had caused chaos within the family residing at Gawsworth Hall. When Ellen had realised that her daughter's courses had not run in either July or August she had taken her aside and questioned her closely. She might as well have talked to the wall for all the answers she got. It was Cissy who finally collapsed under cross-examination and tearfully whispered the name of William Brereton to Mistress Fytton.

'Where there's trouble there's William.' She thought to herself. Not content with aping the actions of his older brothers, he had to go and better them. Bringing the loose ways of the Court to their doorstep! John was ranting like a crazed bull and might have killed the girl with his bare hands if she hadn't got between them. His fury had been frightening. This was the end of his hopes for a Davenport match for the girl. And for her sins Elizabeth was to be incarcerated in the Nunnery at Chester. For life. Ellen had managed to procure a stay of execution on account of the plague which was rampant in the city and she had found that some of the sisters were temporarily living at the hospice on the outskirts of the village of Frodsham. There, at St. Leonard's Elizabeth would be allowed to reside until the birth of her child in the spring. After that, she would travel to St. Mary's Convent in the city and to all intents and purposes leave this earthly life. She would have a lifetime to reflect on the stupidity of her actions.

'I'll be all right, Cissy, never you fear. Will is going to send for me soon. He hasn't deserted me, truly he hasn't. You wait and see.' Elizabeth was supremely confident. Didn't he love her? Hadn't he said so? As soon as he knew about the child he would send for her. Cissy wasn't so sure. Will Brereton was the type to produce a dozen bastards before he'd done. He was too full of his own importance to worry about some silly chit he shared a secluded romp with. More than likely he wouldn't give it a second thought. All the dreams and hopes that the two girls had shared had come to a dramatic end.

There would be no weddings and sharing of news around each other's hearths as they had planned. They would most probably never set eyes on each other again. And so Cissy cried. All the way to Malpas where she was to stay with her aunt until arrangements could be made to have her join her own family.

Elizabeth watched her go with a lump in her throat,. She hadn't wanted it to be like this. Cissy was her best friend. They should stay together. Friends until they died. But they would meet again. They would! She would make it happen with her secret powers. Her mother and her father would not come between her and her wishes. They could do what they liked but she would win in the end.

Leaving Gawsworth Hall was even worse than saying goodbye to Cissy Bulkley. The first golden rays of the sun were just bringing it to life as she said her farewells. It was the only real home she had known and she had always felt a strong bond between herself and it. It was a house of secrets, as she was a woman of secrets, and she felt instinctively that they understood each other. The house would live on with all her secrets and a thousand more besides. It would never tell. As she would never tell. They were the watchers. The hoarders of other people's triumphs and disasters. The dew was still clinging to the cobbles in the courtyard as she turned away for the last time. That picture would remain with her for ever.

Somehow Elizabeth couldn't settle into her temporary home. The all-pervading smell of incense was a constant reminder of that brief taste of fulfilment; those precious moments when carnal lusts were sated and fantasy became reality. She was forced to make some show of praying for the redemption of her sins. If only the sisters had known. All those hours spent kneeling on the cold chapel floor were a blessing in disguise. There she could concentrate with all her energy on the thing which really mattered. William Brereton. She willed him to send for her.

In her imagination she saw him as clearly as if he were there. His golden curls were always untidy; his dark, violet eyes always deep with sincerity and his smile practised enough to charm the birds out of the trees. Sometimes in the night her dream would be so real that she could swear she had touched him. Could he feel it? What was he doing? Who was he with? She was tormented by thoughts of him with other girls. Prettier girls. More fashionable girls. Despite her swollen belly and aching paps she still hungered for him.

The ecstasy which had gripped her in Malpas Church had been so transitory as to have no earthly connection with her present plight. It had been the pinnacle of her attainment. The moment when all her spells and chants to bring him into her arms had come to fruition. The dull pain in her back and cramp in her legs owed nothing to that magic achievement. This was not his fault. She was glad that her couldn't see her so misshapen and clumsy. Soon it would all be over. Soon.

During the last week of March her trials began. As she heaved and sweated the sisters cooled her brow and held her limbs fast to prevent her falling from the narrow bed. She was so young! Or maybe it was that she looked younger than she really was.

'How old is she?'

'Fourteen, I should think. She'll be all right. This one's got the will to live.'

As the day passed into night her thin frame arched against the pain and Elizabeth lost all sense of time and reason. The sisters crossed themselves repeatedly as she howled fiendish curses in some strange foreign tongue, defying the very Devil to drag her into hell. Finally their faces receded on a horrifying wave of pain. Only as the dreadful tearing ceased did Elizabeth realise that in the quietness of the cell, a baby cried.

The child was bloody and its red face wrinkled. It looked older than Old Megan at the end of her life and yet somehow it was Will's face. The miracle struck home. That monstrous aching belly had produced Will's child and as Elizabeth held it in her arms she was overwhelmed by the love she felt for that helpless scrap of life.

It was a girl. Belle, she called her, for that one small token of love which Will had given her, and for one short week mother and daughter were inseparable. Then they took her away. Back into the family, if the sisters were to be believed, though Elizabeth couldn't think that Father would be agreeable to such a move. The pain of the parting was a hundred times as intense as the pain of giving birth. Something wonderful had gone from her life and she knew that it was irreplaceable. It was as if this building had turned her into one of the living dead.

She had to get out of the oppressive atmosphere of Latin chants and ringing chimes calling the faithful to their insane and mindless worship. Desolate and alone she trudged wearily through the gardens and up on to the hill, unthinking and uncaring. She was still weak from the birth and the way was steep, but she had to get away. On that her mind was insistent. Dragging herself up through the wooded slopes, dazed by her loss, she finally emerged to stand, a tiny blurred speck on the edge of a sandstone outcrop. Raised like a massive altar to the gods, it overlooked the cluster of cottages which made the village of Frodsham, and beyond them, the broad sweep of the river marshes. And there, in the hazy distance, crouching like satanic guardians over Megan's homeland, Wales, lay the mountains. Dwarfed by the immensity of the vistas before her, Elizabeth flung her arms to the sky. This was her place of worship. Not some dismal tomb full of skeletal remains. The gods would listen to her here if she reached out to them. Gusts of blustery cold spring air tore at her skirts, chilling her through her thin gown as it whipped her hair about her face. There was a faint smell of the sea. Filling her lungs she removed the last vestiges of incense and freed herself from those past six months of depressing captivity. Wholeheartedly Elizabeth gave thanks for the miracle of life. Yesterday's troubles were over, and tomorrow's not yet arrived. She was free! Despite the milk still oozing through the bodice of her dress and the blood, sticky on her legs, she felt clean again. The whole world lay at her feet. She had survived.

That tantalising taste of freedom was all too short, but it was enough to open her mind to the size and space outside herself. All things were possible, and her life was yet to be lived.

The month of April was spent under the rather more sympathetic eye of Mistress Margaret Talbot in her house at nearby Helsby. Thanks to good food and fresh air Elizabeth soon recovered her usual healthy state, physically, at least. Mentally the loss of her baby took its toll. Only the thought that Will would soon send for her kept her from constant weeping and self-pity. That and the disparaging remarks from Mary Talbot.

'You'll never see him again. I've met his kind before and I shouldn't wonder but he has even forgotten your name by this time.'

Elizabeth refused to be drawn by such baiting. All she had to do was wait and then Mary would see!

'The Court is full of pretty maids. Do you think he will bother his head about one so far away? Where is he now, when you need him? You'll never set eyes on him again!'

It was a struggle to keep her temper when Mary was putting into words the very things which worried Elizabeth.

'He will send for me, Mary, despite your disbelieving smile.'Tis not his fault that he was called away to attend His Majesty, and one day I shall probably wait upon the Queen myself.' She sounded a good deal more confident than she felt. But Will had warned her that it would take time. She just had to be patient. That was all.

It was the first day of May when they took her to St. Mary's. She felt the full impact of the irony in the situation. One year ago today in Yates's Spinney by Congleton Fair. One whole year! How excited she had been by his attentions. How grown up she had felt then. She hadn't realised, she hadn't understood how painful growing up would be or how enduring the heartache after a child was torn screaming from its mother's arms.

Inside St. Mary's Convent the infernal chimes rubbed her nerves raw. Pray! Pray! Pray! That's all they seemed to do. It nearly drove her mad in the first weeks until she found a way to make use of the system herself. After all, they were only calling the faithful to worship. Elizabeth became less loath to join them, though those around her would have been wary of her company had they known who it was she prayed to. Her lips moved in time to their responses, but the words were different. Word would come. It had to. Will couldn't leave her mouldering here for ever.

Only in the night did her fears sometimes get the better of her. Elizabeth had no control over her dreams and her vivid imagination made them as real as dreams will ever be. She felt again his satin-smooth skin pressed passionately against her own and relived once more those precious moments when their bodies had joined and moved as one. When heaven had truly come on earth. Then she would wake. Alone. Deserted. And the fears that she would never see him again would wipe out completely the fleeting glimpse of happier times. With no one to witness her weakness she would cry softly to herself and whisper his name into the darkness, willing him to hear it. To come to her.

Going about her daily tasks, no one would have suspected her desperate longing to be free of the cloistered life. She was as docile as anyone could have wished. Gradually they put less restraint on Elizabeth and if there were any errands to be run, she was the one who was given the task. She became a familiar sight to the traders and their wives and soon learned where the best bread was baked. So, too, she could be guaranteed to find the freshest fish and plumpest fowl.

As the months drifted by Elizabeth began to indulge her passion for drawing. Everything came under scrutiny. The people and the place. The forthright welcome of Agnes, the alewife at the Bluebell, to old Seth the stonemason. She sketched the Market Cross and the round towers of the castle, the city gates, and the graceful spire of White Friars. In her simple convent garb, she herself became a part of the fabric of the city.

It soon became recognised that Elizabeth could make a fair likeness of anyone and she found that men and women alike were flattered to have their pictures as a keepsake. She never kept them. Except the ones she had drawn of Will. She could draw him from memory still, but those she had made of him at Gawsworth were the best. Those, and the silver bell, were all she had now to remember him by. Other things were beginning to fade. Her parents, her sisters, her brother. But Will was as clear in her mind as though she had seen him only yesterday.

It was one of those hot, airless days when a hammering and banging from outside the city walls caught her attention. Men were on the roof of the old Church of St. John attempting to rebuild the spire. She could see them silhouetted against the bright blue cloudless sky as she squinted upwards, and above the din came the shouted instructions of an as yet invisible man who appeared to be in charge. Emerging from the deep, circular hollow between the walls and the church she finally saw where the bellowing was coming from. Mister Bolton, the master-carpenter was as round as he was tall. A shiny-pink pate glistened in the afternoon heat despite the fact that it was mopped by an enormous, if grubby, cloth at the culmination of every sentence.

He made a perfect subject. Settling herself on an unused block of sandstone Elizabeth drew a likeness so exact that even she was unusually pleased with her efforts. The back of his rough work-shirt had wriggled its way out of his breeches and half hung, half poked out behind like the white flash of a rabbit's tail. On the other side, the rotund belly was more reminiscent of some hugely inflated pouter pigeon strutting about its loft on legs which looked far too thin and feeble by comparison. And all the time he crowed like a cock watching the sunrise. Apart from the noise, there he was captured in every detail on the parchment.

It was the sudden silence which made everyone aware that all was not well with Mister Bolton. The hand half raised to mop the brow became diverted to the throat where it struggled ineffectually to remove the knotted shirt ties. The dusty air had somehow stopped his breath at the same time as his big round face took it upon itself to compete with the sun for colour. He never uttered another word. Just one astonished splutter, and he fell. Dead.

Elizabeth couldn't believe her eyes. There he lay, perfectly still, and flat on his back in the sun. Everything seemed to have come to a stop. The men on the roof had turned to stone, their faces as grotesque as the gargoyles they were busily replacing, and even casual passers-by had stopped out of curiosity. Elizabeth was the first to move. Death could be so abrupt. Stark in its brutality.

She ran. She didn't wait to see how they would carry him home, or who would take his place and stand there in the heat shouting orders to men with other things on their minds. Anyone could die. At any time. What if Will had died? What if that was why he hadn't sent for her? How would she know? Who would tell her? She couldn't bear the thought of staying at St. Mary's for ever. Her mind was in such turmoil that she wasn't really looking where she was going and turning a corner ran full tilt into a young man coming in the opposite direction. To save them both from falling he put his arms around her and by lifting her off her feet managed to retain his balance.

It was Christopher Werminsham, the goldsmith's son and apprentice to his father in the trade. Elizabeth had seen him about for some time, and he had had his eye on her for even longer.

'A lucky day for me and no mistake,' he laughed as he set her down on her feet again. 'Chased by the Devil, are you?'

Somehow she gasped out the cause of her hurried passage through the streets. The piece of parchment was still hanging limply from her hand and he took it from her. As he held it up and she saw Mister Bolton, perfectly depicted, the horror of it hit her again and she looked as if she was about to faint. Not one to miss a chance, Christopher played the gentleman and supported her with his arm round her waist until she was safely at the convent gate.

Elizabeth was grateful to him for his obvious concern and after that day they often met, quite by chance, she was sure. Sometimes they walked by the river and talked of their families and friends, their hopes and aspirations. It transpired that Christopher had heard of Will Brereton, the head of that family holding high office in the city of Chester. Doing well for himself at Court, by all accounts. Elizabeth was avid for news. How well? What was his position now? At least he was still alive! Unfortunately, though he furrowed his brow convincingly, Christopher Werminsham could remember little more than he had already said.

There was other news from Court though. The King's romantic younger sister, Mary Brandon had given birth to a daughter, and the Queen had again miscarried. She still had only the Princess Mary to show for all her trials in the King's bed. Rumour had it that the King had now taken a mistress and tongues were wagging nineteen to the dozen.

'Twas said that everyone at Court now had a mistress. Did Will? Elizabeth was terrified of having her worst fears confirmed but she still desperately wanted news of him. Anything was better than nothing and she began to look forward to bumping into the attentive young man, hoping each time that he would have fresh news from London. Usually he had, but never of Will. Mister Wermingsham knew the full story of Elizabeth's disgrace and envied Mister Brereton his luck, but he also realised that the likelihood of that erstwhile lover returning was negligible. Sooner or later Elizabeth would tire of waiting for news which never came and in her straitened circumstances should not look askance at a goldsmith. Although he was only a tradesman, it was an honourable trade and although he was not the handsomest of men he was, when all said and done, a man. Beggars shouldn't be choosers and Christopher had convinced himself that by the time he was no longer apprenticed Elizabeth would be more than eager to give herself over to the joys of a marriage bed.

Was it really six years since she had first stood on this same street corner, watching these same festivities? How different now to then. Then, she had been surrounded by family and friends. Now, she was alone. No Mother. No Cissy. No baby Katherine Parr wriggling and squealing in her arms. Christopher Savage was long since dead. And where was Will?

Today Abbot Birkenshaw led the prayers and the ceremonial sword was carried high before Mayor Rogerson. The wit of the players had scarcely diminished and the ale-sodden crowd was as receptive as ever. Elizabeth was wallowing in nostalgia, completely untouched by the carnival atmosphere, her thoughts in that same place, but in another time. Taken unawares, she was startled to feel a hand on her back. For a split second she thought he had returned. The illusion vanished. No tingle of excitement accompanied the caress. Instead she felt a shudder of revulsion as Christopher Werminsham slid his bony fingers round her waist and tried to insinuate them between the folds of her plain convent habit. The intrusion, coming as it did in the wake of her little day-dream, revolted her. Mister Werminsham had had a deal more wine than was good for him or their friendship! Her feelings must have been written all over her face as she looked at him but he seemed oblivious. His watery eyes gleamed lasciviously over the thin beak of a nose and great gobs of spittle drooled from the fleshy lower lip. She had scarcely noticed it before, but then she had never really looked at him in that way at all. He had only ever been a moderate good friend, and a source of information.

Realising that he was in no mood to listen to reason Elizabeth pushed his hands away roughly and turned into the crowd.

George Darwell, who happened to be standing behind her at that moment, suddenly found himself with an armful of very pretty girl.

'A kiss and a cuddle and we won't argue,' he laughed. 'But anything more and you must bargain with the wife.'

Elizabeth didn't stay long enough even for the promised kiss. Pushing her way past him she scuttled rapidly through the merry-makers, to a lot of suggestive remarks and invitations. Mister Darwell watched her go with a shrug of his muscular shoulders. Lovely eyes! And a splendid ankle as he had observed when she lifted her skirts to run.

Everyone seemed to want to paw at her and make obscene suggestions. It made her feel dirty. As though she were a trollop out selling her wares along Northgate. It sickened her. The sweat of exertion ran like a river from her arm-pits and trickled uncomfortably down between the smooth contours of her well developed breasts. Nothing and no one could stop her until she gained the safety of the convent gardens. There, wet through and gasping, she leaned against the rough brick wall for support as the blood pounded in her head fit to burst it. Her throat constricted, her stomach heaved, and Elizabeth vomited violently onto the mossy path behind the herb garden. It stung her gullet and the back of her nose and the pain of it brought tears to her eyes. Through a nauseous haze the sick girl somehow dragged herself into the coolness of her cell where fevered delirium wiped out logical thought with nightmare hallucinations.

In that ghastly world full of red-hot knives and suffocating heat she saw herself shackled by priests with hollowed eye-sockets full of burning coals. She was chained and bound body and soul, and dressed in the habit of a nun for all eternity. The chants and chimes scraped away at her flesh until it hung raw and bleeding. A sacrifice to their God. Elizabeth fought every inch of the way. For every one of their foul Latin spells she had one of her own to counteract their magic. She would not prostitute herself to satisfy the lusts of men, nor the greater lusts of the Church. She belonged to Will. Only Will.

At the very height of the fever she screamed for him. On and on, until the sisters almost gave up hope for her life. They learned that praying by her bedside made her worse. Much worse. Each time she opened her eyes and saw them standing or kneeling near her she threw herself into a convulsive fit to the accompaniment of evil-sounding foreign words.

The good sisters cooled her body but it was days before the raging inferno in her mind burnt itself out. When it finally did there seemed little left of the old Elizabeth. She was an empty shell. All hope had gone. All coherent thought had gone. She neither knew nor cared who she was or where she was, and every day was the same. She dressed and washed and ate mechanically, but she was no longer capable of walking the city streets alone. She refused to leave the grounds of St. Mary's. Somewhere, deep down inside herself she had accepted that they had captured her. She had become one of the living dead.

It was a warm September day when a miracle brought her back to life. Her eyes were fixed vacantly on nothing at all, when a stranger approached and bowed his greeting.

'Elizabeth Fytton? I beg pardon for this intrusion but I have been entrusted with a letter for you.'

'Sir?' She turned her child-like expression on him.

'William Brereton at your service, Mistress.' He bowed again.

Something sharp prickled her behind her eyes as she focused on him for the first time. William Brereton? Nay. This was not the William Brereton she once knew. This one was too old. And too fat!

'I bring you a message from my namesake and cousin, that other William Brereton who is at present making his way at the Court of King Henry. He charges me to bring you this package and bids you make good speed.' He thrust the package at her as though glad to have completed some awful task and bowed again.

After watching his back view disappearing rapidly into the distance she turned her attention to the vellum packet on her lap. Strange, that William Brereton should appear, like a ghost from the past to disturb her peace. But then it was not her Will, but only one masquerading under his name. And what was this? Her fingers broke open the seal. Gold coins! Who in the world would be sending her money? The letter was written in a bold, neat hand. And Elizabeth had never learnt to read!

Will had sent for her. The fog began to clear and as it did she became convinced that she was right. Will had sent for her at long last. But how to read the letter? Who could she trust? Not the sisters. Not Christopher Werminsham. She never wanted to see him again.

Mistress Talbot calmly sat herself opposite the flustered girl. Elizabeth looked fit to burst with excitement.

'Please, please, please read it to me.' Elizabeth handed her the letter. 'I'm sure it is from Will asking me to join him.'

Just as she said these words Mary Talbot entered the solar. Or rather she swept in! She looked down her nose disdainfully at Elizabeth in her unbecoming garb. 'You've heard then?'

Elizabeth stared blankly at her. 'Heard what?'

'That I am to be married. To none other than Henry Percy, son and heir to Northumberland. I suppose that you have come begging for a position in my household. What would you like? Work in the kitchens? Or perhaps lady of the bed-chamber would suit you better?'

'Mary!' Mistress Talbot's tone was sharp. 'Show a little more charity to one who has not had your good fortune, if you please.' Conscious of Elizabeth's anxiety she unfolded the letter and quickly scanned through it before reading it out loud.

'Bessy Sweet,

'Make haste, for the time has come. Buy yourself clothes for the journey, though not over-many to carry. I have secured a place for you, but you must come early or the chance will be lost. Mary Talbot is to come to Court and I hope that you may be her travelling companion, for your safety and my peace. Come to me now and on my solemn oath we shall never more be parted.

'In His hand, William Brereton Gentleman to His Majesty, King Henry.'

There was a moment's silence before Elizabeth spoke. Then her words came tumbling out over one another like a flood tide.

'Please Mistress, help me. There is no one else I can turn to and if my father found out I should be beaten. He has settled a sum on St. Mary's that I may spend the rest of my life in confinement. But Will has a place for me and his fortunes are rising. Surely you have heard. I shall not be destitute or alone if only I can be with him. I must go to him. Either with Mary in her good fortune, or alone and take my chances on the road unaided.'

Margaret Talbot couldn't abandon the girl to the perils of the road, and though she knew that there would be angry words with her friends at Gawsworth if they ever discovered the way of Elizabeth's escape, she helped the girl to spend her money in good cause. Unknown to anyone she placed her with Mary as her companion and prayed that she was doing the right thing. Will Brereton's star was ascending if all the tales of him were true, and it was a sin to lock away from the world such a lovely young woman as Elizabeth Fytton. There had been precious little romance in Margaret's own life and it pleased her to be able to help these young people to possible happiness. For certain, Elizabeth would not be happy without the lad.

Elizabeth left Chester without a backward glance. How could she have doubted? Hadn't he said it would take time? Or was it that her fevered pleadings had bridged the miles between them and he had heard her frenzied calls?

Mary was welcome to Henry Percy with his wealth and titles. All Elizabeth wanted now was William of the laughing eyes. Forever.

Three

STANDING awkwardly with her few belongings at her feet, Elizabeth looked around hopefully for a friendly face. Everything had been so new and exciting but after Mary had been whisked away to her father Elizabeth had been left alone amid the bustle of the great yard feeling provincial and incongruous. Clothes which had appeared modish in the city of Chester were little better than rustic compared to London fashions. And where could Will be in this vast honeycomb of a building known as Greenwich Palace? She would never find him.

Through the cool sunshine of that autumn afternoon she could hear the distant calls of the boatmen, full of comradeship and belligerence as they skilfully avoided the pitfalls of their trade. She would never have believed the volume of traffic on the water. It was just as chaotic here beside the Palace. Carts were being unloaded at one side of the cobbled court to the accompaniment of light hearted banter, while all around was so much coming and going that Elizabeth began to feel dizzy.

Washerwomen, oval baskets balanced on their hips, sauntered by eyeing her up and down curiously. They saw a lot of oddities arriving from all sorts of outlandish places hoping for work on the fringe of royalty. Elizabeth watched them go. Perhaps she shouldn't have come. If Will didn't find her, what would she do? She could be abducted! Murdered! The knot of anxiety in her stomach began to tighten painfully into panic. Even the pages in their green and white, scurrying in and out of doorways with messages, knew where they were going.

Such changes and developments take place in the years between fourteen and seventeen as adult proportions are achieved that even the best of friends in childhood have, after a short separation, failed to recognise one another and passed in the street like total strangers. Thus, Elizabeth's glance passed over the handsome young man. William Brereton was now grown to his full height and his muscular frame bore evidence of hours of practice at the tilt, while his features had lost the plumpness of extreme youth. And his hair was short. No longer curling on to his collar, and changed from spun gold to golden brown, it altered his looks completely. Only when he swung her from her feet with a delighted yell did she realise that the differences were essentially superficial. He was still the same Will he had always been. Picking up her box and leading her by the hand he laughed and chattered as though they had never been parted.

Elizabeth was completely bemused by it all. He seemed so happy and confident and quite at home in the maze of rooms and passages through which they passed. It wasn't what she expected. The palace was a muddle of buildings which had somehow become joined into one residence and she lost all sense of direction. Eventually, Will drew her into a small chamber where he knew they would be private for a while at least, and there he began to tell her something of Court life.

Elizabeth listened with dismay as he explained how many hours, or sometimes days, and nights, he would be required to be attendant on King Henry. By the sound of things she was not going to see much more of him than she had in the past two years. It seemed that his normal habit was to sleep with the other courtiers, not yet being so well advanced as to have a room of his own, and she would similarly sleep with the other tiring ladies amongst whom she would be working.

Seeing the look on her face Will burst out laughing.

'Don't worry about that, Bess. I have it all arranged and a room is reserved for us in the village for any hours that I should require it.' He was pleased. She was as hot for him as she had ever been and any doubts he might have entertained at sending for her vanished. Will's intimate encounters with the fairer sex had been numerous and varied. Despite this, there had been no one whom he had wanted to keep as his mistress. Some lasted days, some weeks, but none had ever made any permanent marks. It had only been when others of his acquaintance became enamoured of, and financially responsible for their mistresses that he thought seriously of having one of his own. It would be pleasant to know that there was always someone able, ready and willing whenever he should have the time and inclination for a woman. Occasionally he would think back to that time in Malpas Church. How she had moaned and clung to him, his little virgin. He'd never found another. Would she come? He was unsure. After all, he hadn't bothered about leaving her with child nor about her fate afterwards. But then, he had been extremely busy trying to advance himself at Court. She would understand.

Unless she'd changed since they last met there was one certain way to make sure of her. Slipping his arm around her and turning on all his charm he began to kiss her. Suddenly Elizabeth felt safe. They might not be able to live together as her parents had and as she dreamed they would, but he would still be there, close by, to look after her. Oh, how she loved him.

'We'll not have long to wait, Love. When the rest of the Court dines we shall be away to the room I told you of. I've made arrangements with others so that I shall not be missed tonight and your ladies may whistle for your company until tomorrow. Has the time dragged, Bessy, or has someone else been keeping you warm whilst I struggled to make my way in this difficult world?'

He made it sound as if his lot had been the penance and hers merely a holiday. Perhaps he thought that no one else had ever found her attractive and that was why she came running the moment he snapped his fingers. Elizabeth told him of her friendship with Christopher Werminsham, omitting the fact that she found the man repulsive in the extreme. Will only laughed and kissed her more soundly than before. It was no use. She might as well tell him the truth. Mister Werminsham had made her sick. Literally.

'And didn't I?' There was an amused twinkle in his eye at this oblique reference to her pregnancy. For the first time ever Elizabeth felt a twinge of disappointment in him. Had the child, their daughter, really meant as little to him as that? '

It was a girl.' She stammered over the words.

'Aye, and as pretty as her mother too. The same pale skin and wide eyes, though her hair is more a fiery gold than your deep auburn tints.'

'You've seen her? Where is she? Why was I never given word of her?'

'She is part of my brother's family now, just one more in a large brood. My mother and yours made sure that she was well seen to and happy. It was best that you should forget her and leave her to grow up thinking herself in her rightful place, but don't worry. I have not forgotten that she is ours and should I make my way with any success I shall see that she is well provided for.'

Elizabeth felt as though a great weight had been lifted from her shoulders. 'And you knew of my welfare too?'

She looked so trusting. He didn't lie. He kissed her again which, as he realised, she took as the affirmative and clung to him so tightly that he wished it were night already. It was going to be easy, getting his way with this one.

Later, in a tiny room of the village inn, they rediscovered each other's bodies and found that memory had not exaggerated. Indeed, if anything it had sold them short. This time there was no worry of being caught, and no stink of stale sweat or other bodily excretions left by the supposedly celibate priest. As Will had promised her that day there was a real bed with fresh clean sheets, and curtains drawn against prying eyes. They could do anything they wanted without fear of anyone.

It was there, on that first night, that Elizabeth learnt that it was not his intention to marry her. At least, not until he could provide for a wife as he would like to. Elizabeth could have argued that his lack of money didn't matter to her at all. But she didn't. She was content to be there with him after so long alone. She would do whatever he said. The trouble was there was so much to remember. He warned her to say little at first, until she was familiar with the mess of intrigue without which Court life could not survive. She would soon learn who to side with and who against.

Elizabeth listened carefully to his advice, trying to remember it all. It was so difficult! Names without faces. Would she ever survive in such a maelstrom of subversive activity?

Soon after she began in service at the Court Elizabeth made the acquaintance of a girl of her own age to whom she seemed irresistibly drawn. In personality they were complete opposites, Elizabeth being quieter than a church mouse, whilst Anne Boleyn could not be happy unless she was at the centre of a noisy crowd. Despite this difference there was somehow a feeling of sympathy between the two girls. An indefinable rapport. Something Old Megan used to say came back to Elizabeth. 'When true sisters meet, they know it. But some will not acknowledge it. Until the end.' Anne Boleyn had the Power, if she chose to use it. Elizabeth felt certain.

Anne and Elizabeth were opposite not only in nature but in appearance too. Where Elizabeth was well endowed with curves, Anne was singularly lacking in such feminine features. With her long black hair and sallow skin she almost despaired of her looks. This was probably the reason for her determination to be the wittiest and most outrageous girl about the Court.

Gradually the two became friends, a situation which Will encouraged, in view of the fact that Anne Boleyn was well connected. Niece to the Duke of Norfolk. Many a whispered conversation took place between those young girls by the light of a guttering candle, long after everyone else was asleep. Elizabeth told of her undying love for the King's man, William Brereton, of how they had first met, and of all the things which had happened to them since. Anne admitted that she was still a virgin. Oh, she'd had her chances, at the French Court, but never having felt any passion herself she had been disinclined to throw away her virtue simple to satisfy the momentary cravings of some courtier or other. Listening to Elizabeth though, she began to wish that she could experience that overwhelming love for another human being. To want to give herself completely. Somehow she never thought that it would happen. Men loving her! Now that was a different proposition altogether.

Years later Elizabeth was to wonder whether she had been the one to put such thoughts into Anne's mind at a time when she needed to feel that she had someone of her own. Whatever the reason, it wasn't many weeks before Anne was sporting an air of secret excitement. As Elizabeth guessed, she couldn't keep it to herself for very long.

'Oh, he's wonderful, wonderful. Wonderful!' Anne danced about the solar singing the praises of her paragon.

'Who is wonderful?' She had had Elizabeth guessing for ages but she was no nearer now than she had been at the beginning.

'He's the handsomest man at Court. There, that should give you a clue.'

'Will Brereton, 'Elizabeth grinned at her.

'Idiot!' The cushion hit Elizabeth full in the face.

'And has he . . . ?'

'Swived me? Aye. Down by the river last even. Look if you don't believe me. I still have the insect bites to prove it.'

Anne lifted her skirts to show the results of the recent battle.

'Tis to be hoped that only the insects have bitten deeply enough to wound,' Elizabeth said seriously. It would never do for Anne Boleyn to find herself compromised by some eager youth. 'Who is he? To whom you have given your favours so lightly?'

'Not lightly, but with all my heart,' Anne pronounced dramatically. 'Wait until you meet him and all will become clear.' Rushing over to where Elizabeth sat she pulled her friend to her feet. 'Come and meet him now! He mentioned that he might be walking by the river again and it is stuffy in these rooms.'

As it turned out, Harry was passably handsome, Elizabeth conceded, if one liked the quieter, she hesitated to say weak, rather introvert character in a man. In her eyes he could not hold a candle to the rip-roaring rumbustious Will. Harry's steadiness did however suit Anne perfectly. She needed someone like that to stabilize her own volatile moods. One thing was certain; a couple more in love would be difficult to find. They shared those intimate looks which denote lovers everywhere and managed to touch arms and hands on the flimsiest of excuses. It wasn't long before Anne had Harry chasing her through the trailing branches of the willows, teasing him for long enough before giving him his reward in a full impassioned kiss.

Elizabeth looked round anxiously. Anne could never count discretion amongst her virtues. If she were seen playing fast and loose with any Tom, Dick... or Harry, there would be a whole lot of trouble to face of her own making. It was not until the two girls were alone and walking back to the

58

Palace that Elizabeth learned the whole truth.

'You worry too much, Elizabeth. It won't matter if we are caught. Do you think I would throw away my virtue on some low-born lad with not a penny to his name? Surely you know me better than that by now.' Anne put her arm around Elizabeth and lowered her voice. 'We don't want it spread abroad yet until our plans are laid as Harry's father has ideas for his eldest son to marry some mealy-mouthed wench from elsewhere. But if I have anything to do with it, it will be Anne Boleyn who marries Henry Percy, heir to Northumberland.'

When Elizabeth confided the news to Will, however, he advised her to be cautious.

'Anne has some wild schemes at times, you know. What if she doesn't get her own way? What kind of scandal will it create? Until we know which way this thing is going try not go get too involved.'

'Mary Talbot knows nothing of it yet. She is still strutting about the Court as though she owns it, but I should love to see her face when she finds out. It's clear that Harry likes laughter with his passion rather than the haughtiness which is all Mary has to offer.'

Will looked thoughtful. 'Maybe Anne will have her way at that. Have you heard that her family is moving in the highest circles of all these days?'

'How so?' Elizabeth sensed fresh gossip here.

'Well, it would seem that King Henry has given up all hope of having a legitimate son since the birth of his bastard by Bess Blount. He thinks he would only be wasting his time and energy in his wife's bed.'

'You mean he has taken a new mistress?' Elizabeth was not surprised. She knew that Mistress Blount had recently been sent packing with a husband to keep her happy.

'Aye. Anne's sister Mary is known to be keeping him warm at nights, and if Anne wants favours of His Majesty I wouldn't think she'd have a better opportunity than this.'

'I wouldn't argue that Anne can be devious at times, and it's true that she laughed at me for throwing away my virtue on a man of no estate.'

Will interrupted, laughing. 'That sounds typical of Anne.'

'But despite his wealth I think she really has some feelings for Harry. I'm sure she is in love with him.'

'If you ask Anne I'm sure that she would tell you that 'tis as easy to fall in love with a man of means as a pauper.' In Will's opinion love and marriage should never be spoken of in the same breath, but he knew the way Elizabeth's mind was working.

'I didn't look for your purse before I loved you.' Deep down inside Elizabeth knew he was right about Anne, just as she knew that money was the last thing she herself ever worried about.

'And you are not of the Howard family, my sweet, and therein lies the difference.'

The affair between Anne and Harry progressed. It wasn't long before Elizabeth was hearing of illicit meetings and such daring behaviour that the whole thing was bound to be discovered before long.

'I shall never forget that first night we spent together. We wanted to look at each other, so we left the bed open to the moonlight. Oh, the feeling when he touched me!' She shuddered deliciously, 'His skin shone with the soft lustre of an iridescent pearl but you can take my word for it that softness was nowhere in evidence when he took me. And then,' she paused, reliving the vision, 'and then, right at the moment of his ecstasy he gave a little moan which pierced my heart and I swear, joined our souls forever.'

It was all very well for Will to tell her not to get too involved, but Elizabeth couldn't help it. She and Anne were kindred spirits, and if Anne would only learn to control her emotion a little as Elizabeth did, and channel all her thoughts into achieving her aims, everything would be fine. The trouble was that Anne was too easily waylaid by other things and constantly flipped from one activity or pastime to another. And she always had to be the centre of things! If only she could have known Old Megan! Anne knew that Elizabeth worried for her but she only laughed and continued to make her plans. Her family were on the best of terms with the King.

At first the Lady Anne screamed and kicked at everyone who dared approach her. She had left it too late and her sister Mary was no longer the object of the King's affections. Who would have thought that the stupid girl would get herself rejected after so short a time. And as for men! They did not deserve a woman's company or favours. They were braggarts! The lot of them! Brave? Courageous? Never! They were cowardly and weak enough to be blown away by mere words. Fear of losing titles was greater than the counterfeit love of men. Love was a sham and a hypocrisy and by God, men would pay for it. Harry Percy would be the last to get the better of Anne Boleyn! She felt shamed and dirty. She had believed him when he said that he would marry her. She would have her revenge. Somehow!

For days Anne denounced men for every crime imaginable. She didn't care that Harry hadn't stood a chance against his father's wishes, or that if he had been disinherited she would have been the last one to want him for a husband. It was the humiliation which hurt. Elizabeth began to fear for her sanity. If only Anne had known how to harness all that hate! Instead, her ravings merely became wilder and more extreme, without definite direction. Elizabeth prepared a soothing potion to calm her fever and make her sleep.

'This has brought her close to madness,' Elizabeth confided in Will later. 'Sometimes she is scarcely in control of what she says and I swear she was ready to utter treason if I hadn't quietened her when I did.'

'Her fury was misplaced anyway.'

'What do you mean, misplaced?'

'I mean that Harry could do no other. It wasn't that he didn't want to marry Anne. But what else could he do? Could he tell the world that they had been lovers for weeks? Could he drag her name through that kind of mud with Norfolk ready to kill her for disgracing the family and Northumberland incensed at Norfolk's disparaging remarks? The heads of both those families will most certainly not allow the junior members to tell them their business. Harry knew that even if he told the truth and ruined Anne's reputation, they would still not be allowed to wed.'

'Are you trying to say that Harry actually loves her?'

Having heard all Anne's accusations that was hard to believe.

Will nodded.

'And how, pray, have you come by that snippet of information? Do you now also have Harry Percy's ear?'

'Well, not in the normal way of things, no. But on this occasion I happened to be on the spot and we talked.

Will rarely just 'happened to be there'. The best way to acquire information was usually from the horse's mouth and in this instance he had wanted to know exactly where Anne Boleyn's fortunes now stood, and which direction they were likely to be travelling in. He had no wish to be caught up in the aftermath of any upheaval of this sort.

Elizabeth was looking at him in that way women have when they are almost accusing you of something without knowing quite what that something is.

'Miserable as he was after renouncing her publicly, the only thought in his head was to purchase himself some comfort.'

'That certainly doesn't sound much like a man with a broken heart. Are you all so fickle?' Elizabeth had often wondered why Will had bothered to send for her when he was surrounded by any number of Court beauties. But Megan had always promised her the Power and the Strength! Unlike Anne, Elizabeth knew how to direct her thoughts and concentrate them.

'What do you take us all for?' Will was laughing at her. 'Twas the good wine of oblivion he was after. He hadn't the slightest appetite for women that night. And I have to confess, I joined him in his cups and as we poured the wine, out poured the secrets of our hearts.'

'You never told him of us?' Elizabeth couldn't believe that for a moment. Will preferred her to stay well out of the limelight and few people had connected their names together. Or so she believed.

'Not in so many words,' Will admitted, 'but I was sympathetic to his cause and told him a tale of how I had to leave the love of my life because of circumstances. Without mentioning any names.'

Elizabeth snuggled up to him. The love of his life, was she? Almost as good as being his wife, she supposed.

'Anyway, the truth of it is this: Harry is to be wed to Mary Talbot without further delay and arrangements are to be put in hand to marry Anne to one of her Butler cousins. In any event, she is to be removed from the temptations of the Court before she manages to create more havoc. The trouble is that while they can force Harry to wed Mary, he swears that they cannot make him bed her and that he will never take another woman.'

'That must have been the wine talking! A married man not bedding his wife nor any other woman? Aye, some I could believe it of, but not one so eager as Harry was with Anne.'

'At this moment, he believes it, and that is all there is to it. Harry did think that he might have talked his father round, but apparently Thomas More stepped in with a timely piece of advice and he thought better of it. That venerable scholar certainly knew how to prevent Harry making an even bigger fool of himself over a silly woman.'

Elizabeth didn't say a word. It wouldn't be any use anyway. She had always known that it was a man's world and that women should never be allowed to interfere in a man's ambitions.

Will was thinking along the same lines. He's been in the company of Anne and her brother George quite often of late and would prefer the fact to be forgotten for the time being. It was unfortunate that Bessy had become such good friends with Anne but he had thought of a way round the problem.

When he told Elizabeth what he planned she was at first indignant, and then hurt. 'Come to me now and we shall never more be parted.' Wasn't that what he had written? And hadn't she trusted him completely and come running? She always knew it wouldn't last. He must have found himself another mistress.

'Who is she? Is she more beautiful? More loving? Rich?'

He had known all along that she would not be happy with the news. Oh, why were women so predictable! Maybe a rest, or a change, would do him good after all.

'Bessy, my sweet, I do love you. I haven't taken anyone in your place and not am I likely to. There is no one more beautiful, or more loving. As for riches! If you will just do as I ask with a smile instead of a frown, I shall have all the riches I could want in no time. 'Tis only until all this pother over your friend Anne has blown over. No one who wants to rise at Court can afford to let the ground slide from under him. You wouldn't want to stand in my way, would you?'

She wouldn't. It was just that, well, it was difficult to know what to believe. She had seen what the Court was like and she could see the dangers of leaving a man like Will to his own devices for any length of time. If she really faced up to the truth she knew he wouldn't be on his own for very long.

She had to go. He'd made his mind up. But there was no sense in burning his boats. Was there? If things turned out well he might want to bring her back again. Dropping to his knees before her he deftly popped the toe of a fine silk stocking over her foot, and smoothing it up over her leg proceeded to tease Elizabeth from her sulks. The job completed, his touch became a caress and she knew immediately that she would put up no further argument.

It was no use trying to deny him. She knew she couldn't.

'Kiss me,' he coaxed her, 'or I shall be forced to send you away without further favours.' His hand was still on her leg and he watched her eyelids begin to droop as his fingers slid expertly between her thighs. It was the first time she had ever disagreed with him on anything, but he had won.

Four

NORFOLK! The place was completely foreign to Elizabeth. Flatter than the Cheshire plain and scarcely a tree in sight worthy of the name! She knew how prestigious her position in the household of the King's sister was but what on earth was Will up to? Did he have another lover or was this move really to protect his position with the King? Or perhaps little of both! The only consolation was the children.

Frances Brandon was a precocious young madam for her age. Four years old and ruling the roost whenever she thought she could get away with it. Needless to say, she tried out all her wiles and tantrums on the new nurse-maid only to find that Mistress Elizabeth was more than her match when it came to who should have their own way sooner. The hoity-toity manners failed to intimidate Elizabeth for a reason the little girl would never understand. Somewhere along the lanes of Cheshire, or in the deep green of the forests lived another girl. Another four-year-old, just as wilful and independent as this one tried to be! A fiery-headed child, stubborn to a fault, so Will had said. All the high and mighty ways which Frances tried to copy from her elders only served to endear her more to Mistress Fytton who needed someone to love, someone to care for in her enforced separation from her lover.

Henry Brandon was a quite different matter. Two years older than his sister, he was already being groomed for great things. As nephew to King Henry the young man was close to the throne. And could get closer! Certainly his father was as close to the King as any man could be and there was not a father living who did not have ambitions for his children.

Elizabeth was not unduly sorry that she saw much less of Henry than she did of Frances. The boy attended lessons daily in the company of others from local aspiring families, his tutor doing his best to educate him, but often finding himself defeated by the greater attractions of the outdoor life.

Despite her initial loneliness Elizabeth soon settled down, helped by the more pleasant duties in the nursery though occasionally she couldn't help but wish that the children were her own children. She did her best not to dwell on such things. She would just have to wait until Will thought it safe for her to return to Court.

Even the air seemed different here. The wind was sharper. Yet on some days the atmosphere was as sultry and as oppressive as it had ever been in London. Elizabeth was amazed by the vast numbers of game-birds which winged constantly overhead, their throaty call drifting out from the fens and waterways. Flocks of nagging geese argued constantly with the dumpy little ducks whilst the graceful swans fattened themselves in readiness for the dinner table. There was never any shortage of fowl in the Countess Mary's house! Elizabeth had always imagined the King's younger sister to be a beautiful, romantic figure, eloping as she did with the handsome Charles Brandon and so daringly risking her brother's wrath. She was indeed a beautiful woman, but Elizabeth found that she had the Tudor temper, which rather squashed the notions of romance and made it advisable to step warily in her presence. The Duchess had a very nasty tongue in her head.

'A fine evening, Mistress.'

Elizabeth looked up startled. She hadn't heard anyone approaching across the grass.

'Henry Bedinfeld, at your service.' A handsome face. A charming smile. And more than a spark of interest in his eyes.

Elizabeth nodded her acceptance of his presence. 'Are you then kin to young Master William Bedinfeld who takes his lessons with the Master Henry?'

Whoever he was, he had a certain refinement of features which Elizabeth found very attractive. His penetrating brown eyes almost exactly matched the colour of his hair except for the fact that they were curiously flecked with gold. Altogether a fascinating visitor! And very easy to talk to, as Elizabeth soon found out. Henry Bedinfeld had arrived to escort Master William home, an occurrence which was apparently a regular part of the boy's routine, and seeing the beauty of a voluptuous feminine, figure going to waste in the balmy evening the noble youth generously decided to end her loneliness. He had nothing to lose but an empty hour.

As it happened, the two found conversation flowing between them. They were quite unconscious of the charming couple they made as they sat side by side in the setting sun, totally engrossed in each other. But that was only the beginning. Henry found that he had to pass that way at other times than when young William needed an escort, and Elizabeth began to look forward to his visits.

Sometimes she felt guilty. But then again, what was Will doing all this time, back at Court? He would doubtless be up to more mischief than passing the time of day with one pretty woman. So Elizabeth tried to salve her conscience, and thought she had succeeded.

She hadn't expected to be banished to Norfolk for so long, but the weeks turned into months and the months looked like becoming a year. It seemed that William Brereton was up to his old tricks of forgetting all about her but Elizabeth didn't mind quite so much this time. Apart from Henry's visits there was plenty to keep her busy. She enjoyed every day which dawned and much later on was to regard this time in the Brandon home as one of those sweet interludes which sometimes happen in life. A tranquil island, untouched by all that had gone before, remaining untarnished by future's cruel twists.

But how life loves to stamp on our innocent pleasures! All unsuspecting, Henry picked an apple from the overhanging tree as they strolled in the late summer sunshine and after polishing it on his jerkin held it out to his new friend. Her lips, suddenly twitching in a smile, took on a sensual quality which stirred feelings other than mere friendship in the young man. Henry wanted to kiss her and hold her. Catching her fingers as she took the proffered apple he stilled her with a look. Laughter died as she felt the old familiar tingle run across her skin. Bending his head, he paused, just for a second. Then his lips found hers, responsive and warm and for a moment, with her senses all a-quiver, her body moved to his without restraint and she felt his hardness pressed against her.

Then she was running through the hot gardens into the safety of the house, and her bedchamber. Henry Bedinfeld was certainly not Christopher Werminsham! But then again, he was not William Brereton. What on earth was she to do if Will didn't come for her soon? Elizabeth closed her eyes and concentrated all her thoughts to that end. Unless he had deserted her for good this time he had to come now.

It was uncanny. Only days after Elizabeth faced her dilemma Charles Brandon arrived home with a party of friends and amongst the company was William Brereton.

'Are you ready to come back to Court then, Sweet?' he asked, basking in the sheer delight which shone from her face. 'And no more rented rooms! Behold! Your graceful lover has at last charmed his way into the King's bed-chamber. A position which provides an occasional room for my own use. Shall I require it?' To ensure the appropriate answer he entangled his hands in her hair and held her tight against him until her body ached for him.

'I didn't want to live in Norfolk,' she reminded him.

'I had ambition for both of us, Sweetheart, and I have news which I think might have you smiling. Anne is back. What is more, I am elevated by the patronage of Anne's uncle, the Duke of Norfolk. And, I have secured a place for you to work with Anne herself.'

Elizabeth was thrilled at the news but even so it didn't do to appear too eager. 'I don't know,' she said slowly. 'I have quite made a life here, with the new baby Eleanor and all. You know I can't resist babies. I should miss her if I left now. And Frances.'

'You're teasing, Love. If I left without you, wouldn't you miss me? Though my wealth and power don't impress you wouldn't you miss this?' He kissed her.

She had to give in. He was irresistible. Life at Court was going to be very different from now on. With Henry Exeter as Privy Councillor the whole Court had been tipple-a-top-tail for some months whilst the new broom swept clean. Hunting dogs and various hounds had now been reduced to kennels with the horses and as a consequence it was less hazardous for dainty slippers amongst the rushes of the palace floors. Only the ladies' small dogs remained in chambers. Other uninvited guests had fled lest they be flogged, or worse, for living off His Majesty's bounty without just cause.

'As a result of all this economy there are also fewer in the King's bedchamber, and all sworn to secrecy on the King's movements in that suite! This means that my place holds more prestige than previous such positions.'

'Shall I see less of you then, despite the greater convenience of a chamber within the Palace?' Elizabeth didn't relish the thought.

'You'll see all of me when time permits,' he grinned.

'What of the queen?' she asked, wondering that there were so many secrets to be kept for the King.

'Conspicuous by her absence,' Will replied. 'Given overmuch to prayer, though that's no way to bring back youth. More like to age her I should think, frowning over her missal. These days His Majesty surrounds himself with ladies of gaiety and charm who are more than willing to dance the night away, even to the King's tune,' he added with a wink. He wasn't lying. He himself had stayed the pace with the best of them many a long night.

Whether things had simply gone from bad to worse, Elizabeth didn't know. One thing was certain. Holy vows appeared to count for nothing any more, so how could mere promises still hold? Will saw her expression and followed her train of thought. Best change the subject! He didn't want Bessy asking too many pertinent questions. Launching into a graphic description of the comedies of the Court, his natural talent for telling a good tale soon had her laughing so hard that tears ran down her face.

That laughter died so suddenly on seeing Mister Bedinfeld materialise before her that Elizabeth almost choked. Will stood to greet the stranger, his manners impeccable, and to her acute embarrassment she had to introduce them. Noting Henry's puzzled look, and the guilty flush of Elizabeth's cheek, Will guessed the way of things. Amused by the discomfiture he decided to prolong her agony, and slapping Henry heartily on the shoulder begged him to join them

'Any friend of Bessy is a friend of mine!' he declared.

Will had the situation under control and Elizabeth watched amazed as he proceeded to charm Henry into forgetting that she even existed. When at last the two men parted it was as if they had been lifelong comrades who no mere woman could ever come between. There was no doubt about it, Will had a winning way with everyone when he wanted. It was only later, when they were alone, that she realised that he had not been deceived for a moment. He lifted her chin forcing her to look him in the eye.

'Come, Bessy Love, 'tis time to choose for I can see the way it has been.' Even now the twinkle never left his eyes. It was almost as though he found the whole thing amusing.

'There's nought to choose,' she denied hotly. The vehemence of the denial was enough to condemn her.

'Aye there is, and it must be done,' he insisted quietly. 'Has he bedded you, Sweet? I can see that if he hasn't 'tis not for want of trying.'

'He hasn't. I couldn't! Oh, I wanted for love, but not with any man. No matter how great the time or distance is between us I can never divorce myself from you because I love you. You surely must know that?'

He did know. In a tender reunion he bathed her in the ecstasy she craved finding as he did so that all his own recent amorous exploits faded into insignificance. The trouble was that his accusations and his talk of the declining morals of the Court had set her thinking, but when she brought up the subject his reply was nonchalant.

'Where the King leads, others will always follow.'

'And are you joined in his games, Will? You question my conduct, but what of yours? I am perhaps a poor measure against the pretty duckies of the Court today if all you tell me is true?'

'Would you mind then, Sweet?' he asked casually.

He felt her wince as though he had struck her and her hands faltered in their gentle caressing. She should know better than to even dream of cross-examining him in such a way! But still, she had her uses. He felt the roundness of her breasts, the smoothness of her thighs. Remembered all the different ways she knew of pleasing him. His irritation vanished.

'I was only joking. We'll be together always, I promise. It would have been easy enough for me to leave you to Mister Bedinfeld.' Kissing her between words, his mouth moved sensually from her face to her neck. 'You may be cool to the rest of the world but when we are together you are more eager than a whore.'

Elizabeth made to clip him about the ear, but he caught her arm deftly and with a laugh turned her struggles to his own advantage. Try though she might, she had to submit to the needs of her body. Resistance was impossible. The truth was that satisfying him was the only way to satisfy herself. Tonight was no exception.

Lightly bathed in sweat, Will rolled away from her, laughing. 'I've no envy for the King,' he said. 'He merely seeks that which I found many years ago in Malpas Church, though I shall never dare to tell him so for fear he tries you for himself.'

Their passionate love-making had lulled her fears. 'And if he tried I've no doubt that I should be sick over him. Majesty or no, for no one rouses me as you do.'

She was looking forward to a new life at Court in Will's company, and to seeing Anne Boleyn again. It wasn't that she hadn't enjoyed her stay with the Brandons. All things considered, she had enjoyed it more than she had expected and it wouldn't be a final parting from the little girls. As nieces of the King they would often be at Court as they grew older so there was no need at all for heartache in her goodbyes.

Will had not exaggerated. The mood of the Court had indeed changed. Everywhere there were grumbles about the reduced value of money. The Cardinal's new measures to protect the King's treasury were biting deep into the purses of his subjects, so while the fun-loving King rose in popularity the Cardinal was blamed for every new devaluation. King Henry was taking less of an interest in government these days and every hour was filled with some diversion. He played, he rode, he danced and he sang. And at night he had the choice of so many that it was rare for the same one to return. Each new dawn heralded a new adventure.

Yet despite the many differences at Court, the Queen's household had hardly changed, prayer being the overriding order of the day. The Princess Mary was being taught that her devotion to God was the only way of life and that frivolity was an obscene tool of the Devil. Sharing those lessons was a quiet, studious young girl.

Katherine Parr had grown into a lovely young woman and despite the prevalent atmosphere at Court she was not coquettish or capricious as most maids tended to be, hoping to catch the eye of a handsome courtier. When they were both free from their duties they would sit together, Elizabeth drawing her likeness as Kat bowed her head over her books. Through their conversations Elizabeth discovered that Kat was betrothed to a much older man and worried that she would fail in her duties as a wife.

'What shall I have to do? What will he expect of me?' She voiced the very natural fears of a twelve-year-old.

'He will teach you all that he wishes you to know, never fear,' Elizabeth assured her, 'and probably take great pleasure in doing so.' She told Kat the story of her life since the time they had first met in Chester, though Katherine had been too young a baby to have any memories of those days. She described how great a love could be between a man and a woman and how the birth of a child opened up a new vision of life, a fleeting glimpse of some great design in the continuity of creation. Elizabeth gave Kat the benefit of her experience and before long the girl began to think that the marriage bed would not be quite the trial she had thought it.

For Elizabeth these hours were a pleasant respite from the high emotions and capers of William Brereton and the Lady Anne Boleyn in whose service she was now permanent. As Will had become a close friend of Anne and her brother George it meant that not only could Elizabeth see him when he arranged for her to share his bed, but also when he was at his leisure in the company of her mistress. There was a crowd of courtiers who had assembled themselves into a boisterous and inventive group. They were at the heart of all new mischief and entertainment at Henry's Court.

Sitting on the window seat watching the others amuse themselves, her hand made rapid movements across the parchment as she sketched the scene. Margaret Bryant and Mark Smeaton made the music while some danced and others sang. The sun was shining in through the lights as she idly watched the dust motes swirling in partnership with the ladies' skirts. Will was there, and Hal and George, Richard Page, and Francis Weston, that rich young man, newly arrived at Court. Tom Wyatt leaned against the casement looking down at Elizabeth.

'You have a great gift,' he remarked. 'Have you ever been taught by limners?'

Elizabeth coloured slightly as she shook her head. 'I taught myself,' she replied. 'To tell the truth I am poor at learning anything at all and this small skill is my only one.'

Tom raised his eyebrow quizzically at her, meaning that her looks indicated otherwise. She blushed furiously. He was a very attractive man. His hands, she noted moved with all the sensitivity of his artistry, yet the muscles showing hard beneath his hose were of the fighting man. His disarming grin had her stammering over her words.

'All the hours I have spent thus might have yielded more profit had I learnt to read and write.' She raised her candid green eyes to his. 'I've heard some of your rhymes and now regret the times I ran away to draw a leaf or to find whether beetles really have no ears when I could have been learning such lovely words as yours.'

'Aye, the things beyond our reach always seem the most attractive,' he agreed. 'I can only paint my pictures in words.' With an effort he moved his gaze away from Anne Boleyn and leaned over Elizabeth to see her picture more clearly. 'When it comes to the sketch I am all thumbs so no matter how I love my lady she must be content with mere words.'

The dance came to an end. Will picked up a lute and strolled with easy grace to sit beside Elizabeth, plucking out a popular tune as he walked.

'Has Tom been bothering you?' he asked cheerfully. 'Methinks he would try to steal you from beneath my very nose. Away and find another wench, for this one's mine and not likely to be shared for many a day. Find yourself a maid who lacks a lover or you will find yourself with a fight on your hands.' He squared up to Tom as though to prove it. He could afford to joke about it, knowing that Tom's preferences lay elsewhere.

Tom pulled a wry face. 'Hush't, Will Brereton. Don't use foul language before a lady.' He lowered his voice. 'There is one I would take willingly, if only I could get near her. She is pleasant enough to me but always avoids being alone with me. I can't ever find her without her friends surrounding her. You, Will, are always there, for one.'

They all looked across to where Anne sat in animated discussion. Will and Elizabeth exchanged glances.

'You are lost before you begin.' Elizabeth told Tom. 'Even if you were the most handsome man in Christendom, it would be impossible to win that lady. She trusts no man with her heart.'

'She'll not hold out long if only I can be alone with her! Every woman wants what all the others have, and every other woman in the Court these days has a lover. By all that's holy I'm determined that I'll be the one she succumbs to.'

Will shrugged his shoulders and Elizabeth caught the movement. They both knew that the ghost of Harry Percy's love lay cold and unrelenting between Anne Boleyn and the arms of more substantial lovers. From that time on it became understood that where Anne was, so was Tom Wyatt, though for all his wiles they were never alone.

Then one day Tom was suddenly gone home to Kent. The King was chafing for something to interrupt the dullness of his life. Despite the liberal pleasures of the Court, those very pleasures became tedious when repeated too often and His Majesty was in need of some fresh diversion. As he mentioned to his gentlemen, the Lady Anne had a refreshing candour. The hint was usually enough, but knowing how Anne kept men at a distance Will had little hope that she would comply with a request to spend a secluded hour, even with the King.

'Tom has made a timely exit.' Will paced the room. 'He's not one to be caught between the King and his fancies and you can be sure that all our lives will be made miserable if there is any delay. If you first broach the subject she might eventually listen to reason. Will you?'

Elizabeth thought the task impossible, but for Will she would attempt even that. 'I'll try, though I doubt very much whether Anne will ever listen to reason.'

Anne Boleyn shuddered delicately and looked at Elizabeth for understanding. 'As you say, he is handsome and none too old. And he is the King!

But you were there when Harry Percy turned my whole life upside down. I daren't expose myself to that again. The King does not love me. He wants to use me. As he used my sister.' Anne looked uneasy, knowing that it could mean disaster to refuse King Henry, though it might be worse to lie with him and not be able to respond to his caresses.

'You must agree to go to him.' Elizabeth was becoming impatient with Anne's obstinacy. 'No one in their right mind would refuse him.'

'Then say that I am mad! I don't care. Am I mad? Am I mad? Once I would have been constant to just one, but he showed me what men are really like so now I remain constant to myself. I shall use men as they use women, for no man is my better.'

'His Majesty won't take kindly to being spurned like some common lad. If you cross him now he may find a way of punishing you. You know the King!'

People had been banished for less. How could she avoid him.

'I shall plead illness,' she said decisively. 'After so long in the city I am in extremely poor health. Arrangements must be put in hand for me to leave the Court at once.' Her high spirits returned. 'It won't be long before he finds some new fancy and forgets all about me.'

Anne didn't realise that by running away she was unwittingly turning the situation into a game which she could never win. The chase was on, and in this game it would be Henry who made all the rules.

Five

AN AIR of expectancy hung over the formal gardens and there was a certain amount of tension visible in the nervous pacing of Lady Anne Boleyn. Who would have thought that the King would have shown such persistence? Anne had only avoided him at his pleasure but for a long time now he had shown no interest in other ladies of the Court. Whenever he looked at Anne there was an odd gleam of speculation in his eyes. He could not give up the chase now without appearing a fool before the whole of England and Anne knew it.

Laughter preceded the gaily coloured band of men as they emerged into the open areas of the gardens and Elizabeth saw Anne's attitude alter immediately. Suddenly she seemed casual. Nonchalant even. It wasn't until the King was almost within touching distance that she acknowledged his presence at all. Give Anne her due, she had courage. Any other woman would have been bowing and scraping at his feet in worship. Without preamble Henry held out his arm to her and Mistress Boleyn could do no other than accept his invitation and step across the neat lawns with him as he engaged her in earnest conversation.

As her maid watched them go she couldn't help wondering why Anne was so adamant in her refusals. Oh, she insisted that she would never love any man again. But surely the King wasn't just any man? He was still handsome, his hair was still golden in the sun. Added to that, he had now completely put aside Queen Katherine, and Anne had been given a suite of rooms of her own.

Almost by accident, one would think, Will Brereton found himself standing at Elizabeth's side. They too made a handsome couple. Will had developed into one of the most stylish and charming of Henry's courtiers and with the wealth which he was rapidly acquiring it could be judged that before long he would be a force to be reckoned with. Will felt that here was no limit to what he could achieve. On the other hand, Elizabeth was almost invisible. A becoming woman, she was now fully conversant with the ways of London society, yet although she wore all the silks and finery which Will had once promised her, she was in no way ostentatious, effortlessly remaining in the shadows.

They watched as the King led Anne to the seclusion of an arbour.

'Now she will have to give in.' Will spoke as though to himself. 'She has made a stand for virtue which has had Henry chafing at the bit and raring to go. With the news he has for her today she will have no reason to hold out any longer.'

'It isn't just an act, you know.' Elizabeth kept her voice low so that the others would not overhear. 'I can only think that she still loves Harry, despite the fact that she will not have his name mentioned in her presence. Remember Christopher Werminsham? I was sick at his touch because I still loved you. Maybe it is the same with Anne.'

'She is going to have to come to terms with the fact that the King will have her sooner or later. If Anne doesn't see sense she will be in danger of being crushed.' He moved closer. 'Can't you talk to her?'

'Talking doesn't do any good. She isn't a fool. Anne knows the position and despite all the entreaties of her family she simply cannot do it. Look what happened to her sister anyway. Anne has too much pride to follow in her footsteps.'

'She may not have to.' Will bent his head and spoke almost in a whisper.

Elizabeth looked up at him, startled. 'What do you mean?'

Will cleared his throat and glanced around to be certain that they were not being overheard. 'He has it in mind to marry her.'

Elizabeth was silent for a few seconds. 'How? Queen Katherine and the Church will not allow it? He can't.'

Will smiled grimly. 'Today Henry has taken the first steps to cast doubts on the legality of his marriage to his brother's widow. He now blames the death of all their sons on the wrath of God at their unholy alliance.' Will

77

sighed. 'The needs of the King's royal loins have entirely dismissed the needs of England and Henry excuses his madness by virtue of Queen Katherine's failure.'

Will was not lying. The King had indeed told Anne something of his plans. Her initial dismay had quickly turned to cunning as she saw a way to extend her prevarications.

'I am dragged along on the tide of men's ambitions.' Anne's eyes narrowed. 'Give in! Give in. That's all I hear from my father and my uncle who swear that they are only trying to further my cause. Further their own, more like! If, however, I was married then of course I should have to do my duty.' She laughed complacently. 'But there is little chance of that happening. Is there?'

Elizabeth had to agree with Anne. No one in their right minds could imagine the King's long marriage to Katherine to be null and void. And if it was, it had taken him an extraordinary time to discover the fault. No. Katherine being his brother's widow was only an excuse. But as the world was to find out later, Henry had the power to rid himself of cumbersome ties.

'I shall forget the whole weighty business.' Anne cheered up suddenly. 'Nothing will come of it. At least for a long time yet, and life is too short to be miserable. Thank God for my brother and your cousin Will and their friends. If it wasn't for the way they keep me entertained I should go mad.'

Elizabeth wondered whether Anne realised that those friends took such care of her for their own reasons. While the King was smitten with Mistress Boleyn, her friends were well looked after too. It was a sad fact of life.

Compared to Anne's turbulent life and conflicting emotions, Elizabeth's days were serenity and tranquillity. People had begun to hear of her cures and potions and when she was not attending her mistress she could usually be found in the great kitchens, stirring and brewing up concoctions for the afflicted. This was especially true at those times when Will was away on business. He was often away for weeks at a time, returning to tell her humorous tales of things which had occurred on his sojourns. She heard news of home from other quarters too. Since Will's increased affluence and exalted position in the King's household it was not unusual for one or other of his brothers to pay him visits to keep themselves in his mind. One of the more regular faces to turn at board was that of his younger brother, Rian.

Rian was not like Will. He was quieter by nature and slighter in stature and lacked the courtier's polished charm which Will seemed to have acquired so easily in his youth. But one thing he had which Will hadn't. A son. Young William had become Will's ward and looked set fair to follow in his uncle's footsteps. Rian often sought Elizabeth for conversation when his brother's duties kept him at the King's side, and one day, unable to help herself, Elizabeth confessed her disappointment over her lack of children. At that, Rian launched into a description of a sturdy young lady growing up in Cheshire who was obviously the apple of her father's eye.

'Since he has made his way with rather more than a modicum of success, that girl has wanted for nothing. She has a strong look of her father too.'

Elizabeth remembered that screwed-up, screaming baby face as though she had seen it yesterday. Aye, she favoured her father.

'Except in her colouring, perhaps. Her hair has more a fiery tinge and curls out like a burning halo, while her fair skin is speckled over with a fine dusting of golden sand. You can't imagine how she raves against the injustices of fate for the ugliness of her complexion. The truth is that her looks are so striking that she has captured more than her fair share of young men's hearts. And some old ones too,' Rian admitted sheepishly. 'Why don't you go home to see her sometime?'

Oh, how she would love to! But no. It would do no good, and might do harm. Why re-open old wounds and set them bleeding again? Best leave such things be.

'Besides,' she excused herself to Rian, 'If I leave Will alone at Court the chances are that he would find another to replace me.'

'No need to worry on that score,' Rian laughed. 'Will says that only in your company can he relax and take the guard from his tongue, knowing he can command instead of having to serve.'

If only Will had not this great aversion to marriage she could be as happy as any mortal could be. 'No need.' That was all Will ever said on the subject. No need!

The musicians struck up a different tune, and the Court was ready to dance. Rian bowed his excuses and with his neighbour and companion in travel, John Savage, he approached his brother. They would be seeking introductions to the young duckies who were offering services for the night.

Elizabeth watched as the first tentative moves in the nightly mating game were made. Blending with the shadows of the hall she thought herself unnoticed as she took stock of the new alliances being made. But Elizabeth was not the only watcher. Others too had found it profitable, in their own way. She was surprised, however, when George Cavendish took his place beside her and wished her well.

'Your lady is in fine fettle tonight,' he observed, nodding to where Anne was prancing with the King.

Elizabeth didn't trust Mister Cavendish. He was the Cardinal's man and had done his bit to stir up trouble when he could. He was far from innocent of the rumours spread about Anne and Harry Percy years ago, causing the pair so much pain. Now what was his game? What was he fishing after tonight? Anne had been at loggerheads with the Cardinal ever since those humiliating days and by the looks of it things could only get worse. At this minute, Wolsey was sitting with a glum face as he listened to the King's hearty laugh above the general clamour. Anne would appear to be at her witty best, as Cavendish had already said.

'Cardinal Wolsey looks sick. Is he not feeling well this evening? He often retires early these nights whereas previously he would scarcely leave His Majesty's side.' Elizabeth looked anything but sympathetic. 'My Lady says his numerous sins are catching him up and that he visibly quails to meet his maker.' She glanced sideways at him at this reference to the Cardinal's gift to Anne, a conciliatory brace of quails which had done precisely nothing to win Anne over.

Anne had done all in her power to undermine the cardinal's strength. She was playing her game so successfully that Wolsey's reputation as a statesman was rapidly falling. He was in an intolerable position over the

King's secret matter of the divorce, Anne treating his efforts with derision and scorn. Contrary to everyone's belief, Anne had no wish for the Cardinal's mission to be successful.

Cavendish ignored the jibe. 'It isn't his body which ails, but his mind. He is sure that the King is bewitched by the lady, and try as he might he cannot unravel the problem of the Queen.' George Cavendish watched as Anne so easily held the King's attention. 'The Queen rejects all ideas of a divorce on these ridiculous grounds or any others, so he is in trouble with that lady and all who support her. The King urges him to solve the problem with the Holy Church, and the Lady Anne continues to spurn him publicly. He cannot possible win.'

'He is not the only one in that unenviable position,' Elizabeth murmured.

Cavendish looked at her sharply, narrowing his already small, slit eyes. 'It almost seems as though she doesn't want the King.' He paused, watching Elizabeth closely. 'She really must be a witch as they say, to have Henry turn the whole world upside-down for her and not see what she is about behind his back.'

Hearing the implication in his tone Elizabeth was immediately on the defensive. 'Nay, Sir,' she interrupted before he could make further insinuations. 'The lady is neither witch nor whore and if you only knew the truth you would realise that she is always amongst many, and never alone with just one.' Had she said too much? Elizabeth closed her mouth, her lips meeting in a hard angry, line.

'You're quick in her defence,' Mister Cavendish observed slyly. 'Perhaps in consideration of William Brereton being one of her closest paramours?'

'You lie, Sir,' Elizabeth denied his allegations hotly.

Mister Brereton is too fond of her, and of his own neck, to soil their friendship with carnal lust.'

'So you would have yourself believe. And yet by my observations, he is as close to her as any.'

'She has many friends, Sir, and none of them foolish. Nor will you ever get confirmation of your vile inventions from my lips.'

Mister Cavendish rose slowly to make her a mocking bow. 'You may take my word for it,' he said confidently, 'yonder lady has too many fingers deep into too many pies, and if she isn't careful she will one day be burnt.'

***

In the last few weeks things had deteriorated rapidly and the Cardinal feared not only for his reason, but for his life. Anne lived on a knife-edge, balanced precariously between the Cardinal's failure and her family's success, and how she still managed to avoid being carried off into the King's great bed nobody knew.

For the King, the excitement of the chase had given way to an iron determination that he would have his own way, in his own way. He would obtain the divorce! No matter what the cost! The whole issue was now one of pride and Henry would not lose face before the whole world because of the obstinacy of his first wife or the stubborn attitude of the Pope. At times the tension had been unbearable.

Elizabeth had been glad to get away. She filled her lungs with the cold crispness of the winter air and watched as her breath steamed out in front of her in great moist clouds. It was invigorating to be out riding along the open road putting all the petty feuds into perspective and letting the years fall away so that she felt almost youthful again. How eagerly she had grasped at the chance to join this escort into Lincolnshire to conduct Katherine Parr to Court.

Approaching their destination, the travelling party was overtaken by a blanket of dense fog which covered the whole countryside, muffling sounds and obliterating every landmark from sight. For a time they feared that they might be lost and it was with enormous relief that they found themselves entering Gainsborough Hall, where the fire burned brightly to banish darkness, and the ale was being warmed.

Elizabeth embraced Kat Parr before holding her at arm's length and studying her with a critical eye.

'No longer a girl then, Kat?' she chuckled, remembering how the young Kat had been so afraid of marriage. 'How does it feel to be a full-grown woman then?'

Kat laughed happily. 'Full grown, aye, and a widow-woman too!' Black suited her. For all she was 'full grown' she was still only eighteen years old, quiet and demure, and lovely in her widow's weeds.

'The mourning for Edward is over but somehow I have found it hard to put it all behind me and make the effort to start afresh. Thank goodness you were able to come, for if anyone can bestir me it is you.'

Elizabeth's company and sensible advice had helped Katherine enormously during her early years at Court and she hoped that one day she would be able to show her gratitude to the older woman. Kat also respected her for the quiet way she got on with her life without seeming to interfere in all the ins and outs of intrigue which surrounded her. And she was faithful to her man. The fact that Elizabeth had left his side to travel to Lincolnshire proved to Kat just how much her friend cared for her and she would not forget it, but she failed to realised that even she was another sentimental link between Elizabeth and her early memories of Will.

Linking arms companionably the two women moved to sit by the roaring fire and the gossip flowed between them. There was a lot of catching up to do and a lot that Kat wanted to know about the current politics of Court. Queen Katherine, whom she had served before, was not permitted any comforts these days and only allowed the minimum of ladies to wait on her. It would be no use looking to take up her old position now. On the other hand, she could perhaps find a welcome with the Princess Mary.

'Until you find yourself another husband,' Elizabeth laughed. 'I take it that you are not so frightened of that blissful state anymore?'

'Not frightened, no,' Kat answered, 'though I think you rather exaggerated the pleasures of the marriage bed when you tried to set my mind at rest. It certainly wasn't the hot romp you described to me, but I have no complaints.'

'Perhaps your next lover will be young and vigorous and show you some new tricks, then,' Elizabeth winked at her.

Kat only smiled and shook her head. She had been content with her late husband and if there was more to marriage, as Elizabeth implied, then she didn't miss it.

Returning to Court, Elizabeth found that the Christmas festivities were to be louder and more outrageous than ever. She was glad she had been able to warn Kat Parr of the chaos which reigned over Henry's household since the queen had been virtually banished. The Cardinal was now dead and no doubt making his excuses to the gods for all his sins right at that very moment. Anne laughed more wildly than ever to stem the rising tide of panic. Playing. Dancing. Riding. Everything was done at breakneck speed and with so much fiery enthusiasm that it almost seemed as though Anne was trying to burn herself out. There was very little now to keep her from her monarch's couch. King Henry had a new man working on the problem and this time he meant to have results!

Will was only half listening to Elizabeth's observations on Anne's state of mind.

'As time has passed, the revulsion she feels has grown worse. Much worse. When she thinks about what she will one day have to go through with the King she is almost sick. It's no trick. She really can't bear the thought of any man using her like that.'

'She must be mad!' Will had little patience these days with Anne's excuses. 'I know what she is like. Rubbing up to us in the dance. Holding hands just that little bit too long. Smiling all sorts of promises. And not only to the King. She makes men want her, but to her it is only a game. She doesn't want them. And why not? She wants to be Queen. The crown! She is a fool. A grasping little fool. And who knows where her folly will lead us?'

Will sounded disgruntled and Elizabeth couldn't help wondering whether he too had been kept in hopes. She looked at him thoughtfully. Will noticed.

'Don't look like that,' he almost snapped. 'Women always think the same thing. Can't you understand what is happening? The Pope has discounted every claim, and Henry is as determined as ever. The country is split between the King and the Church and one of them will have to break before all this is sorted out. It will mean trouble for everyone. Who knows where it will finish?' Will had made vast profits from his dealings with the abbeys and he could see it all coming to a rapid end if Anne did not give in to the King soon. 'Anne should bear in mind that the future of England may rest on who she can and can't accept as bed-fellow.'

And the future of William Brereton!

There was only one way to take his mind off his problems. Elizabeth kissed him and slipped her fingers inside his shirt to caress his shoulders. It always worked.

Six

PEACE at last! Blessed calm. The rooms were unusually still and silent, littered and empty, as though a storm had whirled its way through them before blowing itself out. The royal party had at last set off for France, and Anne had finally given in. After weeks of dithering and dallying she had been broken by the fierce pressure being brought to bear on all sides. Tortured by doubts she had chewed at her lips until they bled, picked at the lace on her dress until it was beyond repair and picked at her ladies until their nerves were in a similar state. Praise the Lord for soothing potions or Anne would have ended her life locked away and accused of madness of the brain, or thought of as an uncontrolled Bacchante. Part of the problem had been Elizabeth's refusal to attend her on the journey into unexplored territory, where Henry was nonetheless King and Anne was terrified of becoming nothing more than an insignificant subject. But at least the price was right! Certainly she would now be able to command a little more respect from those who still sided with Queen Katherine and a title would go some way to softening the blow of capitulation. If Anne felt she must submit to the indignity of becoming the King's latest mistress she had to have this vestige of respectability to cling to. Endless hours of soul-searching had preceded her decision; long sleepless nights listening to the screech-owl hunt his prey, hovering silently, waiting to pounce on the unsuspecting victim. And then the hoot of derision after the kill was made! Is that how it would be for her? Who the victim and who the victor? She could never follow in her sister Mary's footsteps, to find herself a nonentity, the laughing stock of the Court. In his words of persuasion Henry had promised to make her his Queen. That was the full price. She would accept nothing less. Then they would dance to her tune, those who blamed her for Queen Katherine's failure, losing positions and possessions gained through cunning and conniving during Henry's golden years. When Anne Boleyn became Queen!

Although Elizabeth knew how important the next few weeks were to them all she could not bring herself to cross the turbulent strip of water between England and France. Anne would be all right. Hadn't she given her all the potions she would need? If she followed the instructions, the King would have no just cause for complaint, and who knows? Anne's silly daydreams could even turn into reality. With Henry one could never tell. It wasn't that Elizabeth wanted to desert her mistress at such a time, but the nightmare which had plagued her since childhood kept her in fear of travel over the water.

So it came about that when the Lady Anne sailed across the Channel with her monarch Elizabeth did not accompany her and by the sheer good fortune of having few duties to perform, renewed acquaintance with an old friend.

Will had been more than generous with her since his prospects had improved, and Elizabeth made good use of the Court's absence to make one or two improvements to her wardrobe. The first stage in this process was a visit to a clothier of repute, well known for the quality of his cloth and his patience with the ladies.

Brian Kelsall also required patience. Mistress Fytton would be a time choosing, he well knew. No longer than other ladies of Mister Brereton's acquaintance, to be sure, but time enough for him to contemplate the twitching hips of every female under forty passing the murky portal of the clothier's shop. From the comparative seclusion of the doorway Will's young page watched the whole hotch-potch of humanity go by. Everything from the gentry to beggars and thieves. As he yawned again his eye was caught by the barely concealed alertness of a thin ragged youth who hovered craftily in the shadows across the narrow street. That one was not waiting on his mistress. Loitering. That's what he was doing. Loitering. And with his greedy eyes on a woman's purse, too. Brian watched as the emaciated boy sidled nearer to his victim, his sharp glance constantly flicking this way and that, his eyes bright points of cunning in his dirty face. He waited the chance to snatch and run.

Having taken some considerable time in coming to a decision Elizabeth left the premises in more than a little disarray, the head of the merchant being by now barely visible over the mountain of materials which cascaded from the cutting tables in a seemingly endless flow of colour. He didn't mind. The lady had been persuaded to place not one order, but two, and his patience had been amply rewarded.

Blinking rapidly in the sudden glare of the street Elizabeth was just in time to witness the commotion which was going on with Brian Kelsall right in the middle of it. The young thief took to his heels and ran away empty-handed, realising that he had no chance of loosening Brian's tenacious grip on the stolen purse and that his life would be forfeit if he didn't put his knowledge of London's alleyways to good use immediately. The outraged screams of the unfortunate owner of the purse made everyone in the vicinity aware of the attempted robbery and for several noisy moments the stout, smartly dressed woman was the centre of attention. Elizabeth couldn't believe her eyes. It couldn't be! Could it? The same rosy cheeks, guaranteed to dimple in more jovial circumstances than the present ones; the same rosebud mouth, despite the indignant wails now issuing from it. It was!

'Cissy! Cissy Bulkley!' Without realising it, Elizabeth's feet were propelling her rapidly towards that vociferous ghost from the past, a mixture of excitement and disbelief setting her heart pounding.

Cissy's face was a picture. The distress calls of the plump matronly figure, so stately in its Sunday plumage, fell to a hoarse, strangled whisper before ceasing altogether, leaving her silent mouth wide open and her numerous chins quivering incredulously. That was the face of Elizabeth Fytton, wasn't it? But such elegance! Such refinement! She looked more like some great lady of the Court than the wanton, flaunting maid of Gawsworth Hall.

And then they were in each other's arms. The separate paths their lives had taken had not cut through the threads of a loving childhood friendship and the incidents of birth, marriage and death along the way only seemed to have served as stepping stones to bring them to this moment. It was rapturous. There was no hesitation; no awkwardness. For Elizabeth at least, it brought a feeling of security and a feeling of coming home as she was enveloped in the immediate warmth of Cissy's embrace.

The torrent of words which followed that first gasp of amazement swept them into the commodious apartments above a nearby haberdashery, recently rented by Mister Stumpe for the convenience of himself and his wife Cissy whilst he addressed business in London. As Cissy sent out for refreshment Elizabeth assessed the accommodation. Whatever his line, Mister Stumpe was not without means. The window looked out over a profusion of flowers at the back of the building, bearing witness to the high cost of the rooms. Cissy caught the expression on the other woman's face and it was all she could do to stop herself from preening openly.

'Mister Stumpe has a fine head on his shoulders when it comes to money matters.' She couldn't help feeling proud of her husband's achievements. 'He is in cloth and as you can see he dresses his wife in nothing but the best.' Cissy smoothed the extravagance of her fur-trimmed oyster velvet. 'And all his daughters too, for that matter, though if truth be known it's all in the same cause. We advertise his wares, you see, and bring him further business.' To Elizabeth's mind, Mister Stumpe seemed to be a rather mercenary character; somewhat unloving. Cissy giggled in that oh-so familiar way. Despite the trappings of her husband's success she hadn't changed. 'Don't look so worried,' she said cheerfully. 'We cannot lose by it, though I admit that being the envy of the neighbourhood has caused my girls to err on the side of vanity.'

'You have a large family then?' That one fact could produce more envy in Elizabeth's heart than all the fripperies in the world.

'Aye,' chuckled Cissy. 'And more to come I shouldn't wonder. I've already birthed eight, though two died as babes, and at times the house is more than a little crowded. The more the merrier! Even so, they do try my patience now and then, what with all the dressing and altering and looking constantly for admiration.' Cissy sighed exaggeratedly for the trials brought upon a mother by a large family, which did nothing to dispel Elizabeth's first impression of a contented, respectable matron. The refreshments arrived and the sweet honey cakes scarcely managed to slow the flow of words from Cissy's mouth by a fraction.

'And you, Elizabeth? What happened to you? My aunt told me that you were sent to St. Leonards but from the time I left her house to join my family in Hampshire I never heard one word of you, either good or bad. Indeed I was led to believe that you had died in the birthing and until my own marriage you were held out as a warning to me against disobedience. Many a time I wondered why so many pleasurable pastimes turn out to be nothing more than instruments of the Devil. But you didn't die to roast, did you? What happened after I was sent away?' She leaned towards Elizabeth, curiosity written all over her as she encouraged her friend into explanations. Where had the expensive gown come from? Who had paid for it? There was a mystery here, and Cissy was eager to hear the tale.

Elizabeth couldn't help smiling. No, Cissy hadn't changed one bit. This was the same endless chatter and complete openness which had broken through her own reserve all those years ago and shown her what friendship really was. And now it was time to put her out of her misery.

'It's lucky that the Court is away across the sea or we should never have even met,' she began. 'When Will is in London, or anywhere about the Court you can be sure that I am not far from his side, but on this occasion I couldn't bring myself to cross the open sea for fear of bringing disaster to the venture.'

'Hold!' Cissy interrupted. 'Will? Will Brereton? You married Will Brereton after all? Why, did your father change his mind? What happened to the baby?'

Elizabeth burst out laughing. 'If you keep interrupting we shall never be done this side of Christmas. Be patient and you shall hear it all. In the first place I regret to tell you that we are not wed, save in our own eyes. Make of that what you will but it is the truth.'

Cissy understood. William Brereton's doxy! Yet by the looks of her he was keeping her in fine style. With a magnificent effort she kept her tongue still. Elizabeth continued. 'And as for my little girl, they took her from me when she was only one week old.' The pain, though hidden by Elizabeth's cool manner, was still discernible to someone who knew her as well as Cissy did and her motherly face mirrored the sympathetic sounds which clucked from her throat.

'Took her where?'

She told the whole story from the beginning, interspersed with oohs and aahs from the captivated Cissy who at times had to catch an escaping tear in the dainty embroidered linen kept solely for that purpose. Mistress Stumpe was amazed at the heights to which her friend had risen after such an unpromising start, even without the respectability of a wedding ring. On the other hand, such things were to be expected at King Henry's Court. What else could one expect? Wasn't the great man himself off with the second Boleyn whore at this very moment? Servants have always followed their master's lead, so Cissy supposed that there was nothing unusual in Elizabeth, waiting on the Boleyn. That was society for you!

'So you see, I never have had a home or family of my own. Not even a husband.' There was immense sadness in those few words and Cissy's warm heart went out to her friend.

'Yet didn't that handsome rascal send for you and make a life for you safe in his arms? Hasn't he courted you and cherished you all these years although he could no doubt command a rich wife? Would you have had it any other way, really?'

Elizabeth knew that she wouldn't. Will was not the one to stay by the hearth with only a wife for company. He had to be constantly striving to better himself and she knew in her heart that if he had married her she would have seen less of him than she now did.

'I guarantee that you would not exchange him for Mister Stumpe. He is a good man and a good husband, but steady; not a one to laugh overmuch. Such a life as his would never have suited William Brereton, and therefore would not have suited you either.'

Possibly not, but everyone had their daydreams, those little pockets of fantasy into which they could retreat when the real world became too harsh to bear. But Elizabeth knew that Cissy was only trying to comfort her, to show her the bright side of her life. How different were the paths they had trodden! Yet the love was still there; would always be there. No matter how far apart their destinies kept them, they would always be the best of friends. Cissy felt exactly the same. They were so different in their ways, in their looks, and in their whole approach to living yet the bond of comradeship between the two women was so strong that probably death alone could break it. And Cissy had learnt a lot from Mister Stumpe. It would do no harm at all to have friends in high places.

When the time came for the ladies to make their goodbyes there were a few understandable tears, but Cissy made Elizabeth promise that should she ever find herself near Malmesbury or Newbury she would call on them and meet the family.

***

Will Brereton hummed softly to himself as he made his way toward the newly refitted apartments of Anne Boleyn. His step was light as he went over the idea once more in his mind. He could find no fault in it. Anne adored dressing up and to dress up as a Queen, even a Fairy Queen, in a flimsy gown which would have even Henry's Court gaping, would amuse and delight her. Lost in his thoughts, he failed to notice how deserted and quiet the outer passage was, and tapping on the door, scarcely paused before entering. Only after taking several steps across the floor did he realise that he was alone, and stopping, looked around puzzles. Strange! Anne was not with the King and it was too late to be out riding. Indeed, it was too cold to be out at all! What was going on? As he turned, mystified, to leave again, determined to find Elizabeth for the truth of it, a small sound halted him. Someone was in the room with him, sitting silently in a high-backed chair, hidden from view. Carefully he approached, taking the precaution of placing his hand near the hilt of his dagger in case it should be needed. The sight of a Lady's slipper peeping out from the hem of a skirt assured him that such measures would be quite unnecessary, and with relief he saw that it was Anne sitting there. But so unlike her usual happy self!

'Why so sad? Have you lost an angel and found a groat?'

'Lost an angel and found a goat, more like!' To Will's amazement, he saw that her lashes were damp with tears. And who could resist a woman's tears? Not William Brereton! Sinking to his knees before her he took her slim hand in his and kissed it deferentially.

'Tell me who has hurt you and I shall stick him until he spurts blood with his apologies.' He found that she was clinging to his hand.

'Tis no use. No one can help me.' A sob of self-pity rose in Anne's throat, renewing the trickle of tears down her cheeks. 'I am alone. No one cares. No one loves me, nor ever has. Nor ever will, I shouldn't wonder. They call me a whore. They hate me. Yet I have done nothing wrong. How long did I keep the King at bay, not wishing to demean myself? And when I finally give in, they all hate me. And I doubt whether he will ever give me children. Even had I been the most willing of women I would have only found comfort in tears of frustration.' Her finger-nails dug into the flesh of Will's hand where she still held on to him as if for dear life.

Will looked round uneasily. Dear God, he would lose his head if he should be found alone in such compromising circumstances with the King's mistress. And not just any mistress at that! Anne Boleyn, no less! Feeling him pull away, her bottom lip began to quiver uncontrollably.

'There, you see! Everyone is afraid. Is there not one single friend whom I can turn to? Not even you who have shared so many happy times with me in days gone by?'

The depth of sadness in those beautiful, dark, almond-shaped eyes stirred him to pity. Crying had made her lips deliciously wet and full. Asking to be kissed better! But not here. It would be madness to take the risk. Anne saw the change in him and watched him assess the possibilities as his glance fell on the door of her inner chamber. He was right of course. A little caution would not come amiss. Sliding her other hand up his arm, bringing it to rest on his shoulder, she drew him slowly to her, never taking her eyes from his face for a moment. They pleaded for her; begged him to comfort her; to love her; to hold her and make the loneliness go away.

Will felt pity turn to the hard insistence of his full-blooded masculine desire, heightened by the element of danger in the situation. Many a man had Will Brereton cuckolded, but never the King! This was something new and different. All his senses were now fully alert. By God, he'd do it! It was too

93

good an opportunity to miss. Bedding the King's mistress he could, if only for a moment in his own private world of make-believe, pretend he was the King.

In the comparative privacy of Anne's small dressing room, on the same couch where Elizabeth sometimes slept, his rapacious male appetites urged him on, starting with the sweetest notes of tender loving care which he gradually allowed to rise to a magnificent climax of passion such as Anne had never experienced in her life. At first she remained so quiescent and passive in his arms that he thought he too had failed with her, but then in the final, vibrant moment he felt the woman in her respond instinctively. Head thrown back, eyes closed as though to protect her from the sudden blinding flash which fleetingly illuminated her darkness, Anne Boleyn clung to him. For the merest whisper of time her head no longer ruled.

***

During the last-minute preparations for the Christmas festivities Elizabeth's exuberance almost matched Will's. Enthusiastically he described the form the tableau would take, with Anne draped alluringly in filmy gauze to represent the Queen of the Fairies surrounded by others as the Seasons.

'The part of Mother Nature would be more apt,' Elizabeth laughed. She had a suspicion that Henry's gift from Anne this year would be in the form of good news.

'So?' Will was quick to catch her meaning. Raising one eyebrow in surprise he whistled softly. 'She is with child, is she, Bessy?' His relief was obvious. 'Good news indeed, and guaranteed to keep the King in better temper.'

'Say nothing,' Elizabeth cautioned. 'Even Anne does not suspect yet but I have seen the signs and think it may be so. Promise? You'll keep your tongue still until Anne herself makes it known?' Seeing that he was no longer listening to her she pinched his arm impatiently. But Will was lost in his own thoughts, and rapidly calculating dates inside his head.

'Are you listening, Will Brereton?' He came back to the present.

'Aye, I'm listening, woman, but there is a price for silence and it must

94

be paid this instant.'

'He couldn't be more excited if it were his own child,' Elizabeth thought to herself happily. What a wonderful thing friendship was. And as the two fell into that luscious state of long-accustomed mates, moaning softly in their ecstasy and smiling in their pleasure, Will celebrated the joyful tidings in time-honoured fashion. But alas, not with the mother of the coming child.

It was impossible for Will to keep the news to himself and mentioning it to Hal Norris, in the strictest confidence of course, the two decided that a jug of wine was called for. Thinking about it later, Hal required confirmation of the tale, and who better to ask than George, prospective uncle of the child? George had heard nothing, but rumours were always rife at Court, weren't they? His wife would know, being one of Anne's ladies and her sister-in-law to boot!

Jane was in fact the last one Anne would have confided such momentous news to, knowing how bitterly jealous Jane was of the close friendship which existed between her husband and his sister. Resentment had writhed and chewed away at her peace of mind like a clutch of maggots for long enough, poisoning her thoughts against the pair of them. In a Court where licentiousness was often the norm, depravity was only one twisted invention away. There were many who had been insulted or ignored by Anne, and plenty who thought her attitude too high and mighty for a whore, so that Jane had no difficulty in finding a sympathetic ear for her complaints and accusations.

'How was it,' she asked, 'that the King's courtiers seemed to know more about the condition of Anne's belly than the King? Certain ones are always at her beck and call.'

'Always?'

'Aye. Who but the King's closest friends would know the whereabouts of His Majesty at any time of the day or night? His courtiers are her most intimate friends! Never far from her side! Any of them.'

But everyone knew that plots and intrigue were a way of life at Court, and nothing to panic over.

Anne was just as overjoyed as Will had been. 'It is true then, and not just imagination?' She looked at Elizabeth delightedly. 'I really am with child?' Was there perhaps just a hint of hysteria in the wild laughter?

'It will put my smart young cousin Mary's nose right out of joint and no mistake. Henry Fitzroy will remain the King's bastard, and his wife no better in my opinion. My son will confound all her hopes of ever becoming Queen. Mark my words; the King will make sure he is born in wedlock!'

Elizabeth decided that Anne would benefit from a good night's sleep and began searching out the little bottle of recently made preparation. As if the King would really marry her! Could marry her! Wasn't he still married to Queen Katherine? The news of the coming child had most certainly turned Anne's mind.

'Is it in there? Truly?' Anne held her hand to her flat belly for any sign of swelling. There was none, but she had to believe Elizabeth's confident smile. 'So this is why my paps ache and feel as though a thousand needles prick them' Anne flopped down on to a mound of feather cushions. 'And I thought it was the lateness of my course which had brought on the vomits! You must be right, and suddenly I feel better than I have for days. I want apples! Fresh, juicy apples. Send down for some, Elizabeth. I need the taste of apples!

'They'll be none too juicy in January but more likely to be as wrinkled as a crone,' Elizabeth told her wryly, rising from her chair. 'You'd just as well take this potion I've brewed for you.'

'Apples!' Anne insisted laughing. 'You really mustn't upset me, you know.'

Elizabeth called to a page from the doorway. 'Go to the kitchens,' she instructed him, 'and ask for apples. If anyone questions your sanity, find John Thynne and tell him they are for the Lady Anne. Look sharp, now, or there will be trouble.'

Too late she saw a movement on the other stair, and heard the rustle of skirts as Jane of the sour face scurried off with confirmation of rumour for the ears of her friends.

Anne immediately told the King of her suspicions before he heard from other quarters.

'He was so delighted with his skill that he pranced about his chamber like a child,' she told Elizabeth scathingly. 'And if it were possible he would pluck the moon from her place in the Heavens for his Lady to wear on her breast. Nothing is too good for Anne Boleyn now.' For just one split second her eyes held a sly, secretive look and Elizabeth barely caught her next words. 'Are all men fools?' Then that laugh rang out again, slightly tainted with madness. 'What shall I demand as payment? A priceless jewel? A castle? Or a crown?'

Elizabeth shook her head. 'In your place I should settle for a castle. A home of my own. Somewhere safe and secure.'

Anne looked at her pityingly. 'I could never cut myself off from the glamour of the Court, or the thrills to be found here. I would die of boredom to be shut away by my own keys. No, not a paltry castle! The mother of a prince deserves a crown and nothing less!'

'That can't be,' Elizabeth began a little incautiously. 'Even after all these years of trying to be rid of her, Queen Katherine is still his lawful wife, for all it killed the Cardinal, and for all of Mister Secretary's promises.'

'He will not see his son born a bastard,' Anne insisted forcefully. 'Nor will I see a child of mine called bastard.'

This last was spoken slowly, deliberately, emphasising each word in turn. 'My child will be born to rule over England. Make no mistake about that.' Her look was as hard as steel, daring Elizabeth to argue. 'The plans are already in hand and you shall bear witness to the truth of what I say. In two days time you shall see His Majesty's full intent.

***

'God hasn't blessed a couple in such strange circumstances before.' She lay in the smooth warmth of Will's arms and whispered into the dark. 'The tower room was as cold as the grave in a black silence before the dawn, and Anne was so muffled with furs that she looked more like a traveller than a bride. At the same time, His Majesty had the air of a boy who was daring to steal apples from the orchard of his enemy. It was not an honest marriage. I could feel the constant presence of the King's true wife, a spectre in the shadows, watching every move and condemning the pair to hell.'

Will had heard Elizabeth's fanciful imaginings before and though he would never have admitted it, they made him nervous. He couldn't fully understand her strange sensitivity to atmosphere or the apparent ease with which she diagnosed ill humours. 'If it satisfies those two, what does it matter? Our secret vows have held, haven't they? And no man would dare to speak out against the King unless he sought instant martyrdom.' He spoke quickly to push any thoughts of her strange notions from his mind. When he had first heard the news of the secret wedding he had been dumbfounded. Then terrified. For days he had been as jumpy as a virgin in a brothel. Fortunately Elizabeth had put it down to all the secrecy in which the King's gentlemen had lately been involved. She didn't suspect. Why should she? Why should anyone? Anne would never tell. It had even crossed his mind that she had planned the whole thing. And no one else knew, did they? But with Anne made Queen the child could one day become King. It was an awesome thought and one which had been causing nightmares.

'This wasn't done in love as ours was. We were young and foolish with more faith than the wise. These two have lived longer in the world and should know right from wrong and not do slyly what we did in innocence.'

Will allowed himself a smile. Had he ever been as innocent as Elizabeth chose to believe? 'It's not a good beginning,' she continued, 'and in the face of such iniquity I fear for the future.'

Will's thought followed similar lines. Anne Boleyn was a strange one and no mistake. She had so needed comfort that night. Had it really happened? She had given no sign of it after. It was as though he had imagined the whole thing. But from what she had told him then there was no love in her for the King at all. She could hardly bring herself to touch him. Or so she insisted. And by her totally indifferent attitude since, she didn't have passionate feelings for Will Brereton either. She had cried and made him pity her. Pleaded with her every gesture for help. For Love! But even when he had so chivalrously obliged the lady, she seemed cold.

For the first time in his life, Will felt used. His delight in the news of the child had been obliterated by the news of the wedding. 'I doubt he will ever give me children.' Those were her words. Oh aye, he was certain he had been used! If Bessy only knew it, there was cause to fear for the future with Anne willing to take such risks. King Henry was not a man to trifle with but whatever the dangers, Will knew that his fate was now inextricable tangled with that of Anne Boleyn, and his only consolation was that with Bessy so firmly entrenched in the Queen's camp he was certain of being forewarned of any further madness. And thinking of consolations, wasn't that why Bessy was in his bed right now?

Elizabeth stretched deliciously, responding to his movements. She felt sorry for Anne, married to the King. He was past forty now and not nearly as handsome as he had been. And not so active, though he still forced himself to keep up with the youth of the Court with whom he liked to be surrounded. Will was not turning to fat, or slowing his pace at all. Rather, the opposite. These days he seemed to have more schemes afoot than ever and his rapidly increasing wealth paid tribute to their success. He was wonderful. If only Anne could know the strength of such a lover instead of looking for men's weaknesses she would be a well contented woman. Woman? She was now Queen! It was incredible.

'Where will it all end?' She spoke aloud.

***

Elizabeth attended to the gold thread which had been impertinent enough to scratch the Queen's royal arm.

'The people will now see a true Queen, not some sombre religious who usurped the title and duped the country for years. It shall be brought home to the people that Katherine's was a false marriage and sinful before God. To say otherwise is now treason, and I won't have doubts of my own marriage encouraged by the foul slander that the Spaniard was ever Queen.'

Despite the venom with which these words were spoken Elizabeth knew that Anne still didn't like to think of herself as Henry's wife, but as the King's Queen. Even so, she was his wife and had to endure all that it entailed, the result being that she was often fractious and out of sorts with her women.

'Was it so bad then last night?' Elizabeth guessed the reason for her bad temper.

'Not one single night, not one, have I been allowed to rest alone, and the pretence is a thousand times harder to bear since the deed is done and the seed already planted.'

Her expression showed the disgust she felt at this treatment.

'His member is a monstrous thing, veined and purple, and even when at last I fall asleep it interrupts with nightmares of further intrusion. Believe me, it's no instrument of joy, but one of torture, and I worry for my son. There are so many who would laugh to see me ruined, but at times I wonder how long I can submit to it.'

'Is it worth the price?' Elizabeth asked softly.

Anne looked down at the gorgeous gown, just one of the advantages of being Queen, and her maid saw with relief that she was smiling.

Yet when Anne Boleyn rode out, the dazzling cloth of gold and silver tissue brought no gasps of admiration from the crowd. Instead, the spectacle was greeted with almost total silence The words which rumbled through the crush of people, mouth to ear, were those best kept well away from the proud figure of the King.

'Whore. Harlot. Slut. Witch.'

Men had been cut down for less! Elizabeth trembled to see the mounting fury in the King, but there was nothing he could do. Even Henry could not force a crowd to adulation.

Anne's body was rigid; her face frozen in a smile which failed dismally to hide the humiliating effect of the insult meted out by the citizens of London. Her dark eyes flashed hate. Hate for all the world! What had she done to deserve such treatment from this scum? No one knew what she had suffered nightly for the privilege of being there! They should admire her courage; marvel at her bravery and stand awe-struck in her presence. Didn't they realise the miracle before them? How many of them could endure the indecency of incessant rape without abandoning hope? Which of them in her place would not demand the crown?

The King might pay her price, but London would not toss her a farthing if she were destitute. Should Anne Boleyn ever be in need of friends, this was not the place to seek them.

***

'There are so many weddings Will, that it's surely the season for it.' Elizabeth looked at him meaningfully.

'Aye,' he replied, yawning, unimpressed. 'And just as sure there's a reason for it. Advancement!' He lay fully clothed on the bed, the jewelled edges of his velvet doublet peeled back to expose the fine embroidered linen shirt beneath. He looked so young. Boyish, despite the scar on his lip, won during a careless moment in the joust. Through knowing this one man her life had colour and meaning. Without him there would have been nothing! Seeing him there, so relaxed and contented, she had to agree. What did they need with marriage? He came to her more often than most men visited their wives. And not only to satisfy his lusts. He liked the pleasure of her company, and her conversation, though she had little to talk of but the trials and tribulations of Queen Anne. Will didn't seem to mind.

'Praise God that Anne is past the dangerous month. She seems set fair to have a healthy child.'

Will smiled, almost to himself. 'No reason why not,' he said jauntily. 'Anne is so determined to carry a prince that even God would tremble to gainsay her. I am sure that He is as much hers to command as the next man.'

'It's not like you to be so blasphemous.' Elizabeth smiled. 'Is your God away on other business this week? Or have you joined me?'

Will laughed. 'Nay. Bessy. God won't take offence at my feeble jests when such blasphemies are about these days that he must be listening in amazement to some of England's prayers. Our monarch is now as close to God as that.' He crossed two fingers of his right hand. 'He has dispensed with the Pope as mediator and should any object to the new arrangement Henry will probably give them every opportunity to state their case to God face to face.

'Put himself above the Pope?' Elizabeth looked puzzled.

'Aye. Someone has pointed out how wealthy the Church is, so Henry

101

will now be head of that Church. There will be no one now to tell him who he can or cannot divorce. Or marry for that matter. But some of us will have to tread warily. I no more want to lose my gains to Henry than the next man. Witness the way Cardinal Wolsey was relieved of Hampton Court.'

Elizabeth had difficulty in assimilating such radical new ideas. 'What will the people think? She asked.

'They have worshipped their golden king for years so he slips into the role of God very comfortably.' Will assured her. 'And trouble-makers will be given short shrift. You have had little time for the Church yourself but the avarice of its incumbents is negligible when compared to Henry's greed. One thing you can be sure of: Cranmer is the King's man in this, and coming straight from the Howard altar will do his best to see the Queen right. And that could prove providential for some of us.'

'Always change! Nothing stays the same for long,' Elizabeth grumbled. 'Why, even Frances Brandon is now grown enough to become a wife, though if she still has as many tantrums she will lead Henry Grey a merry dance.' Her mind wandered back to those peaceful days in Norfolk, to a time before she had known just how vitriolic a tongue the King's youngest sister had. Days of wild geese and tranquillity. And Henry Bedinfeld. The memories transferred their pleasure to the corners of her mouth, which turned in a smile. Startled from her secrets she blinked nervously as Will lifted her chin with his fingers.

'Come away, Bessy Sweet. Yesterday is gone and I am here instead.' She blushed, laughing in her embarrassment.

'How can you see into my mind when no one else even notices my presence?'

'No magic art,' he told her affectionately. 'It's done with love, and no more than you have often done with me. I sometimes wonder if I have any secrets from you at all. Was that smile for your lost lover? Do you wish to turn the years back, Love, and be in his arms at Westhorpe still?'

'Nay, Will.' Her voice was scarce above a whisper as she put away her drawing materials now that he had moved.

He couldn't help noticing the guarded look which had come over her.

That was strange. What was she hiding? Sitting down beside her Will slipped his arm round her waist. Elizabeth concentrated on folding the parchment.

'Don't hide it from me, Bess.' He wasn't joking any more. Obstinately she shook her head. Some things were better not spoken of. Murder was an ugly word. Especially as the victim still lived. And yet the deed was as good as done. But Elizabeth had reckoned without Will's insistence and she glimpsed the ruthless tenacity which had lifted him so high in Court circles.

'There were rumours being spread,' she said at last. 'It was before Frances Brandon's wedding. Her mother, Mary, was in total sympathy with the Princess Mary over the treatment of Queen Katherine and the two were vociferous in their condemnation of Anne. But when the King's sister openly declared that the coming child would not, nay, could not look in the least like His Majesty, Anne's enemies began to prick up their ears.'

'Who then would he favour?'

Elizabeth hesitated. 'Several names were suggested.' She had no need to spell it out for him.

'You surely don't believe any of it?'

She shook her head. 'I don't, but it isn't me you should be afraid of. If the King should hear the slightest hint of this from his sister, or if Charles Brandon were to repeat it in the King's presence, there is little doubt about the outcome.'

'Then what else are you not telling me?' Will refused to give in until he knew the full story.

'Mary Brandon is ill. Mortally ill.' Elizabeth fixed her eyes firmly on her hands, clasped together on her lap. 'The wicked humours from her mind have now overflowed into the fabric of her body and she will waste away quickly. Her tongue will soon be as still as the air in her tomb.' She lapsed into silence.

For what seemed like an eternity Will didn't move. And then she felt his arm tighten round her.

'Eleanor has grown into a clever child.' Elizabeth spoke as if she was in some far-off world of her own. 'She put me in mind of another child, long ago, listening to those self-same remedies at the knee of Megan ap Y. And there was nothing Old Megan didn't know about cures for all afflictions, including several which are guaranteed to stop a flux of words. Eleanor loves her mother and will remedy her well. There is no need to worry. Those who don't jostle for position in the Court have no more substance than a will-o'-the- wisp and the potion is so natural a thing that nothing will even be suspected.'

At last Will was moved to action. He grasped her by the shoulders, his fingers digging into her flesh harder than he realised as their eyes met in a look of mutual understanding. God, how this woman must love him! But poison! What dangerous games they played!

His lips caressed hers briefly before he bent to pull on his boots. 'I must leave to attend my duties.' And find out how far this ugly rumour had travelled. Time enough for real thanks later.

'Wait for me tomorrow, Bess, and I swear that then I'll pay you proper tribute.'

So he left the lodgings in Mark Lane somewhat abruptly to pursue his business and Elizabeth sat on alone wondering how she had come to tell him what she had done. She hadn't meant to.

On the first of May the sun rose to bring the promise of a fine day for the maying, and Will presented Elizabeth with a jewelled ring.

'Emerald, the jewel of constancy, and framed in gold,' he told her. 'It's a poor reflection of nature. Nowhere could I find one to match the depth of colour in your eyes or the gold to match their chestnut frame but I can only hope that it will serve to remind you of my constant joy in you, my sweeting.'

There was no need for so precious a jewel. She was only too pleased to be at his side when there were so many other beauties available at Court. All she asked was that he didn't desert her and she would help him in any way she could.

'No more sadness now?' he asked her, looking deep into her eyes. Sadness was the word he used. Not guilt. Some things were best not spoken of ever again.

Elizabeth didn't answer. She was overwhelmed, not by the costliness of the gift, but by the thought. Constancy. The word dispelled the niggling doubts still lurking in the dark recesses of her inner mind. The trouble was that she knew him too well. But even Will, for all his appetites, would never be so foolish. She saw that now. Ambition had its limits! It only went to show how easily stupid rumours could take hold and be believed; how downright lies could be believed! If friends could be swayed by them, enemies would certainly have a field day. The odd thing was, she could feel no remorse for what she had done. Will was the only one who mattered and if it was in her power to help him in any way at all, then right and wrong didn't even enter into it. But it would soon be over and with luck the evil slanders would die with the King's sister. She had done what she could, thanks to an ancient Welsh remedy!

The air was crystal clear; fresh, unsullied, and oh how sweet it was to be alive and happy. It would be a day of lamb's–tails and hawthorn sprigs and the pungent smell of lush grasslands crushed and trampled underfoot. May the first.

That brought thrilling memories of her first real kiss when love was young and life was still a virgin patch of snow. When cascading emotions had swept sanity away and launched her into her future. With Will. At Congleton Fair. She watched him now, sharpening his wits on George Boleyn as the King's laugh boomed out with every thrust and parry. Today he declared his constancy. May the first. A day to remember! As the thought formed in her mind a cold shudder of presentiment ran through her. Someone walking on her grave. The shadowy, half-formed premonition clouded the present with pain. Then the emerald glinted in the sunlight, focusing her attention on today, and the moment passed into oblivion.

Seven

THROUGHOUT the summer of 1533 Elizabeth Fytton needed all the patience she could muster. After the excitement of her coronation at the end of May, Queen Anne's volatile and erratic temperament drove her serving women to distraction. The fact that the causes were easy to see didn't make her any easier to live with. Sometimes she would be wild with joy, thinking of the heir to the throne lying safe and snug within her womb. Katherine must be livid. She had failed time after time where Anne Boleyn would succeed at the first attempt! And the Princess Mary could look to her laurels too, when her brother, the prince was born! Anne was impatient for the event and as the hot weather at Windsor dragged on and her belly grew more round and cumbersome her discomfort frayed her temper.

'Another cushion, Elizabeth!' Anne was scowling again as she tried to make herself comfortable. 'I don't recall others being so ungainly. Look at Jane Dudley! Why do I ache so while she shows no signs at all of discomfort?'

'It isn't her first, ' Elizabeth plumped the cushions around her mistress. 'She already has sons and knows that they arrive in their own good time.'

'Patience has never been my bed-fellow.' Anne allowed a smile.

'It will be worse before it is better, and for the moment it will do no good to fight it. Live with it and let your body rest around it. This will ease the ache and help the child to a gentler disposition.'

Anne sighed. 'It's taking all my strength to smile at Henry and feign happiness at my grotesque shape. He thinks me more beautiful than before and can hardly keep his hands from my swollen belly. My stomach turns at his pawing.'

'You are Queen,' Elizabeth reminded her quietly.

'I feel like an animal, and I'm sure this monstrous swelling contains not one prince but a litter. My problem is that the King still considers me to be a bitch on heat. It takes all my wiles to persuade him to hunt so that I can forget my couch for a time.'

'And while you forget yours, I must also forget mine as Will rides at His Majesty's side constantly. Have you no thought for your friends?'

'No thought for them? They are constantly in my thoughts. I price their friendship above pearls for the service they do me in distracting the King for a time.' She placed her hands tenderly on her distended stomach, her frowns gone, replaced by a gently smile. 'It won't be long before Will is laughing and in your arms at Richmond, and then at Greenwich for the birthing of the prince.'

It seemed that the whole of Greenwich Palace was being turned inside out in the frenzy of activity which announced the arrival of the royal party. The grass and rushes on the floor were swept aside. Hangings and drapes were taken out and beaten. Tapestries were shown the light of day for the first time in years and the beetles and mites evicted from their ancestral homes. Then sweet summer grasses mixed with wild flowers and herbs were strewn thickly on to the floors of the rooms and the furnishings returned in splendour to their posts. And the cradle was made ready.

When Anne first saw it she looked at it silently for some moments. She turned to Elizabeth as though she had only just realised that a real child was about to make its entrance. It suddenly dawned on her that the fantasy prince whom she had talked of for months was not the dream-child of her imagination, but would soon be lying there. Real flesh and blood. Crying and laughing, drinking and sleeping. What would he really look like? Would he be dark, like his mother, or golden-haired like his father? Would his skin be fair, or sallow like hers? What colour his eyes? What shape his nose? Who was he, this child of hers?

'Before long a babe will lie there.' She sounded amazed at the thought. Then a dazzling smile lit her face. 'And all my discomfort gone!' August had been a miserable month, spent shut away from the Court while she awaited her lying in. Anne was tired of women's talk.

'Did you think you carried a lump of dough, then?' laughed Elizabeth.
'It's certainly risen like one,' Anne replied, displaying it to its full extent and demonstrating her rolling gait, her hands pressed to her aching back. 'Though it feels more like a nest of writhing snakes.'

On the fifth day of September Anne complained of belly cramps and an air of expectancy pervaded her rooms. On the sixth day of September she could not stay still but walked about the chambers incessantly, her hands arranging and rearranging cushions to no useful purpose until the early evening. She stood stock still as the ever widening pool of water seeped round her slippers and across the floor. It was time.

As they persuaded Anne to her, bed, Elizabeth saw panic in her eyes. Stark, naked terror masked her face. 'Has the King been sent for?' she asked.

Elizabeth nodded. 'Though there'll be nothing to see for many an hour yet.'

Despite Henry's impatience, the child was in no great hurry to greet its father. Anne held on to Elizabeth's hand as though it was a lifeline. She was wet through with sweat as the pains contorted her delicate frame. Elizabeth worried silently. In her agony Anne tried to twist on to her knees to gain more leverage, but the women held her down. Her legs jerked upwards, bending to press themselves against her swollen abdomen as she panted in desperation. The eyes of Henry and his courtiers bored into her, every vestige of privacy stripped from her, her womanhood splayed open before them all. Elizabeth felt Anne's burning shame with her. She knew that the Queen would rather be dead than exposed like this to friends and enemies alike. She had always been insistent that her flesh belonged to no one but herself. Since Harry Percy! Anne was fighting the pain and fighting the birth. Why didn't they all go away?

'Stop it!' her eyes implored. 'Stop it! Stop it!'

But there was no stopping it. She had to go on before them all, in her own private hell. Then the pain changed and she felt as though every muscle in her body was intent on turning her inside out. There was no fighting this! Anne found herself putting all her strength into aiding the process, the watchers quite forgotten, and as her limbs trembled with her efforts she felt cool hands urgently trying to assist her. Again she had to bear down with all her might until she felt her own flesh being torn apart. She screamed out loud as her body rebelled and stopped its forceful straining.

'Just once more!' Elizabeth all but yelled at her. 'Please Anne, for the love of...' She never finished. As the muscles contracted fiercely again and she felt the tearing begin, Anne called out a single word, like a prayer. 'Harry!'

And the effort was enough, for the desperation in that word was so eloquent that it birthed the baby's head, and the bloodstained body slid easily from its mother's womb. Elizabeth looked across the room and caught Will's eye.

During the whole of Anne's labour Will had been careful to hide his agitation. Only Elizabeth had noted his nervousness by the way he constantly chewed at the scarred edge of his lip. In fact, as the labour had become more and more protracted, he had seemed more concerned even than Henry!

'He's worried,' Elizabeth thought to herself. 'What will happen if after all this the child dies? What will the King do then? And what possessed Anne to call for Harry?'

That one word had had more impact on some observers than others. Will's face had flushed scarlet. He looked almost angry! And so did Thomas Percy! His brother's success with Anne gnawed away at his guts constantly. How he would love to see them both in hell! The King, on the other hand, was beaming ear to ear like a simpleton. Harry! He thought that she had called for him. King Harry!

And for all Anne's convictions, it was a girl. Even that fact could not dampen Henry's spirits at that moment. He only knew that Anne had called for him.

Elizabeth wrapped the baby in its clothes and held her gently as the King spoke to his Queen. She looked down at the tiny wrinkled face. It was? No! It couldn't be. A light fuzz of red hair. A tiny toothless mouth quivering tremulously.

The years fell away. Elizabeth was fourteen again, looking at her own baby for the first time and seeing Will's face. They could have been sisters, those two innocents. Her eyes focused on Will. He was staring at her. Staring fixedly at the child she held. So many things began to fall into place. No wonder he had been so worried. What if Anne had spoken? Lunacy! The whole thing was sheer, depraved lunacy! Elizabeth felt as though she had been stabbed in the back. She looked again at that lovely baby. It hurt. Oh, how it hurt!

'A girl?' The Queen looked up at Henry. She was too tired to hold back the tears.

'Aye, and a lusty one,' Henry smiled. 'But what I have heard today assures me that there will be many more to follow. Boys too!'

Anne closed her eyes. She was in no mood for jokes. Go through it again?

But Henry's thoughts had turned to the child and he rose to take the baby. As he did so he saw Elizabeth, as though for the first time. Before him stood a fetchingly voluptuous woman, elegantly dressed, and with a candid gaze. The pain reflected in those misty green eyes was unnerving. His interest moved to the rise and fall of her smooth, white, cushioned breasts, and the slight tremble of the exposed flesh as her heart pounded violently. The lady must be overawed. She shook at the close proximity of her Monarch!

Not insensible to his own attractions, the King leaned towards her in the easy, charming manner he had with women. There was no need to be afraid, his smile reassured her. Joy in his wife and pride in his new daughter had wiped the age-lines from his face and Elizabeth briefly glimpsed the handsome youth of former years.

'What is your name?' His voice was gentle.

'Elizabeth, Sire.' She replied, sinking low before him. 'I was named for your gracious mother, the Queen, if it pleases your Majesty.'

'Elizabeth, for my Mother,' he repeated slowly. 'Aye, it pleases me very well.' Turning to his wife and holding out the tiny Princess, he smiled. 'I give you the Princess Elizabeth, for my sainted mother's memory.' And still smiling, he raised Elizabeth Fytton from her knees.

***

'The King tries too hard to please her.' Will lounged in his chair before the fire, his shoes removed and his silk-clad legs raised high upon the fire-piece edge.

'He does no more than he should.' Elizabeth defended her mistress's viewpoint. 'She is certainly more secure since the King has declared the royal succession to her issue, but with Katherine hovering in the shadows Anne is forever looking round, fearing a mortal blow from her enemies.'

'She is her own enemy, Sweet,' Will answered absently. 'We have made a wager in outer chamber on when the King will tire of trying to possess her. A lesser man would have turned to more loving arms before now.'

'Will Brereton!' she admonished. 'How could you wager on a woman's fate? And that woman a special friend, despite her being Queen of England!' Since the birth of the princess, Elizabeth had watched Will closely when he was near Anne. They had always been close, laughing at the same things, inventing new diversion and enjoying each other's company. Their touch had never lingered. Their eyes had never held that secret look of love; of carnal lust. They were not lovers, of that she was assured. Had they ever been? She still wasn't sure. Best not to think of it!

Early in the year Anne had been ill and full of black depression. She had collapsed before the great hearth in her room, unable to move and when her women had undressed her the bright red stains had splashed her skirts and soaked the linen of the bed.

'Was it another child?' Anne had asked desperately. Elizabeth knew what fears lay in her mind, seeing before her the sad spectre of Katherine. It had been too soon to tell. In the months which had followed, Elizabeth had fed her broth and remedies for the strengthening of the blood, and gradually she had returned to something like her old self. In Henry's bed it had been a different matter.

'His touch makes me shudder.' Anne had told her in confidence. 'Try as I may I cannot overcome this horror whenever he comes near. What is wrong with me? Even wine cannot dull this revulsion which I feel.' Was it the same for her with all men? Except Harry? Elizabeth didn't know, but one thing was certain, she had never loved King Henry. What was more, she couldn't help not loving him. A fine thing then for the courtiers to wager on! How long before Henry looked elsewhere?

'It's a merry wager! Only a jest,' Will explained. 'She'll soon be won over by her husband. Who in this world could resist a fine new palace of her own? Or a man so enamoured of her that he will stand against the Pope? One who would cast off his wife of nearly twenty years, and degrade his eldest daughter in the service of her baby sister. Anne must surely see that she has Henry, and so England, to mould as clay within her palm. She cannot fail to love him!

'How can you, of all people, sit there and say that! Does not contrary evidence now stare you in the face?'

'How so?' He settled his head on the cushioned chair and turned his dark eyes on her.

'When I came to you, it was for love,' she said softly. 'You had no firm position, and certainly no money! We shared nothing but stolen hours in shabby rooms, and that was more than enough. I know that I now own silks and furs finer than I ever dreamed of, thanks to your good management and generosity, and that I drink the best wines and even sup at the King's own table on occasion but these things are only trappings. They owe nothing to the feelings of my heart.

'And Anne?' he asked.

'That's the other side of the coin,' she replied. 'When the heart is untouched by love's arrows no amount of palaces and furs will make it beat with passions of the flesh. And you should know better than most that Anne cannot love as others love. She has no heart left to give and despises men for their base lusts. She needs man not for pleasure, but for heirs.'

Something in her tone made Will sit up and look at her sharply. 'Henry is incapable of that?' he asked as though the thought had just struck him.

'Don't worry. He has been up to now, and see how he adores the Princess Elizabeth. The trouble is that Anne gives him no encouragement and from what she tells me he is sometimes in sore need of all the help he can get to gain full satisfaction in her bed. She must conceive again.' Elizabeth paused. 'It is a tragedy that the princess was not a prince.'

Their eyes met and held. A blazing log broke through the silence as it burnt, splitting apart in a shower of red and gold. Will busied himself with the fire-irons, his face devoid of all expression, his thoughts impenetrable. Money lost in a wager was negligible compared to some gambles. One crazy gambol could cost much more than riches. It could cost life itself should the truth be known, he thought wryly.

At last the dreary winter was washed away by the fresh spring rains. Everyone was glad to rid themselves of the gloom and despondency of those cheerless months, rediscovering the joys of life with Mother Nature's great revival. Will begged leave to visit his estate, always conscious of the need to remind his workers of his existence.

Anne was as querulous as ever, a state which was becoming the common order of things, and which Elizabeth put down to nerves. They worried that the Queen's courses were becoming increasingly irregular, sometimes making slight appearance, sometimes none at all. The presence of Frances Grey in her retinue did nothing to relieve the tension.

'Her eyes pry everywhere,' Anne complained. 'I swear she misses nothing, and every move I make is passed on to her husband. If I put one foot wrong the King will know of it in minutes, so great is her ambition for Henry Grey.'

Elizabeth remembered Frances and her high and mighty ways of old. Too much pride! A common fault nowadays! Even so, she had made it very clear that she had no great liking for Queen Anne and Elizabeth wondered how much she had believed of the rumours spread by her mother. As Elizabeth had predicted, Mary had not lived long after her trip to Court the previous summer, but in some quarters the damage had already been done. Anne Boleyn's quick tongue had made her many enemies and the power wielded by her family encouraged untold jealousies. Slander could hurt. It could even bring downfall if the fates so ordained.

'She mourns her brother,' Elizabeth remarked, thinking of the handsome youth who had followed his mother to the grave. 'Suffolk too mourns the lad and I hear that the King has plans for him to remarry to take his mind from ill-fortune.'

'Aye, nothing must be allowed to spoil Charles Brandon's fun.' Anne's voice held a harsh note. 'Kate Willoughby is no more than a child, and he is as old as the King.'

'Perhaps a man turned forty needs such exquisite diversions,' Anne was continuing. There was a question, a plea for reassurance in her words.

'Only if he has lost his wife,' Elizabeth was quick to answer. 'The King has not looked at children, or even buxom maids about the Court, though many a one has cast her eye on him.'

'You're right.' Anne's frown cleared. 'I am so anxious that I'm beginning to see spectres where there are none.' It had not helped her any to find that Jane Dudley was once more with child, her last one, Robert, being the same age as the Princess Elizabeth. Five sons! And another on the way. It was almost too much for Anne to accept.

Elizabeth spent her free time sketching scenes around the Palace and gardens to while away the hours and take her mind from her absent lover. A shadow fell across her as she painstakingly reproduced the fragile beauty of a spider's web, caught like a delicate wisp of fairy lace across the spiny talons of the brier rose. Startled, she looked up into the inquisitive eyes of the man beside her. Then she blushed furiously. It was the great man himself. How often she had stood in awe, admiring his work and wishing that she possessed a fraction of his talent. Hans Holbein was, to her, beyond compare.

He nodded, smiling. Squinting through half-closed eyes he saw how nearly she had matched the original, and approved. 'You have more than a little skill Mistress,' he observed. 'as I have previously noticed. Though I fear the spider is a poor substitute for Mister Brereton! You seem singularly lacking in models, saving that one.' The lines of his face folded themselves together in a tracery of impish humour.

'Sir, you mock me cruelly.' Her cheeks burned under his gaze. 'My best efforts could never equal even those pictures which you discard as failed.'

'You are too modest.' Mister Holbein leaned further over her, inspecting her work more closely. 'It is a brave likeness to the little spinner there, but I admit to seeing several portraits of William Brereton which could only have been drawn by extraordinary skill, or an excess of love, or some mystic blending of the two.'

Elizabeth was convinced that he was making sport of her and made to leave. He stopped her, his hand upon her arm. 'Don't take offence.' He looked sincere. 'I mean it. I have admired your efforts, and to make amends for my clumsiness in approaching you thus, I would be honoured if you would grace my poor rooms by the river with a visit.'

Elizabeth completely mistook his meaning and her face blazed redder at what she thought was an impudent suggestion, no doubt encouraged by Will's absence in the north. 'Sir,' she said sharply, 'I am not in the habit.'

Realising her mistake he laughed out loud 'Nor did I think you were. I have admired your work,' he insisted, 'and envy Mister Brereton his acquaintance with you, but I only wish to be friends with you in art. I thought to demonstrate my colours to you, and spend an hour or two discussing pigments and perspectives.' His voice trailed off, waiting for her reaction.

Elizabeth stood looking at him feeling quite ridiculous at mistaking his intentions. She would never get such a chance as this again. Sinking low at his feet she lifted her face. 'I shall be most honoured, Sir, for your portraits are beyond compare, and so I most humbly accept your invitation.'

Taking her hand, he raised her and bowed his thanks, but before he could take his leave she caught his arm.

'I apologise, Sir, for my manners. I can only think it was your speech of Mister Brereton which unnerved me. No one has ever linked his name with mine before this, and so you startled me.'

'My eyes are all, my tongue is as nought,' he said smiling. 'And I am no gossip to reveal another's privacy before the malice of the world.'

And so saying, Hans Holbein left her in a happy state of confusion at the encounter.

To Elizabeth's dismay, the Queen's problems seemed to be going from bad to worse and she could see no way of helping, especially as Anne had sworn her to secrecy. She sat alone on the window seat, her small frame silhouetted against the evening twilight with the first silver stars shining their promise of a fine night. Her friends laughed and shouted joyfully as the dice rolled across the wooden floor, apparently without a care in the world. It was a wonder to her that the Queen could hide her worries so convincingly from them all. Elizabeth smiled, glad to see her happy for once, even if the respite was brief. Will had not long since returned from his business in the north and his reappearance had brought a little gaiety into their lives.

After they had supped with Anne, her women had been dismissed. Except Elizabeth. Now she watched as Hal and Will, with Anne and her brother George, played their games. For a time they could forget the prying eyes and jealous ears, relaxed in the certain knowledge of each other's loyalty. Unknown to them all it was about to be tested to the hilt in the coming months.

Mark Smeaton plucked out an old tune and sang a ballad, hoping to increase Anne's merriment.

'Once yet again
Of you I would refrain
Why come ye not to Court?'

Anne threw back her head, laughing, exposing her slim white neck. A pulse spot dimpled appealingly at the base of her throat. She was so attractive when she wanted to be! As the dice rolled towards her she nimbly lifted her skirts and skipped out of the way, accidentally bumping into Will who had been standing beside her. Cheerfully he made to bow his apologies, seeing as he did so the sudden flash of pain crease the Queen's face. Will immediately put his arm out to support her but she shook her head, pretending that it was nothing and made as if to continue the game. But Anne's health was important. Very important to those who had made themselves her allies! George was promptly at her side demanding to know what ailed her.

'Tis nought,' she laughed unsteadily.

'Don't conceal your ills from me.' George put his arm about her tiny waist. 'If anything is wrong I want to know of it. Are you sick?'

'You are with friends, Anne.' Hal Norris joined George in his pleas. Everyone waited expectantly; all looked worried.

Anne cast one despairing glance at Elizabeth before shrugging her shoulders resignedly. 'Then I shall show you if I must, but believe me there is nothing that you or anyone can do. Elizabeth alone can ease my discomfort, secretly with her salves.' At this Anne Boleyn raised her skirt to show first her calf, and then higher revealing her thigh to her brother. In some parts it was tinged with ugly purple wealds dappled with sore red patches, and in others shaded blue and yellow where the bruises had faded to more delicate hues.

George was on his knees with his hand upon the injured limb and a look of total disbelief upon his handsome features. Hal's response was to place a protective arm about her shoulders as Will's worried frown gave way to an expressive twist of disgust.

'Sweet Jesus!' The sound came involuntarily from George's lips and Anne's own mouth trembled with unshed tears. The question in his eyes as he looked up at his sister needed no words.

At that very moment the door opened suddenly, almost as though someone had been waiting outside for this tableau to assemble and hold position. For an instant the group froze, trying to come to terms with this new aspect of the King's marriage. Then Anne dropped her skirt to her ankles, leaving George awkward on his knees before her as Hal stepped back, quickly releasing his Queen from his embrace. Six heads turned to see Jane Morley, George's miserable wife, framed in the doorway. With the briefest of acknowledgements Jane surveyed the little scene, then, with an unnatural smile distorting her pale face, she turned and pulled the door closed behind her without a word.

'The witch!' Anne screamed after her. 'The sly eavesdropping whore!' She swung away from the others, her body shaking with anger. 'Did she see? Did she? What rumours will now begin?' She looked from one dismayed face to another.

George was the first to recover his composure. Leading his furious sister to a large seat he picked her up gently and sat her on his knee, his arms folded round her comfortingly. At his show of love Anne's temper cooled as quickly as it had flared, and with her face buried in his shoulder allowed herself to relieve her pent-up emotions in hot, wet tears. George rocked her tenderly and Will led Elizabeth and Hal to the shadows of the window seat.

'You knew of this then, Sweet?' he asked Elizabeth quietly.

'Aye, for several weeks,' she whispered. 'The first time I found marks on her they were no more than lovers inflict upon one another in the excitement of the moment and I teased her about them saying that she must now be rousing His Majesty to greater enthusiasm than previously. She made excuse of her clumsiness but I knew her to be lying, though why, I didn't know.'

Will and Hal looked at each other helplessly, recognising that no man could interfere in the disputes of a marriage without injury, and if it were the King's marriage it would be sure to end in more than a bloodied nose.

'How in God's name has it happened?' Will glanced at the woman sobbing like a hopeless child on her brother's knee.

'It has all come about because of Anne's lack of passion in the King's bed.' Elizabeth kept her voice low. 'The first small marks were caused when the King lost his temper and slapped her for her unfeeling manner. His anger cooled immediately he saw the red hand-prints on her skin and he was all contrition. Anne accepted this treatment, realising that she was at fault and the Kind found himself able to take he with ease. He didn't call on her services for several days, but when he did he slapped her with his hands immediately, yet he was very careful that he only marked the flesh which would be covered by her gown. In moments he again pleaded remorse and begged her forgiveness, proving his penitence by forcing himself upon her until exhaustion overtook him. This abuse only made Anne shrink from him all the more. For a few nights he keeps away, but when he reappears she cringes and so makes things even worse.' Elizabeth whispered.

There was a gentle tap on the door before it opened to admit the young maid, Jane Seymour. She curtseyed low and her eyes widened at the sight of the Queen wrapped in the arms of her brother, sitting cosily on his knee before the hearth. She didn't see the others standing in the shadows

'Begging your pardon.' Jane bowed again, more insolently 'The ladies request leave to retire, unless your Majesty requires further service?' Her look showed that in her opinion Her Majesty had more to service her than was modest.

Elizabeth stepped forward to confront the girl. 'That will be all, Jane,' she said quietly. 'I shall attend and the ladies may go to their rest.'

Anne was desperately trying to regain her composure, smoothing her gown into some sort of order as she rose. 'Yes, tell them to go,' she agreed, her voice still wavering from a throat full of tears. Jane left silently without another word, gliding away as though she were a ghostly fabrication rather than a maid of flesh and blood.

'She shall be dismissed.' Anne 's face had become pink at the glance from Jane's cool eyes, and then red as her anger once more took hold. 'Prodding! Prying! Peering! Watching and listening all the time! They repeat and exaggerate everything! I shall go mad. I am alone in this nightmare, surrounded by hate and not knowing which way to turn for my own safety.'

Dramatically, Hal Norris fell on to his knee and took her hand.

'Never fear that you are alone whilst I am at your Court. I cannot challenge your husband on these matters but you can be assured that I am, and always will be, your most loyal servant and friend.'

Anne was indeed a pitiful sight, a tragic maiden in distress, guaranteed to bring out the chivalry of any noble knight. George followed Hal's lead, as did William Brereton, and they all pledged themselves to their hurt and bewildered Queen. Mark Smeaton, not to be outdone by those of higher rank laid down his lute and offered similar obedience to her cause. Anne had to smile at his earnest young face framed by his dark curling locks. By the radiance shining from him it was easy to see that he had found an altar at which to worship.

'Good friends,' Anne smiled sadly. 'I am only happy in your company. Your loyalty is beyond question and your help has been invaluable to my cause. Without it I would have been lost long before this.'

She looked directly at Will and he flushed with what Elizabeth could only think was embarrassment. 'I sometimes think that the King would see me dead, and even if that is the truth, you are right when you say that there is nothing you can do in the matter. There is, however one way in which your loyalty can be demonstrated.' They only waited to obey. 'Get rid of that sly Seymour wench. I cannot stand the sight of her.'

'An easy task,' Will kissed her hand. 'Her brother Henry leaves tomorrow to return to his lands and he may escort her to her father on his way, though you can be sure that John of Savernake will be far from pleased with her disgrace.'

As the summer ended and the Court settled once more into London town, Elizabeth stayed close to Anne's side, trying to prevent the worries in her mind from festering and poisoning her whole life. It was a difficult task but she was aided in it by those courtiers who knew of the Queen's sufferings. They formed a tight and friendly band around her, making merriment out of nothing to distract her and protect her from those she thought of as enemies. But they could not protect her from the King!

Elizabeth sat alone in an outer chamber. Late in the afternoon the King had arrived, summarily dismissing all Anne's ladies, but she had stayed behind, knowing full well that when Henry left the Queen's bedchamber in case her salves and sympathy would be needed. Whiling away the hour at pricking out a part-made tapestry cushion she could hear the shouts and rude oaths of the other men as they too practised their arts of sword and lance. Albeit at the tilt, rather than between the sheets.

At length she heard the chamber door creak. Glancing up she saw the King emerge and laid the tapestry aside. Noticing the movement Henry flushed with anger at her presence and in a couple of strides stood tall above her frowning, his fists clenched hard upon his hips. Elizabeth slipped from her seat and bowed so low that her forehead almost touched the waxed floorboards. Her heart pounded so hard in her ears that she thought that they were going to burst.

'Rise!' The command vibrated like a death knell. 'I would see what manner of spy is so tardy as to be observed at her task.'

She trembled before him, her face scarlet from the pressure of blood inside her head and the fear in her downcast eyes hidden by her thick auburn lashes. The King stepped close, lifting her chin with a forceful hand so that he could look full at her. A flicker of recognition registered in his features and he slowly leaned closer until she could feel his hot breath on her mouth.

'Elizabeth, is it not?'

She was so surprised that he had remembered her name that she could only nod her head dumbly like some empty simpleton.

'Perhaps I was a little hasty in my judgement,' he said softly. Too softly. The expression in those small blue close-set eyes changed frighteningly. Lewd. Lascivious. If this was a spy it came dressed in a most provocative manner! How could those eyes remain so innocent above such a titillating body? They held nothing bur purity, while the rest of her flaunted every desirable attribute known to woman!

'Such eyes as yours hold promise of delight,' he murmured, his voice catching in his throat as his gaze lowered, coming to rest on the plumpness of her matronly breasts swelling over the rich bodice of her gown. His hand moved slowly, caressingly, down the smooth length of her neck, coming to a halt on her soft, inviting paps. Squeezing. Testing. Enjoying. Elizabeth stood immobilised.

'Sweet duckies,' he almost whispered. 'Soft and yielding as your full red lips, glistening damp and begging to be kissed. Art wed?' he asked somewhat sharply as the thick wined fumes of his breath washed over her again. The King let his intrusive hand fall away and Elizabeth lowered herself into another graceful obeisance.

'If it please you, Sire, nay.' Her voice sounded too loud in the empty room. Her nervousness made it so, for though she looked calm enough her heart pounded against her ribs. The King didn't reply but the interest still gleaming in his eyes and the smug expression on his face showed her that it pleased him very well indeed. She had never wanted this! His Queen must be failing miserably if he could come straight from her bed only to have his interest caught by the first lowly serving woman his eye happened to fall on!

As Henry hesitated to put his thoughts into words the creaking door broke the silence. He turned to see the incredulous look on Anne's flushed face as she watched the little scene, recognising the leering hunter in her husband's stance. The King turned his back on her.

'Take good care of your mistress.' His voice was loud enough for Anne to hear clearly. 'We are in sore need of ministrations such as yours.' With those words he turned on his heels and left the two women staring at each other, Elizabeth wondering whether she had imagined the whole thing, and Anne convinced that the inevitable had happened. Henry was again looking at other women for his pleasures.

Will finally persuaded her that she had read more into the King's words than had been meant. As groom of the bedchamber he assured her that he would be the first to know if the King had shown any inclination for such games and though the courtiers were surprised, Henry had so far remained faithful to his wife. All the same, she kept well out of the King's way. It meant foregoing the pleasure of seeing Will across the room as he sat by His Majesty, but she was frightened. She had the awful feeling that she was being watched. Will laughed at her, covering her mouth with his own to stop her worries.

'You've been around Anne too long,' he told her. 'She has been looking over her shoulder for years trying to catch evil eyes casting their spells. It's only my loving gaze which you feel. I'll not let the ghouls and demons get at you, Bessy!'

But Elizabeth knew that she was not mistaken. One evening as she made her way through the passages to Anne's chamber she was stopped by a young page, his manner unsure as he addressed her.

'Begging your pardon, Mistress,' he stammered, 'Are you the one they call Elizabeth? The one who heals?'

'Aye,' she smiled at him. 'And who is so hurt that they send at dusk for me?'

'My master bids you tend him with all speed for only you can stop his hurts this night.' The words came out as though he had learnt them by rote, and beckoning her to follow him he sped off down the gloomy corridors. At length he stopped outside a chamber door and tapped on its oak panels. Without waiting for an answer he pushed it open and stepped back to allow Elizabeth through. Wondering at the wound she must attend she entered the small darkened chamber, dimly lit by the glow from the fire in the hearth.

As the King turned to look at her she hid her dismay in the folds of her skirt, dipping into a deep curtsey. His footsteps as he came towards her were deadened by the thickness of the rugs so that his soft voice bidding her to rise startled her. Trembling, she stood. The hairs prickled on the back of her neck as they had these last few weeks and tiny beads of sweat broke out on her brow as she fought the sickness which lay heavy in her stomach. Pray God it does not rise to drench his royal Majesty!

Taking her hand he led her to a seat beside the fire and she sat down gratefully, certain that her legs would not have held her had she been obliged to stand for any length of time. Then she realised that the King was intending to sit beside her. Her cheeks glowed crimson as she felt his hand slide round her waist.

'May the gods give me strength!' she prayed silently. Visions of Anne's bruised flesh swam before her. Visions of Will! No other man had ever taken her in her life, and there was no magic in Henry's touch. Only lust which would have been sharply dealt with from anyone else. Was this how Anne felt?

'Do something,' she urged herself. But what could she do? Nothing! Except try to control her rapid breathing in case the King took it as a sign of her desire. Or her fear! Either would be wrong Her eyes remained lowered, fixed on her hands as they lay clasped together in an unconscious attitude of supplication.

'Such modesty becomes you, Mistress,' Henry whispered.' But I would prefer a welcome smile from those sweet lips, and more.'

Elizabeth swallowed the rising bile though try as she might she could not stop trembling as the King's hand move roughly, impatiently, across her bodice to where her breasts rose pale above the dark velvet of her gown.

'Come! Offer your King the sweetness of your mouth that he may drink at the fountain of innocence which shines so pure from the compelling depths of those lovely eyes.'

Obediently she turned to face him. She could do no other. Henry's small mouth sought out hers. The greedy lower lip was wet and fleshy, but the thin, hard line of the upper one all but bruised her with its unyielding strength. Elizabeth closed her eyes helplessly as his mouth left hers to move to where his hands were busily at work removing her full breasts from the safety of her clothing. The tip of his tongue traced the outline of the nipple before his mouth engulfed it. Terrified, she held her breath. At last he lifted his head. Between kisses to her neck and ears he murmured all the things he wanted of her. All the things he found lacking in his wife. 'You are so pure,' he kept saying. 'Untouched. Unsullied by vile appetites. Free of guile and deceit. A maiden still, in the fullness of her years. Treasure, just for me.'

'The man must be mad! She thought. Still a virgin after twenty years with Will?'

'You have been watched these many weeks and the reports I have had indicate no wantonness in your nature. You have not been seen to lust after or make free with any men about the Court. Unlike some!'

Elizabeth heard the bitterness creep into his voice, as though his mind had suddenly been jerked back to Anne. What had he been told? By whom?

'And you have helped her in her madness!' He stared hard, trying to read her mind. She kept her gaze steady. If it wavered she was lost. Anne's injuries, her own lover's identity, the uncanny resemblance between the Princess Elizabeth and her own lost daughter. And Mary Brandon's rapid end. Kings had ways and means of finding out secrets!

Seeing that she remained unflinching before him, despite the half-naked disarray in which he had left her, he continued. 'Aye, her madness! If I had known that she was possessed by the Devil I would have avoided her black arts like the plague. Damn this abyss which is swallowing me!' There was desperation in his words as though he was at odds with his conscience over his ill-treatment of his wife.

'If it please you, Sire,' Elizabeth kept her voice low and soothing, 'I am but a humble serving wench whom you graciously honour far above her merits. I have not the arts with which to ensnare, nor even the wit or conversation. I can scarce read the written word and my part in life is simply to serve my master and mistress in loyalty, and in any way I can find.'

The King's shrewd eyes watched her intently. 'As with all women, you see only a King. Can't you look beyond the crown and see the man? Think of me tonight as just a man.'

Elizabeth knew he was playing games. Henry could never be just another man. His word was law, and he would have no one forget it! Not for one moment must she let her guard slip.

'I cannot believe, Sire, that anyone could be insensible to so handsome a man. The crown with all its jewels is dull by comparison. It may be that some stand in awe of a being so majestic as to seem more god than man but having only mortals to compare you with, they can surely be forgiven their mistake. Everyone loves you, Your Majesty.' His hands had again begun to enjoy the smoothness of her exposed flesh.

'Except one!' He dug his nails into her sensitive skin at the thought. The vision of his dark-haired wife shadowed the passion from his face. 'The Devil must be beaten from her! I'll have no witch within my chambers!'

Elizabeth watched as the deep, angry colour suffused those flaccid jowls at the recollection of his last attempt to exorcise the demon. And then the passion ebbed away. He looked at her strangely, as though he had forgotten why he had sent for her. His fingers slipped from her breasts uselessly as he stood up. Rising, she waited in the awkward silence. A log fell in the hearth with a crash, setting all her nerves a-jangle and at her sudden indrawn breath Henry put his hand out to her throat before pulling her to him and holding her close. Crushingly close. Kissing her again with that cruel narrow mouth she felt his body press against her, rubbing at her thighs and belly, trying to arouse those feelings in his loins which were almost impossible to find with Anne.

Elizabeth stayed pliant in his grasp. She resisted all her instincts to fight him off. He was the King! Nausea washed over her. It was no use! Maybe he tried too hard. Certainly nothing had risen that night except his hopes. Panic gripped her, tearing at her guts more powerfully than the King's hands tore at her clothing. How could she avoid the recriminations which must surely follow his failure? She was not the Queen, so who would care if she was beaten to within an inch of her life? Instinctive cunning for self-preservation came to her aid and Elizabeth fell down on to her knees, lifting her face imploringly, her whole attitude apologising for the unhappy situation.

'I beg you, Sire, forgive me for my stupidity. I am a simple maid and no fit company for the gods. I am witless in these matters and know not the ways of kings.' That he believed her a virgin must now be used to her advantage. 'Allow, Sire, that I may retire to hide my abject shame from the world, but even in my failure I beg you not to banish me from the Court for I would die were I not able to serve Your Majesty.'

The King looked at the dishevelled figure grovelling at his feet. Her hands were held out to him, palms upward, making no effort to repair the damage or restore her modesty. The woman must indeed be witless. A good-looking woman who had reached perhaps thirty? And still no husband! She really must be lacking somewhere! Magnanimously he raised her to her feet.

'To have remained a maid so long is certainly not natural, but if it is God's will, then God's will be done.' Henry felt almost pious, beneficent. Aye, God's will be done!

Relief flooded through Elizabeth as she correctly read his thoughts. She bent her head to kiss his hand in a rush of gratitude which was not altogether feigned. 'You are most generous, Sire,' she whispered, 'I shall never forget your kindness to me, the most lowly of your servants.'

Backing away to the door, she left the King alone with his thoughts, his bulky silhouette dark against the red glow of the burning logs, and then she ran, as though chased by goblins, through the corridors of White Hall to the beloved familiar surroundings of her room.

Eight

ELIZABETH watched the capers of Queen Anne's Court from the quiet shadows of the solar. Will Brereton and Hall Norris had devised an entertainment for the Christmas festivities and each of the friends was reading his part amongst much merriment. First one postured about the room muddling his line, only to be followed by another even more inept player, which reduced the audience to merry tears. Then Richard Page and Will came to the part where they had to fight for the honour of the Moon Goddess and tripping over scabbards, cloaks, and their own toes proceeded to make it more the jest than the joust. It was a relief to see Will once more like his old happy self.

When she had told him of the King's abortive attempts at making love to her he had been angry. Yes, angry!

'Dear God, Bessy! You could have made some effort! Haven't I told you for years that you have the most pleasurable body I have ever come across, and the most delicate of touches with which to encourage every last drop of nectar from even the most stubborn horn of plenty? And why lie to him? Why tell him you have never bedded? If he ever finds out the truth of the matter you may be certain that I shall be made to pay for it one way or another!'

What had he expected? She had never had personal ambition, and certainly not the crude ambitions of a whore. Since that time, he had taken to meeting her only in lodgings as in the early days of her Court life, taking no notice of her when they were in the company of others. But he still wanted her, and that was all she asked. And now with Christmas fast approaching, he seemed as carefree as he had ever been. Anne too was all smiles as she sat watching their antics. George lounged on a stool at her feet shelling nuts and sharing them with his sister. Elizabeth noticed that in her present mood she had even forgotten vanity, making a game out of taking the kernels from his fingers with her teeth, which she was usually at pains to keep covered, her pretty pouting lips disguising their unevenness.

It was almost the end of another year, and so much had changed in Elizabeth's world that she began to fear what would happen next. It was often weeks between the King's visits to Anne and he seemed to be more closeted with Mister Cromwell than with his Queen. He was now head of his own Church and fast embroiled in conflict with its former leaders and champions. Henry was becoming a stranger to those who had thought him a friend for many years. The handsome, youthful monarch had been devoured by this domineering, brutal ruler of all England. When he laughed it was just a hollow echo of his former hearty bellow and others made haste to join in it from fear and not from any pleasure. Where once he had led entertainment, he now sat at its centre and waited to be entertained. Forcing gaiety had become a way of life for Anne but she had learnt to enjoy herself when the King was absent, and these days it seemed that he had matters of state on his mind.

Elizabeth sighed to herself. Youth and careless joy were fleeing them all. And Henry was more loath than most to let it go. She watched Will. In her eyes he still looked young, and his energy and invention were as lively as ever. She could see why she still loved him.

Holding the sketch she had just completed at arms' length, she squinted at it with a critical eye. It didn't do him justice, but then, it was almost impossible to capture his vitality in the stillness of a drawing. She picked another from the pile. She smiled at it absently her mind wandering to the day when she had fulfilled her promise to Mister Holbein. With a page to guide her she had gone to his rooms down on the waterfront before he once more left this country on his travels. Crossing the cobbles and entering the low doorway she had stepped down the several treads into the room. It smelt of oils, and earths, and woods and so many things that she could only guess at. And there he had shown her his arts, and she had found so much pleasure in that one visit that it made her shiver to remember it. Before she left him she had been in possession of a fair sketch of herself, of which she was more proud than anything she owned, except the emerald and silver bell, tokens of Will's love. Thinking of it, she unrolled the picture to enjoy again the work of the craftsman. There she was, looking out from beneath the point of her cap. She was glad she had worn the new style favoured by the Queen! And he had not drawn in her full breasts, explaining with a twinkle in his eye that he had no wish to cross Mister Brereton in the matter. Although he had only been teasing her she had blushed at the time, her instincts telling her that he found her pleasing to look at.

As she gazed at the picture, noting every line, the company in the room broke off their singing of a festive song. The King had entered, accompanied by John Dudley and Henry Grey and several of his courtiers whose presence these days seemed indispensable. Everyone in the room bowed low until Henry bade them rise with an impatient gesture. He went immediately to Anne and kissed her on the mouth.

'You are looking well,' he noted, deciding to remain with her for the night.

'As are you, my Lord,' she answered smiling. 'And we are honoured that you care to join us, lightening the dullness of this dismal evening.' She sent for more wine and comforts for the King.

Elizabeth moved to assist in these matters and in doing so caught the corner of the drawings where they rested on the seat and sent them scattering to the floor. One of the King's newly favoured courtiers was immediately at her side helping her to retrieve the pieces. She recognised him as one of the Court's great seducers and one who had no cause to love the Queen. Jane Seymour's brother, Thomas had an intuitive feel for timeliness and lately he had been keeping close company with those who counted themselves members of the King's intimate circle of friends. He quickly scanned the separate sheets as he picked them up. Every one a detailed likeness of William Brereton! Elizabeth was never quite sure how it happened but something caught the King's eye and attracted his curiosity. In three strides he was at her side. The memory of his rude probing and futile lust danced in her head as she fought for self-control but his eyes bored into her mercilessly, searching for the slightest sign of insolence or derision. Her expression remained docile; her eyes downcast; her whole aspect, submissive. At last he spoke.

'What's this, Mistress?' He took the Holbein drawing from her hand. 'By the Gods, 'tis a fair likeness, and from the hand of Holbein, 'less I am mistook!'

'Your Majesty is always most astute in matters of the arts,' Elizabeth murmured as she curtsied low before him. The King still held the picture, appraising it at arms' length. There was only one thing to do. 'Would your gracious Majesty be pleased to accept it as my humble gift, this surely being the season for it?' Elizabeth cursed silently at fate for allowing the King's gaze to fall on the precious piece.

'Aye, indeed I shall accept, for it is well designed.' A chuckle was rising in Henry's throat when his glance fell on the other sketches which Thomas now held prominently before him. 'And these?' he asked, holding out his hand for them.

Elizabeth's face flooded crimson to the roots of her hair. Thomas Seymour's knowing smile had her heart beating at double its normal rate. What was it about the man? He set her nerves all on edge.

If only the floor would open and swallow her. 'Those are merely some attempts of my own in which I thought to emulate the master,' Elizabeth stammered, 'And in which I singularly failed.'

Henry scrutinized the drawings, and then her embarrassment. 'Indeed, Mistress, they are well done.' His eyes glittered frighteningly as he carelessly threw the sheaf down on the seat. 'I thank you for your gift. I shall keep it by me as a reminder of my most trusty and loyal servants, with whom it seems, I am surrounded.' He turned, looking directly at Will as he joined his wife beside the fire. For the rest of the evening William Brereton was studiously ignored by his King.

A couple of days later Will found it necessary to travel to the north on business, leaving Elizabeth in a distressed state, thinking that it was all her fault. Things were not well. She could feel strange under currents of hostility around, even more so than usual. What was happening? Will left her with a word of warning.

'Keep away from Thomas Seymour! He is a clever fox in intrigue, and always has an eye for a pretty woman. The less he knows of my life, the better.'

But the incident had put new ideas into Henry's head. He would look into the affairs of Mister Brereton. Financial and otherwise.

It was several weeks before Will returned to Court but within a few days of his arrival she was eating beef and mutton and spiced rabbit pie with him in rented rooms above the Quill. As the ale was served to them by the ale-wife's long suffering husband, Will told her of the incidents which had occurred on his travels which he knew would have her laughing. She was happy again.

Yet later, in the bed, with the hangings drawn against the ill-humoured draughts of the inn, he became silent and she heard him sigh into her hair. She waited. He would tell her in his own good time.

'I have lately had Norbury make a settlement on our daughter,' he revealed at last. 'He is a good man and will do it discreetly. I would not see her without provision now that she is of an age to wed, despite the risk of its coming to the King's notice.'

Elizabeth tried to imagine that tiny child grown to womanhood but even the memories of her baby were partly obscured by the superimposed picture of the Princess Elizabeth.

'What is she like?'

'She is the kind of person who will always have her own way, though it is rare for her to scold or frown. Whatever she wants she gets by way of guile and a smile.'

'So like her father, then.' Elizabeth turned to kiss his shoulder.

'Yet I fear that this time it will take more than a jest to bring me back to favour. It's true that I have sometimes incurred the King's displeasure over some small mischief, and as soon had him laughingly dismiss it. But this now is too near his privacy. He wonders if we made a fool of him over your virginity. I know too many of his secrets and he is plagued by the thought that I took from you that which he could not. It is a sensitive issue. No man likes to be reminded of his failures and especially not Henry!'

'What can you do?' She held him a little more tightly.

'Perhaps he can be persuaded that yours is an unrequited love and that I have never had designs upon you at all. You said that he thought you simple minded, didn't you? Then he will no longer look on me as a rival. It will not pay me to have him look too closely into my accounts. The King has an avid eye for the wealth of others and mine is now considerable.'

Elizabeth was quiet for a moment trying to grasp the full meaning of what he was trying to tell her. 'Are you saying that we shall never meet like this again. Must I really only gaze at you across the body of the Court? Must we turn this myth of unrequited love into reality?'

'That would perhaps be best.' It had occasionally crossed his mind that one day he would get rid of her but he had never thought that he would find it difficult. It had to be done. The arrangements were already in hand! Do it gently then, and with emotion!

'Bessy, if there were any other way, I would have found it. There is no other way. I shall miss you, Sweet.' He let a hoarseness creep into his voice.

'Dear God! I won't be able to bear it. To see you and never touch you. To want you and never have you. And where will you go for your pleasure?'

The silence was suffocating. He drew her closer and kissed her so sweetly that tears started in her eyes. It could not be at an end!

'I am to be married.'

Elizabeth didn't move. Married? What did he mean, married? The word was meaningless. How often had he said there was no need?

Worried at her total lack of response, Will kissed her again. She clung to him, prolonging the kiss, kissing him again and again in a vain effort to wipe away those dreadful words. She wanted him desperately. Now and forever.

'Take me! Take me now! Say you didn't mean it. Please! I love you. You are my life. Take me. Show me that you love me too.'

In the face of such throbbing agonising emotion he could do no other and together they rode on the highest waves of ecstasy, blinded by the pulsating lights of their momentary heaven.

'Tell me that you love me,' she pleaded, still holding him tightly as though she expected him to disappear instantly.

'I do love you Bessy. Listen.' He held her head to his chest. 'That heart beats only for you.' He stroked her hair tenderly. The woman really did love him. He had expected her to cry. To argue. To scream and shout maybe. But not to plead, to cling, to tremble with fear, to react with passion. This was not like the calm and collected woman he saw silent about the Court. Not even like the warm responsive lover of so many years. This was a raw and primitive love, exposed in all its wounded nakedness, slashed and bleeding. He found himself trying to explain. To justify this marriage.

'I am doing it for you as much as for myself. There have been so many ugly rumours of late, concerning Anne.' He paused. 'And I have some small evidence that the King has had enquiries made about my wealth. If this is so, who knows what else may be explored and probed? His interest in my affairs seems to have stemmed from his interest in you and the last thing I would want is to see any harm come to my sweet Bessy.' He kissed her lovingly, knowing by the quiver of her lips that she was crying silently. 'With things going from bad to worse between their Majesties it is best to be prudent. It is too easy to make a sudden end these days. I'm sorry, Love.'

Elizabeth's body was convulsed with sobs. Her hands were touching him, caressing him. Then she raised one hand to the back of his neck and pulled his mouth down on to hers. It was wet with the tears, her lips swollen into luscious fullness with her efforts to bite back all the ugly recriminations which had sprung into her mid. This last night was too precious to spoil.

Will understood her needs. She wanted to be loved. And so he loved her. Gently, carefully and patiently, drawing on all his skill to prolong the final moment.

She never spoke of William Brereton's wife. Not even to Queen Anne. Elizabeth couldn't help but wonder at his choice though. If he was so worried about becoming too rich for his own comfort, why had he married a wealthy widow, and the daughter of an earl at that? Had it only been an excuse after all, to be rid of her. How often had he been in her company on his frequent journeys home, supposedly on business? Will had become ward to her young son on the death of his father. Elizabeth remembered John Savage, a close friend of the Breretons, especially Rian. The family home was not far from Frodsham where her own baby had been born. 'Rock Savage' they called it for its elevated position, across the valley from that high pinnacle where she had once given thanks for her own safe deliverance. Elizabeth Savage. Now known to all the world as Mistress Brereton! All Elizabeth Fytton could do was pray that his affluence would not be his downfall.

The night she knew him wed was the longest the gods had ever visited upon this earth. Elizabeth could bear neither sight nor sound of another living soul. Creeping down to a small cosy where she had often whiled away an hour in his company she sat by the window and watched the stately progress of the moon across the floodlit dome of night. How could the moon still shine? Didn't she know that all light had been extinguished in Elizabeth's life that day? The uneven surface of the glass distorted the world beyond.

'So shall my world now be,' she thought. 'My direction is unclear. There is no one to guide me. Nought for me to follow.' Flinging open the window she breathed deeply of the cold night air, indifferent to the demons of the dark.

What did he do to pleasure her, his wife?

The thought crept into her mind uninvited. Once the question had formed there was no way to undo it, despite the sharp pain which cut into the pit of her stomach.

All through that long, lonely night she sat alone, heedless of the draughts which slowly chilled her to the marrow. Her mind tormented her with a million scenes of Will in consummation until the emptiness grew to a physical pain deep inside her heart. A pain which only death could cure. Her finger constantly traced the grain of wood around the window glass. A small incessant movement. Round and round, like the torment in her head.

The sun at last took pity on her loneliness, ending her futile vigil by turning the sky to grey and then to pearl. The night was over. Other nights would reflect the pain of this, the first. Her cold skin felt unnatural, like the skin of the dead before mortification, yet by the time Queen Anne's ladies had roused themselves, yawning and stretching from their slumbers, Elizabeth was outwardly her normal self and so assured that no one remarked, or even thought about William Brereton's marriage.

Except Anne. The Queen saw the blue shadows beneath her maid's eyes and noticed a certain listlessness in her movements. How cruel was fate! She knew better than to attach any blame for what had happened to Will. Despite everything, Elizabeth would not hear one word said against him. Knowing how she herself had felt on learning of Harry Percy's marriage to Mary Talbot she let Elizabeth be, making no demands on her and allowing her time to heal her wounds in peace.

The early summer grew out of spring and with her mind shut tight against the vagaries of men Elizabeth watched the birds and beetles busy about their lives. Solitary in the woods she watched the leaves unfold upon each bough, and flowers peep from long-forgotten corners like friends of yesteryear. Nature soothed her sadness with its continuity but it could not tempt her to smile. More often she sighed. She had no more appetite for food than for company and as her cheeks became thin and pinched her figure lost its beauteous fullness so that it looked as though she wore the cast-offs of a larger woman. Her once glowing eyes mirrored nothing more than apathy.

Nothing of the Court could penetrate her introspection until Anne pleaded for her help.

'I cannot conceal my hurts without your powers for healing. I am surrounded by spies who would delight in whispering about the Court. If it was taken back to the King's ears you may be sure he would look for a scapegoat and some poor unfortunate would be made to take the blame and lose his life unjustly. To say nothing of mine!'

Elizabeth was immediately sorry for her selfishness 'All these weeks I have thought of nothing but my own loss, and mine so simple compared to your problems.'

Anne smiled at her sadly. 'Yours are still as pained and buried deep where no sweet salve can reach them whilst mine can be mended in moments with your aid. Indeed I am only grateful that the King has at last returned to my bed. His absence has tormented me with ideas that he plots against me.'

Elizabeth looked at her questioningly.

'All is not well between the King and his old friends,' Anne explained. 'Sir Thomas More is the biggest thorn in his side, refusing to bow to Henry as the head of the Church. So my husband fumes and frets and accuses everyone at hand of treachery, emphasising the fact that he is King and warning them all never to forget it. The threats are very thinly veiled and every member of his Court is treading warily.'

'Too much power corrupts even kings,' Elizabeth observed. To keep the peace Will had been forced to marry where he had no wish to, she convinced herself. Sir Thomas's faith was being tried to the limit, and Anne's flesh used as a whipping post to relieve his frustrations and his lusts.

'Your pride only serves to make him worse,' remarked the maid, smoothing oils into the bruise. 'Would that I could do to our beloved Henry just half the hurt he does to us. He demands his love, he commands his friends, and he himself loves nothing save King Henry and the power of the crown.'

Anne was quick to caution her. 'Have a care what you say. You can never be certain that you will not be overheard! I find him pitiable. There he stands, so tall and powerful a man, who is really no man at all. My brother and his friends are now my strength. They give me the will to fight, to carry on. Yet even this has been misconstrued by some.

'How so?' asked Elizabeth. 'Surely no one could doubt your brother's love?'

'It seems that even friendship can be a worry.' Anne sighed. 'One day as we strolled in the gardens Tom Percy gave me his arm and begged word. Thinking it to be some private petition I stepped aside with him to listen and was amazed to hear him court me in the most impertinent manner which left no doubt that he would come willingly to my bed!'

'What made him dare to utter such treason?' Elizabeth looked shocked. 'What gave him cause to think he had a case?'

'It seems that my dear brother has been careless with his tongue.' The frown lines on Anne's face became deep furrows. 'He has joked that Henry is no longer the man he was and that it would take more than the King to satisfy any woman. He thought himself among friends at the time but the gossip was spread. Tom Percy was sly. He said he wished he had been born first and named for the King so that I might call his name out with such emotion. He knows, Elizabeth, or at least guesses about the loss of my maidenhood to his brother Harry, and now extends George's words to mean that I am eager for lovers.'

'The whole world is going mad,' Elizabeth exclaimed. 'What did you say?'

'Nothing. By one disdainful look I caused him to feel as tall as a dwarf and about as desirable as a hobgoblin, but since that time I have had the feeling that I have made another enemy.'

Gradually, Elizabeth resumed her normal duties but kept away from any place where she might bump into Will. He was in her thoughts night and day but she avoided any sight of him until the day when Anne insisted that she join the ladies at supper with the Court. Commanding Jane Dudley to make sure she attended, the Queen led the way to the great hall.

As soon as she entered her eye fell on Will Brereton as though drawn there by magic. He was leaning casually against Francis Weston's shoulder, laughing as he explained some story, his hand expressive in the air to emphasise a point. Her stomach lurched within her at the sight of his face but as the men rose to greet the Queen and her company Elizabeth dropped her eyes to the floor and could not bear to raise them throughout the meal. Seeing him there looking just the same as ever, handsome and relaxed, laughing happily with no sign that he had been tormented by their parting, the hurt of her loss had returned tenfold. Had it all been a silly dream? Had he never really loved her? The question tore into the very fabric of her being, leaving even her memories in twisted, tattered shreds. And yet, as they ate, she was sure she was being watched.

The conversation all around her was of Thomas More and John Fisher, some calling them fools, others, martyrs. Elizabeth thought that Sir Thomas was so good a man that no lasting harm could possibly come to him, especially as he was now so advanced in years. Yet he was stubborn in his faith, a fact which Elizabeth could scarcely comprehend. Her early experiences of churchmen had been mostly of wine and good living, not saintly aspects at all. But now it seemed their God was punishing her for her sins and misuse of His Holy Church. He had blessed Will's union with another woman. Made her his lawful wife!

The dish of unwanted food wavered before her tear-filled eyes as she choked back a sob. God was having his revenge. And what of Will? What payment must he eventually make for his sins? The few mouthfuls she had swallowed churned within her and she hurriedly excused herself to Jane.

Escaping from the palace rooms she entered the darkened chapel. There she sank to her knees on the hard stone and tried to pray. There was nothing. How could she pray for forgiveness when she knew that, given the opportunity, she would do the same thing all over again? The smell of incense was all about her, evoking memories of a tumbled straw pallet and the stink of the priest from long ago.

'Dear God, I love him. Is that so wrong?' Was that the cause of all her troubles? She had lied for him and schemed for him. Suspected him of treason and said nothing; even hastening the end of the King's sister in his cause. Murder? No! Say rather a blessed release for poor Mary. Even so, was Megan's way the right way? For the first time in her life Elizabeth's faith wavered. Perhaps his God would be merciful. Should she try? There was nothing left to lose. But who would confess her? Who could she allow to confess her? Who were the King's men and who were not? The confessional was not always the private place it should be.

Devilish demons of guilt and sorrow twisted her worries round their horns and tails until Elizabeth became quietly demented. Hardly conscious of what she was doing, she wandered from the palace grounds, her feet leading her on to the road to London. As luck would have it she was overtaken by a family of merchants who were on their way back home from a satisfactory outing to distribute their wares about the Court and before she knew it the women had made room for her in the cart and Elizabeth was on her way with more speed and comfort than she had hoped for.

On parting from her travelling companions she quickly made her way to the house where Sir Thomas More's daughter lived. Margaret scarcely recognised Elizabeth. A mere shadow of her former self, she seemed rather vague as to why she was there at all. Margaret took her in and fussed over her, encouraging her to eat some of the good wholesome food which she had prepared, and it was then that she learnt of Elizabeth's wish to be confessed. By Sir Thomas! He was imprisoned, but his daughter visited him regularly and after some initial hesitation she agreed to take Elizabeth with her in the guise of a maid.

Thomas More was an old man now, his hair wispy and white, and though he was almost certain of the outcome of his imprisonment he had a serenity borne of his unshakable faith. This one was most certainly not the King's man. He was God's man first and foremost. No secrets of the confessional would ever be torn from his lips, even under torture. In a heart-rending torrent the pent-up words poured out covering her sins, real and imagined, of nearly twenty years. From her desecration of God's Holy Church to the sins of pride and jealousy when she lost her lover to another woman.

Sir Thomas listened gravely but his expression showed no trace of condemnation. This woman was a pitiful sight. Her inner torment was etched in the lines of her thin face. The stooped back and the nervously plucking fingers were the outward signs of enormous difficulties with which she had been wrestling so ineffectually. What unhappy states King Henry brought his subjects to! He should never have married Anne Boleyn! And there the old man felt himself at fault. He had known at the time of the romps she had with Harry Percy and had even used his knowledge to persuade the young man of the dire consequences of disobeying his father. If only he had known that Henry would take a fancy to the girl his action might have been different. Kings of England should only marry virgins. Women who had never been betrothed. Look at the problems of succession caused throughout history by kings who thought they knew better. And Henry certainly thought he knew best. In everything! Ah well! What's done can't be undone now. All he could do was adhere to his faith no matter what it cost. He knew what it would cost, but he was ready to meet his Maker. The young woman on her knees before him was, however, not in that same situation. She had a long way to go and many more trials and tribulations yet to face. He stretched out his hand and placed it on her head, absolving her.

As she raised her eyes to look up at the venerable old man she fancied that he was surrounded by an aura of golden light. Elizabeth blinked rapidly.

'The gods be with you. Always.'

Was that what he had really said? Or had she misheard? Suddenly she was more awake and more aware than she had been for weeks. They had almost trapped her! The Church had kidnapped Will and she had almost fallen for their trick! She really had been like one of their living dead for months. But Thomas More was a man of strength, and he had given her the will to carry on. Elizabeth Fytton still believed.

Back at Court, Anne welcomed her with open arms and flaying tongue. They had searched high and low for Elizabeth and had feared her murdered at least.

'I lost my way.' She didn't explain how or why, and that was all she would say on the subject. It was immediately noticeable however, that she was more like her old self after her mysterious disappearance. Once more she could be found in the pungent steam of her brews, muttering and mumbling unintelligible words under her breath. Had she been old and warty some might have thought that she was casting spells! Even had she wanted to, Elizabeth knew that it would have been unwise to mention where she had been. It would not have been very clever to let slip that she had been visiting the King's prisoner!

Anne was only too pleased to have her back and did not press the point.

'At least you've returned, and that's the main thing. I can't manage without your help, especially as we are soon to leave on a progress west, keeping ahead of the plague and making it a holiday for the Court.' The

Queen looked at her thoughtfully. 'You are now well enough to resume your full duties?'

This, of course, would entail being in Anne's company when Will was present. Elizabeth accepted that she couldn't avoid him forever. She nodded. It would be difficult but now that she had faced the fact that she had lost him, it wouldn't be impossible.

When the moment came, it was every bit as hard as she expected. Her breathing seemed to stop and the banging of her heart felt as though it would shake her to pieces. Elizabeth concentrated on controlling her trembling hands, hoping against hope that no one noticed the flush of apprehension warming her skin. She was more than glad when it was time for Anne to return to her own chamber.

'The King seems more pleasant than a few weeks ago,' Elizabeth observed as she undressed her mistress.

'Mister Cromwell is to be thanked for that, I believe,' Anne told her. 'He has assured the King that he is omnipotent in all matters of state.' She smiled ruefully. 'If only he were not so impotent in other matters! Fortunately George and Hal have been ahead of themselves in flattery of His Majesty lately and my punishment has been less severe. 'No husband is so careful of his wife,' she mimicked. 'No husband is so beloved for his care, and none so adored for his wit and conversation. And a husband more loving and less demanding of his wife must surely be a saint!' Anne sighed with mock humility rolling her eyes heaven wards before breaking into peals of laughter. 'And so they go on and on, telling him how all the Court sees him as a model of perfection. He is coming to believe it!'

'How does he use Will?' Elizabeth almost whispered the name.

'Well, I think. How did you think he looked today?'

'There are shadows under his eyes.' Elizabeth blushed furiously after she had said it. Such shadows were only caused by sleepless nights.

'He said the same of you.' Anne watched her closely, looking for her reaction. Elizabeth went white. She seemed about to faint.

'He spoke of me?' She was incredulous.

'Aye. He wondered where those rosy cheeks had gone, and the full inviting duckies, for you really are only half the woman William loved for so long.' Anne yawned, dismissing the subject of Elizabeth's lost love. 'Take the dress away and tomorrow you may choose another.'

That night Mistress Fytton slept very little. The hours were spent in absolute concentration.

She rose with the dawn, standing for a moment to watch the first golden rays suffuse the summer sky through the window of the Queen's bed-chamber. Another day. So near to him, and yet so far removed for fear of Henry's renewed disfavour, and the barrier which holy wedlock had put between them. Somehow life had to go on. Behind her the chamber door creaked slowly open. Turning, she was surprised to see George Boleyn tip-toe in, carrying in his arms an enormous pannier of fruit. The drapes about the bed were not closed, the night having been warm, and a deep chuckle rose in his throat as his sister stretched sleepily. Opening her dark eyes she squealed with pretended indignation and modesty as he approached her.

'Breakfast for my beloved Queen,' he laughed, piling the fruit around her before lying lazily across the foot of her bed and helping himself to a ripe, juicy pear.

'You are irreverent, Sir.' Her smile belied the words. 'What would your dear wife Jane think if she saw you now? Creeping in at dawn, and me still with the sleep upon my face! Imagine how the tongues would wag around that titbit of gossip?'

'Jealousy. Sheer jealousy.' George laughed wickedly. 'There isn't a woman in the Court today who wouldn't jump at the chance of sharing a bed with the King's brother-in-law.'

'But I am your sister,' Anne giggled. ''Tis a pleasure which I fear I must regretfully decline. There is enough spice in the stories spread about me as it is. You shouldn't tempt fate!'

George put his finger to his lips and winked at her. 'This is in a good cause,' he whispered. 'Elizabeth.' He turned his impish grin on her. 'Go to the robe-room now and find something to suit. But be silent. We wouldn't wish our little escapade to be discovered!'

Elizabeth nodded, smiling at his boyish enthusiasm. Crossing the outer chamber she opened the door of the robe room quietly and slid gracefully through, wondering what would please the Queen today. She gasped as a hand gripped her arm and another clamped firmly over her mouth, stifling her cry of fear. Struggling to escape, her eyes widened with disbelief as she looked up into his laughing face. Her taut muscles slackened and he released her. As he took her in his arms her response was instant and predictable. Sanity and reason drowned in the flood tide of her love as she tasted the sweetness of his kisses, the lovely familiar scent of his skin again filling her nostrils. It had to be a dream! Reality broke through the shimmering haze of his nearness and she tried ineffectually to pull her belly away from him, at the same time, pushing at the strength of his shoulders with her tiny, wasted hands. At last he let her go. Smiling down at her he waited for the questions which would follow. But she was stunned.

He held out his arms to her. 'Bessy sweet.' 'Twas all he said, but it was enough to make her fling her arms round his neck and kiss him again and again with all the fervour she could muster. Letting her hands rove over the hardness of his shoulders and chest to his narrow waist and down to his legs, her fingers revelled in the familiar shapes as desire played havoc with her common-sense. She groaned aloud at the desperate need to feel his weight crushing her and to feel the sweat of satisfaction damp between them.

'Is this just to torment me further?' She kissed him again. 'I love you more than life but you can never be mine. You have a wife!'

He heard the harshness as she said the word.

His face was only inches from hers. Gazing into those deep wood-violet eyes she had the feeling that she was looking right into his soul. It was an intimate, moving moment.

'Dull gold cannot compare with the blinding rays of the sun. I have been a fool. You have every right to send me away to paddle in the stagnant pond my life has recently become. I didn't know until you weren't there that your love has been the mainstream of my whole existence. I must have been blind! I thought you were my mistress; that you were there for my enjoyment. That you didn't really matter! It hit me hard to find that I needed you and I tried to forget, to pretend to myself that you were nothing special, to ignore the fact that you even existed. I began to think that I was succeeding, and then I saw you with Anne's ladies at board.'

Elizabeth remembered. By his attitude that night he certainly had succeeded.

'You were so thin and looked so ill. I wanted to hold you and comfort you. To make you well again. I couldn't take my eyes off you and at last I admitted to myself that you were my true wife. We share so many memories. You have stood by me even when you knew me in the wrong. You have loved me in spite of my faults, which I own are many, kept my secrets, covered my disasters and been constant to me through it all. And in return I have cheated you, and lied to you, left you to bear a child alone, sent you away when you stood in the way of some small ambition, and in the end, deserted you.'

Tears streamed silently down Elizabeth's face. She had known him for a long time and as he said, she knew his faults. She had known when he had strayed for an evening and said nothing. What man at Henry's Court didn't have occasional fancies? Never by one single look had she ever let him know that she understood him so well. He had always returned. None of his amorous adventures had ever been serious. Until he decided to get married.

'Forgive me, Bess, but I cannot live without you. When you disappeared I was frantic with worry and I vowed to God that if he spared you I would fulfil my promise made that day in Malpas Church and stay with you until death. If you will have me?'

'There is nothing to forgive.' Her look was tender through her tears. Let him believe in his promises to his God. She knew the real reason he had not been able to forget her. She had used her strength. Her power. So why did she still find it so hard to believe that he was here, holding her? What of his wife?

'My greatest torture has been your marriage bed,' she admitted. 'In my mind you have caressed her, and kissed her,' she paused. 'Loved her. Do you love her, Will? Was it the same with her?' They had been too close for too long for her not to ask him.

144

'I would lie if I said it was nothing. My body fulfilled its obligations, but it wasn't the same. We never got close. We were not one. Even after, instead of contented sleep, you haunted me. Beckoned me to come to you. To take you. You must be a witch to have ensnared me so. You have become part of me. Part of the good times, and the bad. Teasing me and tempting me until I couldn't stay away any longer.' His kiss was as insistent as his words, the hungry pressure of his lips forcing hers apart to invade the privacy of her mouth set her blood on fire.

'My body fulfilled its obligations.' The words were like a knife twisting in her breast, re-opening the ragged wounds of jealousy. But it had not been the same! With that she had to be content. One thing was certain: after this there would be no secrets and no barriers between them ever again. They had been through too much together for that. So far as Elizabeth Fytton was concerned, from this moment on, she was his wife. Lawful or not, she was his wife.

Will looked at her strangely. 'You sometimes make me wonder whether my whole life has been wasted. What good is power if no one loves you? What good is wealth with no one to share it? Ambition has been my driving force, corruption my tool, and there isn't a friend who hasn't been used to further my aims in one way or another. So really I have no friends. Except you. And Anne, perhaps. Until recently I truly believed that it didn't matter. The enormity of my conceit was unbelievable. Whatever happens now I shall not desert the Queen. In the future she will need every one of her friends and I have learnt my lesson. Love and friendship are worth more, much more, than wealth or power. Will you have me, despite the dangers which I fear my convictions will lead me into?'

'Shall I come to you tonight?'

It was the answer he wanted. She was with him, all the way, just as she had always been. But it was time for him to leave her or, as he observed, he would land George in trouble if the ladies of the Court found him in his sister's bedchamber at such an early hour.

'Until tonight!' With one last kiss, he was gone. Elizabeth raised her fingers to her bruised mouth, staring transfixed at the door through which he had just vanished from sight. The whole thing was incredible. Unbelievable! Had he really changed? Distanced from his charismatic personality she began to come back down to earth as elation gave way to misgivings and doubts. He was always so plausible and, loving him as she did, it was only too easy to believe every word he uttered. But did it matter? He wanted her back and that was all she cared about at that moment. Accepting the fact that she would never be his wife had been difficult. Accepting that she could be his mistress for life was so much easier, and whether it was for love, or some other more basic emotion didn't really matter at all. If she wanted to continue sharing his bed then she could. If pride prevented her from swallowing the bitter pill of his marriage she knew him well enough to realise that he could soon find someone else to satisfy him when his wife was not at Court. Perhaps she was being unjust. Perhaps he did mean what he said. It was simply that she was no longer the gullible young girl she had been, no longer blinded by infatuation, no longer thinking him perfect. Elizabeth sighed. Knowing all his faults didn't stop her loving him. She would be his mistress, and willingly. The Devil take the King and his suspicions! As Will said, they had all been friends for a long time and it would be a sad world if friends couldn't stick together.

Let Henry do his worst! They could make themselves a happy life without his patronage.

Elizabeth drifted through the day in a dream. She waited on the Queen, visited the kitchens to prepare her brews and potions, ate a little, walked a little, and all the time she wondered why the day passed by so slowly. It seemed as though night would never come. How many times did she shudder with anticipation? She had been a long while without her man and her mind ran riot with erotic fantasies throughout the seemingly endless hours.

'Twas as though they had never been apart. Her hands caressed his body constantly, as gently as silks rippling in the breeze. Her fingers fondled him intimately with that special seductive quality he had searched for and failed to find in anyone else.

'Ah, Bess, my sweet whore.' He restrained himself, laughing with his mouth against her slender neck, his teeth teasing her skin as though he wanted to eat her, to hurt her. To rape her. 'Bless those fingers. There are no others like them in the whole world. You are an angel of the night sent on to earth to dismiss the problems from men's minds.'

'One man only,' she corrected him softly, and her body arched beneath him causing his immediate capitulation. The rhythmic movements of her silken thighs brought him steadily, inexorably, to a glorious pulsating peak where their bodies blended in a passion as complete as the reuniting of their souls.

Sadly, the elusive nature of heaven makes it impossible to grasp and hold on to, especially in such dangerous times as these. The only consolation Elizabeth had was that Will talked to her, told her of his problems and his worries.

'Something is going badly wrong.' They were sitting on the grassy bank beneath the willows which rustled and swayed around them, silvery green in their full-length gowns of rippling foliage.

'The King is up to something but I can't seem to put my finger on what it might be. Whatever it is, he wants me out of the way. And quickly. Ireland! Of all the places he could have sent me to it had to be Ireland!'

Elizabeth slipped her hand into his. 'You really don't know why?'

Will shook his head. 'Someone has been prying into my affairs. I only wish I knew who!' His voice rose angrily. 'It is the same for all of us. George and Hal, Richard and Francis. Even Tom Wyatt has found it convenient to go home for a while. Everyone is on edge. Looking over their shoulders. Spy-catching.'

'Now you sound like the Queen.' Elizabeth stroked the back of his hand with the petals of a golden buttercup. 'It may be safer for you to be out of sight, even if it is across the sea.' Memories of her recurrent nightmare sent a sudden shiver through her. The gods keep him safe! There were perils on all sides. She thought of Sir Thomas More, that venerable old man whose head now rotted in the heat of the city for all to see. So Henry rewards those who had served him longest! Better Ireland!

'There is a rumour that the King looks to divorce Anne,' Will spoke slowly. 'If only he could find a quick and easy way to do it. I doubt that he'd want the trouble he had of ridding himself of Katherine all over again, but certainly something is in the wind.'

'He wouldn't dare divorce her,' Elizabeth stated firmly. 'Do you think he would want it all to come out in Court? And do you think Anne would remain silent? She could tell a fine tale of impotent rage, unnatural lusts and frequent failures.'

'She would never get the chance to speak. Cromwell would see to that,' Will frowned. 'He is behind all this, I'm sure. The ideas are his, the spies are his, and such a revolution has been set in motion by his interference that even he himself has every chance of falling victim to it in the end. Change is all around. I can feel it.'

Nine

WILL had gone and the Court made its progress westward across England. There was an air of gaiety about the whole thing and the King was in fine spirits. Anne joined him in the hunting parties looking fitter and healthier than she had for some time and it almost seemed as though the clock had been turned back to those happy days of their courtship. There were no embarrassing bruises to be dressed and the change of scene did them all good as the King appeared to shrug off the cares of state, leading everyone in a rollicking good time.

It happened that their Majesties were to spend several days at their Manor of Thornbury and realising that they would pass close by Malmesbury Elizabeth begged leave to visit her old friend Cissy, Mistress Stumpe. She had been plump the last time Elizabeth had seen her but now Cissy was positively stout. Her sedate walk had become a rolling gait and the slightest incline in the path caused her to pant for breath. She rarely left the house. Consequently, she was delighted to welcome Elizabeth, not only as an old friend but as an enviable source of news and gossip.

'Twill be a veritable feast for me to hear all the tales of Court and London for my husband retains so little gossip in his head that I am starved of the things we women grow fat on.' Elizabeth laughed with her. Anyone less starved was difficult to imagine! The questions came thick and fast. Everything from savouries to scandals, from comfits to courtiers.

'Fine ladies and gentlemen don't always make the best friends,' Elizabeth assured her. 'Everyone seeks only his or her own advancement. They may seem to be your dearest confidant one day only to be tittle-tattling your secrets to the world the next. And the stakes are high. Many a one has entered Heaven head in hand, with the King's blessing, thanks to some friend or other's kind intervention in his affairs. Sometimes nerves are stretched to breaking–point wondering where the axe will fall next whilst at the same time they can't resist inching forward in the ranks for a closer view of the gallows. Some seem to thrive on dangerous games'

'And Will Brereton?' Cissy asked, 'Isn't he as close to King Henry as any? How does he fare?'

Elizabeth took a deep breath. She would have to tell the truth. 'He is married to the widow Savage.'

'Married to another!' Cissy was incredulous. 'So many years together and he married someone else! Why, in God's name?'

The story was told. Not the whole story of course. Treason and murder could not be breathed, even to one's oldest and most trusted friend. That much she had already explained. But she told of how the King had taken a brief fancy to her and of how he thought her a virgin, and how Will had taken that drastic step to deflect any suspicion of his involvement in the King's personal affairs. Just how personal, Elizabeth didn't say.

'I take it this is why you look so thin and pale? It seems to me that you are as well off without him.' Cissy was quite indignant at Will's treatment of her. 'Good riddance, I should say!'

'You don't understand,' Elizabeth smiled at her friend's defensive attitude. 'The intrigues of the Court are more twisted than the honeysuckle and smell not near as sweet. I am his mistress again.'

'You are? You still love him? How could you?'

'Without him I have nothing' Elizabeth answered simply. 'I have no home except the Court; no family except Will. How could I see him every day and not want him? And where else could I go?'

'You have a home here with us whenever you want it,' Cissy insisted firmly. 'At any time.'

It was a tempting thought. The house at Malmesbury was fairly large but as it was always full of young ladies, and sometimes the young men who came calling on them, there was scarcely room to lay your hat down at times. To Elizabeth it was sheer heaven. A real family home, just as she had always wanted, full to bursting with movement and laughter. If only! But it was no use wishing. Her life was at Court with her man, just as Cissy's was here with her husband and children.

It was over all too soon and the young ladies didn't try to hide their disappointment when Elizabeth had to leave to rejoin the royal party. They gave her as a parting gift a fine wool cloak which they had embroidered with briers and pansies entwined, symbols of Will's family and her own. She was touched by the gesture and promised that she would never forget them, and that if ever she could assist them in any way at all then they had only to ask. Mister Stumpe was profuse in his apologies for not being able to accompany her on the road.

'Business, you see,' he explained. All week he had been desperately trying to have his selection ready to present to the royal party. But all to no avail. He would have to follow behind. Even so, with a friend so close to the throne who could tell what advantage might not be gained? And so in his rather clumsy way he tried to impress himself on Elizabeth's memory.

Later, she wondered at his servile flattery but happy memories of that precious week when she had once again felt herself part of a real family swamped all other thoughts. How lucky Cissy was! And how wonderful it was to find out that her life had turned out so well. Pictures of the previous seven days tumbled across her inner mind in a kaleidoscope of coloured fragments, every one a treasure to sustain her through the coming weeks of her lover's absence.

For Anne the summer had been a great success. Henry had enjoyed his hunting and the lavish hospitality which had been shown him at the many manors en route. He had been so replete with food and entertainment that his more unnatural appetites had been somewhat quelled.

Anne smiled at Elizabeth happily. 'It has been the strangest time. Most nights he lay with me without even trying me, and when he did 'twas gentle, more playful than forceful.'

'He lay with you to prevent rumours of your differences being bandied about, I shouldn't wonder,' Elizabeth guessed. 'And had he tried to rouse himself in his usual manner, mere rumour would have become an avalanche of speculation. His desires are more in his head than in his loins these days, but at least he has not turned his attention to pages as some are known to do.'

Anne pulled a face at that. 'If Henry had any thoughts in that direction I should suspect Suffolk above others. They are scarcely out of each other's pockets for a moment!'

Her jealousy of Charles Brandon was showing again. A dangerous trait that, as the King would not have one word uttered against his friend, besides which, Charles was still so enamoured of his young bride Kate that the thought was ridiculous. Elizabeth shuddered as though the air around her had suddenly turned cool. As though the ghost of Suffolk's first wife still hovered somewhere near! She shook herself determinedly. It was no use dwelling on the past. What's done is done and can't be undone! It was just that with young Henry Brandon dead, his two sisters were now more at Court to prick her conscience with their motherless state. She told herself time and again that Mary's illness in itself had been fatal even without the potions she had given Eleanor for her mother's relief. It didn't lessen the guilt. But how could she make amends? She could see no way yet and so Eleanor's fragile beauty, reminiscent of Mary's as it was, continued to haunt Elizabeth in Will's absence into the first golden days of autumn.

If only he would return! Strange undercurrents could be detected about the King in the days after the progress ended but there was nothing tangible. No one person or event could be singled out as the cause of the whispers, nods and winks which seemed to abound. Anne was apprehensive. Something was afoot. But what? And then the King was gone, leaving his Queen and her retinue behind. Elizabeth had caught sight of the small party as they set out. Why so few? Where was the King off to so soon after his return? Thomas Seymour had leaned across to the King's horse as they left and obviously made some witty remark about the fitness of the royal mount. The King threw back his head as the courtyard rang with his laughter. It had sounded ominous to those who were left behind and Elizabeth remembered Will's warning.

'Keep away from Thomas Seymour.'

It was easy enough for Elizabeth to carry out those instructions but the King had been won over by that young man's charm and between Thomas and his brother Edward there was hardly room for anyone else to get within three feet of Henry these days. It didn't bode well for Will.

'At least he has left us pleasant company,' Anne brightened, pushing aside her worries once her husband was out of sight. 'We shall dance and sing and make merry whilst the King seeks his enjoyment elsewhere.'

Elizabeth was used to her sudden changes of mood and smiled to herself, thinking that at times her mistress was no more than a wilful child. Without Henry she would happily fill her time with fripperies, surrounded by those courtiers who knew of her sufferings. They had protected her as best they could for months and raised her hopes and spirits when it seemed that everyone at Henry's Court hated her.

Then in October, two days before the King returned, Will came home. Elizabeth flung herself at him in crazy delight, kissing his travel-stained face. He was weary and she noted that his eyes were tired and his brow more lined than when he left. She would soon have him feeling better. Before he knew what was happening she had ordered buckets of hot water to be brought and to his vast amusement she stripped him of his dirty clothes and filled a tub before the great fire in his room. There she bathed away the sweat and grit of weeks. A foaming jug of hot water poured over his head had Will spluttering and splashing her playfully in return until the droplets gathered themselves together to run down between her breasts. She was already roused by his nakedness without his encouragement. Their lips met. Wet, and warm, and sensual. Skin glistened in the firelight as water cascaded down into the tub. Will stood before her like some ancient Greek god.

'Bless you, my sweet. I should think that I am far less likely to cause a stink about the Court after that. And more able to face Henry.' She could see by the expression on his face that he had other things on his mind. Henry could wait. And so could the rest of the Court. 'But now I must repay you for your kindness.' With a yell he lifted her bodily into his wet arms and carried her, squealing, to the bed where he had all her laces undone in a matter of moments.

'You've practised that these last months!' she accused him jokingly.

'Not me, Bess,' he assured her. 'I'd as soon tumble old Megan as the wild, unkempt women of Ireland. There is no elegance or subtlety in that part of the world to tempt me. I had too many problems with the men folk to worry overmuch about the women.'

All had not gone well then. Now that he was refreshed, the only thing to do was to try to take his mind away from such dull troubles. Running her fingers through his curls, still damp from their washing, Elizabeth proceeded to remind him why he had left the tub for the greater space of the big, carved bed.

***

'What in God's name is happening?' Hal Norris looked from one blank face to another. No one had the answer.

'Something is going on if Henry's pleasant attitude is anything to go by.' Francis pushed absently at a burning log in the hearth with his foot.

'It seems that his hunting trip was successful.' Anne wasn't looking too hard for reasons. Henry was in a good mood and that was all she asked. If only she could get herself with child again, all her worries would be over.

'He found rare game in Wiltshire, and satisfaction enough to leave the kill for another day.'

'Where did he hunt?' Will had his suspicions, knowing who Henry's companions had been. Frowning, he waited for her answer.

'Savernake Forest, for the most part, I think.' Anne tried to remember Henry's exact words. 'Game a-plenty in Brail Wood. That's what he said. Game a-plenty in Brail Wood.'

Elizabeth noticed Will and Hal exchanging a knowing look, though neither said a word. Something was amiss. Something which they had guessed at, but before Anne could sense that anything was wrong, they changed the subject. Inviting the Queen to show them the intricate steps of a new dance which had lately been devised, the whole lot of them were soon leaping around like frogs and had Anne laughing until she nearly cried. They too could keep their secrets when they wanted to.

The scene which greeted King Henry as he arrived with his courtiers was one of hilarity. It stopped immediately on his unexpected entrance.

'I shall try this myself, good wife.' Henry smiled with his mouth only. His eyes remained unmoved. 'Come.' He took Anne's hand. 'If Norris will give me leave. There was a heavy pause before he continued. 'You shall instruct me.' It sounded like a royal command rather than a friendly request of a husband to his wife.

Elizabeth slipped from the room, her heart pounding with some undefined worry. There was something cruel about the king's look. She didn't like it. It was as if he were the playwright and director and the central actor too. Only he knew the final scene and how it would be played.

Elizabeth remembered how he had been when she had first seen him. Was it really fifteen years since she had come to Court? It seemed no time at all! Then he had been so much younger and handsome, and full of boyish fun. When had it all changed? She didn't even have to think. It was when he bedded Anne Boleyn. After Katherine's tender love, he had been first hurt and then angry at Anne's hard and unresponsive attitude which never altered for all the gifts and favours which he showered on her. She had bewitched him with her gaiety and forthright nature but he had seen too late the madness beneath the laughter. Anne had never forgotten that Harry Percy had rejected her. And for Mary Talbot! It rankled even now so that her husband still could not pleasure her.

Tonight Henry had looked at Anne as though he tried a horse for fitness, a look which weighed the points against what? Or whom? She made her way quietly to the room she would later share with Will and set the fire blazing. Pouring the ale ready for his return she settled in the warmth and considered how strange the world was that it revolved around who bedded with whom. If she hadn't mounted the steps to Malpas church she'd not be sitting here now. Nor would her daughter be laughing with her own child upon her knee in Cheshire's green forests. So would future generations be forever changed by the love she shared with Will. So too with Anne. Had she never bedded with Harry Percy perhaps she could have felt some passion for the King and he would not have deviated from the normal ways of loving.

155

Elizabeth sighed. Poor Mary Talbot. She had been so proud of her proposed husband and yet for all their years together there was no child of the marriage. It seemed that he had been true to his first love. Anne and Harry. What a tragic couple they made. Both had withheld the wonder of their bodies from their spouses and brought nothing but misery on themselves as a result. If Anne had loved her husband then Henry would not have tried to fumble Elizabeth Fytton and so never cared that William bedded her. Then Will need not have married. Her head spun with the thoughts circling in it. Round and round they went, like the people on God's earth. Round and round, bumping first one and then another. Some would overbalance, forcing others down. Then more and more would fall to destruction. Destruction wrought on man by his fellow men and all began with a bedding. She felt the rising tide of panic in her throat and looked frantically around for Will. He was not there. Only Henry! Whichever way she looked she saw Henry. Laughing louder and louder. Growing taller and taller, blotting out the sun.

The door opened suddenly, jerking her awake with fear still showing in her eyes. Fear caused by that terrible half-real dream. It was Will come at last and as he sat heavily on the seat beside her she handed him his ale.

'You feared me, Will. I was nearly asleep with the strangest things all jumbled in my head.' He stroked her hair absently, only half listening. 'Whether the world would continue or not depended entirely on who would bed together and everywhere I looked I saw the King. It seemed that Henry held the whip and he laughed louder and louder, demanding that he should bed them all. And so was the world to end.'

Will felt her shiver though the fire blazed high. He put his arm around her shoulders. Few things frightened him, but Elizabeth's odd premonitions and almost eerie sensitivity to atmosphere unnerved him. It would never do to show it though. Witchcraft was best ignored so he smiled at her.

'While you were having your dream I was talking with Hal about the King's strange manner these days. Savernake was the clue. We now believe that Thomas Seymour took Henry to stay at Wolf Hall, his family home. That very place where we returned his sister Jane when Anne begged us to be rid of her!'

'Aye, Anne didn't like the girl. She thought her sly.' Elizabeth paused, realising what Will was insinuating. 'Jane! She is hardly the one for the King. So insignificant and quiet! Nay, Will.'

And aren't you quiet in company?' Will asked. 'Perhaps Jane is like you, hiding her light by day but bright and hot as a beacon by night.'

'But what about Anne?'

'I don't know,' he answered her. 'Henry made this marriage so legal after his divorce that he will not easily find the means again.'

'It took years to remove Queen Katherine,.' Elizabeth voiced his worries.

'He's different now. He won't wait so long again. He's a different man altogether. If only Anne could learn to please him it might not be too late even now. Can you impress the need on her, Bessy? George will caution her and we hope she will listen to his advice, but you know what she is like! We could lose everything we have gained in one move. Jane will not miss her chance. Her brothers will not let her. Anne must charm her husband or she is lost. Think to warn her.' Will became aware of her hands, and his voice softened. 'But I am in need of your service now.' He pulled her to her feet. 'So first you shall seduce these plaguey problems from my mind through your sweet finger-tips.'

Elizabeth went early to Queen Anne's chambers only to find her mistress already awake.

Seeing that it was Elizabeth and not one of the other women, Anne relaxed back against the pillows pulled herself up with a sigh.

'I've hardly slept.' The words were whispered through clenched teeth. 'Something is wrong and I don't know what. Dress me quickly before my ladies Pry, Sly and Spy arrive to mock me.'

'What happened?'

'Not very much,' Anne answered wryly. 'He tried to be gentle with me at first but his royal member remained soft and small. It nuzzled me with its wormy warmth, making my very skin scream out in protest at its touch.'

Elizabeth remembered that same feeling when the King had tried to rouse himself with her. Poor Anne!

'Couldn't you have at least pretended and brought him to contentment?' Even as she said the words she knew how impossible that would be.

'How?' Anne demanded. 'How can I when I shrink from his every movement? His clutching hands make me feel unclean and when his body crushes mine it puts me in mind of a serpent suffocating its prey. His breath on me makes me turn my head away or I would scream my revulsion to his face.' The memory of the heaving sweaty body caused Anne to tremble. 'I turned away. I couldn't help it. I clenched my fists, hoping that he wouldn't notice Warm. Flabby. Useless! I have known what it is like to be taken, magnificently taken, in moments.' She could have bitten her tongue off.

Elizabeth concentrated on the damaged thigh. Neither looked at the other but Elizabeth had a sudden mental picture of the little Princess Elizabeth. Anne was getting careless. Such talk was dangerous.

Anne cut short the silence. 'Then he got angry. He struck me with his hand for my lack of warmth. If he can't move me in love then he'll do so in hate. Watching my struggles had the effect he sought. Finding himself to be a man, if only briefly, he conquered my body with his cruelty.'

'Is there nothing at all that you can do to stop this madness?'

'Years ago I tried. I was determined to gain as much purchase from my position as I could. I thought that I could use men as they appeared to use women. I took as much as I could at as little cost as I could manage but I am beginning to fear that I was nothing but a fool. Cromwell has shown Henry that everything his heart desires is his for the taking. Everything except Anne Boleyn.'

'Hush now!' Elizabeth made sure that the door was still firmly closed. If such talk got back to the King's ears it would be the end. 'Would it not be to your own advantage to have the King's son? Would you not like a son?' Her voice was soothing.

Anne calmed down immediately. She did want a prince. Commonsense told her that it was the easiest way out of her predicament but Henry was not the easiest of men to conceive a son by. This time she kept her thoughts to herself. She didn't want to arouse Elizabeth's suspicions, and anyway another daughter would be no use. Some men only fathered daughters and this time it had to be a son!

'Aye, I should like a son,' she smiled sweetly at her maid. 'And if God is merciful I shall live to reap the fruits of last night's labours.' Only let it be known that the King had for once succeeded in the marriage bed!

From that time on Elizabeth became increasingly worried about Anne's state of mind. No one who had resided at the Court of King Henry during the previous eight years could claim to have lived pure and innocent lives. It had not been the fashion since the King had tired of Queen Katherine, or maybe even before, considering Mistress Blount, but if Anne continued to talk so glibly of her amorous exploits, the world would collapse. With the King in his present mood the slightest hint of treason would have those intent on advancement scurrying to whisper in his ear. Anne had always been erratic in her behaviour. Where truth ended and fantasy began was no longer discernible even for someone who lived so close to her.

'Harry Percy, you have a lot to answer for!' Elizabeth murmured to herself. It had been as much Anne's fault as Harry's. And they had been young. Youth was the time to fall in love if one was ever going to, but in this case the consequences had been so far reaching that the Devil must surely have had a hand in the affair rather than Cupid.

When some weeks later Elizabeth was able to confirm that the Queen was indeed with child there was great relief amongst her friends. Elizabeth was as overjoyed at the news as Anne herself. This child would not revive ghosts from the past for her, of that she was certain. Will had been as good as his word in most respects since he had invited her back into his bed. He had shown kindness and consideration to Anne during her fits of black depression. He had kept her close company, singing and dancing and trying to make her laugh, but he had always been sure that others were present too.

Although Will was treading carefully and keeping well away from trouble, others were not so fortunate. Ever since the first time that Anne had shown her injuries to her brother and his friends, Mark Smeaton had been like an adoring lap-dog, making excuses to be in her company and forever bringing her small gifts to cheer her up. It did cheer her and Anne had often been surprised and delighted by his thoughtfulness in so many little ways. She was playing the same game she had played for so long, encouraging the men around her in their friendship, having them dance attendance on her whilst still holding them at arm's length. Unless it otherwise suited her purpose! So it happened that Mark presented her one morning with a jar of preserved fruit, knowing how sweet a tooth she had, and on leaving the Queen's chamber encountered Tom Percy loitering in the passage outside. Tom's animosity towards Anne was well known, having been rejected when he thought others were given favours, and to Mark's way of thinking there could only be one reason for him being there. He was spying!

'Watch for the draughts at door cracks. They have been known to cause pains in the head which turn to mortal sickness.' Mark was not one to pick a fight in the usual way of things, but he knew that Tom Percy skulking around her rooms meant nothing but trouble. Tom was equally belligerent.

'I'll take a chance on that, being grateful that I have a head with which to feel. You are early visiting? Does Her Majesty now take to dancing in the early morn? Is she as addle-pated as her courtiers that she jigs before breakfast with a servant?'

At the insult to Anne Mark's face flushed scarlet, but on hearing Tom call him a servant his control broke and he lunged at his taunting adversary. Mark hated above all else to be thought of as a servant. He had no noble blood in his veins, but he had always tried to dress and act as though he had. Tom side-stepped the wildly aimed blow delivering his own thrusts verbally.

'You seem to be losing your head.' Tom's eyes narrowed viciously. 'You break the law by presuming to raise your hand against me within the precincts of the Court. I shall have my revenge on you, scum.'

Mark was shaken by the look of pure evil which sat on Tom like a mask. He blanched, realising that he should have kept his temper rather than make such an enemy, and when Elizabeth opened the door of the Queen's chamber to enquire about the noise she found him leaning weakly against the wall! This was a pretty kettle of fish! As if things weren't bad enough already. Somehow she managed to shoo him away before anyone else came prying. The boy really was lacking in sense as well as courage by the look of him and Elizabeth returned to her mistress shaking her head at the sheer folly of Mark Smeaton.

The King heard the news of the forthcoming child quietly. Here was no great celebration as when the princess was expected. Instead he had Tom Seymour present his sister to Queen Anne and insisted that she take the girl into her retinue. Anne could do nothing but accept her.

The King's great laugh echoed strangely through the rooms, bringing joy to some who heard it, and fear to others. Anne was petulant and sulky. So much so that her brother had quarrelled with her in his worry, reducing her to tears. Her relatives had pleaded, cajoled and then threatened her, realising that she was losing her last hold on the King's affections.

'How can I make merry?' Anne asked her brother, her wayward temper bursting through her sniffles. 'I am sick every day with the coming child, my paps ache and I am so tired that I have scarcely the energy to rise in the mornings, let alone gallop about as though I were still a girl in the rudest of health. The King hardly speaks to me. He makes merry with all others around but never me! I'd as soon not be there at all!'

'And have you noticed who it is that makes him laugh these days?' Her brother's voice rose to match her own. ''Tis not my Lord your brother, nor yet Norris nor Brereton. John Dudley and Edward Seymour now have favours for the asking. Have you seen them bow and scrape? And who provides the wit and humour and leads Henry into more exciting pastimes than his wife is willing to provide? Why, Thomas Seymour, the greatest libertine of all! And where am I? Nowhere, thanks to you!'

'You think your hurts and slights could ever compare with mine this last year?' Anne shouted at him. 'Ask Elizabeth and you doubt them. Many a morning has she eased my pains that I may dance to His Majesty's tune and smile with all.' Fresh tears ran down her face and from her reddened nose. George's temper at once subsided.

'Forgive me, Love. 'Tis not your fault alone, I admit.'

He kissed her brow. It would not help his cause to have Anne parading about the Court with a face swollen from crying. Praise be that at least she was fertile and breeding.

'Don't complain at the soreness and sickness. This child will be our salvation and when he'is born you will see mere fancies and blow-by-nights melt away, never to be seen again. Make yourself lovely for me. Pretty your face and we'll merry the evening away. Together.'

The music and the dancing had the desired effect and their differences were patched for the time being. She was pleasant in the company George observed. How she loved being Queen. Arguments were certainly not the way to get round Anne and he would have to watch himself in future. It was so nerve-racking to be dependent on someone else's high position for one's own!

They had all passed a happy hour when the slight frame of Jane Seymour appeared. She curtseyed to the Queen and dislike of the girl could be seen on Anne's face.

'Forgive me, Your Majesty.' Jane's tone always held a touch of insolence. 'I felt unwell and so retired to rest a while.'

Anne looked at the girl's flushed cheeks and bright eyes.

'Aye,' she was forced to admit. ''Tis most unlike your normal pallor. Are you fevered?'

''Tis nothing to worry about.' A secretive smile played about her mouth. 'I feel in good heart now. In excellent spirits.'

Anne stared hard at her. What was the sly creature up to now? What had brought such unnatural colour to her cheeks? Perhaps it was simply her courses, nothing more than that. Well, it came to them all. Time to worry when it didn't. The Queen dismissed Jane from her knees to join the others at their music.

Only moments later the King arrived, surrounded by his new favourites and smiling beneficently down on them all. What's more, he made a great fuss over Anne and her ladies, accepting their homage with goodwill and cordially inviting them to continue with their activities.

'So that's the way of it,' Will whispered in Elizabeth's ear. He looked from where the King now sat to Jane, her face flushed prettily and her eyes downcast. 'I would guess that Jane is more than happy to do her brothers' bidding and our King has the look of one who hugs a secret. We must have a care! See how his grooms no longer have his ear? Those who are with the Queen are without the King. What in God's name can we do about it?'

'Pray for a boy, 'Elizabeth murmured. 'Pray for a boy!'

Ten

ANNE was making a brave attempt to keep what little of the King's interest in her remained. It was unfortunate for her that she suffered such dreadful sickness during the early months of child-bearing. It did nothing for her looks at all. In addition her nerves were frayed by the constant acting, and gaiety. The minute that they were alone the mask fell and on more than one occasion Elizabeth had warned her to have a care.

'You never know who is watching these days!'

'You're right as usual.' Anne sighed. 'Even Jane Dudley follows her husband's lead in this. Jane Morely creeps about as she always did and now Jane Seymour taunts me with her slimy looks! I can never relax for a single moment except in your company, and that of my few friends. If Will and Hal did not praise me so ridiculously and flatter me to the skies I'm sure that I would go mad. Thank God for loyal friends!'

'The men who love you will never desert you,' Elizabeth assured her. 'We were all young together, sharing those silly hopes and dreams. We fell in love, we laughed and cried and shared in each others' triumphs for weeks and months and years.' She hesitated. 'We have involved each other in our mistakes and in errors of judgement, too. Our lives are as closely interwoven as our destinies are unavoidable. Only death can bring such friendships to an end.'

'Not even death.' Anne seemed to be gazing out into the future, her eyes glazed like the old soothsayer. 'In death we shall be together for eternity.' She roused herself with some difficulty. 'Would that those carefree days were back!' The Queen had quite forgotten the pain of Harry's rejection, refusing to admit that since that time she had been unable to love any man with her heart. She remembered only the dazzling clothes of her coronation, the jewels and the feeling of power which had acted like a drug, an opiate to deaden the raw wounds of her loss. Anne placed her hand upon her belly.

'When the prince is born I shall be fully restored to favour. See how he swells already?' Her eyes gleamed at the prospect of being feted as the mother of a prince.

'Perhaps it is another princess.'

'It is not!' Anne spoke sharply. 'It feels nothing like the time when I carried Elizabeth. It is a prince!'

Realising that she had made a mistake Elizabeth turned the subject slightly. 'She is a lovely child.'

No one could disagree with that statement. The Princess was a lively and intelligent little girl. Despite her rounded baby features she had her mother's slight frame and her mother's forthright nature. On the other hand she could sense when it was best to keep silent. And those eyes! Elizabeth could not mistake those eyes. It was perhaps as well that the birth of a boy would relegate her to second place in the succession. And further boys would place her further down still. That would after all be the best.

'Aye, she is quicker than many a boy.' Anne was proud of her daughter. 'But this one will outshine even her, mark my words.' She began to laugh.

It was a hysterical sound which grated on Elizabeth. What did Anne mean by that? Surely to God this one would favour her husband the King? If not, then Heaven help the lot of them. She must be truly mad.

In January Queen Katherine died.

'The messenger thought that he was bringing some small, sad news and he was startled out of his wits when the King burst out laughing.' Will continued to speak through the mouthfuls of pie as Elizabeth poured the hot spiced wine into his cup. 'And he was well rewarded too. If Henry is so happy at Katherine's demise you may be sure that it is a bad day's work for our cause.'

'How so?' Things had been so bad of late that Elizabeth couldn't imagine them becoming much worse. 'You surely don't mean that he wished her dead? She could do no harm, locked away as she was.'

Will pressed two fingers across his lips in the well-known gesture used by all to indicate treasonable utterance. 'Best not ask just how she died.' He winked solemnly. Elizabeth knew how easy it was to administer potions for a chill or to dull the bone-ache. The King's new friends would do his bidding without even having to be asked.

'But why? What is to be gained by Queen Katherine's death?'

William Brereton put down his empty cup and looked thoughtful.

'There you have the answer. Queen Katherine. How can there be two Queens? Half of the King's subjects still think of Katherine as the true Queen. This has been the big thorn in his side for years. Even in the beginning when Henry loved Anne, the people didn't. Now it seems that he agrees with them, but have you thought? How could he possibly be rid of Anne and marry again with Katherine still alive? That would make three living Queens of England and make our monarch the laughing stock of the world.'

'He can't mean to marry Jane?' Elizabeth had never thought that far. 'She is only a passing fancy, surely?'

'She would have been had she not had such ambitious brothers.'

That was true enough. Edward, Henry and Thomas Seymour were using Jane to further their own ends. As George had done with Anne! The pattern was always the same. Ruthless men used any means to climb the ladder of success.

A thought struck her. 'He won't divorce Anne. She is carrying a child. A prince, she insists. There's nothing the Seymours can do to alter that fact. Even when the prince is born Henry won't dare to rid himself of Anne. Tis unthinkable.'

Will was not so certain. The King was not the man he had once been and he had despatched so many people, friends and enemies alike, these last years that nothing, nothing at all, was impossible.

'No sense in brooding over what has not yet happened.' Will pulled her to her feet. 'We must be in the company to protect our own interests. The King is dressing in his brightest clothes and commands us all to do likewise that we may make merry and dance with the ladies tonight. It would be foolish to leave the floor entirely to the Seymour family.'

'Dance attendance on the ladies, or My Lady Jane?' Elizabeth looked sideways at him. Even if he had wanted to she knew that Will had no hope of changing sides in the silent struggle taking place on the Court battlefield. The Seymours were not the kind to share the spoils of war!

He read her mind. 'At best we can distract Anne so that she is seen to her best advantage. In her better moods she can outshine Jane easily but when the depression settles on her Jane must seem like a haven to the King. We have to keep her spirits up at all costs.'

'Aye. There'll be fear fluttering in Anne's belly tonight,' Elizabeth observed as she made ready to leave the room, 'and hope a-fluttering in Jane's.'

As it happened, Henry's bizarre deviations from the norm weaned him back to his wife and temporarily left Jane standing in the wings. Her brothers were furious at the turn of events. Life had its pitfalls, even for those who thought their schemes infallible! It was only a small setback, they assured themselves, and Jane was kept in readiness to make her entrance right on cue.

The King could not resist a woman swollen with child. His child! It proved he was as good a man as the next, didn't it?

Look what he had done to her. Look at the markedly expanding breasts, the nipples already proud and moist. See the widening girth as his seed raped her from within, distorting her natural curves to the pagan shape of the old fertility goddess. He had done that! Henry found it impossible to keep from her. Touching it, kissing it, he knelt before the smooth swollen whiteness as though it was an altar at which to worship. He wanted to penetrate those holy precincts time and time again. If only he could!

Anne suffered silently, terrified of the fanatical gleam in her husband's eyes. His touch repelled her, making her skin crawl. She wanted peace and solitude in her bed but she knew that could not be. The consequences of denying him were unimaginable. She couldn't help him and sooner or later the visual stimulation failed Without her participation it simply wasn't enough. Frustration turned the King against her, humiliated and unsatisfied.

After one such hour Anne relaxed as the King's harsh breathing turned to rasping snores. The suppressed tears flooded from her eyes to flatten the plumpness from the feather pillow. Why did no one understand or seem to care? George kissed her better and then sent her back for more of the same, saying it was her duty. Her duty to him! He was loath to lose any favours no matter what it cost his sister. Men! They were all the same, all using her for something. They never saw her, the person, Anne Boleyn.

'I wouldn't offend your ears with the things he said.' Anne paled at the memory. Although it was well past the cold wintry hour of dawn she made no effort to rise. 'He says I haven't the feelings of his favourite bitch. At least she ruts in season. With him, I wouldn't doubt.' Her face was ugly with hate. 'His face fused purple with anger at his failure, for which he blamed me entirely, until at last he was grown white and cold with the silent rage of defeat. As he left he said that his strength was better spent at the tilt, for there at least he was sure to penetrate his foe and come away with honour. It is the end. I will not be subject to such treatment any more. Not George nor Norfolk nor any man living will persuade me to bed with that monster again.'

Elizabeth could see that as Anne's anger abated it was replaced by one of her black depressions. 'Hush now and rest easy.' The worried maid fussed her. 'Think on your precious child!'

'I am.' A frown creased the Queen's face. 'My back aches with a nagging pain, duller than my wounds, but a deal more insistent.'

Elizabeth placed a cushion beneath Anne's feet as she lay in the great bed with the gold-embroidered green and white hangings, and as the other ladies came in to keep her entertained Mistress Fytton left silently to give her lover a word to the wise.

'Lord have mercy on us all!' Will threw himself into a chair, his whole body as taut as a primed bow-string ready to let fly. 'She's bringing disaster on herself and no mistake. That those two ever wed must surely be the Devil's work and if her actions are anything to go by Anne has been in league with him for years.'

'You can't blame her entirely, Will,' Elizabeth admonished him. 'It would have needed a miracle to save the baby. It's a sin against God to defile a woman so when she is with child so the King is as much to blame. No one in England knows it. Everyone blames Anne. They always have. If anyone speaks out against the King they find themselves dismissed, and some are never seen again. Stay silent and stay the axe! It is an apt saying these days. You would pity her if you could see her now, pale and empty, weeping alone. It is strange how many of her so-called friends have found themselves urgently called away just now. They told her that Henry had fallen in the tilt-yard. As she made to rise the first pain struck her and she clutched disbelieving at her belly. We all knew it was far too early for the child to have a chance of life. All through the labour she berated Henry and cursed him for her son's death.'

'Was it a son?'

'Aye, the boy she longed for. He was so tiny but perfectly formed. Miniature hands, with the smallest fingers imaginable. But he never made a cry. It was too soon.'

Tears welled in Elizabeth's eyes at the recollection.

'Hush, Bessy Sweet.' Will pulled her to him and held her tight. 'Tears will get us nowhere now. Leave the crying to Anne.'

'What did happen to the King?' Elizabeth sniffed, wiping her eyes with the back of her hand.

'He looked as though the Devil had his tail. First he sat with his ministers, and then alone with Mister Cromwell. Even when he finally emerged his temper was as hot as ever and he commanded us to the tilt. It was as if he fought the infidel single-handed. He swung and lifted with such force that men stood and gaped at his display. Then he miscalculated and coming round suddenly on another horse, his mount reared and threw him to the ground. He fell heavily and his leg was all but broke.'

'The Devil pays his own,' Elizabeth said without sympathy, 'Or it would have been his neck, as some would have had Anne believe!'

'Were you there when he went to see her?'

Elizabeth nodded. 'Aye. Such hate! It was malignant. Evil! No one was in any doubt that it would be Henry's last visit to her. What happens now?'

'God only knows! Would that I could shield you from the harm which Anne has brought about this day, but we are too deep in. I know that Henry has had his eye on my revenue for some time. If he needs any excuse to rearrange the order of things the Queen has given him a good enough one today. All we can do is sit tight and pray that the worst will pass us by.'

William Brereton was no fool. He knew that Henry needed little reason to deprive men of their living. It had happened too often before, and mostly to those who had the greatest assets. The Seymours had no great love for him either, hovering like vultures to win the best pickings. What rumours could they revive if they had a mind? What gossip would be resurrected now to further their aims and precipitate Anne's downfall? It had all been so exciting in the beginning. So much fun and laughter! And Henry himself had led them into dissipation. Somehow it hadn't seemed wrong when everyone did it. But now? Now was the time of reckoning. He turned to find Elizabeth's trusting green eyes fixed on him. She was simplicity itself, looking for the good in people all the time. Cruel reality would come upon her like a thunderbolt. If only he could regain the King's affection! The trouble was that there was no getting near to Jane without tripping over one or other of her brothers.

Elizabeth gripped his arm. 'Are you thinking of leaving Court? You'd not desert Anne?'

Could she really read his mind? 'Nay, Sweet. I'll not leave you now. It would be the worst time to be absent. A poor defence against the enemy is better than no defence at all. There is no way the King can divorce Anne yet awhile so we still have time to breathe and think what to do next. Thank God he made it so legal after tearing so many holes in his first marriage contract, but we shall have to keep our wits about us. Henry is nothing if not devious.'

Anne Boleyn never recovered from the loss of her son. Her face remained pale and drawn with deep purple shadows beneath her eyes. Her charm was completely gone. Seeing Jane Seymour kept close to the King, bringing him a cushion for his foot or wine for his comfort did nothing to help her disposition. Her hatred of the girl grew and Elizabeth could only watch helplessly as the situation deteriorated even further. Henry only had to compare the two. Jane was the one to welcome him with a gentle smile, whilst Anne became more jealous and shrewish by the minute. Her body was slow to heal from the birthing, a distressing flow of blood making her daily life a misery. Henry needed no more excuse. Anne kept dolefully to her rooms and her husband kept away, constantly surrounded by Seymours. It was like the old days when the Court had been split by the differences between the King and Queen Katherine except that now, instead of Katherine's firm insistence on her rights through the offices of the Church there was Anne, a mad woman by comparison. Elizabeth sighed to herself. So is the victor vanquished!

One morning as she prepared some simples in the clutter of the great kitchens Elizabeth was surprised to find herself summoned to the King's corridor. She was even more surprised to find that it was Thomas Seymour who awaited her, sitting elegantly draped across a seat as his dark eyes, vibrant as hot coals, assessed every passing female. Something about the man fascinated her, as a snake fascinates its prey. He was a woman's man through and through, ready with his smiles and honeyed compliments, and too handsome not to know it. There weren't many young girls at Court who had not looked doe-eyed in his direction, and Tom was not the man to disappoint them, having no need to boast of his prowess. They were only too proud to boast for him and he walked with the easy grace of one who knows himself admired, charming to a fault, and with so much confidence that would-be rivals automatically backed away from him,. So it was that Will had warned her to stay away from Thomas Seymour. It affected Elizabeth strangely to think that he was the enemy. In close proximity it was almost unbelievable.

'Sit down, Mistress.'

The smile he gave her was enough to turn one's knees to water. 'My sister Jane tells me you carry potions which can heal the flesh and dismiss the evil humours of the blood. Is't so?'

'Aye , Sir, I have some small skill in those matters.'

Elizabeth perched her backside on the edge of the proffered chair, poised like a bird, ready to take flight at the slightest provocation. The corridor was crowded with the flotsam of the outside world, all apparently waiting to petition His Majesty on matters dear to their hearts, but merely trivial to everyone else, and Elizabeth was very conscious of the knowing glances thrown in her direction.

'I have always tried to help my friends in times of sickness.'

'And are you a friend of His Majesty?' His penetrating gaze pierced her soul causing extreme discomfort.

'Aye, Sir,' she stammered. 'These many years.' God but the man was arrogant. Too sure of his position. It was easy to dislike him.

'Then come. You shall have the honour to tend the King's wound which has been slow to heal, and your arts may yet work miracles.'

Taking her arm Thomas led her courteously through the crowds and across the outer chamber. Will Brereton turned his head, dismayed, in her direction. Her face flamed red but she could not possibly stop to explain. All she could do was to follow Thomas Seymour, who was fully cognisant of the raised eyebrows, through to the King's inner chamber.

The sight which greeted Elizabeth shocked her to the core.

Sitting on the King's own cushions, sharing his great chair and being fed sweetmeats by the royal fingers, was Jane Seymour. Her attitude was one of docile adoration and Henry was smiling at her as though he had discovered one of God's angels on earth. At once Elizabeth understood what Will had been hinting at for months. Now she knew why he had been growing more morose, more silent and brooding. It seemed all over with Anne, and it was easy to see why Henry no longer visited his tearful wife with the viperfish tongue and the scornful eye.

She curtseyed low as Thomas made the introduction and somehow the King managed to tear himself away from Jane's limpid gaze. The glittering sapphire eyes bore into her as she raised her head.

'Methinks we have met before.' His smile seemed to harden as he cast his mind back. 'You have always drawn poison and consorted with ill humours. Am I not right?'

Elizabeth broke out in a sweat of panic at this dreadful reference to Will. The King had forgotten nothing. What should she do? What could she do?

Jane realized immediately that the King associated Elizabeth with Anne and her friends and quickly interceded.

'Allow her, Sire, to tend your wound.' Her gentle voice broke the tense silence.

'Hrrmmph,' Henry grunted before his face relaxed into a semblance of a smile. Little Jane should have her way. How she pleased him! He motioned Elizabeth forward to examine the damage.

'How did you first come to Court?' Henry was suddenly curious about this shadowy figure with the skilful hands. She popped up at the most unexpected times!

'I came as tiring woman to Lady Clere and Lady Shelton some years ago.' Elizabeth kept her voice low as she avoided the question.

'Then where did you learn this healing? Not at Court?'

He was watching her intently as she examined the yellow oozing wound on his leg.

'As a child in Cheshire,' she answered carefully, pushing at the poisoned flesh gently.

'Cheshire? Ah yes. Cheshire. My Chamberlain of Chester is one Randolph Brereton. You know of him, I take it?' The King's voice was heavy with sarcasm and she noticed that he didn't mention Randolph's brother William who was at that moment standing only yards away in the outer chamber.

'He is my cousin, Sire.' Elizabeth focused her concentration on her work, trying to ignore the tight knot of fear in her chest and the uncomfortable clamminess of her palms.

'So!' Henry whistled slowly. 'He is your cousin.'

This time he referred to Will. For years Elizabeth had kept out of the limelight, frightened of being dragged back to Chester by her family, and then later to avoid hampering Will in his grand designs. And now, thanks to Jane and Thomas Seymour, she was once again brought to the King's notice. What did they hope for? What titbit of information did they hope to glean from her about William Brereton? Did they really think that she would be a party to his downfall? If so, they had picked the wrong one this time. Elizabeth had no personal ambition and consequently could not be bought. Not at any price!

Anger made her prod the King's sore leg a little harder than she intended. She could feel the indentation in the bone, though it was not broken. That was where the poison was exuding from. There was no doubt about that. Henry winced.

'Canst heal the plaguey thing?' The irritation caused by illness grated in his voice.

It would be useless to lie.

'The flesh can be healed.' Her wide eyes looked up at him solemnly, 'But the bone will only mend in God's own time, and with a lot of patience.' Elizabeth noticed how Jane hid her smile. The King could be called many things, but never patient.

'Then heal it, Madam. Heal it!' Weeks of inactivity had caused Henry to grow stouter and she could tell that his digestion was suffering as a consequence. Megan's training came into its own and she attended the King regularly for the following weeks, binding his leg and administering her herbs to promote a feeling of well-being in her monarch. And so before long Henry felt the need for exercise and declared that he would celebrate the Easter Mass in London town. To no one's surprise, Anne and her friends were left to their own devices while the King made merry elsewhere. Elizabeth thought that her embarrassing duties were at an end, but on the King's return Jane once more requested her to make simples for His Majesty's continued good health.

'So you are now physician to the King.' Will smiled at her, kissing her fingers.

They sat together in the window seat of Anne's solar, the fresh blue sky of spring outside becoming tinged with pink and crimson as the sun began its descent behind the trees. Elizabeth giggled as he tickled her palm with his tongue, not even trying to remove her hand from captivity.

'Hardly physician.' He had lifted his head and she saw the speculation in his eyes. 'Though I do admit that I have managed to improve his leg somewhat.'

'And what does he talk of, Bess?'

He meant 'What does he ask of me?' She shook her head as he gripped her hand more tightly. 'He never speaks of you, nor of your family since that first time. Nor of Anne. Nor any of her friends.' Elizabeth couldn't work out whether that was good or bad. Was it better to be ignored than slandered?

'And Tom Seymour? Does he ask questions? Or has he tried seduction as a quicker means to an end?' He kept his tone light but she could hear the underlying worry.

'Idiot! Who do you take me for?' She leaned forward to kiss him softly. 'Besides he is too thin and scrawny for my tastes, and I'm a deal too old for his.' It was a well-known fact that Thomas liked them young. The younger the better! 'You don't really doubt me, do you? After nineteen years of loving you, you think I would betray you by one single word?'

'You might be tempted to have your revenge on me for all the times I have let you down.'

He meant the times he had dallied with his brief fancies, but more especially the pain he had inflicted on her by his marriage to Elizabeth Savage, and the all-too-clear expression in a young princess's eyes. These were monumental hurts which might have broken a lesser woman and driven her to revenge as he suggested, but Elizabeth had long understood him, faults and all. There was no rhyme or reason to love.

'You came back.' It was a simple statement of fact but it embodied all the forgiveness in the world.

'Dear God, I don't deserve you.' Will crushed her hands in his and for the first time she knew that he was sincere.

This was no act, no courtier's practised charm. A warm glow spread through Elizabeth and a lump in her throat threatened to burst in a deluge of tears. She choked it back. Will would think her mad.

Tom Seymour could try every trick he knew to have her implicate Will in treasonable acts but he would try till God's Kingdom came on earth without success. She had loved William Brereton all her life without much hope of him loving her to the same extent but at last she felt that the bond which had been forged so slowly through the years was strong enough to withstand even the malevolence generated by Court life. How strange that in this dark hour, persecuted by spite and malice as they were, she should feel as though her heart was about to burst with happiness. And yet it was appropriate. To-morrow there was to be a carnival; a joust to celebrate the May, and the first day of May had always been their special day. A day to remember the kisses and promises of long ago in Yates's Spinney on the Park at Congleton Fair.

As it happened, Queen Anne retired early that night and Elizabeth pre-pared herself for a long wait for Will alone in their room. But he too was early. She detected his restlessness immediately.

'What is it?'

Will shook his head. 'Rumours! Rumours and more rumours! One page tells another that he was told by someone else that secret messengers are scurrying across London by the minute. No one seems to have the truth of it but Kingston's man was mentioned.'

Elizabeth felt her blood turn to ice. That meant the Tower! The place where fiction became fact in moments in the face of pain and torture. 'Who?' she began.

'We don't know. And we don't know what. It may be nothing at all, but if so, why did Henry dismiss us? Anne has heard nothing ?'

'No. We saw no one after you left. Now that I think about it that in itself is strange. Everyone just seemed to melt away.'

'Don't worry. We'll find out tomorrow in the field. The answer will be somewhere there amongst the riff-raff that surrounds the Court on such oc-casions. Someone will talk, no matter how much he has been paid to keep his mouth shut.'

What could she do? Tonight there was only one way to take his mind off the troubles of the day. Besides, she wanted to consummate their new-found closeness, to show just how much he meant to her and to feel that he truly loved her in return. She undid the fastenings of his heavy brocade jerkin and entwined her fingers around the cross-band laces of his shirt to caress the skin beneath. Will was still frowning as she untied his points, but as she caressed him rather more intimately he began to chuckle.

'Harlot!'

Elizabeth saw that his mind was at last on the present and she moved away to slowly undress herself. Tempting him. Tantalising him. She learnt not to hurry in the arts of love. Patience increases pleasure, and so she revealed her body teasingly, inch by inch so that he could look before he touched. It was a feast in which greed played no part as they savoured every morsel to the full, each small movement calculated to whet the appetite as mouth tasted hungry mouth before moving to other sweet delights. Through the hoarse whispers of her endearments she heard his breath become ragged with desire; felt the muscles of his belly tighten as he fought to control his urges through the ecstasy which was carrying them rapidly into oblivion. And then he surged against her, over her, inside her, rising like the swell of a great tidal wave, remaining suspended for one breathtaking, awe-inspiring moment before crashing down to flood her whole being with an overpowering sense of oneness.

'If only life could always be as sweet.' Will's voice came muffled through the thickness of her hair. Ah, if only it could!

Elizabeth moved against him, enjoying the contented lethargy of her body, raising her hands to stroke the curls at the nape of his neck. He sounded tired now and she watched him lovingly as his eyelids drooped sleepily, the long dark lashes shadowing his cheeks, and the lines of worry hidden by the softness of the candlelight. Long after he slept she stayed, propped on one elbow, watching him. Every vein and mark on his body was as familiar to her as her own blemishes and even in the dimness she could see the small white scar on his lip. The pain of wanting to hold him tightly, never to let him go, was physical, but she didn't disturb him. Will was weary from the worries of the world and he looked so peaceful, one arm thrown back across the pillow and the covers still tumbled from their love-making to reveal his nakedness. He looked so vulnerable. Elizabeth worshipped him, but he would never understand how much. Words were not enough. Kissing him so softly that he didn't even move she lay down beside him, happy and frightened at the same time. What would tomorrow bring? The question tormented her till dawn. The dawn which heralded the month of May.

A fresh breeze fluttered the multi-coloured favours worn by every knight and nobleman on the field and flapped the pennants noisily against the canvas. But the sun shone, and later Elizabeth was to remember the day as a series of well-defined cameos, a bright patchwork of events seemingly unconnected but which, when joined together, made a whole.

As the day wore on it looked as though the rumours of the previous day were simply that. Rumours. The lads sent to listen to idle gossip had uncovered nothing untoward and even Hal Norris's horse-cope, whose ears normally missed nothing had little of importance to report. The usual chaotic frivolity of the Court abounded amongst the sweat, and sometimes panic, of the men who strove to have the mounts ready and the armour slick, the weapons polished and the devices prepared.

In the absence of any evidence of imminent danger the men surrounding Queen Anne gradually relaxed and Will winked more than once at Elizabeth. It was a thing he often did when they were separated by the company, when it would have been improper to touch or hold hands, or kiss. It was instead of all those things, bridging the space between them, showing that he was thinking of the night they would later spend and keeping her thoughts from straying to others. There was no danger of that. He looked extremely handsome in a suit of blue velvet cut with silver, colours which reminded her of home. Of Gawsworth. The same blue and silver of the family crest. That was all so long ago. A memory of the house shimmered before her mind's eye, a ghost from the past intent on haunting her. It had been a happy home with a secret heart and she remembered how she had almost felt that she was part of it; that she belonged there for ever and ever. Elizabeth shook herself. That had been a silly, childish dream. Nothing in this life lasted. She knew that now. Her glance fell on Will where he stood sharing some lewd joke with Tom Wyatt and an icy finger of premonition touched her briefly. It was gone as soon as it had formed. She had felt that same thing before but when or where she could not for the life of her remember.

The holiday atmosphere was infectious and even Anne was enjoying herself, George keeping her amused in the absence of the King's attention. Henry seemed more intent on the outcome of the tournament. All around was a hubbub of noise interspersed with gasps and squeals as riders were unhorsed, and cheers for the victors.

Anne reached for a sweetmeat and the action brought a frown to her face. 'What can have become of Mark? It's not like him to miss a spectacle. Did he say where he was going?'

Now that Elizabeth thought about it, she hadn't seen Mark Smeaton for a couple of days. She shook her head. As Anne said, it was most unlike him. He was usually the first at hand to offer dainties, trying all the time to anticipate her needs. He would probably arrive shortly, full of apologies for being late. Elizabeth unconsciously scanned the crowd although it was impossible to imagine Mark mixing with the common herd. On the rare occasions when he did have to speak with such people he was known to have more edge than a broken chamber-pot, a fact which amused some of higher rank but did nothing to bring him friends.

The gaudy dress of a harlequin tumbler caught Elizabeth's eye as he rolled and tossed himself about like a rag doll to entertain a small crowd. He was good. Foreign by the look of him. The little group applauded him as he finished and he gathered coins and compliments happily, every inch a showman. One bystander seemed unimpressed. In fact he seemed rather out of place and not to be enjoying the holiday at all. He had the air of a watcher. Not watching the main events or side-shows, but watching the people. A burly fellow with bushy, glowering brows.

'The likes of him should stay at home,' Elizabeth thought to herself. He was like a dark cloud hovering. Waiting to cast its shadow over the proceedings. There was still no sign of Mark though, and after a while she forgot about him again, and about the gloomy stranger.

It must have been after four o'clock when something made her look across to where the King sat. Thomas Seymour was bending to whisper some secret into Henry's ear, nodding as he did so towards Tom Percy who was at that moment pushing his way through the crowds. Elizabeth turned to catch Will's eye but he was deep in conversation with Hal Norris who looked guardedly towards the King. What was going on?

George Boleyn struggled to his feet but his shouted warning came too late. They were surrounded. Suddenly everything was as clear as day to Elizabeth. The strange man in the crowd hadn't been the only one. They were the constables, on duty, waiting for the signal to surround the quarry and conduct it to a predetermined place. The Tower.

Will twisted round as though to come to her. His hand stretched out in her direction, a fleeting movement cut short as strong hands reached out to pin his arms to his sides. In those seconds before they dragged him away time seemed suspended. Everyone around faded into the background and the noise of the people became a dull whisper. The whole world slowed and then stopped. Silence. Nothing existed except the look Will gave her then. It would last through all eternity. Their eyes held as though for the last time on earth, until the anguish became unbearable. Then he was gone.

The raucous laughter of the crowds continued as though nothing had happened. It all began to move again and no one but Elizabeth appeared to notice anything unusual at all. She couldn't believe it. William Brereton was not the only one taken. George Boleyn. Hal Norris. Tom Wyatt. Francis Weston. Richard Page. All gone.

And then it was Anne's turn. There was no panic. The Queen held herself proudly as she was taken away but her maid was shaking in her shoes. She could hear the King laughing as his orders were so efficiently carried out. The laughter of insanity. It had to be! He seemed to loom over the Court like some great fiend. A madman. The awful bellow echoed in her head and she thought that she was going to faint. It was just like that strange dream she kept having. Henry. Mad dictator of the world, until the world ended. And as far as Elizabeth was concerned, it had just happened. Catastrophically.

The evidence against the Queen had been flimsy to say the least. Nothing more than the spiteful gossip of females who had kept close company for too long. Jane Morley's jealousy of her sister-in –law had become obsessive and her malicious tongue had slandered Anne and her brother at every opportunity. 'My husband had his hand upon her naked thigh while at the same time Hal Norris embraced her.'

Jane Seymour told her brothers of how she had found the Queen sitting on George's knee, her arms around his neck and her head on his shoulder. Hal Norris and Will Brereton had been there at the time. Collusion!

Mary Lascelles told of how she had walked unexpectedly into the Queen's bed-chamber to find George Boleyn lying across the bed eating fruit as Anne, still in her night clothes, made much of him. She also told of how she had seen Will Brereton leave the Queen's chamber very late one evening and on entering the room had found Her Majesty alone and looking like the cat who has stolen the cream. But that had been before Their Majesties married. Some weeks before that secret wedding over three years ago. And if you wanted to go that far back, Tom Wyatt was not blameless. He had made no secret of his feelings for Anne Boleyn. Francis Weston was another always in her company. His family had immense wealth and Francis had done his best to obtain equal power through the Queen, a task which had not been unpleasant when she had appeared so witty and flamboyant and so much fun.

But tittle-tattle on its own was not enough, and Anne still had some friends. Elizabeth Fytton had never uttered a single word against any of them despite being given every opportunity and being shown how great the rewards could be. Even Thomas Seymour's charm had failed to win her over. Harry Percy's mouth had remained firmly closed too, and not just out of fear. There was no incriminating evidence against him left, Thomas More being long since dead. No, it wasn't that. Even in these days of greed and cruelty a few, a very few, knew the meaning of love.

Inside an ill-lit, sparsely furnished room within the confines of the Tower Mark Smeaton continued to retch weakly. One eye bulged from its socket, bloodshot and staring, whilst the other was hidden in folds of puffy red and purple skin. The trickle of blood from his nose continued persistently and he wiped it on the back of his hand. For someone so fastidious, it was disgusting. But he had told them!

'Let's see how the music master sings.'

Music master! Didn't they realise just who it was that they spoke to?

Anne treated him like a friend. A close friend. As close as any. As close as Page ore Weston, or Tom Wyatt. Aye as close as Norris and Brereton.

'As close as My Lord her brother?'

'Aye, even as close as George Boleyn.'

'How close? Was it true that George had placed his hand upon his sister's naked thigh? Lain on her bed with her an hour before dawn? Kissed and cuddled her in front of others? And how would a servant know of these things?'

Servant! He was rather more than a servant. Hadn't he been in Queen Anne's confidence for years? There was nothing she didn't tell him. He too had been to her chamber early. Very early, and alone!

But that wasn't enough. They wanted details. Sordid details. And his goddess didn't deserve that of him. He had stopped his boasting, but it was too late. He had said too much for them to let him go and not quite enough for their satisfaction. He had tried to be brave but had never been a fighting man and before long pain not only loosened his tongue but fired his imagination too. They had their evidence. Tom Percy had his revenge on the arrogant upstart, and it had only taken two days. Pity! He would have liked the torture to continue somewhat longer. However, there was still the execution! Hung, drawn and quartered! That's how commoners ended up.

The waiting had been the worst. The wondering. What had gone wrong with all those golden dreams of youth? If they could live it all again what would they change? Elizabeth couldn't think straight. How had they made so many enemies? Barely remembered incidents were dredged up from the past, innocent things which now were made to appear sinister in their implications And not one word of Henry's cruelty. Such a thing was unthinkable. A complete fabrication. And besides, none of the prosecution wished to cross the chamber to swell the numbers in the dock.

The trial was a farce. The Queen accused of fornication with half the men at Court. It was laughable. What had His Majesty been doing all the time his wife had been otherwise engaged? Looking the other way?

The black comedy played itself out as the sentences were passed. Death.

Tom Wyatt and Richard Page were released for lack of evidence but Anne's enemies had done enough and five lovers were plenty to condemn her. Anne had loved only once. Crazily, madly and with all her heart. When that love had been destroyed she had wreaked her vengeance on the rest of mankind, playing up to them, captivating them and then using them for her own ends. She had loved the clothes and jewels and desperately wanted everyone to admire and envy her, to show Harry Percy again and again what he had missed by not marrying her. But it had all gone sour and the price she had been expected to pay for being Queen had been untenable. Why did no one love her? Why did no one even like her very much? She was under no illusions. Even these few friends who were to lose their lives for her own failings had used her to further their own causes as she had used them to satisfy her own craving for love and attention But even so! The axe!

Her request was granted. Anne Boleyn would die by the sword. A French sword would swing in the expert hand of a French swordsman but to Elizabeth's dazed mind one was as bad as the other. Such things only happened to others. Will couldn't die. Anne couldn't die. She was the Queen. Even Henry for all his perversions, for all his degenerate lusts, couldn't glean satisfaction from beheading her. Not even his depraved mind could ask this, the ultimate brutality, to stimulate his abominable corruptions. No. In the end he wouldn't kill her. But what of the others?

The rattle of keys in the door announced the arrival of a meal. Elizabeth knew many of the ordinary people who had worked in and around the King's palaces and castles and Dorothy, the jailer's wife, was one of these. They had first met in one of the kitchens where Elizabeth had regularly brewed her herbal remedies and had indulged in harmless female gossip for many an hour as they worked. Elizabeth seized the opportunity to have a quiet word.

Dorothy nodded. 'Aye. No sooner said than done.' Her sympathies lay with the dark-haired tragic Queen who looked so pale and hollow-eyed since the birth of her dead son. Even now, so many months later, the bleeding could not be staunched.

And so it was that Elizabeth was able to go out from the Tower to bring clean linens and good strong wines to make her mistress more comfortable.

She also brought back a second wicker. Anne was unlikely to need such garments as cross-banded shirts with matching hose! How many children had she cured of the fever? How many cuts had she healed? How many women eased through childbirth? Numerous people had cause to be grateful to Elizabeth Fytton and she knew that no door would be barred to her in any of the King's buildings. Not even the Tower of London.

Will leaned against the hard edge of the window casually scratching at the stone with the point of his small dagger and tears stung Elizabeth's eyes as he welcomed her. She blinked them back rapidly, having promised herself that his last sight of her would not be spoilt by her weakness. Hal and Francis rose. Their game of cards had seemed rather pointless anyway but it had served to fill the time. George never moved from where he lounged before the hearth. Their smiles on seeing her were wide enough, the others calling Will a lucky dog to have home comforts brought to him in such an attractive package. They had not lost their spirit, then.

Will left them to their food and led Elizabeth through to the sleeping-chamber, to a lot of ribald comments from his friends.

In silence they sat side by side on the hard straw pallet, finding no words to use in the hopelessness of their thoughts. He pulled her to him, roughly, all but crushing her in the ferocity of his embrace and she clung to him, revelling in the pain. If only she could die with him!

'This time our separation may be longer, God willing.'

'No! There will be nothing to keep me in this foul world when you are gone.' Despite her good intentions hot salt tears ran silently down her face, falling to shine like liquid diamonds on the blue velvet of his doublet.

'Forgive me for the years of your life which I wasted, for the time we spent apart when we should have been together. Forgive me for not recognising what I had in you until it was too late.'

Elizabeth shook her head. He had been forgiven long ago. She couldn't speak. Emotion gagged her. Threatened to choke her. All she could do was cling harder.

'Come on, now. It's too late for tears.' Will was actually laughing at her. 'And with luck God has a place awaiting this poor sinner in His Heaven, though it will be a mean kind of heaven without you.'

For his sake she tried. 'Will you wait for me, then?'

At this he laughed out loud. How many times had he said those self-same words to her? And she had always waited.

'Till Doomsday if I have to, Bessy Sweet.'

For the first time since she arrived he kissed her. His soft lips brushed hers gently before the pressure gradually increased, forcing her mouth open until she could taste the sweetness of his tongue between her teeth. She sucked it carefully, sensuously, rhythmically. But that was not enough. It didn't matter that the others were only feet away, on the far side of the door. It wouldn't have mattered if they had come in. Those two were completely lost in each other. If the world had ended there and then they would not have noticed.

For the last time! The last time. The last time. She touched him, kissed him, wrapped herself around him and braced herself against him. And when he entered she surrounded him, enveloped him in a warmth as soft and pro-tective as his mother's womb, holding him there. Making the moment last. Last! The last time! No. It couldn't be. Again. Again. And then never again. Never again as long as she lived would Elizabeth Fytton give herself to any man.

She couldn't take her eyes from him. 'How has it all happened? How are we come to this?'

'Maybe I deserved it. The wages of sin!' Bitterness crept into his voice. 'I was a fool. A weak, stupid fool to give in to her. The fact that I would have been condemned out of hand anyway does nothing to make me feel better at this moment. At least Henry hasn't disowned the child, but there again, that may only be a matter of time. His purpose is served well enough with a clutch of lovers for his wife without looking further. God, what a mess! The King mocks us all. He well knows how poor a comfort Anne was between the covers and that any man should lose his head for so little is re-ally very comical. It's Henry's most subtle cruelty yet. His voice trailed off.

'Don't, Will. Don't torture yourself.' Elizabeth kissed him. A flurry of little kisses, on his eyes, his nose, his ears, his mouth.

'It didn't take much to make that popinjay Smeaton squawk, by all accounts. Still, I wonder how much he really said and how much they added afterwards? Harry Percy looked ill at the trial. Gaunt and haggard as an old man. What's more, he never spoke one word against Anne. Unlike his brother Tom!'

'Perhaps he still loves her.' Elizabeth wanted to think so. Surrounded by hate as they were, she needed to believe that love still existed.

Will looked into her eyes and saw there all the helplessness and hopelessness that she was feeling. What could he say to help her? There was no antidote to grief.

'Don't fear for me, Bess. 'Tis only a small step to death, and one which everyone must take sooner or later. I'd rather die like this than by the wasting sickness or coughing out my life-blood in a raging fever. Don't worry about my body. Pray for my soul that my sins may be forgiven by the Almighty so that in His Grace we may one day be united.' The inbuilt courtier's charm came to his aid as he gave her one of his most dazzling smiles.

'How can you?' she asked. 'How can you be so calm when everything you know is ending?' She gripped his shirt as an infant clings to its mother's skirts. 'They are going to hurt you.' Her voice fell to a whisper. 'They are going to kill you.' Elizabeth shuddered violently and he covered her mouth with his, letting it linger, long and gentle to soothe her agonies.

'Hush, Bess. Twill be quick, and no man can ask better than that. I shall be smiling then, seeing nothing but the prospect of eternity with you where no one can divide our souls again. My one regret is that I realised too late but this I know: our lives have touched in beauty the like of which too few are privileged to own. It has a mystic quality, the reflections of which will float forever in the mists of time. Others not yet born may one day catch a glimpse of the truth of our love through our daughter, and our daughter's children. Our love will be reborn with every generation.'

Looking into those beloved eyes Elizabeth had a desperate yearning to believe him. It was not the end. Their love would be eternal, both in the embrace of her gods and here on earth, where their descendants would live and play in the forests of Will's Cheshire lands for a thousand years.

Hearing the iron rattle of the keys in the lock she knew the time had come. She held his head in her hands, twisting her fingers in his hair and kissed him desperately, one last time.

'I shall pray for your soul, Will, if that is what I must do, but I shall also pray that my death may shortly follow yours. I would not want to keep you waiting long!' Elizabeth made a brave attempt at a smile, holding his gaze for one agonising moment to imprint his image firmly and forever in her mind. Stinging tears began again to make the picture waver and blur and she turned away without another word.

Unable to bear it she flew from him, her skirts rustling panic round her ankles. She couldn't bring herself to say goodbye.

Eleven

PRAY for Him! It was the last promise she had made him and Elizabeth was determined that she would keep it. The trouble was that her mind kept wandering away from prayers of salvation to Will. Will as he had been when she first knew him. Will as a devil-may-care youth, always in and out of scrapes; Will as a courtier, charming, elegant, and dissolute at times. Will in maturity, sincere and loving. And in death, brave. Braver than Elizabeth could comprehend.

Incidents from their life together swam in and out of her mind, completely destroying what little concentration she had, each one hanging for a moment of poignant recollection before fading, to allow another scene to replace it. Congleton Fair. Chester's fair city. Greenwich Palace' Windsor Castle.White Hall. And now, the Tower of London. She saw him dance and joke with Anne; ride out, handsome in the King's company; share his supper with her in some private room; lie with her in a big feather bed, curtained with tapestry hangings as he had once promised. Elizabeth twisted the emerald ring round and round on her finger. All gone! It was all gone.

Time and time again she brought her thoughts back to her prayers only to have them slip away. Throughout the night she knelt on the hard floor, immobilised as though she were made of stone. She felt no physical discomfort. Her body was numbed by terror as her mind raged back and forth through time and space in love and hate and prayer.

All too soon the sun rose, its first bright rays dousing the fragile flicker of the candle which had been her night's comfort in the chapel. Unwelcome sounds from outside on the green forced their way in on her vigil as she searched her mind for words of supplication. There was nothing. Panic began to eat its way into her brain. Where had all the words gone? Caught in the grip of uncontrollable fear her eyes stared blankly at the section of cold stone wall below the image of Our Martyred Lord. Crevices and cracks made long ago by a workman's chisel stared back at her like gaping empty eye-sockets, totally unmoved by what was going on outside, only yards away. But Elizabeth could not ignore the growing clamour echoing through the stillness of the dawn.

Time would not stand still. It marched relentlessly forward, step by step, the seconds hammering away inside her head like an extension of the heart-beat thudding painfully at her ribs. Trying to get out! There was no escape. The horror of the moment pounded in her eyes, in her ears, and in her throat, with the stoic rhythm of the funeral drum, rising to tighten in an iron band of torture, a skull-crushing agony of despair.

Then silence! Instinctively Elizabeth held her breath. The resounding crack felt like a staggering blow between the eyes and she watched, mesmerised, the crimson blood splashed with vivid clarity across the rough grey wall of the chapel. She should never have come here. Why had she come? Despite all Megan's teachings she had stumbled blindly into this so called House of God. What God? Would their God allow indiscriminate murder and still expect to be worshipped? Still expect unquestioned faith? Only a saint could follow such ridiculous teachings. Like Thomas More? Old Megan knew what she was about. There are certainly more ways than one to skin a cat, and prayer would seem to be the least effective method. Great scarlet drops spattered the floor on which she knelt, pouring out from her nose and throat in choking hollow sickliness. She bled with him. William Brereton no longer graced this earth and in that knowledge, Elizabeth Fytton swore to avenge him. Sooner or later. When the time came. She would be ready.

She was not the only one to feel the pent-up anger of frustration. Ice-cold words of hate had spilled from Anne's mouth like poison, cursing Henry and promising him every slow and painful death imaginable. His flesh was to rot with open sores as maggots ate him from the inside, chewing at his carcass whilst he still tried to live in it, until his limbs spewed yellow pus and his mouth black vomit.

Hell fires would be too good for him! First he must suffer a living hell, with Queen Anne's blessing. It had gone on and on. Hysterical laughter interspersed with even more venomous curses. Those who had always scorned witchcraft began to look uneasy and retreated to the far side of the room. As Anne's skin burned with a dry heat her eyes became glazed, conjuring up all the powers of evil to do her bidding. Only Elizabeth would go near her as she rocked backward and forward, staring at nothing, muttering incantations in some long-dead primitive chant, mostly unintelligible. Except to her maid.

Elizabeth held her hand tightly. This was it. The consummate hate which had more potency than prayer! The King deserved all that was coming to him. And not only from the spell now being woven. If Anne's words needed any practical assistance Elizabeth would willingly supply the ingredients. She too had sworn revenge.

Then it was Tom Seymour's turn. Concentrating their thoughts the two women decreed that he would lose everything. Everything! Including his handsome head! That insolent whelp would pay in full. As would his descendants. No absolution! Not until the last of his line was licked clean by the very fires of Hell. Tom Seymour's hopes and lusts would all end as fine grey ash. The magic was strong. There could be no escape. No escape.

Anne slumped forward in her seat, drained of energy and pathetically ill. Sad, purple shadows under her eyes scarred the sallow skin like bruises, denoting the massive strain of the past three weeks. The bubble of hate had burst.

'What did I do wrong?' Anne looked genuinely puzzled as she sipped a sleeping draught placed in her hand by Elizabeth. 'They used to love me.'

She was thinking back to the early days when she had been the centre of attraction, when every man at Court had vied for one dance, or a pleasant word, or just a smile from Anne Boleyn. They had been like bees round a honey pot, and Anne had played up to them very sweetly. How she had revelled in it all, selfishly giving no thought to anyone but herself for years. It was only during the last few years that she had been renowned for her generosity to the poor, and her charitable works. Far too late to buy the people's love! Far too late to try to outdo Queen Katherine in that respect. Sometimes it almost looked as though she was trying to make up for lost time. But not any more. The jewel-encrusted cover of the French prayer book lay closed on the table and so far as Anne was concerned, the candles could have remained unlit. She had other things on which to set her mind. Other things which revenge had swelled to greater importance than her own soul.

But now the drug was beginning to make her drowsy.

'I only ever wanted to be loved. But I never was. Not by my father, my brother, my uncle, or my husband.'

Elizabeth couldn't disagree, but she thought that it would do no harm at this late date to tell her of one who had loved her.

'Harry loved you.'

'No more than the others, if his hurried exit from my life into the arms of Mary Talbot was anything to go by.' Bitterness could still be heard in her tone.

As the two women sat together in the lengthening shadows, gathering dusk around them like a cloak to ward off the dawn, Elizabeth repeated Will's words from long ago. It helped her to be able to speak his name; to remember his voice; to keep him there, alive, inside her. And it might help Anne to know that at least one man still cared. Had always cared!

'So,' concluded Elizabeth quietly, 'I believe he has kept the vow he made then and that he has never bedded Mary Talbot to this day. Nor any other woman on this earth since he bedded Anne Boleyn. Certainly he has no heirs.'

The soothing potion had weakened Anne's guard and her tired eyes filled with glistening rears, reflecting a lifetime's pain. Her hopeless, endless search for love had been neither methodical nor calm, but eager, then anxious, and finally, desperate.

'Why?' Anne simply didn't understand. 'He never showed it by so much as a single word. Why?'

'How could he have shown his love for you? There was no way, except the way he chose. He tried to protect your honour all those years ago and loved you enough to let you go. You saw him at the trial. Gaunt and haggard. It is killing him to see you suffer like this and him not able to help you. Harry Percy still loves his Anne Boleyn. To the end.'

191

The tears overflowed in silent anguish.

'Lord, oh Lord, what a silly, grasping fool I've been. How can he still love me after watching all my childish stupidity?' She blushed at the thought, seeing herself for the first time as someone who loved her might see her. How she must have hurt him when she flirted with everyone but him. And then when she married! And the rumours about her moral laxity! Had he believed it? Any of it? He knew how hot she had been when she was young. When he first made love to her. Did he imagine that she had been the same with the King? And others?

'His love was entirely misplaced. Wasted! I can see now that no one loved me because I didn't deserve to be loved!'

'Love is never wasted,' Elizabeth assured her. 'Harry didn't ask to love you. It just happened. It wasn't his fault that he couldn't marry you. All he wanted was your happiness, and that's why he grieves to see you now. He didn't use you. He asked nothing. He only loved you.' She paused. 'As I loved Will.'

Something in her tone made Anne look at her closely in the gloom. 'But Will didn't . . . ' Her voice trailed off. After all, William Brereton had left Elizabeth for a time when he married Elizabeth Savage. He had been far from faithful as Anne well knew, but Elizabeth Fytton couldn't possibly know about all his escapades. Could she?

'Will did. Many times. As you know.'

There was a deep silence, broken only by the slow creak of an old tree outside the window as it complained against the wind.

Did her maid know? Anne couldn't be sure. But if she did then there were some people who were born to love with all their hearts and souls. As Harry Percy had loved her. Why had she never felt it? Real love, like Harry? Like Elizabeth? Was it too late? Even now?

'I cannot know what history will say of me, but one thing they'll not say. They'll not be able to call me a coward. They'll not see Queen Anne flinch from death. If I can do no more to recognise Harry's love, I can die with my head held high as my friends did today. Compared to my husband the King, I am innocent. Compared to half the Court I am innocent!' If she had found nothing to live for, Anne had at least found just a little something to die for. And it was never easy to die.

'For Harry, then.' And Anne Boleyn slept.

Fate was not kind. The Frenchman and his sword were late and the execution delayed. Tension became almost tangible. Nerves made everyone jumpy. There was little to do in the absence of prayer and since Anne had acknowledged a greater power, taking strength with each sip from Elizabeth's cup, there was no need to pray. Carefully, Anne chose the clothes she would wear, determined to die as she had lived. Brightly and defiantly.

The glowing red of her gold-embroidered kirtle would blaze brilliantly against the cut away of her dove-grey gown with its intricate filigree of silver lace. And the cap! Red to match the kirtle, criss-crossed with a diamond-lattice pattern of golden thread. She couldn't be seen without her cap! Except that she would have to remove it, wouldn't she? Then her long, dark hair would fall about her shoulders, as like as not. It would be a nuisance. Anne didn't want the poor man to have the vision of his target obscured. It would not do to have him miss his aim after travelling so far to perform the service! The women solved the problem by devising a linen cap, adapted from a night-cap, to bind her hair tightly to her head beneath her normal headpiece and Anne finally declared that she was happy with it. Happy with it! It was almost macabre and yet such details had to be attended to. It was something one didn't think about until the time arrived. Elizabeth noticed how throughout the day Anne's slim tapered fingers insisted on straying to her neck, touching it, feeling the softness of the white skin, the little folds across her throat which had deepened with age. The Queen was now past thirty. At least she would not suffer the penalties of old age, but that was no consolation to any of them as the last night of all drew on and the Queen continued to stroke the hollow at the base of her throat. Was that where it would be severed?

Although sentence had been passed and understood the whole thing still seemed unreal. It didn't seem possible. Were they really going to cut her head off? Even as they led her out it was hard to believe.

She looked so frail and tiny, but her back was ramrod straight and her head held high as a murmur rippled through the crowd at her approach. Most had come in less than friendship and not one person in the gathering could take their eyes from the fragility of the delicate neck. It would not need too heavy a blow. It would be over in no time. The bravado of her red kirtle stood out boldly in defiance of her treatment while the exquisite simplicity of her gown had the stamp of elegance for which Anne Boleyn had been renowned. All her fashions had been assiduously copied by the ladies of the Court for years. Elizabeth watched the proud, haughty indifference of her friend as she turned to face those come to watch. This was no terrified woman, frightened of the fires of hell. She was not bowed or cowed by guilt but looked ready to meet her end with as clear a conscience as any of them. Her enemies were disappointed. They had come to see the whore grovel and plead for mercy but what they saw was a Queen, ready and willing to die with dignity.

Everything about that morning looked clear and sharp, as though God had painted the picture with more care than usual, gilding the edges with sunlight. The early rays lit the dew-drops still scattered on the grass, turning them into diamonds sewn upon the Tudor green, sparkling in the stillness. There was not one hint of a breeze. It was as though the whole world waited with bated breath to watch the final act of Henry's cruelty. No one had thought it possible to execute a Queen and many a wager was lost on the outcome of the day.

Anne's voice rang out strong and true but Elizabeth couldn't understand a single word. Her mind would not accept the scene set out before her eyes. She saw her friend of many years, so slight a figure that she could scarcely have had the strength to hurt a fly, standing calmly as she removed the little red cap. Before Elizabeth realised what was happening she saw the sun glisten on the silver blade, heard the common intake of breath by those around her, and then the weapon sliced the air. Her hand flew out towards the group enacting the tragedy. She opened her mouth, as though to insist that there must be some mistake, when a joyful cry went up.

What was that bloody horror? Where had Anne gone? Elizabeth watched in dreadful fascination as the spurting blood died to a trickle from the severed vessels of the little neck and the slender limbs of the headless body twitched their death-throes in the straw. The black shoe scraped its toe ineffectually on the wooden boards in one last macabre dance before it jerked to eternal stillness.

As the others moved away the big guns rang out their news. Elizabeth continued to stare at Anne's ghastly, distorted face, the lips turning blue as they oozed a sinister message, and the dark eyes gazing sightlessly through dilated pupils into the perfect summer sky. She never knew how long she stood there. Her mind had closed out recognition and the increasing buzz of flies around the congealing pools and raw flesh meant nothing to her. Mister Constantine, well meaning, took her by the arm and led her to a seat against the old house wall. The poor woman must be demented! Probably the first time she had witnessed a Queen dying. He smiled to himself. But wasn't it something new for them all? And if rumour were true he wouldn't like to be wearing Jane Seymour's shoes right now!

Hours later, or so it seemed, Elizabeth bestirred herself and walked slowly out of the Tower of London and into the stinking bustle of the streets. How she made her way safely through the thieves and vagabonds alone she never knew but her body seemed to move by instinct. Her mind was blank. Not one single thought was in it, either that day or for many a day afterwards. She must have continued to live as she had always done, on the edge of Court life, but it was done mechanically, without any planning on her part. And she waited.

Meanwhile, the Court moved around her in a chaotic urgency of preparation which completely failed to puncture the barrier between her inner mind and the real world. If she knew when Henry married Jane she gave no sign and soon words got around that she was a harmless simpleton. Queen Jane told her ladies to let Elizabeth be. She had healed the King and many more besides in her time and if she still had the sense to practise her arts then it would be sensible not to bother her.

Even the arrival of Princess Mary at Court did not surprise her. It was all one to Elizabeth now. Something fluttered through her brain when she heard the ladies whispering that Princess Elizabeth was now rechristened bastard and rightly so. For a moment she thought that this news should hold some significance for her but she couldn't grasp it so how hard she tried. It slipped from her and was gone. Her life was lived in swirling mists of some half-conscious world from which all pain had been eliminated.

Winter came on with the river-ice causing hazards to boatmen plying their trades and the frozen streets being the cause of many a broken limb. The very old and the very young suffered most. Here today and gone tomorrow as the freezing winds cut like sharp blades into any flesh caught out without its wraps. Thick white frosts rimed roofs and windows and great pointed spears of ice hung motionless from every ledge, menacing those who scurried beneath the huddled buildings.

Elizabeth noticed nothing. She inhabited a lonely, garish world of nightmare hallucinations and half-remembered horrors which overlapped and blended into their own strange and frenzied hell.

Flickering lights of altar candles threw grotesque shadows around the suffocating interior of the church. Dark-cowled figures shuffled menacingly nearer. Nearer and nearer. The flat, sightless eyes of the living dead pierced her with the points of a thousand tortuous needles as the vague, faceless form beside her turned.

His mouth opened. Wider. Wider. No sound. And then the blood gushed out, hot and molten, it splashed her gown, soaking through to her flesh and washing across the cold floor of the church. It was no use trying to scream. There was no one to help her now. The church began to spin. Faster and faster, with the sea of blood frothing into white-topped waves, until the building became a storm-tossed vessel. Drowning. And all the time she could hear the crazy laughter of a madman echoing round and round. Father? Was it Father? Had he returned at last to avenge Thomas Davenport? Or was it? Who? He was causing the storm and bidding the waves rise to swallow the church and all who had taken refuge within its walls.

And then nothing. The monster had faded away. The church had gone.

The faithful had drowned. The nightmare always ended the same, with Elizabeth alone, staring out in silence over an endless, glassy sea, stained to a thick, glossy crimson by the last dying rays of the setting sun.

Alone? Not quite. As darkness settled like a soothing mantle around her Elizabeth watched as the merest traces of fine grey evening mist gathered themselves together, swirling gracefully and light as gossamer until at last she could make out the shape and beckoning arm of Old Megan ap Y. The lilting chants fell softly on her ears, full of meaning, full of wisdom. The old ways were best and Elizabeth believed. This was her salvation and when the long, healing hibernation of winter was over she would be once more ready to face the cruel world. And seek revenge.

Twelve

ELIZABETH Fytton stood silent and still, frozen in time. The only movement was the breeze catching a wayward lock of hair as she gazed out over the wide vista before her. Here on the high vantage point of the Chute she could wonder at the vast enormity of the sky, bluer than blue today above the deep green of the woodland below.

How had she come to this? Once, long ago she had stood on a cliff, despairing at the loss of both child and lover. Today, twenty five years later, her heart was nothing but an empty void. Broken beyond compare. Her mind was full. Of hate! For months nightmares had plagued her as she relived the horrors of King Henry's Court. Dead! Everyone of them. Hall Norris, Francis Weston, George Boleyn. And Will Brereton. Her love. Her only love. Necks severed by the axe. Blood spurting and seeping into the straw-strewn boards. And Mark Smeaton! Hung until his eardrums burst, his eyes bulged from their sockets, his protruding tongue swollen and black. Then cut down and revived to watch them slit his belly, holding up his entrails for him to see. Those piercing screams still haunted in the dead of night,

Elizabeth Fytton had sat with Anne Boleyn the night before she died. How the Queen had cursed! She quietly wished her husband a slow and agonising death, his limbs spewing yellow puss and his mouth the black vomit.

Elizabeth cursed too. Not at the King but at that arrogant usurper Thomas Seymour. He had schemed to bring about Will's downfall, making sure his sister caught the King's eye. He had stirred up trouble, started rumours and worse, falsified evidence. And now, high on that hill near Malmesbury she cursed him again. If she still had the power he would die. Her spells would show him no mercy, conjuring up the Devil himself. In the icy chill that had surrounded her she had cursed not only the man but all that he held dear. No love of his would survive. Not wife, nor child. All would be consigned to the fires of Hell.

Was the power given to her by Old Megan in the smoke-filled hovel near her childhood home still strong? Her green eyes sparkled in the setting sun as she cursed him silently again, those old almost forgotten words echoing from the distant past.

'Marw... marwolaeth! Distryw.'

'Mistress Fytton!'

Elizabeth starting from her reverie , turned to see young Mary Stumpe, flushed and smiling and almost running, followed by a curly-headed youth with a grin equally as wide.

'You haven't been up to anything you shouldn't?' She tilted her head, eyebrows raised at the pair.

'Yes and no,' Mary responded cheekily. 'I'll not bed him till I've wed him,' she laughed. 'As you told me. But he has asked me!'

'Asked you?' Elizabeth felt a smile twitch her lips.

'To marry him.' Mary held out her hand and Jack Winchcombe took it eagerly.

'And what will your father say to that?'

'Mother will win him round.' Mary was confident.

No doubt, Elizabeth thought. Mary's mother was the reason she was here in Malmesbury instead of wandering mindlessly through the foetid streets of London without help or hope. Mary's mother was Cissy. Cissy Stumpe who had once been Cissy Bulkley, her best friend all those years ago when she fell for the inescapable charms of a young and passionate William Brereton at Gawsworth Hall.

'Should you ever be on the streets,' Cissy had told her, 'You will always find a bed in my house.'

They'd laughed at that. Elizabeth was maid to a Queen and Cissy merely the wife of a clothier, although an ambitious one. They hadn't realised how things could change so drastically. But change they do. Beyond all imagination. And so, one foggy day as the nights were drawing in Cissy opened her front door to a somewhat frail and bedraggled Elizabeth, desperate for the warmth and comfort of a loving family home.

Three years later she was still there, helping Cissy raise her five daughters, making potions and herbal remedies to keep them fit and healthy. Mr Stumpe had no say in the matter and truth to tell he put so much effort into the financial support of his family that he was often away "doing business" and seemed glad his wife had someone else to chatter endlessly to, as women do.

'Is Father home?' Mary stood apprehensively before her mother, Jack hovering in the kitchen doorway, nervously swaying from one foot to the other.

'Not yet.' Cissy paused to put the kneaded dough trough in the hearth to rise. 'He's gone over to Newbury.' She nodded towards Jack. 'To see Jack's father, as it happens. All of a bluster he was. Something to do with that last trip to London, but in such a state that he hadn't the time to tell his wife. What a husband! His women-folk seem to count for very little in the scheme of things.' Cissy shook her head and chuckled. 'So are you going to tell me your news or must I wait until your father gets home?'

Elizabeth sat down and began to chop the mound of bright parsley on the table.

'Might as well get it off your chest,' she advised.

Mary looked from one woman to the other, still unsure. Then with a deep breath her news spilt out in a torrent.

'I'd like to be… I want…' she swallowed hard. 'Jack has asked me to marry him. And I said yes. Can I? Will Father…?'

Cissy bit her bottom lip to prevent herself laughing out loud. They'd seen this coming months ago but neither family had seen any need to push the youngsters, preferring to let them get there in their own good time.

'Why now?' she asked her daughter. 'Why now?'

It was Jack who answered, stepping forward to take Mary's hand.

'I have employment. I shall be able to support a wife.'

'With your father?'

'No. Not the family business. My brothers have taken any work needed there. So when we are wed, Mary will join me at Littlecote where I shall manage Mr Darrell's household, and my wife will work with his house-keeper in the kitchens. Mary's a good cook and we shall do very well.' Jack straightened his shoulders and waited for a verdict, squeezing Mary's hand so hard she felt her knuckles crack.

'I'm sure you shall.' Cissy stood and kissed her daughter and then a re-lieved Jack Winchcombe. 'And if I'm not mistaken I think you father has ar-rived, Mary.'

Mr Stumpe flung off his coat and slapped his fine leather gloves down on the kitchen dresser.

'Oh, what a day. What a day!' He rubbed his hands together excitedly.

'Indeed it is, my love,' Cissy agreed. 'If you can just take a breath and listen for a moment, Mary and Jack have news for you.'

'Ah, Jack. Yes. Employment with landowner Darrell. Your father told me. Off very soon, I hear.'

'As you say, Dear,' Cissy interrupted. 'Off very soon and our Mary would like to go with him. Married. Right away. With your blessing.'

A silence fell, but only for a moment.

'Married? Mary and Jack? Of course they shall be married. And don't you know? My ship has finally come in. We shall have wedding cake and ale. And wine! Bottles of wine, my Dear.'

Elizabeth and Cissy exchanged an incredulous glance. His ship must certainly have come in. Jack's arms were round Mary and they kissed in a haze of happiness, shutting out the older generation who could not possibly know what true love was.

'So are you going to tell us?' Cissy asked as her husband sank into the chair beside the hearth.

'I have a commission. I am a made man.' His chin raised itself proudly.

'Who with? Where? Here?'

'Not here! I said I am a made man. A commission in London!'

'At Court?' Elizabeth was curious.

'At Court indeed.' Mr Stumpe's chin lifted even higher. 'None other than Lady Latimer. The rich widow Latimer,' he said grandly.

Elizabeth trembled, hope shivering her spine as she took in this unexpected piece of information.

'The widow Latimer,' she breathed softly. Kat! Katherine Parr. The baby she had once bounced on her knee in a garden in Chester as that handsome show-off William Brereton turned somersaults for her entertainment. For a moment she was back there, crowds thronging the streets to watch the parade. The music and noise of a Holy Day with half the people drunk and the other half set to join them. A happy day.

Elizabeth remembered that later, at the King's Court, when the frightened thirteen-year-old was about to wed a much older man she had calmed the girl's fears and helped her face her future. At eighteen Kat was widowed and again married an aging man. And now Latimer too was dead, leaving her once more widowed.

What was the Court like now? Where once there was Will Brereton, Hall Norris and George Boleyn there would be the Seymours. How she had cursed them. Thomas Seymour especially, and his ambition had already received a body-blow. His sister Jane, Queen of England, had died only days after giving birth to Henry's longed-for son, Prince Edward, so Thomas was now uncle to the heir to the throne. But still, he would never reach the heights he dreamed of. He and all his line were cursed so deeply that it could never be reversed.

How Elizabeth would revel in his downfall. Delight in the head being removed from that handsome frame. And watch as his children and his children's children were devoured by the flames of Hell.

Mary and Jack Wichcombe were married in the late September sun just as the rippling leaves of the silver birch were turning gold, setting off to begin their new life in Littlecote Manor. And within days Elizabeth was setting off in the company of Mr Stumpe as he made his joyous way back to London with a sumptuous cargo of fine silks, damasks and furs for that elegant Lady Latimer.

Thirteen

THE silken waters of the Thames glided quietly by and the newly arrived maid, idle for once, watched the wavering reflections of the little landing stage. The majestic river eased its graceful way towards the city, the Court, the King, and the sycophants who surrounded him. With luck she would soon be part of it again, quiet and unobserved, going about her work for Kat.

'Dreaming dreams or scheming schemes?' Kat joined her with a smile.

Elizabeth returned to smile, seeing the lovely sophisticated woman Katherine Parr had become. She had been welcomed with open arms, knowing more about the pitfalls of Court than most, with Katherine recognising that, as a widow and prospective bride, the more allies she had surrounding her the better.

'Dreaming mostly. Not much to scheme about here, though when we go to Court I think things may change.'

'If the women continue sewing at the rate they are I shall be out of widow's weeds in no time.'

'And then?' Elizabeth enquired. 'Another husband? How old this time?' There was a gleam of mischief in her eye.

'God help me!' Kat laughed. 'One with a little more vigour I hope. As soon as my new wardrobe is complete I shall face the Court with its waspish ways and viperfish tongues, and who knows? Maybe Mr Stumpe with soon be furnishing me with a soft, seductive trousseau.'

The Court had certainly changed and yet, when rubbing shoulders with courtiers who had stayed the course while she recovered mind, body and soul in Cissy's company, it was strangely the same. Whispered asides; knowing glances and a thread of fear that could not be untangled from the truth.

Only My Lady of Cleves seemed to have weathered the storm. Fourth wife of Henry, she had somehow overcome his aversion to her, calming his disappointment and anger by becoming more sister than wife, occasionally beating him at cards and helping him to laugh at life's vagaries.

So it was that King Henry, light-hearted and ready for romance, cast his eye on a child bride, and the Howards gained favour with His Majesty once more. Anne Boleyn's fall from grace was buried in the past as Anne's cousin Katherine Howard became the new Queen of England. Young, doe-eyed and mischievous, she had the King wallowing in the novelty of a pretty nubile virgin in his bed.

It wasn't long before Katherine, Lady Latimer was called to Court to wait upon the Queen and Elizabeth Fytton accompanied her, renewing the acquaintance of those she had known in happier times.

Red tinted leaves had fallen in drifts, every pathway rustling with brittleness as the Court settled into London. The sudden unexpected chill of morning frost soon cleared to sparkling days but the rooms had roaring fires half way up the chimney, warming groups of women as they toasted their toes in the hearth, cracking nuts and baking sweet apples, chins wagging so fast they scarce had time to eat.

Immersed in her own thoughts, Elizabeth lost the thread of conversation as it dwindled into whispers, and then silence.

'The Queen's headaches provide her with more sport than the hunt did for the King.' Bess Tyrwhit's voice was barely audible above the sudden patter of raindrops against the darkened window.

Heads nodded in agreement.

'She must be mad. Henry indulges her every whim, mesmerised by her youth and innocence.'

'A Howard innocent? Age has impaired his memory. That gleam in her eye isn't for her husband nor the show of ankle just for him. Dareham is a fool.'

Anne Herbert and Joan Denny couldn't hide the smiles at that.

'What is a delight for a common maid of fourteen should be shunned by a Queen. If she wants to keep her head. She's gone from childhood romps with Manox to fun and games with Dareham. And Culpepper!'

Elizabeth spoke for the first time. 'Those who boast of a Queen's favours can meet a very painful end. Dareham should look to the past.'

Tom Percy had tortured Mark Smeaton, but Thomas Seymour had reaped the benefits, and now, as Prince Edward's uncle, he had another axe to grind. He'd rid the Court of the Howard clan at a stroke if he could, and take his place at the King's right hand.

A log spitting on the fire disturbed Kat's hound from his slumbers on the hearth and sitting up to shake himself awake, scratched a persistent flea behind his ear and nuzzled his mistress. Receiving a reassuring pat he decided all was well and with a contented sigh was soon asleep once more.

Elizabeth watched Kat brush nut shells from her skirts into the rushes on the floor. What was she thinking?

'Culpepper plays a dangerous game,' she murmured. 'Is the Queen so stupid? Who will be dragged with her in to the mire? God help us all! Had she any sense she would see she only needs patience. Nature has a way of leaving young wives widows.'

Lips trembled with amusement. If anyone should know that it was the Widow Latimer.

Kat's quiet demeanour and elegant manner, and no doubt her wealth, had made her a target for almost every eligible man at Court and Elizabeth was dismayed to notice that one of the most prominent was Thomas Seymour. Kat was well aware of that family's ambitions, but she was not immune to the charms of a handsome, charismatic courtier of considerable standing. Away from Court it wasn't long before her maid's suspicions were confirmed.

It was late when that most prominent of the King's circle strolled into the house, removing the dampness of his cloak as he did so. Thick November fog swirled eerily into the hall behind him as Elizabeth went out to close the door. Hearing his voice Kat ran from the cosy where the apple-wood fire burned high against the chill evening, leading him by the hand to warm himself. After hanging the cloak to dry Elizabeth turned to leave the room, but Kat stopped her.

'Stay, Elizabeth.' Kat motioned with her hand for her maid to resume her seat where she had previously been occupied with plain sewing.

'Aye.' Tom was all agreement. 'Might as well hear it from me as have Katherine repeat it all later.' He lifted Kat's chin and kissed her lightly. 'The secret is out!'

He was almost laughing as he stretched his feet towards the fire comfortably, the smile etched into the handsome features. Suddenly he sat forward, holding out his hands to the leaping flames, the flickering firelight exploding a brilliant burst of colour in the great jewel on his finger.

'It's all over with the Queen, and lucky you were away from Court when it happened. She screamed for mercy, begging for an audience with the King. Pitiful it was.' The grin on his face didn't match the terrible meaning behind the words. 'Henry had tears in his eyes, it's true, but he wouldn't see her.' Tom rubbed his hands together, presumably to warm them, but the action was almost gleeful.

'Who told?' Kat knew it wouldn't have been Tom. He'd never anger the King, even in his own interests.

'Cranmer.'

'What will the King do?'

He had no need to answer. The block was always ready these days, the King seeing enemies everywhere and they all knew very well how the system worked. Keep your wits and keep your head. Truer now than ever.

'We need to be vigilant. Tread carefully. The Howards are on the wrong foot again but the Seymours are ready.' He took Kat's hand in his kissing it slowly and meaningfully. 'And unfortunately my own plans must now be delayed.'

'Plans?' Kat was curious.

'Our plans.' He kissed the back of her hand more seductively. 'These stolen hours are not enough for either of us.'

Had Kat stopped breathing?

'I've had it in mind to take a wife. If I thought for a moment you'd be willing.'

Willing? Was this the proposal she'd waited so long for. Not an old husband, but a handsome man in his prime

'Willing?' Kat blushed. Her voice was no louder than a sigh. 'More than willing.'

'But now we have a problem.' Tom stood, moving to look sightlessly through the window into the swirling mists of night. 'It's hardly time to be speaking to the King of weddings.' He turned to look at Kat, his expression deadly serious. 'This mess has to be sorted out to the King's satisfaction. Evidences to be sworn. Witnesses to question. Trials to organise and supervise. Nothing must be left to chance.'

Elizabeth, quiet in her corner, saw a crafty look come into his eyes. When had Tom Seymour ever left anything to chance?

'The King must not be left to brood and I think I have just the solution.' He moved to take Kat's hand once more, lifting it to his mouth to caress the palm with the tip of his tongue. 'Can you distract him from the stupidity of the Howard girl and keep him sweet-tempered towards me? Will you try?'

After almost a proposal of marriage Katherine would attempt to fly if Thomas Seymour asked her to.

Elizabeth, sickened by his duplicity slipped silently from the room. She had no need to watch the charade played out, preferring to slice through the supper meat with a cleaver, wishing it was Mister Seymour's aristocratic neck. If Katherine had not been sharing the meal it would have been so easy to slip an extra special herb into the stuffing or the sauce. But no! Thomas was to die by the axe. Trembling before the block. As Will once had. The spell could not be broken. She too would have to bide her time.

As she approached the cosy to ask where supper should be served her mind was still focussed on thoughts of Mister Seymour's death. They didn't hear the soft tread of her kid slippers on the stone slabs of the hall floor. Or notice that the door was slightly ajar. Beside the thick tapestried wall Elizabeth Fytton was almost invisible.

The smoothly curved hollow in the small of his back formed a dark, mysterious pool of shadow on an otherwise perfectly visible, perfectly formed male body. The skin glowed with honeyed vibrancy, the muscles of his shoulders and arms had surely been moulded from those of a god. Frozen

207

to the spot, Elizabeth couldn't even close her eyes to blot out the sight of him making love to Kat, the rippling motion of his naked back easing the palely rounded buttocks into a totally sensuous movement that tore a whimper, then a moan from the woman clinging to him.

How Elizabeth hated him. Because of him she was left to spend each night in a cold and lonely bed with no-one to hold her or kiss the loneliness away. No man to touch her with affection. Only tears into a sodden pillow before dreams brought Will back into her arms, perfect and devoid of all human failings. He had been taken from her by the man now tasting those delights with a rich woman he had set his sights on. A willing and euphoric Katherine Parr.

Elizabeth called on all the powers at her disposal. May the gods keep Katherine from his evil clutches. May he fail in his endeavours. May he die in fear!

She slipped silently away, back to the familiarity of the kitchen and the magic herbs that would help her in her quest It would be a long night, but she would succeed. She had to.

Fourteen

THE heavy rose-coloured damask of Kat's skirts rustled interminably as she paced the waxed boards of her day solar, fiddling with the gold ring on her finger and chewing at her bottom lip. Too studious, Will had once said. Well, maybe she was for some, but her barely controlled excitement as she waited for her lover gave her a youthful look that was really rather fetching. A variety of incidents had occupied the elusive Mister Seymour and Katherine had seen less and less of him as the months went by. It was now some time since they had been alone together as Kat had been keeping the King distracted from the loss of his foolish little wife, joining him in the many discussions he lately enjoyed with the academics of the church and University.

The King was changed man. His health had deteriorated after Katherine Howard's execution and he seemed disinclined to seek a replacement. The whole Court had a more sombre attitude, Henry frowning on wanton behaviour amongst his courtiers and his own bawdy jokes had degenerated into the crude observations of an envious and bitter old man. Lack of physical agility had brought him to the point where he could only prove himself in debate, the sports of his youth having become a ludicrous farce as his opponents desperately tried not to better him without seeming to lose on purpose.

Katherine Parr shone in this atmosphere. She was in her element and being widely read she had no difficulty in taking an active role in the intense intercourse which sometimes developed. Especially on the merits of the new religion as opposed to the old. What's more, her rich apparel added sparkle to the company amongst the drab and dusty velvets of the scholars. At times, the King was entirely distracted.

Kat enjoyed the debates despite Thomas being largely absent and therefore not in a position to bring up the subject of marriage to the King. There had been problems with the Scots and other minor uprisings but to Elizabeth's mind his prolonged absences were suspicious. He was untrustworthy, but Kat could never see it. If love is not absolutely blind, it certainly wears blinkers. Warnings did no good. Tom's charm had always been a force to be reckoned with.

Then Kat was gone. Her ears must have been straining for the sound of the oars and the scraping of the boat against the landing stage. Watching through the window Elizabeth thought how lovely she looked. Lovely and in love, despite being thirty years old.

Tom, as immaculate as ever was already approaching the house across the cropped grass as Kat ran out to greet him. The welcome was unmistakable as she skipped across the lawn, hands outstretched and an ecstatic smile illuminating her normally serious features. Mister Seymour's smile was more guarded, his steps purposeful, his demeanour determined.

Still, he kissed the proffered mouth as he slipped a strong protective arm about Kat's slim white shoulders to lead her to the shady seclusion of a garden seat.

'Don't make it so obvious,' Elizabeth murmured to herself.

'No! No!' Kat was tearing herself from him as though she had been struck, shaking her head violently.

Something was terribly wrong. What had that monster done now? Abandoned her to wed elsewhere? Elizabeth wouldn't put anything past him.

The outer door banged against the wall with noisy violence before the sound of Kat's slippered feet pattered past the solar and up towards the bed chamber. The silence was as heavy and fraught with emotion as before the first fork of lightning rips across the sky in fury. Then Katherine's pain tore itself from her body in a terrifying scream.

Elizabeth's heart, which only moments before had turned to lead, hit the pit of her stomach with a sickening thud.

'Damn Tom Seymour to eternal hell fires!' Elizabeth snatched open the door. Where had his filthy scheming led them this time? Rushing into the hallway, where Kat's screams were magnified by the cavernous stone of walls and floor, she ran headlong into the glowering figure of Tom Seymour himself.

Menacingly he barred the way, a dark flush of anger accentuating fierce lights in his eyes. Bright splinters of steel aimed directly at Elizabeth.

'Mistress!' He spat the word out. 'Katherine must be made to see reason. And soon!' His voice shook with anger. 'No more romantic notions. Tell her something of real life for a change. Tell her, if you will, what happens to those who disobey the King. She may care nothing for her own life but remind her that I would be sure to lose mine too. You remember what it is like to see your lover kneel before the block. To see his life ooze away with his blood. Tell her! Tell her how easy it is for secret whispers to reach the King's ears.'

'What?' Elizabeth struggled to understand.

Tom took a step towards her, controlling his anger.

'She has the honour to be chosen as Henry's next bride. She will be the next Queen.' There was an edge of sarcasm to his tone. 'But My Lady declines the offer. What's more, she wants to tell the King the reason. She is to wed Tom Seymour, if you please. Can you imagine?'

Elizabeth could. Will had always warned that Tom was slyer than a fox. He had kept Kat well away from other suitors and held her enthralled at the prospect of marrying him. Had this been his plan all along? Having Henry's Queen in love with him and every little move and conversation reported. How could he? How could he initiate Kat in the arts of love and then present her to an aging, impotent mound of stinking flesh with a reputation for decapitating wives.

'Make her see the sense of it unless she wants to see me dead!'

He was so close. Elizabeth could see her own wide-eyed expression reflected in his steady gaze which held her rooted to the spot. How she would love to see him dead!

'She will be Queen of England! And besides, is certain to outlive the King by many years.'

His breath was warm and moist against Elizabeth's cheek. 'Tell her I'll be waiting. If she plays the part of Queen to perfection she will not let me, or herself down.'

Elizabeth felt the pressure of his hand increase purposefully. His mouth was only inches away from hers She closed her eyes to shut out the memory of kisses once enjoyed and when she opened themTom's tentative half smile said it all. He had won. As he raised Mistress Fytton's hand to his mouth Thomas Seymour thanked God for the gift of being able to handle women and for this proof that he was master of them all. His place at the King's side was safe and he had set in motion the first part of a grandiose plan of spectacular proportions.

On a hot summer day in July 1543 Katherine Parr became the sixth wife of King Henry. As she remarked somewhat wryly to Elizabeth, marriage was becoming something of a habit with her as well as Henry. He was her third husband but, God willing, he wouldn't be her last. Naturally such treasonable thoughts were kept well hidden and from the day of the wedding ceremony at Hampton Court Katherine, Queen of England never once looked at Thomas Seymour in a way that could give rise to even the slightest rumour. Instead, to take her mind from the lover she had lost Kat immersed herself deeper and deeper in theological discussion, taking her Erasmian piety to such a degree that she almost became a religious zealot.

Perhaps she took her zeal too far. There were always enemies, and in Katherine's case the one set against her was the Lord Chancellor Wriothesley. They had crossed swords on more than one occasion but he had not got the better of her yet. However, he only waited for his chance.

Elizabeth turned as Kat entered the bedchamber, her face flushed with pleasure.

'The King is in good heart, then?'

Katherine looked surprised. 'In good heart? I suppose so. Certainly we had a long and enjoyable discussion and I really feel I have begun to show him greater depth than he thought possible to the New Learning. He sometimes fails to grasp the full implications of the new books and sermons, but I've studied them closely and tonight was able to point out diverse aspects, some of which I intend to write about and see published.'

Kat positively glowed. All these new works, these new ideas, stimulated her mind and gripped her imagination. She deliberately used her intellectual interests to subdue her physical needs, turning thoughts from things yet forbidden. Things the King could never guess at. That night neither Kat nor Elizabeth had the slightest suspicion that all was not well.

It was the next evening as Elizabeth scoured the herb garden for fresh young leaves that they got the first indication that the King had not been so enthralled with the discourse as his wife had been. Looking up she was curious to see the squat figure of Dr Wendye, his face set in a grim expression making a deliberate beeline for this secluded corner of the garden. He did not mince his words.

'Put you mistress on her guard. Things are afoot which concern her, the gravity of which she must not under-estimate.'

'What things?' Elizabeth frowned. 'The King?'

'Aye. The King. And Wriothesley. I've just left His Majesty and he told me the whole tale. Last night, after some heated debate with the Queen, the King felt slighted by her superior knowledge in certain matters touching on new attitudes to religion. He was annoyed with himself at letting her lecture him, and angry with her for daring to do so. 'To come to my old age to be taught by my wife!' These were his words and the Lord Chancellor, ever quick to take his chance, suggested that a search of the Queen's apartments might reveal documents which could amount to heresy.'

Elizabeth felt the blood drain from her face. Heresy? No.

'Is there hope? What can the Queen do?' Elizabeth's mind was racing. She would not see Katherine destroyed for some imagined hurt she had done Henry. How that man would suffer if Elizabeth Fytton ever got her hands on him!

'She can take hope that the King has mentioned it to me, albeit swearing me to secrecy. Perhaps he already regrets his anger but doesn't know how to stop Wriothseley without losing face, But I might be wrong. He might want her arrested.'

Dusk was falling rapidly and Elizabeth shivered in the sudden breeze. She had to go to Katherine at once. Stammering her thanks she made to leave but Dr Wendye stopped her with a hand on her arm.

'Follow me and keep an eye out for the messenger as he leaves the King's apartments.'

Without another word he turned on his heels and almost trotted back along the path towards the building, glowing amber now in the last rays of the setting sun. With his short legs thrusting purposefully forward beneath the swirl of his second-best cloak, the curved feather in his cap twitching jerkily with every step, reminding Elizabeth of a ridiculous mummers play she had seen as a child where all the men were dressed as crowing cocks. For some absurd reason she wanted to giggle. Desperately she fought the urge. It was the beginning of hysterics as panic held her in its painful grip. She should be thanking the doctor, not mocking his shortcomings.

Mercifully they were soon inside the now almost deserted corridor, dimly lit by smoking torches high in their iron sconces. It seemed that Dr Wendye knew who to look for and as the King's man passed he engaged him in some quiet conversation. Elizabeth waited in the shadows, her heart beating madly and frozen with fear.

The two men walked slowly by, deep in some earnest talk. She never took her eyes from them and almost missed the very thing she was there for. Carelessly dropped, and even more carelessly pushed by a passing toe half under a wooden seat, lay a loosely rolled parchment. It was inside Elizabeth's sleeve and on its way to the Queen's suite in seconds.

Katherine, Queen of England was in despair. In her hand was a warrant for her arrest and if her maid was to be believed men were already gathering to search her rooms.

'Is it so easy to fall into a trap? After all the patience I have shown him. After all I gave up to become his wife! Why? Why want me branded a heretic after all the fine enlightening discussions we have shared?' She collapsed weakly onto a chair.

Elizabeth had regained some of her usual calm and unobtrusively made arrangements for the lost document to be found again.

'All your books and papers must be removed from your apartments immediately. Anything at all that could be classed as subversive. Now!'

The urgency in her voice roused Kat from her shocked state.

'Yes. You're right. They must find no evidence against me. None at all.'

Drawers were cleared, cupboards emptied and all shelves carefully checked in a frenzy of activity, and they finished the task with only minutes to spare. The men sent to search found nothing. Nothing at all. Katherine didn't hide her distress at this treatment but it was to no avail. The men were only carrying out orders. And orders had to be obeyed.

They were no sooner gone, empty-handed, than Elizabeth was pouring a cup of special cordial for Kat to drink. One thing was certain: she must not lose control. Henry must somehow be persuaded to change his mind. And quickly.

'Is it at all possible to remain Queen for more than five minutes in the country of ours? Does he really mean to see an end to me? I was so careful of the one thing I thought to be a danger.'

She meant her feelings for Tom Seymour.

'At night I lie awake, wondering. Tom is not one to sleep alone. I try hard not to think who he might be with while my husband insists on fumbling me and kissing me, pretending to himself that he is still a man. And then he falls asleep leaving me with my body inflamed for a real lover. My lover! But I never wavered. Never let him see. Knowing that would be my downfall. And now this!'

Katherine plucked nervously at the edge of her gown. 'In trying to occupy my mind I have fallen foul of the King in another way altogether. Were his other wives guilty as charged? Or was their only crime marrying a King?'

'You'll not end up on the dung-heap like the others,' Elizabeth told her firmly. 'You're too shrewd to let the likes of the Lord Chancellor get the better of you over something as silly as the way you choose to worship your God.' Elizabeth had her own gods and was completely at a loss to understand what all the fuss was about anyway. 'You've studied the subject to take your mind off other worries, so couldn't this be the reason for engaging the King in lively debate? To take his mind from other worries? From the pain in his leg? And the fact that ill health keeps him tied to England when he would rather be away fighting his wars?'

The King had recently had to cancel a trip to Calais on his doctor's orders so Katherine saw the sense in this.

'Elizabeth, you are a marvel. So calm in a crisis. Is my dress tidy? My cap straight? I must go to him at once, late though it is. Henry mustn't go to sleep brooding or I'll find myself in the Tower tomorrow.'

Without further ado she was gone in a flurry of skirts and petticoats leaving Elizabeth to nervously await the outcome of the day's events. Tom Seymour would not be pleased. Elizabeth was convinced he had put it into the King's mind to marry Katherine, knowing she would tell him everything the King was thinking. He should have realised no woman on earth could satisfy the King on every level, especially as the curses made against him were now all coming to fruition. Today the King's body was covered with putrid wheals of flesh and open, running sores. Katherine had been forced by Tom to marry Henry and keep him occupied. Now she was in mortal danger for obeying those orders. If only the King would die. Elizabeth mentally cast a spell. Would it work? Or would something more practical be needed?

Katherine was lucky. Hearing her apology and her explanation for engaging him so boldly in conversation he actually smiled, accepting that she had only acted in that over-knowledgeable way to distract him from his many problems. Perhaps Dr Wendye had been right. Perhaps he regretted his impulsive show of anger in front to Wriothesley. Whatever the workings of the King's mind, Katherine had been reprieved. Not only that but she was again considered good company for her husband and had been asked, almost commanded, to join him for his afternoon stroll the following day.

Elizabeth heard the full tale later that evening. Kat had worn her newest and brightest gown for the outing knowing that the King did not take kindly to dowdy women. They seemed to revive memories of his first Queen who had taken to prayer in the most severe manner, denouncing all things frivolous, even colours. Clothed entirely in golden buttercup yellow, embroidered in several shades of blue and turquoise silks and with a stiffened bodice a sparkle of sapphires, Katherine looked enchanting. What is more, she managed to be so entertaining that the King threw back his head and laughed heartily. A thing he rarely did these days. Slim and light, she had been a perfect foil for the thickset, limping old man, who but for the richness of his crimson velvet and the glitter of his jewels would not have been given a second glance.

This charming tableau, this engaging scene of domestic bliss, was the unexpected sight which stopped the Lord Chancellor and forty men-at-arms in their tracks. Wriothesley's face fell. He stood, out of place and ill at ease, dismay written all over him. His plan had failed. He didn't know how or why. He only knew that he had failed.

Queen Katherine hoped he had. Prayed that he had. Even so, as the King stepped across to speak quietly and privately with Wriothesley she held her breath. Would her husband change his mind again? Which way would the Guard be ordered to march? The suspense seemed endless but at last the uniformed phalanx turned on its heel and disappeared from view as it had arrived. Without the Queen.

Katherine felt exhausted. She wanted to sleep. Sleep for a week and forget this nerve-racking tightrope which had to be walked daily.

'If only he could be made well enough to travel with his fleet to France, leaving us in peace and safety.'

Watching Elizabeth pour her a goblet of her evening comfort, a hopeful expression crossed her face.

'Will none of your special salves help him? See him on his way?'

Katherine meant on his way to France but Elizabeth put an altogether different meaning to the words. A tremor of excitement ran the length of her spine. It would require nerves of cold steel, but how many times had she gone over the possibilities?

'You healed him once before. Wasn't it Queen Jane who introduced you then?'

Aye. It had been Jane and her brother Thomas tempting her to talk. To condemn Will Brereton and the others to treason. She had healed the King's leg but her lips had remained tightly sealed.

'Will he remember that I healed him? Or that I was Will Brereton's wench and part of Queen Anne's household?'

'I'll tell him how I have known you since I was a child and that you have

217

been known to perform miracles with you salves and potions. He'll see you. If I ask him.'

The figure of the King was gross in its obesity. Muscle had degenerated to superfluous fat, swaddling him from head to foot and keeping him as incumbent as a new born babe swollen to a monstrous size and propped uncomfortably in its chair. Only the eyes remained the same. Blue as sapphires. Hard as diamonds. Glittering jewels set into a red, pulpy mass of over-indulged flesh. Shiny portholes through which that still-sharp intelligence peered myopically at Elizabeth, making her wish she had had the presence of mind to visit the privy before being summoned. Added to that she had the desperate urge to sneeze, the dust from the hem of her skirts tickling its way up her nostrils as she remained in a deep curtsey before her monarch. The command was so slow in coming that she began to think the King had fallen asleep. Or died! But no. Henry cleared his throat, a gurgling phlegmy sound, thick and wheezy.

'Sit with us.' Despite the ragged edges of that once-firm voice, it still held more authority than most achieved in a lifetime. It still demanded to be obeyed.

Elizabeth rose as gracefully as she could as Kat smiled encouragement. The three of them were quite alone and she could feel the King watching her through those tiny windows. Those spy-holes sunk into a bloated, rotting carcass. How Katherine must suffer.

Suddenly the King leaned forward startling her like frightened rabbit. Henry missed nothing. Worried eh? She had every right to be. Always popping up when least expected. Probably dabbling in things that shouldn't concern her. Dabbled in herbs though, and if memory served him true, she had been more successful than those idiots calling themselves doctors. No harm in letting her try then even though she had once been Anne's woman. And William Brereton's. It was all coming back to him now. Wasn't the woman something of a simpleton. An almost forgotten picture came to him. This woman. Dress torn to expose her naked breasts and hair escaping from her cap. Thick auburn hair. Wide green eyes. She had apologised. He'd had some good times with Brereton and Norris. Wrong place, wrong time. But the ends had justified the means and Jane had given him as fine a son as a man could wish for. And here she was again, an old maid, with his wife, the Queen.

'You say she is of great assistance to you, Wife?'

Somewhere in the distance Elizabeth could hear Kat's voice extolling her virtues, but she herself was in another world. This quivering dung-heap of a king had murdered Will. Killed him without a second thought to rid himself of Queen Anne. But now he would suffer long and slow just like his sister Mary all those years ago. But first he would seem to improve. A brief respite from pain would seem like the road to recovery. Then the fatal dose, its symptoms remaining hidden for many weeks giving her time to put him back into the hands of the doctors. The reversal would then be put down to their well-known incompetence.

'It's settled then.'

Elizabeth realised that her silence had been taken as affirmative that she would alleviate the King's pains.

Only when he spoke did Elizabeth notice that Henry's manner had softened. The moisture in his eye couldn't be down to sentiment? Probably just the rheumy trickle of advancing years.

She would have been surprised if she could have read the invalid's thoughts. That strangely vacant expression in her clear sage-green eyes and the magnificent swell of her still shapely bosom had unleashed a frantic carnival of memories, vivid colours, raucous noises and sweetly tender moments of those early, happy days. Merry masques and gargantuan feasts when his legs never ached and his digestion could cope with peacock, swan and suckling pig, hare, venison and fowl with scarcely more than a belch.

Oh, to be well again! To be able to ride without the tender swellings in his groin causing untold agonies. To have the breath to play at tennis. And oh, to have the power to be a husband to his wife. Elizabeth Fytton had performed that miracle once before and he had a son to show for it. By God's Wounds she would be well rewarded if she could do the same again.

Make him well? Have him slake his filthy lusts on her sweet Katherine?

She'd see him in Hell first. Elizabeth kept these thoughts hidden, gazing at the King with a trusting simplicity, a naivity that seemed almost divine yet calm and totally confident.

Henry couldn't help having more faith in her than in his physicians.

'This time your reward will be just.'

What did he mean by that? Not sorry for murdering Will after all these years? Too late. Far too late. Worried about answering to his God? To late for that too! In spite of herself, she smiled. She would have her revenge for all the lonely nights she had hungered for her lover, but truth to tell, William Brereton had taken his own revenge. That, unknown and unsuspected by everyone except Elizabeth Fytton, could only be seen in the sun-gold hair and violet eyes of the Princess Elizabeth Tudor.

Kat filled the silence.

'Allow her to prepare her potions, Sire, and let her help you. Then Mistress Fytton may be persuaded that some small reward is justified.'

Elizabeth cast her a grateful glance. The awful stink of rotten flesh and a cloying mixture of oils and perfumes was settling on her stomach making her feel decidedly sick.

Later, when they were alone, Elizabeth was adamant that she would not accept even the smallest reward from the King but Kat had other ideas.

'Refuse him for yourself, by all means, but what of others? Aren't there those to whom you are indebted? Would they not be grateful?'

Indeed! Why hadn't Elizabeth thought of that herself? The first that came to mind was that of Will's nephew, also called William Brereton. Will had treated him like the son he never had. The boy had been raised in high hopes, only to have them dashed as his uncle lost his head. Then there was her own brother, Edward Fytton, master of Gawsworth Hall these many years. How she had disliked him for his high-and-mighty attitude, the result of being the eldest son and knowing just how much he would inherit. In the scorn and derision he had poured on her on learning of her disgrace he had only been following their father's lead. All the childhood arguments and squabbles, in retrospect, seemed so pointless. Now, she might use her influence for the good of her family.

And there was one other. She felt very much indebted to Mr Stumpe for the years of hospitality he had shown her. The man had a burning ambition to clothe the King himself, and now even that was possible.

The King's health gradually improved until at last he was fit enough to travel and Katherine got her wish. As she waved him off to Calais, despite one or two setbacks caused by lack of seaworthiness of his flagship, she was able to inform Elizabeth that the King had been given three names deserving honours on her behalf.

King Henry was not one to rush into things, but on this occasion he kept his wife's words in mind. The green-eyed woman had done her work well and did merit a reward. He would keep an eye on Brereton and Fytton as they carried out orders in France and perhaps when they returned measures could be taken.

So it came about that before one year had passed William Brereton and Edward Fytton were Knights of the Realm and Mister Stumpe had met his Monarch and made his fortune.

Fifteen

THE improvement in the King's health became so apparent that Elizabeth's reputation was assured and whenever anyone was ill it was her name carried to the sick-bed as a cure-all. No-one spoke of her powers openly. Magic is a thing to steer clear of except when one is ill, so these days Elizabeth needed no excuse to install herself in some handy corner of the kitchens, preparing her brews and chanting over her potions, all but disappearing in the clouds of pungent steam rising from her boiling bowls.

Katherine had learned her lesson. Still active in debate, she knew when to defer to her husband and when to hold her tongue. She was far too clever to lose her head through pride, and besides, it meant that the King was willing to give way in certain other matters. Like filling the Court full to bursting with children. Loving books the way she did Kat saw no reason why the children shouldn't learn to love them too, and the only way to do that was by lessons.

When Elizabeth's duties permitted she could always be found chattering to the nursemaids as they watched over their charges grappling with Latin, Greek and mathematics. But it wasn't all work. There was plenty of time for play.

A new generation had arrived almost overnight, it seemed. Off-spring of the people she had known about the Court for so long, growing up to take their parents' places, and some who no doubt, would make a better end than others. Take the Dudley boys for example. Elizabeth watched the group with interest.

Of all Jane Dudley's boys, Guildford was the most handsome. The trouble was, he knew it, and almost gave the impression that he was shallow and empty-headed, all vanity, assured that his garb fitted perfectly and that the flawless symmetry of his features was admired.

If Guildford was somewhat lacking in personality it was the last thing anyone would say about his brother Robert. He entertained them all and danced for pleasure, holding centre stage with ease and beguiling his contemporaries with an attractive, wayward fascination. Robert would never be out of place, Elizabeth was certain.

Then there was Mary Dudley, sweet-natured, the image of her mother when she was young. How Anne Boleyn had raved at the ease with which Jane Dudley had produced children. And five boys! Fate can be so unkind.

Henry Sidney was whispering in Mary's ear, making her blush to the roots of her hair. These youngsters were growing up fast and some forming partnerships already. Away from the older ones little Jane Grey was being shown how to spin a top by Prince Edward. There was no doubt that those two would one day make a match, if Thomas Seymour had anything to do with it. He'd been making tentative enquiries into the ward-ship of Frances Brandon's eldest daughter and Thomas never did anything without reason. Jane looked healthy enough but Prince Edward had been ill during the winter months, coughing and full of fever and though Elizabeth's salves had worked, he still had a frailty about him. She doubted he would make old bones but, the gods being willing, he would live long enough to marry and produce an heir.

A shaft of bright sunlight cut through the shadows of the room, illuminating the circle of children. Diamond panes of glass dispersed the rays in miniature rainbows over their heads and in their midst, leading them in their game was the Princess, Elizabeth Tudor. Slim and straight, her hair glinted gold, rivalling the sun for brilliance, giving her the aura of a delicate, untouchable Celestielle. Pale complexion. The finest bone-structure. But it was the eyes that drew attention. Unfathomable. Sometimes as light and phosphorescent as the sparkle of sea spry, sometimes as clear as moonlight on the lake. And sometimes deep, shaded and dark as the velvet petals of violets in the wood. It all depended on her mood and those who knew her well could use this strange phenomenon as a barometer to forecast calm or stormy days. Add to this an astute brain and a very determined nature. A formidable combination. Anne would have been proud of her daughter. To Elizabeth Fytton, she was the daughter she had lost all those years ago in Chester. Will's daughter.

At that moment a bright-eyed bundle flung itself at her and climbed up onto her knee. Margaret Clifford knew where she would be welcome. Eleanor Brandon had died young, leaving the one child of her brief marriage motherless and Elizabeth had taken the tiny girl to her heart. She was someone to cuddle, someone who would kiss her in return and make her feel less lonely. Meg Clifford became a substitute for so many things. Her lover, her child, and Anne's child all rolled into one, so Meg scarcely felt the loss of her own mother at all. And she loved to help, stirring the pot into which Elizabeth put leaves and roots and flowers.

But there were times when Meg was not allowed to help with the preparations. Sometimes the brew smelt evil and she was sent to play elsewhere. Those were the days when Mistress Fytton muttered strange words and lived in a far off world of her own, putting her most secret plan into operation.

The King was very well. The poultices had done wonders for his sores and after this last, special application Elizabeth could hand him back to the tender mercies of his physicians. Then it was only a matter of time.

***

Anne Boleyn's final wish had been fulfilled. The corpulent body of the King was horribly diseased and he had lingered painfully before, on a dark and bitter January day he slid unwillingly to his final judgement. England sighed for the passing of the man, though whether in respect or relief was hard to say. Henry had long since gone from golden boy to grisly grey-beard under the awesome weight of the jewelled crown. After that monumental sigh the country held its breath as every eye looked to the throne where the young King Edward sat, flanked on either side by his two powerful uncles, Edward and Thomas Seymour. Their day had arrived.

Kat had known for some time that her husband would not remain long on this earth and had had the foresight to order yards of fine black silk intricately embroidered with gold thread, from that now wealthy merchant, Mister Stumpe. Some may have wondered at such mourning luxury but from the widowed Queen's point of view Henry's funeral was a celebration. With her fair looks she knew that black suited her better than the white she could have chosen, and now, more than at any time Katherine wanted to look her best.

Elizabeth marvelled at the full swirl of the skirts and deep sheen of material rustling out behind her as she walked. At the back the dress flowed to the ground in tapered folds, trailing slightly to give added poise to the wearer and where the sleeves gripped the forearms the embroidery was as thick as that encrusting the stiffened panel of the bodice. Under the matching cap Kat's face looked pale and lovely as befitted a grieving wife, but the expression in her eyes ruined the whole effect.

'Best lower your eyelids,' Elizabeth told her bluntly.

Kat had the grace to blush but try as she might she couldn't help the hint of a smile playing on her lips. Thomas Seymour had been the first at her side with the news of Henry's death, solicitously escorting the rather less than distraught Queen to her chambers, speaking quiet words of comfort and keeping a steady grip on her arm to support her. Some thought it touching to see his concern over Katherine when it had been supposed his first move would be towards the new King Edward. They should have remembered that Thomas did nothing without good reason.

Later, when they were finally alone, Kat dismissing her ladies on the pretext of needing a soothing draught to alleviate her suffering, the pretence was over and the widow danced around the room clapping her hands and laughing as though it was Christmas all over again.

.If anyone should see you now, dancing on your husband's grave, tongues would wag faster than dogs' tails at dinner,' Elizabeth laughed.

'The wait is over,' Kat sang joyfully. 'No more restraint. No more lies. No more deceit. I am free to think as I like. Free to love where I like.'

'I might have guessed that Mister Seymour was behind all this.' Elizabeth felt a quiver of fear run through her. 'You will observe the mourning?'

'Not for long,' Kat answered mischievously. 'Tom is going to approach the boy King on the subject of our marriage. He can no more wait than I can and is certain his nephew will raise no objections. He loves his Uncle

Thomas too much for that.'

Elizabeth wondered whether life was just one huge joke with which the gods chose to amuse themselves. She had hated Henry for destroying her lover and that hate had given her the will to go on living. It had given her the courage to provide Anne Boleyn's curse with a helping hand. She had cursed Tom Seymour too for his part in the cruel charade, but the gods had put a massive sting in that particular scorpion's tail. Thomas Seymour, dissolute, licentious, lewd, and cursed, was now in a position to marry Katherine Parr, that gentle woman who had never knowingly hurt anyone in her life. Why? She had been far from secure as Henry's Queen but what dangers would Thomas with his ruthless ambitions lead her into? If she tied herself to Tom the future would break her heart. And if they had children! That pact with the Devil didn't bear thinking about.

'Don't marry him, Kat.' Even as she said the words Elizabeth knew they were futile. Would this be the outcome of her curse? How could she have known that these two, one her friend and one her enemy, would get together?

'The wait has been a long one. You wouldn't deny me happiness at last? Why do you distrust men so? Was William such a monster? Was he guilty as charged?'

'Most certainly not! He loved me. After the fashion of men.' Elizabeth was adamant.

'And what is that supposed to mean?'

'Oh, he loved me,' Elizabeth told her in a matter-of-fact voice. 'Yet for two years I was left to wonder what had become of him after the birth of our daughter. Then again when it suited his needs I was sent to loiter at Westhorpe in the Brandon household. Later, to curry favour with the King he married the Widow Savage after telling me for years that he had no wish to marry. But he loved me. After the fashion of men.'

'But Tom is marrying me. Very soon. So I have to send my ladies away after we've supped.'

Elizabeth looked at her sharply. 'Tonight?' she asked, startled. 'Will the King agree?'

'Haven't I been as a mother to him these last years? Brought in friends for his company? He won't deny his beloved uncle permission to marry his beloved mother.'

Elizabeth was bemused. It must have been planned down to the smallest detail. If even she didn't know then no-one else will have guessed. Kat had played a dangerous game. If anyone had realised!

'Aye. We should have lost our lives as well as each other and that was reason enough for extreme caution. But now we may throw caution to the winds. The long, long wait is over.'

'But so soon!' Elizabeth shook her head.

'How could I refuse him? My body aches for him. I've waited and prayed for this blessed day. If you think we can wait a moment longer then you have never been in love.'

Elizabeth paused before answering. 'You know I have so I beg you take care. Hearts are all too easily broken, and impossible to mend. Love is a madness which shuns good sense and is so often our undoing. And where does Edward Seymour figure in these plans? Has he been informed?'

Kat shook her head. 'No-one knows. No-one at all. And no-one shall until we have the King's permission. It is no concern of anyone else.'

Elizabeth thought differently. Rivalry between brothers was always the most bitter and Edward would not take kindly to Tom making these arrangements behind his back. Such manoeuvres had ended in bloodshed before now. Would this be the fulfilment of her curse? And was Kat about to be drawn into it all? One thing was certain, Katherine would not listen to the warnings of a woman whose beliefs were older than time itself. More than a religion, it was a way of life some called witchcraft and other laughed at as superstition, but Elizabeth believed and in doing so, feared. What hope was there for Thomas Seymour? Or his children? Kat's children, if children were born? Elizabeth would protect them with her life so far as she was able, but how strong a shield would she prove to be against a pact struck with the Devil?

Even the day set for the wedding seemed like an ill omen. The first day of May. Exactly thirty years since that young page William Brereton had kissed a tender virgin beneath the silver birches of Yates' Spinney by Congleton Park and inflamed her blood with a passion that would no be ignored. And years later, on that very same date they had dragged him away from the joust to the Tower. Those had been the first steps on the twisting, winding trail that had led her to today and she knew the journey was far from over. No good would come of today's events. No good at all.

Despite her worries Elizabeth settled down in the new household at Chelsea Palace where Kat gathered children around her like some pagan goddess of motherhood. As ever, the gardens were a delight and Elizabeth was in her element, pounding and brewing to her heart's content, constantly muttering to herself as she stirred the aromatic potions. Virtually hanging onto her apron strings would be Meg Clifford. It was ironic that of all the children in the Palace it should be this one, Mary Brandon's grand-daughter who was taking an interest in medicines and magic.

'Who teached you?' Two big eyes as brown as buttons and as round as pennies looked up at her.

Elizabeth smiled down affectionately. 'It was a long, long time ago before even your mother was born,' she told her. 'And the woman who taught me was very old even then. Megan ap Y.'

'And was she?' Meg dipped her chubby little finger into the mixture for a taste.

'Was she what?'

'Happy.'

Elizabeth laughed. 'I believe she was, in the end.'

Megan had often said how she had made an old woman happy by learning the old ways which must never die out. And now it was Elizabeth's turn to pass them on. What better pupil could she have wished for as life turned full circle? Old Megan would be pleased to know that the ritual continued and that more was gained than lost with each successive transfer. As she grew, Meg Clifford began the laborious task of writing down the mysteries and magic for the first time in their history and as they worked together Elizabeth Fytton learned a skill she never thought to master. She learnt to read.

***

There were other changes too amongst the youngsters as they grew from children into the first tremulous stages of adulthood, and one damp and dismal day Robert Dudley found himself in somewhat heated conversation with Elizabeth Tudor.

'I am,' Robert insisted. 'I am a man. And if you cannot understand what I mean then you are not yet a woman.'

Princess Elizabeth blazed with anger. Her fists were clenched. She would love to hit him.

'We're the same age. Why shouldn't I understand? I probably know more about such things than you do.'

'Do you?' Robert took a measured step towards her, watching her bristle in her usual forceful way. Slowly he reached out his hand, never taking his eyes from hers. Then he was touching her newly forming breast, gently, with his fingertips.

The princess froze, staring, her mouth relaxing from the anger it had been ready to throw at him.

'I suppose you hate me now?' A slight grin tilted his mouth as he stood, head on one side, waiting for a reaction.

'N…no.' she stumbled over the word. Her body tingled with a vaguely pleasant feeling. Why? What had he done? Whatever it was she would show no sign of it.

Stepping back he thrust his thumbs into the slits of his amber-coloured jerkin. 'You see, I do know. I have older brothers who showed me more in an hour as I thought to learn in a lifetime. My education, Ambrose called it.'

The Princess stood stock still and took a deep breath, still shaken by the strange feelings his touch had caused. 'I am not so despicable that I would shout about such education for all and sundry to gossip over. It is a very private matter.'

'So private as to be no more than a dream.' Robert seemed determined to have her in tears. 'You are always closeted with Grindal for your 'education'. Is he the one? Grindal? A dusty old tutor? He's the only one

229

Mistress Ashley will let near you. You can't deceive me, dear Elizabeth. You are still a child and must remain ignorant until the day you marry.'

Princess Elizabeth looked at him stonily, refusing to let her anger turn to tears and wondering whether she actually wanted to remain ignorant. His touch had set in motion feelings she had never experienced before.

'You will see,' she retorted hotly, not to be beaten 'I would never consort with rabble.' She gave him such a withering look that he was under no illusions as to who the rabble might be. 'You will see, Robert Dudley. You will see.' And with those words she flounced out of the room leaving her young tormentor wondering whether it was all bravado or whether perhaps there was more to that fiery-headed girl than he had realised.

Had Elizabeth Fytton known of the incident she would have smiled to herself. The Princess would not allow Robert or any other young courtier to better her if she could help it and what Robert had said was true. The girl was never far from the sight of Cat Ashley and so wouldn't know a lover intimately until the day she wed. All the same, she was not the only girl to be changing subtly into a woman. There was Robert's own sister, Mary, and Frances Brandon's girls, Jane and Katherine Grey amongst others.

As Elizabeth observed to Kat, 'So many young ladies. And your husband takes such an interest in their welfare.' Mistress Fytton was suspicious of the hearty benevolence Tom Seymour displayed when young ladies were in the company. She remembered his predilection for girl-children from way back. Not that he would be such a fool in his own household with his wife looking on. Yet he was not naturally the jovial father figure type. He was an impeccable, courteous charmer through and through and no doubt some of the young ladies would be flattered. New emotions, as unfamiliar as the delicate budding of their tiny breasts must have set pulses racing and hope burgeoning in their innocent hearts.

While Elizabeth worried, Kat watched it all happily. 'Tom loves to have them laughing and dancing attendance on him. They have become rivals for his affection ands vie for a turn upon his knee and I shall make this house a home for all of them.'

Elizabeth frowned, but at least the Princess would come to no harm, remaining as she did under the watchful eye of Cat Ashley. She knew of Kat's plan. She wanted to give the Princess Mary some recognition alongside her sister, and the following Christmas saw that ambition fulfilled.

For the first time in many years the three royal children slept under one roof. It was an achievement to be proud of Elizabeth thought as she surveyed the scene, looking from the new faces to the old familiar ones who had been around for as long as she could remember.

King Edward was surrounded by the men he depended on for so much. The Seymour brothers and John Dudley, now made Earl of Warwick, stood resplendent in their honoured positions, haughty in their envied status and watchful, ever watchful in the direction of their enemies.

The ladies were decked out in a glittering array of velvets, silks and jewels, creating as much visual clamour as the sound of their ceaseless gossiping did on the ear. A cheerful minstrel rendering was almost drowned out by the clack of tongues against teeth. Or is some case, gums. Pungent woodsmoke from the fires and heavily spiced foods assailed the nostrils, mingling with the over-sweet odours of oils and unguents with which the fastidious hoped to eradicate their natural excremental stenches. In this they failed.

There was Frances, more high and mighty than ever, her eldest daughter having hopes of becoming Edward's Queen. Kat's sister, Anne Herbert seemed to be only half listening to Jane Dudley as Joan Denny took note of every little thing around her. Gossip to be spilled out later to her husband and maybe used to advantage.

Then there were the young ones. Tom Wyatt was conspiring with the Dudley boys, Robert having his arm around Tom's shoulders as they plotted an adventure, bursting into laughter at some joke. Guildford barely smiled, glancing round to see how many were admiring him. That boy was pure vanity.

Meanwhile, Tom Wyatt's interest had turned to excitement and Elizabeth noticed how like his father he was becoming. She remembered the poet with affection. He had been in love with Anne Boleyn once but had been far too prudent to stick his neck out for the headsman. She was glad he had managed to die abed. She gave a rueful smile. That in itself was an achievement in Henry's reign.

'That is a contented smile.'

Elizabeth turned, startled from her thoughts. She hadn't heard Kat approach.

'I was thinking how time is flying. Once we were like that and now a whole new generation is taking our place.'

'And more to follow,' Kat announced cryptically.

'Aye, no doubt,' Elizabeth agreed, her mind still not entirely on the present.

'And soon!'

Elizabeth heard the muted elation in Kat's voice and raised her eyebrows quizzically.

'Really? Are you sure?'

Kat nodded happily. 'Positive! Tingling. Nausea.' She squeezed her maid's hand. 'And tonight I shall tell my husband we are to be a family.'

Fate is in control of destiny, Elizabeth was convinced. She remembered the night she had made that spell so clearly. She had called upon satanic influences to guide Tom Seymour to the block. Why hadn't she left it there? Why had she gone on to condemn those as yet unborn? His children. And his children's children. The curse would only end when one of his descendents burned on the fires of Hell.

She remembered why. Will had been so worried in those weeks before his arrest. Worried in case Thomas Seymour had seduced the truth out of her. She could still see the terrible anxiety in those wood-violet eyes. But the future is always hidden. How could she have known that the baby they had laughing that day in Chester would be caught up in the intrigue of Thomas Seymour so many years later? Was there anything she could do to avert disaster?

But soon there were other, more urgent worries.

'That man is a fornicating villain. A perverted philanderer. An abomination!'

Hell take him for causing this distress! She rocked the Princess Elizabeth in her arms, letting her cry her heart out. The bodice of Elizabeth's dress was wet through from the deluge of tears to which there seemed no end.

'Hush, child,' Elizabeth comforted her, wiping the worst of the wetness from the puffy eyelids and the sticky, swollen mouth. 'It's not the end of the world, though I'm sure it feels like it at this moment. Such things are soon forgotten and no harm done.'

The eyes that looked into hers were dark-shaded violets drowning in pools of sorrow, but at long last the tears were beginning to subside as Elizabeth Tudor tried understand why the punishment was so severe. The tingling when Robert Dudley had touched her had been magnified a thousand times with Lord Thomas. He had made a habit of coming to her bed-chamber to tickle her awake, having her laughing till she cried. And then the tickles had become gentler. The kisses softer.

'She is sending me away. Furious she was. And now I shall never see him again.'

Two large tears rolled in stately procession down her cheeks to merge at the tip of the little pointed chin, remaining suspended for a brief moment, a crystal pendent vibrating to catch the light before falling to be mopped up by her already sodden gown.

'You will understand when you are older and be grateful to Mistress Seymour.'

Kat had been furious with Tom yet verbally blaming the girl for what had happened. There had been other indiscretions since the marriage but they might never have happened so far as Katherine was concerned, and even now, caught red-handed, she blamed the girl and not her husband.

Maybe the princess had flaunted herself at him after Robert's taunts, but Tom Seymour should have shown more restraint. At his age he should have been more aware of what could be construed as treason. Unless he had an eye for the future? Henry's daughter instead of his widow?

'I'll never understand.' The Princess sounded heartbroken.

Elizabeth Fytton rested her face against the Princess's hair. The child wasn't the first to be affected by Mister Seymour's charm. Given time the heart would mend, but had there been more serious damage?

'Did he love you, child? As though you were his wife?'

It would not take long to make the necessary mixture if her worst fears were confirmed. An involuntary shudder ran the full length of the girl's body as the tears began again. Silently this time.

'He tried.' She collapsed against Elizabeth's shoulder once more. 'There must be something wrong with me. He tried… but he couldn't…' Her voice trailed off.

Elizabeth sighed with relief. No harm done then.

'Hush, now. Hush. He is only a man you know. Not a god. Scarcely worth ruining you life for. He's a married man and you are a Princess of the Realm. One day you will look back and realise what a lucky escape you have had.'

How could this woman possibly know that? Then something Cat Ashley had told her made her think again.

'Weren't you once maid to…?' She didn't finish the sentence.

'Aye. Your mother. When we were all young together. It seems like a thousand years ago.'

'Did you have lovers too?'

It was obvious that the child thought her mother the guilty one, King Henry being held as blameless. How could it be otherwise? Only a fool would have spoken against the King.

'I only had one lover in all my life. He was my life, and when he was taken I stopped living for a long, long time.'

There was a lump in her throat as the princess held her gaze. She believed there was still a part of William Brereton left on earth and Thomas Seymour had nearly brought disaster on the girl. He would never change. She knew had been right to curse him and mark his throat for the blade of the axe.

'Some things are best not spoken of. I was there. I saw it all and many others about the Court saw it too.'

'What was his name? Your lover?'

'Will. William Brereton.'

The princess's eyes widened. Beheaded. Along with her mother. Was he guilty as charged?

Elizabeth said nothing. The gods had their reasons and it was not for her to question them. Elizabeth Tudor was destined to be part of some great plan. This, Elizabeth believed, and in believing would willingly lay down her life for the young princess. As Will had done.

Sixteen

WITHIN days the Princess Elizabeth had been sent off to Cheshunt in the capable hands of Joan and Antony Denny with Cat Ashley in a terrible state, blaming herself for what had happened. The fact that she had been very ill of the fever, which everyone thought might be the plague, rampant at the time, did nothing to lessen her guilt. One thing was certain. If Cat Ashley had anything to do with it, Tom Seymour would be the first and last man to ever lay a finger on her charge.

Elizabeth Fytton was not so sure. What's in the blood will out and if the girl was like her father Cat would have her work cut out. Or would she favour her mother, forever craving the arms of a first love cruelly taken from her. Would she too use all men as pawns in a game?

There was little time to reflect on these things in the upheaval of the weeks that followed. The whole household was on the move, bag and baggage to Tom's manor at Sudeley. On arrival the accommodation was found to be rather cramped, the result of the enormous number of ladies Kat had decided must accompany her for the birth of her first child. Plans for a new wing were immediately put into operation and the builders moved in.

Whether it was the noise and dust of the workmen or the discomfort of the pregnancy nothing could please Katherine. Elizabeth blamed Tom. Since his misadventure with the princess Kat had been less blind to his faults, seeing for the first time the man behind the handsome, genial exterior, the avarice behind the polished manner and the selfish ambition that lurked behind those dark seductive eyes.

Elizabeth watched sadly as Kat's disappointment grew, keeping pace with the swelling of her belly. The first flush of love was well and truly over. It was almost as if the years of anticipation had been more rewarding than the eventual fulfilment of her desires.

Tom's excuse for being away so often was the trouble he was having with his brother Edward and with his nephew the King. Elizabeth was not surprised. He was beginning to reap what he had sown. He was now rushing headlong towards his fate, and Elizabeth knew what that fate would be. The headsman waited patiently.

Sitting in the lee of the old stable wall, away from the incessant clack of women's voices, Elizabeth surveyed the landscape though half-closed eyes. Dark green summer foliage threw patches of welcome shadow across the parched meadow-lands of Gloucestershire, shimmering in the dry, motionless air. The only sounds were of insects, busy about their own business; the huge furry bee, buzzing his wings faster than the eye could see and the spasmodic chirrup of a well-concealed grasshopper not far away.

It was a day for dreaming dreams and being lazy. For remembering the long hot summers of her youth, shared with Cissy Bulkley. Poor Cissy. Mr Stumpe had sent word that Cissy had died. Suddenly. One minute she was ordering the kitchen maid about her business, and the next she had fallen in a heap on the stone floor and expired. She must send condolences, both to Mr Stumpe and to his daughter Mary at Littlecote Manor. She should pay her a visit once Kat's baby was born and see how she was enjoying married life with Jack Winchcombe. Mary was such a lovely girl. How those happy days had flown!

Her eyes had slowly closed to blot out the white glare of the sun, her head cushioned on the cool, moss-covered wall as thoughts and memories merged. The mullioned windows of Gawsworth Hall glinted in the early morning sunlight, the rooftop gilded by the dawn and dew still clinging to the cobbled yard

'Mistress.'

Elizabeth jerked awake at the sudden sound of his voice. Will? For a moment she thought she was still dreaming. But it was Thomas Seymour silhouetted against the dazzling brightness of the afternoon sky. Caught napping. What an idiot she felt. Much to her surprise he motioned her to stay where she was as he carefully pulled a piece of grass from a dry tussock beside him and placing it between his teeth began to chew. His dogs padded round them, noses to the ground and long flag tails waving as they investigated the immediate vicinity, panting heavily and slobbering over everything before flopping down close to their master.

'Not gossiping with my wife then?' His voice had that hard edge of irony which had become common of late. 'No secrets to divulge? No wish to hear the latest scandal?'

Elizabeth had already heard about the kitchen maid. It was nothing new where this man was concerned. So what was he hinting at? What trouble had he got himself into this time?

Thomas Seymour studied her expression carefully. Had she always been the spy within his walls? Would she give evidence against him? He'd given her ample cause in the past and the past was rapidly catching up with him. But would she betray him? He leaned closer, slowly removing the grass from his lips as his mouth slackened imperceptibly. Was it a trick of the light? For the merest fraction of a second he could have sworn he saw curling tongues of scarlet flame leaping and flickering in the depths of her eyes. Cold fear made is scalp prickle. He had never been made to feel so uneasy by a woman, but then the ghostly flames died, leaving her face devoid of all emotion.

Elizabeth stared, her gaze unwavering. He had every reason to be afraid of her. For the evil he had done to Will. And to the Princess Elizabeth. And to his wife, Katherine Parr. Yet he needn't fear that she would speak against him. There was no need. Sorcery was more powerful than speech and so he would be made to pay with his life. Their eyes locked in speculation as a strange foreboding overshadowed her mind. For a second, time ceased to exist. A premonition thrust itself on her and stayed. Somehow their deaths would be linked. Her curse would see an end to him, but it would continue long after he was gone, dragging her too into the next world. Heaven? Or Hell?

In the torrid heat of that August afternoon, Elizabeth Fytton suddenly knew that one day she would be destroyed in the backlash of her own powerful curse. They were firmly on the road to destruction and she pitied him. He had everything to lose. She had very little.

'Mistress?' There was something malevolent in the look she gave him.

Elizabeth gave a wry smile. 'Life, Sir, is little more than a game of chance, so I believe. For all our plots and schemes we may just as well make choice on the toss of a coin.'

'And tails I win,' he grinned, turning away. After all he was the Lord High Admiral of England, married to the King's widow and uncle to King Edward. He was entitled to wag his tail.

'Alas, Tom, heads you lose.'

He didn't hear. When the axe fell the biggest blow would be to his self esteem and for Elizabeth Fytton, her work on this earth would be over.

In addition to Tom's indiscretions and potentially dangerous feuding with his brother, the weather was unkind to Kat in her advanced pregnancy. The sultry heat of August sapped her energy and bloated her face to a parody of its previous delicate charm, her fingers so swollen that her rings were stuck fast, embedded painfully in the soft pink flesh. Aching all over she became more and more depressed with the state of her life as time dragged slowly on.

'It's no wonder Tom looks elsewhere for his comforts.' Kat's voice was bitter with disappointment. She could hardly remember those far off days when they had been lovers, when she had hung on his every word and gone weak at the sight of him. The years of longing when she had been married to the King. The patience and dedication to his cause. All for this! He couldn't even say no to a kitchen maid.

'Is she dismissed?'

Elizabeth nodded, following Kat's train of thought. It had not been the girl's fault. There wasn't a woman in the land who could refuse Thomas Seymour.

'My Lady Sussex sent her packing after boxing her ears in no uncertain manner. She was nothing more than a silly trollop who thought to make some purchase out of working in your household. I suspect it was nothing more than a figment of her imagination from start to finish.'

They both new that Elizabeth was trying to bring comfort and Kat smiled gratefully. No one could have a more loyal or truer friend.

At that moment a sharp blade of pain shot from the small of Katherine's back to the point between her legs where the child would make an entrance. Her head jerked forward in surprise as she clutched at the pain, trying to remove it as if it was a pike sticking through her guts. All other worries paled as the women rushed her to her aid and persuaded Kat to bed. Her time had come.

Katherine panted and heaved to no avail for hours, praying aloud each time the pains turned her whole body rigid with their agonising intensity. In the birthing room the fire burned high and the windows remained closed against ill-humours despite the blazing sun which shone relentlessly down outside. Sweat trickled from armpit and crotch as the women worked frantically on the rapidly weakening woman to bring a living child into the world.

It was with a huge sigh of relief that at last the infant was hauled unceremoniously into view by a triumphant midwife to give its first feeble cries. A baby girl.

'Her name is Mary,' Kat smiled at the tiny red face peeping peacefully from the swaddling. 'Mary Seymour.'

Elizabeth witnessed again the miracle of love that comes after pain. And no tears this time. Not as there would have been had Kat still been married to Henry. A daughter would have seen the end of her but the wife of the Lord High Admiral of England was quite content with a sweet baby girl.

'Isn't she beautiful?' Elizabeth smiled at her mistress.

Kat wrinkled her nose. 'She has a look of her father,' she pronounced. 'Let's hope she is more prudent in her lifestyle.'

For all that the baby looked like its out of favour father it was hugged and cuddled and crooned over as all new babies should be. To Elizabeth's delight she was put in charge of the little mite and was as happy as a pig in squalor, as the saying goes. How long was it since she had held this babe's mother in her arms in Chester? It must be all of thirty-five years yet it seemed that only last week she had been a carefree ten-year-old. But in other ways it was a life-time away, and now, strangely, she was nursemaid to Katherine's daughter. To Thomas Seymour's daughter.

'You'll never leave her?' Kat was weary after the birth, her eyelids heavy with sleep. 'Promise?'

'Oh, I promise.' Elizabeth was busy wiping the first baby dribbles from the corner of the miniature mouth. 'I'm a prisoner for life to this innocent gaoler, and happy to be so. I shall serve her until the day I die and would die for her without hesitation.'

Kat gave into exhaustion and closed her eyes knowing her daughter was in the best of hands and the contented maid took herself and her charge off to the new nursery wing where she supervised everything down to the smallest detail. The child could do nothing but thrive. Elizabeth took her responsibilities so seriously that she left the care of the mother, by and large, to the other women.

Three days after the birth Kat complained of a great thirst, but Elizabeth was not told. On the third day the fever broke so fiercely that nothing anyone could do cooled her until at last, on the fourth day of September Mistress Fytton was finally called to the sick-bed where she saw with horror the illness which held Kat in a vice-like grip, pulling her into the next world.

'Elizabeth!' Her lips were rimed with white, as though her tongue was too dry to moisten them, her voice hoarse in a throat which barely had the strength to swallow. Holding out her hand she strained to speak.

'I fear my happiness was short-lived, but at least I am to be spared the heartache of living with the dream destroyed. God in His Wisdom calls me.'

'Nay, Kat.' Elizabeth was quick, too quick with her denials. 'I'll have you well in no time.' She pulled her hand away to find a soothing draught but Katherine protested so much that she took hold of it again. The skin was dry. Arid as a desert.

'Do not deny me,' Kat smiled weakly. 'I have something for you.' She motioned Lady Sussex to approach and Elizabeth saw that she carried Kat's own bible.

'Take it,' Kat insisted.

Elizabeth hesitated. She viewed anything connected with orthodox religion with abhorrence. Old Megan had told such hair-raising tales of priests claiming the souls of children and turning them into mindless beings. The living dead! Her skin turned to gooseflesh. Someone walking on her grave.

'Take it. Please.'

Hesitantly Elizabeth held out her hand for the Holy Book. But for Kat seeming so close to death she would have refused.

'Look after my daughter for as long as she needs you and when she is old enough give her my good book. So I would have her learn of God, who I now know is merciful and wise. He sent you for a purpose. I trust you will do His will. Keep Mary in the New Faith and make her understand how much this means to her mother and father. Do this for my memory.'

'Don't think of death,' Elizabeth implored her. 'I'll bring something to cool you.'

Kat shook her head. 'Too late. You have always been there for me. Kept me safe from Henry's wrath. Warned me against marrying Tom, although to no avail. And now I beg you, do this last thing for me. Take care of my daughter as only you can. Protect her. Advise her. And love her. Love her as a mother would. Should you be in need, Lady Sussex will help you." Kat was visibly tired with the effort. "Never leave her. Tell her how I loved her, and of how I loved her father.'

'Aye.' Elizabeth was in tears. 'I shall care for her better than I would my own and love her until my last breath. Of that you can be certain.'

'God bless you, Elizabeth Fytton.'

Elizabeth shivered. She wanted no such blessing, especially from a dying woman. But the promise had been made. It would not be broken.

On the fifth day of September Katherine Seymour died, praying to her God in her mother tongue, and with a certain amount of trepidation her maid shouldered the burden she had taken on for love.

Although Lord Thomas remained at Court, embroiled in who knows what mess of intrigue, most of the ladies who had accompanied Kat to her last resting place stayed on at Sudeley. When this latest bit of bother had blown over Thomas was bound to come home and no-one wanted to miss the chance of looking the part of Mistress of the House. The exception was young Jane Grey whose prospects of becoming Queen were rapidly diminishing as the feud between Thomas and his brother went from bad to worse. Her parents judiciously removed her from the ward-ship of the Lord High Admiral.

It wasn't until after Christmas that the true picture of his downfall began to emerge. Lord Thomas was arrested and was to be brought to trial on a charge of treason. Elizabeth felt a surge of relief. She still had the power and this was the moment she had waited for. Revenge. At last.

The word came that the Princess Elizabeth had been questioned. Had anything improper occurred? All those who had been at Chelsea Palace at the time were closely interrogated. Was the princess guilty? Sir Robert Tyrwhit did his best to extract a confession from the girl in the hope of converting it into a death warrant.

At Sudeley Mistress Fytton boiled a special potage in a corner of the kitchen and after letting it go cold, skimmed the scum from the surface leaving it mirror clear and black as night. Later, at the witching hour, when all respectable citizens were fast asleep, she crept down through the silent house and surrounded her wide-rimmed chalice with burning tallow. Gazing steadily into the flickering reflections she invoked the spirits of her gods until at length the pictures she had hoped for began to form. Motionless, she sat and watched the images shimmer into life and fade again into obscurity. She began the ancient chant, sprinkling the liquid mirror with powerful herbs to protect the girl. Elizabeth Tudor. Thomas Seymour must not be allowed to destroy another generation. Elizabeth was numb with cold by the time she had finished her strange and eerie task, but she was satisfied.

Later they heard the whole story. Thomas had tried to remove the King from his brother, the Protector's, custody, the plot only being foiled when the King's dog barked a warning. Tom's enemies had him at their mercy. He had plotted to have not only the King, but all the children of Royal blood in his charge. That was the real reason Jane Grey had been hurriedly removed from Sudeley. Frances Brandon had been assured that her daughter was but a step away from the Crown and so should be at hand and ready. With his wife now dead Thomas had also sent overtures of marriage to Princess Elizabeth at Hatfield, arrogantly seeing him self as a prospective heir to the throne.

This time Tom had overstepped the mark. The Princess was more fortunate. Although Cat Ashley was imprisoned for a while nothing either she or the Princess said could be construed as the slightest bit incriminating. They could find nothing worthy of an arrest.

Elizabeth Fytton knew why. The gods had listened and the Princess had been saved. What's more, Elizabeth Tudor had learned a valuable lesson which would stand her in good stead. She had learnt not to let her heart rule her head and if for that reason alone that ruthless, ambitious reprobate had not lived in vain. And now he faced the axe. As her beloved Will had done. It was a day she had worked towards for years.

Now it would be over. Gazing out over the blustery landscape, the sleeping baby in her arms, Elizabeth wondered what the princess thought at that moment. She would never forget the man who had first aroused those adult emotions in a child's body. First love was never forgotten, no matter what the outcome. Elizabeth Tudor was clever beyond her years. She would know that his end was justified.

In her mind she heard the tree within the confines of the Tower creaking and groaning overhead as the wind howled round the ancient grey stone walls. She saw the block, and the headsman with his polished axe, the crowds come to watch shuffling their feet impatiently, heard the rattle of arms as the guard marched out. And the monotonous beat of the funeral drum.

Every detail of the scene was stamped on her memory. On that May day in '36 the weather had been warm, spectators lingering near the bloody mess, discussing the last gory moments of those brought on to provide the day's spectacle. Today, the sharp wind would have them clutching at their cloaks and scurrying back to the hearth or tavern to decide Tom's last emotions. In his stance, indifference. In his face, arrogance. In his eyes? Fear! Who did not fear death? He did not go willingly.

Mary Seymour stretched her chubby fists and yawned, completely unaware that as she slept she had become an orphan, disposed of her father's lands and wealth, all now confiscated by the Crown. Penniless. And that meant friendless. The nurse-maid's eyes focussed on the distant horizon. Trees were nothing but a blur and fields merged together in nondescript colour under the dark grey overcast sky. Forked lightning ripped like the Devil's tail through the murky atmosphere, changing dull uniformity into a stark fantasy of black and white. Lucifer banged his drums in an ear-splitting clap of thunder that shook the house to its very foundations. That noble head was finally parted from its body. How many blows had it taken? Three was usual. Sometimes five.

Mary opened her still toothless mouth and screamed. Was it just the thunder, or had she smelt a sudden stench of brimstone wafting through the rooms? Hugging the child to her breast Elizabeth began to laugh hysterically. Tom Seymour might be dead, but the last of his line would burn on the fires of Hell. The Devil's price for the death of the Lord High Admiral.

She had promised this child's mother that she would guard her with her life and that promise to a dying woman would not be broken, curse or no curse.

'What are we to do now?'

Elizabeth had no idea. All the ladies had departed, having made their several ways back to Court. No one wanted the responsibility of a child overshadowed by treason. There would be nothing gained from taking on the task of rearing the infant so it was left entirely to Elizabeth to make any plans she thought fit. Lady Sussex gave her a gift of money for the baby's welfare, hiding her guilt behind excuses of being called away suddenly. So suddenly that there was no room for the child or its nurse.

Had it not been for Elizabeth Fytton Mary Seymour would probably not have lived past infancy. Even if one of the high and mighty ladies of the Court had accepted her they would have had little reason to take particular care of her and no one would have questioned another infant death. Elizabeth had promised. She would rear her. Somehow.

And what then? Elizabeth knew how quickly fortunes could change in Court circles.

Mary was daughter of a Queen and cousin to the present King. What would happen as she grew? Who would try to use her for their advancement? Would her life be made a misery by it all? She had seen it all before. The child would be better kept from intrigue, and danger. But where could they go to be safe?

As soon as the spring storms had blown themselves out, Elizabeth slipped silently from Sudeley Manor without anyone knowing or caring, taking the seven month old baby into obscurity. The early April sun was warm as they crossed the open, chalky downs. Birds were mating and Mother Nature donned her fresh green mantle after the barren months of winter. The world had been washed clean by the rains and the weary woman took new heart as she neared the end of her journey.

Elizabeth Fytton had begun life in the warmth and prosperity of Gawsworth Hall, the impressive country home of that gentleman farmer, John Fytton, her father. William Brereton, had shown her a very different way of life at the Court of King Henry. Elegance and lavish hospitality in draughty castles and palaces befouled by households too large to be cleanly managed, yet there had been more comfort in the modest home of a merchant clothier and his wife than she ever had in the King's imposing mansions. So today she once more made her way to the door of a country house where she would be no better than a lowly servant, earning her keep as best she could. If they would have her at all.

The first sight of Littlecote Manor had Elizabeth rooted to the spot. She had never been there before, but had she dreamed about the place? The House, the gardens and the surrounding trees were all so familiar. And over to the left? She knew if she walked in that direction she would come to the slow-flowing river, and the old dry well beneath the trees. And inside the house itself?

Elizabeth shuddered in the bright spring sunlight, her eyes drawn to an upper window. Something evil lurked there. She could feel it in her bones.

It all looked so peaceful yet she had to fight the urge to run away. To escape her destiny. To escape damnation as it lay crouched, long and low, waiting to pounce.

Disturbed by Elizabeth's agitation the baby began to whimper in her arms.

'Oh, Mary. Mary! What have I brought you to? What have I done?'

Black foreboding blotted out the sun as dark shadows of the unknown future enveloped her. But there could be no turning back The circumstances of her life had brought her steadily forward to this place, in this time. Whatever her fate she must face it bravely.

Slowly, hesitantly, carrying the child she had promised Katherine Parr she would care for until death, Elizabeth Fytton mad her way round to the kitchen door and there enquired after Mistress Winchcombe.

Seventeen

ELIZABETH Fytton's arrival amongst the lower echelons of the Darrell household caused scarcely a ripple in the smooth-running management, thanks to Mistress Mary Winchcombe. She welcomed her mother's friend with open arms and at least a thousand questions.

'Where have you been since you left Malmesbury? Have you been to Court? Have you seen the young King? They say he is the prettiest boy in Christendom.'

But of course, the biggest mystery was the child.

'Whose baby is it? Why have you taken her? How old is she? What is her name?'

'I call her Kitty, but who she is and where she comes from I cannot say. She is an orphan, I promise you and the child's mother gave me charge of her before she died.'

By changing the baby's name Elizabeth covered her tracks completely. She never mentioned either Katherine Parr or Thomas Seymour to a soul and no one ever knew she had been living at Sudeley. So far as those in the world she had left knew, she and the child were as good as dead.

Her skill with both culinary and medicinal herbs made Elizabeth a welcome addition to the household and she began as she always did by re-stocking her own corner of the garden. It was not too difficult. She scoured these same areas during the time she had been a guest of Cissy and her husband, and in a few short weeks she had everything she might need at her fingertips.

Mary's son, Robert was two years older than Kitty, and her daughter Edith the same age. As they grew together, playing and occasionally quar-relling, Robert began to show a fiercely protective side to his nature where

Kitty was concerned. Mary Winchcombe nodded knowingly and made a mental note to keep a close eye on those two as they developed.

After the full-scale dramas of life amongst the aristocracy there was little to disturb the peaceful existence of Kitty's early years and Elizabeth felt so remote from the bustle and constant upheaval of the Court that she might as well have been living on the moon. Together they wandered through the pastures of Wiltshire counting the colours of butterflies and picking wildflower posies for the stone jug on the kitchen shelf. From baby to toddler to child, Kitty ran happily through the summer grasses, barefoot and unrestrained. Yet Elizabeth had not forgotten her promise to Kat and made sure the growing girl received instruction in the English Bible as her mother would have wished. Many a twilit evening would find her with Kitty on her knee, listening as she recited the lessons she had learnt.

There was, alas, a barbed and dangerous thorn amongst this bed of roses. The young master, William Darrell, could put the fear of God into anyone, and often did. Spoilt and selfish had turned to malicious and cruel as he grew from boy to man, and from venting his spleen on animals turned his temper onto peasant children and the like. His idea of fun had been to cut the legs off small birds and dance around their agonised flutterings in the yard before stamping them to death with the heel of his boot. Cat's tails were tied together so that he could watch them scratch each others eyes out. Sometimes their injuries were such that they became poisoned in the blood, dying after days of pain and misery. On one occasion Jack Winchcombe heard such a thrashing about in the pig-sty that he thought the old sow already murdered. But no. It was young Darrell up to his tricks again, grinning all over his callous face as the pig tried to escape the besom handle being thrust forcefully up its backside.

If the boy had been born evil, the man he was becoming was worse. Fortunately Elizabeth was able to deal with the injuries meted out by stick or whip but for the most part the women kept the children out of Mister Darrell's way.

Tales from the Court occasionally filtered through to this other world where Elizabeth now resided. Jane Grey had married Guildford Dudley.

Now there was a surprise. Frances Brandon had failed to see her daughter as Queen on the throne of England. Elizabeth felt sorry for the girl. Gentle Jane would never be happy with that young popinjay. Still, with Guildford's parents now styled Duke and Duchess of Northumberland and Henry and Frances Grey the new Duke and Duchess of Suffolk, it must have seemed a suitable match.

One year later there was unexpected news. Robert Winchcombe ran into the kitchen where his mother and Elizabeth were working, bursting with the tale.

'The King is dead!' he shouted. 'The King is dead!'

Elizabeth and Mary looked at each other in consternation.

'Oh, Lordy. A Papist on the throne.'

Mary had put Elizabeth's thoughts into words. The linen and thread on which she had been working fell from her hands.

'Is it true? Where did you hear it?'

'In the stable yard before the messenger went into Mister Darrell. And there is other news. Conflicting news.

The two women exchanged worried glances.

'I'll go and find the truth of it.' Mary hurried towards the door. They would have to be careful if the Princess Mary took the Crown. Her loyalty to the English prayer book was very much in doubt and it was said that her belief in the old form of religion was unshakable.

Wandering to the window Elizabeth stood looking out into the dusty heat of the cobbled yard. Kitty and Edith ran squealing past as they were chased by a grubby little urchin with a wide grin. The son of one of the farm workers amused them with a game of touch and run. Surely nothing could harm Kitty here? There was nothing to connect her with her parents, those advocates of the New Learning. Except Kat's bible. If rumour turned out to be truth then the Good Book would have to be put away out of sight. And Kitty would have to be warned.

As she watched, Elizabeth saw the girl collapse against the stone mounting-block, flushed and out of breath. She was a lovely child. Dark flashing eyes and creamy pale skin and the glossiest black hair Elizabeth had ever seen. There was no mistaking whose daughter she was. Even now, with the finely modelled features softened by puppy-fat it was his face reflecting charm, grace, wit and love of life. May the gods endow her with better judgement than her father had especially if Princess Mary, only child of Katherine of Aragon was now Queen of England.

After the years of peaceful seclusion Elizabeth realised that there could be worrying times ahead, with the country being torn apart again. In the name of God!

She turned sharply as the door was flung open. Mary rushed in all of a lather, her face red and her hands smoothing her apron repeatedly.

'They seek to lay the Crown upon Jane Grey!'

'Jane? They cannot.' Elizabeth thought of Frances Brandon and her mighty ideas. It would seem she still had plans to be mother of a Queen despite her failure to ensnare the young King Edward.

'Princess Mary won't allow that! She'll see them all dead first, and she'll find more than enough followers to champion her cause. Mark my words, Guildford Dudley will ne'er be King of England and those two will be made to suffer for their parents' vanity.'

Time proved Elizabeth right, and indeed it was no time at all, for within a fortnight news was brought that the two pretenders were safe within the confines of the Tower and Mary was Queen of England.

In the autumn she was crowned and as Elizabeth feared, the first command was for Mass to be said in churches throughout the Kingdom. Hiding Kat's bible away at the bottom of her clothes chest Mistress Fytton realised that it was time to have a talk to Kitty. Childhood would seem to be at an end. It was time for her to start growing up.

Not surprisingly Kitty became curious about the Queen and the sudden changes in her lessons. Why was it different? Why was the Pope now Head of the Church instead of the Queen? And why was it so important for Kitty to keep secretly to her own way of worship?

The girl was intelligent. There was some great mystery here and she determined to get to the bottom of it. One thing led to another and it wasn't long before she was asking about her parents. Who were they? Why had

Mistress Fytton never told her of them?

Elizabeth was able to successfully side-step the issue until the following summer when the whole population erupted in a welter of excitement. The Queen was to marry the King of Spain and the ceremony was to take place in Winchester. Everyone wanted to be there. Including Kitty.

She was a quiver of excitement and anticipation at seeing the Queen, bounding from room to room, garden to stable and back again. The Queen! The real Queen. She had to see her. Didn't Elizabeth understand?

Elizabeth did. The likeness to her father was more than skin deep. He had not been able to resist the glitter of the crown either. While Kitty lived, Tom Seymour would not be dead and Elizabeth found herself giving in to the girl's demands. They would go to Winchester for the Queen's wedding. But first, a word or two of caution.

'The trouble is…' The trouble was she had no idea where to begin. 'You see, I used to live at Court, but I would hate to be recognised by those who might remember me.'

'Why not?' Kitty was curious.

'Because some things are best forgotten. And you are one such.'

'Me? Forgotten?'

'Your mother died three days after you were born and I was entrusted to care for you. And your father died soon after.' Elizabeth paused.

'So I was made an orphan when I was a baby? But if I have been forgotten, who were my parents? I don't understand.'

It was no use. The time had come and the girl had to know. Elizabeth took a deep breath and began to tell the whole story, from the beginning. She told of how she first knew Katherine Parr as a baby, and then at Court when Kat had shared the school-room with the woman who was now Queen. Of how Katherine twice married old men and became a rich widow, and then the sixth Queen of King Henry. Of how she loved her fourth husband more than all the others put together and of the lovely baby daughter she had known for just a few short days before she died.

'She entrusted me with the care of the child and with her dying breath begged me to see that she was brought up in the New Faith and that she learned her lessons from her mother's own bible.'

By the time the tale was told Kitty had stopped fidgeting and was listening intently.

'My mother was a Queen.' The words were softly spoken. 'And my father?'

Elizabeth did not mince her words. 'Beheaded. For treason. Which is why you must remain forgotten. There are those at Court who would use you for their own purposes and most likely see an unsavoury end to you like poor Jane Grey. You disappeared, and who would have thought of looking for you in the kitchen of a modest house like this?' She frowned. 'Queen Mary's reforms will not be achieved without bloodshed and we've heard that in London the carnage has begun.'

'So we can't go to Winchester?'

It was a once in a lifetime's chance. Queen Mary would only marry the King of Spain once. What a spectacle it would be. Elizabeth felt a wave of nostalgia. How many would she recognise from the days when she was all part of that great parade? She was old now and the chances of anyone recognising her were remote and it was so long since she had been part of Thomas Seymour's household that memories of her must have faded.

Why not? The outing would do them both good.

The regular inhabitants of the City might have resented the huge number of travel-stained bodies flooding onto the streets and filling every available nook and cranny if they hadn't had the wit to use the situation to advantage. The price of bread soared and late arrivals couldn't get a place to lay their heads for love nor money. In the streets merchants smilingly invited individuals from the milling crowd into their various establishments, bowing and scraping to ingratiate themselves with those willing to be parted from their coinage. At the same time they swore and shouted at the travelling pedlars who threatened to steal their business.

It was chaotic, and Elizabeth had trouble making sure that Kitty was not completely squashed by the dense crush of people. Pickpockets were out in force too and many a cut-purse made his getaway in the colourful, noisy jumble of humanity. The warm air was thick with the smell of sweat and damp wool as a light summer drizzle first misted their clothes and then soaked them through until at last the jovial and sometimes truculent crowd, heard cheering in the distance. And music.

'She's coming! She's coming!' Kitty danced up and down, disturbing a crown of glittering raindrops on her dark hair, sending them cascading down onto her cloak.

'Keep your hood forward, Kitty,' Elizabeth warned, pulling her own half across her face. There was no need to court disaster.

The cheering grew louder, the sound of music came closer and then the City dignitaries led the procession into view. King Philip of Spain wore sombre clothing for a wedding. Cut strangely too. Foreign. Still he was a Spaniard, but a handsome one as Spaniards go. The crowds cheered him but then most of them were drunk by this time, the ale-wives having done even better trading than the merchants.

By contrast Queen Mary looked every inch the radiant bride, smiling and waving to her people, obviously proud of the husband she had managed to acquire, seeming totally unaware of the incongruous couple they made. Never having been beautiful and not tall enough to be elegant, she was now becoming positively fat. Dumpy was the word to describe her perfectly.

Despite the buffeting crowds Kitty's eyes never left the Queen. She had grown very still. The spectacle had her staring. Transfixed. Such richness! Such grandeur. Elizabeth could almost read her mind. If her parents had still been alive! If they had been willing to change their religion she, Kitty, could have been up there, riding behind the Queen. How she would have loved it. Her back became just a little bit straighter. Her head a fraction higher. And the dark, flashing eyes had a proud, almost haughty expression.

The tail end of the procession was making its way towards the arched gate in the distance when a small incident occurred which in all probability altered the course of history. As the crowd began to disperse, those in the city all wanting to leave at the same time, to Elizabeth's dismay her hood became jostled from her head. It was too much for the drunken peasant who happened to be passing. His squint eyes leering unpleasantly, he slobbered at her for a kiss. Snatching the hood back into position she turned away. Pulling Kitty through the crowds into the comparative seclusion of a niche between two buildings, she managed to avoid him. He was either too drunk or too simple-minded to follow, but Elizabeth found she wasn't the only one to be keeping herself from public view.

The tavern's custom had spilled out onto the roadway and two halberdiers were doing their best not to be noticed with flagons in their hands. Where they should have been on duty was anyone's guess but it had obviously been thirsty work so they'd risked their hides by slipping away for a drink. Or maybe two. Something had loosened their tongues, at any rate.

'It won't be long before that one follows Jane Grey,' He nodded his head sagely. 'I'd wager the wife on it.'

'Not much of a wager." His friend poked him in the ribs with his elbow, laughing, before choking on phlegm which he spat noisily against the wall. "Did you see Jane go? Wouldn't have thought you could fit so much blood into such a small person. A spurting tap, she was.'

The first man shook his head. 'Missed that one, but I'll make sure of seeing the Whore's daughter axed. Thinks to wriggle out of it nicely, she does. Denies being in with Wyatt. Does she take the Queen for a simpleton?'

Young Tom Wyatt had not had his father's good fortune to die abed, his involvement with Jane and Guildford costing him his head. Elizabeth remembered his scheming with the Dudley boys all those years ago, and now Tom and Guildford had laid their heads upon the block. Only Robert had escaped, but who knew for how long? How did any of this involve the Princess Elizabeth Tudor?

'The new law will have her done for, and not before time. She's a heretic if ever I saw one. Won't go to Mass, they say. That's where the Queen will have her.' He tapped the side of his nose. 'Mark my words.'

'Where is she now? Still in the Bell Tower?'

'Not any more.' He shook his head. 'Woodstock. Custody given to Sir Henry Bedinfeld, and him not liking it one bit, so I've heard. Frightened to death of anyone getting to her. He's a right to be scared though 'cause she'd overthrow the Queen soon as look. That's why I say it won't be long before she follows Jane Grey.'

Elizabeth had heard enough. It didn't surprise her to hear that Elizabeth Tudor had refused the Mass but she also knew that the girl was intelligent. She had to be warned. If it was simply a case of bowing one knee instead of the other to save her neck then she would be wise to swallow her prejudices and pay lip-service to her sister's religion.

There was likely more than a grain of truth in the halberdier's conversation. Those men had ears at every door. And once more the gods had smiled on her. If Henry Bedinfeld was gaoler to the princess, then Elizabeth Fytton, of all the people in the world should have at least half a chance of speaking with the prisoner.

She wondered how much he had changed. They were so long ago, those balmy summer evenings spent in each other's company in the gardens and orchards of Westhorpe and if memory wasn't playing tricks he'd taken quite a fancy to her. Then Will Brereton had turned up right out of the blue like some knight-errant, carrying her away from the Brandon household and putting an end to any notions she might have had about becoming Mistress Bedinfeld. Would Henry remember?

Queen Mary had married on the twenty-fifth day of July, 1554 but it was not until the end of August that Mistress Fytton stood at the gates of Woodstock Park, wondering at the reception she would be given. Would her powers of persuasion and the fading memory of a youthful flirtation be enough to gain her admittance?

Unknown to Elizabeth, fear and seclusion had been weighing heavily on the Princess as the summer dragged silently on. She seemed to have been a prisoner since early adolescence. Since the day Queen Katherine had packed her off with Sir Antony Denny and his wife Joan. Now, Queen Mary, her sister, refused to have any communication with her and God only knew what lies and rumours were being whispered. If only that fool Bedinfeld would allow her to write to the Council, but he was carrying his orders to the letter. Frightened of his own shadow in case it carried messages from her to the outside world.

As she walked in the orchard, unaware that at that moment her mother's trusty maid was completing the last few miles of her long journey, the Princess Elizabeth heard the happy sound of a milkmaid as she went about her work.

"Would that I could exchange my weary life for hers. At least she gets to walk in the park whilst I am confined to the gardens."

The strain of not knowing what the future held or how long that future might be was telling on her nerves and later that afternoon the sight of Henry Bedinfeld unlocking and locking the garden gates behind her as she went became too much.

'What? Am I likely to charge you and make good my escape when men guard every exit? Do I look to be an idiot? If my mind is so deranged should I not be locked in an empty room and fed gruel until I am sane? Should not the Devil be beaten out of me? See how the gaoler keeps the mad woman caged? With all his keys and spies, even if I were sane when we first met I should be mad by the time we parted. I can only leave my cause to God, and whatever you, or anyone, may do to me, I shall remain the Queen's true subject.'

Henry Bedinfeld was shaken by the passion with which the words were spoken. The truth was that he admired the young woman and was always conscious of his lowly status in comparison to hers, the daughter of King Henry. He'd tried to grant as many requests as he could without stepping outside the rules laid down for him to follow. And now this outburst!

'Madam, I am your officer, not your gaoler and have been appointed to take care of you. Her Majesty has commissioned me to watch over you and protect you from injury. I swear my only fear is for your safety.'

He knew how precarious the Princess's position was, but he also knew how easy it was for ordinary mortals to fall foul of Royalty. He had no wish to incur the Queen's anger, but who knew what tomorrow would bring? King Edward had produced no heir. Would Mary? If she didn't then who would wear the crown? Mister Bedinfeld wished to keep the Princess Elizabeth sweet.

His chance was not long in coming. Elizabeth Fytton's nervousness was well under control as she waited for the interview with the man she had last seen as a gallant, handsome youth.

She would have known him anywhere. The hair was slightly grizzled and the beard tougher than she remembered, but his amber eyes were still curiously flecked with gold. Pure gold which caught the light like tiny gilded threads reflecting sun. And his lips. She well remembered the warmth of that kiss!

Henry rose as she entered and she noticed that although his figure had thickened a little with age his leg was still as shapely as ever.

'Mistress? I was told that your business was of a private nature?'

It was only as she silently glided towards him without appearing to have any means of propulsion that a fragment of some long-dead past rose up to meet him. Those eyes. Where had he encountered them? Norfolk? That was it. Westhorpe. She had held a strange fascination for him. She had been so desirable. Full-bosomed. Wet-lipped. Inviting. And then? Ah, yes! William Brereton had claimed her as though he had every right to her. Well maybe he had. But what could she want now, a lifetime later?

Such a small favour. Elizabeth had happened to be passing on the road and had heard the Princess Elizabeth was residing here. Hadn't she known the girl since the day she was born? Hadn't she been for years at the Court, even putting healing poultices on the King's leg, so much in favour had she been. Would it be possible for her to have a word with the Princess? It seemed such a shame to pass so close without calling to pay her respects.

Henry pondered the problem for a moment. He wasn't going to lose his head through any woman's wiles. Elizabeth saw the doubt on his face.

'You may search me yourself.' She smiled invitingly. 'I carry no documents or weapons but you are welcome to be sure.'

He remembered the feline grace of the young Mistress Fytton. There were still some remnants of it left. Search her? He was sure there was no real need. But it was best to be certain.

The search was thorough and Henry found himself rising to the occasion almost instantly. The bosom was still as handsome and the lips still wet and warm. And he knew the Princess would enjoy a short talk with an old friend. After yesterday's confrontation it would do no harm to show a little leniency. Elizabeth Tudor might one day be in position to remember such things.

'You have no thoughts of treason? No messages giving her hope of escape?'

'On my word of honour. Nothing is further from my mind. Indeed, I would only try to persuade the princess to make her peace with her sister in any way she can. And why would I want to make trouble for a man I once had thoughts of marrying? I have thought of you with affection often, truly I have, and wouldn't want to sully so precious a memory. Not for anything.'

So Henry Bedinfeld made a sort of uneasy peace with his prisoner and Elizabeth Fytton was able to tell her of the rumours that were rife amongst the Queen's men-at-arms.

'It is such a little sacrifice. We all have to make them from time to time.' Elizabeth was thinking of the entry fee she had just paid. 'Attend the Mass and think your own thoughts. Who will know the difference? No one. Certainly not the Queen. A small price for freedom, eh? And if those two topers at the Winchester ale-house are to be believed, what price a life?'

To Elizabeth Fytton the life of Elizabeth Tudor was more precious even than salvation. She had witnessed men die for their faith and nothing could convince her that it was anything but a complete waste. She thought of Thomas More. Venerable. Kind. And as stubborn in his beliefs as a man could be. His head had rotted slowly in the summer heat, displayed for everyone to see. Who would Mary make martyrs?

The following February the burning of heretics began in earnest. As the Queen's confidence increased with her pregnancy, so the smell of burning flesh hung ever more thickly over England. No one was immune. The young, the old, the blind and the lame, men and women both. One, an expectant mother herself. If heresy could be half-way proved, the victim could hold out no hope.

Though frustrated and angry the people held their tongues through fear and Queen Mary was quite unaware, carried away by religious fervour as she was that she was rapidly losing the respect of her subjects. All the hurts and injustices brought to bear on her mother by King Henry were now being paid by fire. Sin expiated by fire. Souls cleansed by fire. Famous and infamous suffered unimaginable pain and a hellish death. Hooper, Latimer, Ridley, Cranmer, and a host of lesser names not noted and never heard of since.

They never did find out who warned the Princess before the trickle became an onslaught. They only knew that in the month of September she began to take Communion according to the rite of the Holy Roman Church, and Stephen Gardiner, the Queen's Lord Chancellor, found that all his plots and schemes to have her removed from this earth had been thwarted. As her sister's religious fury was given full vent, encouraged by the discovery that hopes of a pregnancy were unfounded, Elizabeth Tudor thanked God she still had friends.

Elizabeth Fytton gave thanks too. For the halberdier's loose talk. For putting Henry Bedinfeld as gaoler. For everything.

The only worry now was Kitty. Would she, well versed in the New Learning, be caught up in this sacrificial net? William Brereton's death would not be avenged until? What were the words? Until the last of Tom Seymour's line had burned alive. Licked clean by the fires of Hell. But that must not happen. She had kept the Princess Elizabeth safe, and she would do the same for Kitty. She had promised Kat, but despite the comfort of their anonymity, she trembled as she rode out the storm in the backwater of Littlecote Manor.

With the encroachment of old age both mind and body had become less agile, so a few daily drops of her comfort sometimes brought her almost to a standstill. She would have her work cut out to look after the vivacious young woman Kitty had developed into. That girl was her father's daughter and no mistake. Coils of shining black hair hung heavily on her shoulders and long silky lashes framed the most fascinating eyes Elizabeth had seen for many a year. Creamy white skin begged to be caressed and a petty pouting mouth unconsciously invited kisses.

260

Mary Winchcome had warned Robert to be careful. That girl was as much a mystery as ever but Mary knew she was not simply some low-born orphan and she knew it was none of her business. Except when it came to her son. And Robert was in love with Mistress Fyttons charge. Still, she could thank her lucky stars that they were well away from London out of sight and sound of the martyrs' screams and when Elizabeth muttered in that strange tongue under her breath, Mary turned a deaf ear. If she ignored it, that side of the old woman would go away. She was worse when she had been at her drop of comfort, chanting in that lilting sing-song voice to send shivers down Mary's spine. It was eerie. Ghostly. Like a song of death.

Mary was not far from the truth. Had she understood those tattered remnants of the old Welsh woman's teachings she might not have been surprised when the news eventually came.

The November fog had been thick over the River Kennet for three days and, unknown to the inhabitants of Littlecote, covered half the country as well. The message was therefore slow in arriving and the messenger tired and bedraggled after being lost on the way, But it was true. Queen Mary was dead. Katherine and Thomas Seymour's daughter was safe.

Eighteen

IN HER worry over Kitty's eminent suitability to be branded heretic Elizabeth had pushed the thought of the succession to the back of her mind. Only when the local populace began composing songs to the glory of Queen Elizabeth did she face up to the fact. Anne Boleyn's daughter was the rightful Queen of England. How many strange twists of fate had combined to bring that golden-haired child to the throne? Even her birth had been something of a miracle. Desperation on the part of her mother and an inability to say no to any woman on the part of her father. And who could have predicted that both Edward and Mary would die without issue, leaving a vacancy only Anne's daughter could fill?

Will's fair colouring had been only a shade darker than the King's, and his flamboyance, talent and rhetoric raised him to greater heights of wealth and power than Elizabeth would have thought possible. Elizabeth Tudor had those same violet eyes. And only Elizabeth Fytton guessed at the truth. She knew beyond a shadow of a doubt that the new Queen had not a single drop of royal blood in her veins. But who was she to question when the gods had willed it?

Kitty too had high ideas. Since finding out about her parentage she had decided that the daughter of a Queen should not spend her life in the kitchens of some rustic manor far away from the glamour and wealth of the Court. She should be eating off polished oak, not scrubbed white board. Sitting in the solar, not the kitchen with the maids. She should be waited on and admired. What right had they to keep her away? She was in no danger now that Queen Mary was dead. Mistress Fytton was often drifting away in some dream world of her own these days anyway. She could not make decisions any more.

Elizabeth was not as blind as Kitty imagined. What plot was the girl hatching? How did she hope to change her life? Robert Winchcombe hung around her like a love-sick calf whenever he had the chance, but would he help her in some foolhardy plan? No. His mother had warned him often enough.

Kitty knew he would. She twitched her hips at him. Fluttered her eyelids at him. And one quiet sultry afternoon let him find her alone in the stables.

He couldn't believe his luck. She returned his kisses. Encouraged his caresses. And it seemed that all his dreams had come true.

'Wait.' Kitty fondled the hair at the nape of his neck. 'Do you love me?'

'You know I do.' Robert's heart pounded and his head swam with overpowering lust. 'I want you.'

'And I want you.' Kitty sighed. 'Truly.'

'But?' He could feel it coming. What was going to be the problem?

'I cannot stay here. I have to go.'

'Where?' Robert frowned. Why would she want to leave the place she had grown up in? Where they had work and a roof over their heads? William Darrell was not the nicest of men, but if you kept out of his way and did all that was expected of you, you were fed and watered without question.

'To Queen Elizabeth's Court.'

'You're mad. We know no one at Court. We would be left to starve. I doubt we could live by our wits.'

'I shall know those at Court. I was not born to be a kitchen maid. I was born of higher parentage than you could ever imagine and when the courtiers realise they will all want to be my protector. You'll see. But I can't do it on my own. If we take one of the horses and ride away without being caught I promise you your life will be one of luxury.'

'Have you really lost your senses? Who gave you this idea that you belong at Court? It's a madness. And as for stealing one of Darrell's horses! We'd be hung. Or worse.'

'Then we shan't get caught. When Mister Darrel finds out who he has been sheltering he will no doubt be more than pleased.' Kitty was all eagerness, clinging on to him. She kissed him again. 'Just for me. We shall be together and your mother won't be able to keep us apart.'

'How can we steal a horse?' Robert was perplexed.

'Dead of night, and away before anyone knows. A whole new world awaits us, I promise. And when we are taken into the Queen's household we shall send the horse back.'

'Oh, will you now?' William Darrell stood, feet apart, riding crop in his right hand slapping the palm of his left. 'Ungrateful bitch.'

The riding crop struck her across the face to leave a deep welt on her cheek. Kitty yelled and turned away but not quickly enough. The second blow hit her across the shoulders despite Robert trying to shield her.

'And as for you!' Darrell turned on the youth. Grabbing him by the collar he dragged him out into the stable yard and laid into him without mercy. Robert was beaten to within an inch of his life and there was nothing Kitty or anyone else could do to save him.

At length it was over and Mistress Fytton and Mary Winchcombe were left to pick up the pieces.

'What possessed you?' Elizabeth treated the wounds with salve.

Kitty raised her grimy tearstained face, her dark, flashing eyes sparking hate. 'I hate this place. And I hate you!'

'And you?' Mary asked her son, washing the blood from his skin.

He winced. 'Ask Kitty. High ideas about running away to Court. Reckons she belongs there and wanted me to borrow one of Darrell's horses to get us there.'

'Then you deserve a whipping, my lad. What on earth possessed the pair of you?'

Elizabeth kept her mouth shut. She knew. And she also knew that Kitty could no longer stay at Littlecote. It was time to move on. But where to?

'You'll have to leave,' Mary told Robert. 'You can't stay here or your mother and father will be forced out too. My God. What a mess.'

'Don't worry, I'll go,' Robert told her. 'I shall go to sea. Plymouth. There are ships there waiting to travel the world in search of bounty.'

'Pirates?' His mother was shocked.

'A life on the ocean, wherever that leads. It has to be better than this.'

He glanced at Kitty. All hopes of her had been well and truly shattered, so he was prepared to leave this life behind for ever.

Life changed for Kitty too. The child of Queen Katherine and the one time Lord High Admiral of England had burned her boats and Elizabeth had to think long and hard. The girl could not be trusted to hold her tongue and she would make a very sad end if she did not. What could be done?

The only safe thing to do was to hide her in full view. At the Court of Queen Elizabeth. There she would have to toe the line, keep her own council and do the Queen's bidding. So far as the old woman could see, it was the only way. She was now too old to keep such a lively young woman in check. Others would do the job much better and if the Queen knew the girl's birthright she might be grateful to have her where she could keep an eye on her. She must remember how good Kat was to her when she was young and foolish. She would see Kat's daughter right, Elizabeth was sure.

***

Greenwich Palace was as much of a maze as it had been forty-two years previously when a green-eyed wraith of a girl, somewhat rustic in appearance and with a broad Cheshire accent had stood there for the first time apprehensively waiting for her lover. She had travelled a long way since those days. No longer overawed by the fine ladies of the Court. No longer nervous of doing or saying the wrong thing. She had long ago learnt to keep her mouth shut. In King Henry's day it had been the only way to stay healthy, and probably still was. She had warned Kitty over and over again but whether the message had gone home to the girl she had no way of knowing.

Kitty was entranced, glancing covertly at the men and women passing through the corridors and chambers of the Palace. In the crowded passages where they waited, organised chaos reigned, as it always had done. People came and went, or lounged about waiting to be called. It was all so familiar. Even some of the faces were familiar to Elizabeth. Young courtiers milled around creating a hotchpotch of scent and colour as they stood first with one and then another, listening to the latest gossip, subtly embellishing it before passing it on. So rumours started and plots thickened. The Court thrived on it. Had she done the right thing bringing Kitty into it? What else could she have done? It was the lesser evil.

As first one courtier bowed a greeting and another lady nodded as she passed, Kitty began to appreciate that the woman who had taken care of her from birth had once been part and parcel of this fascinating display of wealth and colour. But surely Mistress Fytton could have kept her here rather than hide her away in Wiltshire. Still, she was here now and that was what mattered.

Just then they were swooped upon by an excitable young woman who squealed with delight as she kissed Elizabeth, trying to hold her hands and hug her at the same time. Elizabeth laughed at Meg Clifford's enthusiasm, and holding her at arms length studied the fashionable figure critically. Then she nodded.

'You'll do," Elizabeth pronounced "You should make old bones and keep the Devil waiting.'

'Aye, Mistress,' Meg grinned at her. 'I've remembered everything you taught me, and practised hard those things you said would need more concentration. Some curses…' she hesitated over the word, 'Take a long time to work.'

The look that passed between the two women set Kitty's teeth on edge. Although Kitty had been forced to learn her scriptures and attend church she knew that Elizabeth avoided both like the plague. Once she had seen the old woman with a bowl and tallows, her hair bedraggled in the pungent steam, chanting on and on in a low monotonous tone. The room had been full of shadows, every one a ghost or spectre, a spirit of the dead. The only thing she had seen with any clarity had been Elizabeth's eyes. Glittering green, illuminated in the wavering tallow-light. Witches eyes.

Meg glanced down at the girl and winked. 'Take no notice of us, Deary. Mistress Fytton was my teacher, but sadly we parted before my education was complete, and I still have much to learn. Who is she?' she asked Elizabeth. 'Very pretty. Tell her to be wary They'll be like flies round a honey pot.'

'This is my ward, Mary. Mary, this is a dear friend of mine, Margaret Clifford, grand-daughter of King Henry's sister.'

The two bowed formally to each other, Kitty assessing the fact that here was someone else related to Royalty.

'Lady Strange, actually. I am married.' She smiled at Kitty from her position of five years seniority. 'It's difficult coming to Court for the first time and I've seen many a young girl get herself in trouble. Be wary of Her Majesty. She has strict rules for her ladies. Of all ages. But don't worry. I'll look after you until you find your feet and if you have the wit you'll find it an interesting life at Court.' And with a reassuring wave Lady Strange went on her way.

The young Queen was an awesome sight. Slim as a lath, she had the same rather boyish figure that had been the despair of her mother Anne. But the poise! The assurance! And the rich trappings of her exalted position which she wore with enviable ease and grace. Elizabeth Tudor was every inch a Queen, and one to be respected.

All this Elizabeth saw at a glance before falling in a deep curtsey before the woman she had last seen as an angry and frustrated prisoner of Henry Bedinfeld. Queen Elizabeth might have the slight figure of Anne Boleyn but her colouring, and most of all her eyes brought precious memories of the long-dead past rushing helter-skelter into her mind. From that handsome inventive youth so full of wit and charm had grown a shrewd financier. William Brereton had become a hard-headed, ambitious politician prepared to go to extremes to achieve his purpose. As had the woman now on England's throne.

Mary Seymour couldn't help staring. The Queen seemed to shimmer from head to foot in jewels and pearls. In her hair. On her hands. And rounds her delicate white throat. A dress latticed with golden thread and trimmed with silver lace gave an impression of frosting over deep carmine silk. And just to think! Her mother had been Queen. Had she looked like this? And wealthy? Mistress Fytton had said her mother had been wealthy. Had her father not met such a violent end, would she, Mary Seymour, now have jewels, gowns and palaces to rival the Queen? Oh, if only things could have been different.

When Mary was at last able to tear her eyes from the splendour of the Queen she noticed that across the room, others were present. A man and woman stood a little distance away, talking quietly. He was tall. Dark. With black flashing eyes, like a gypsy. This was no boy like Robert Winchcombe. This was the courtier she had imagined in her dreams. A man of status. A man of means. And the most handsome she had ever seen in her life.

Somehow an awareness that the conversation between the Queen and Mistress Fytton had ceased roused her from her mesmerised state as she realised she was now the centre of attention.

'Come here, child. Let me look at you.'

It was a royal command. Queen Elizabeth's white, tapered fingers lifted Mary's dimpled chin for a closer examination. The pressure of those fingers turned her head from left to right as first the eyes, then nose, then mouth and creamy complexion came under scrutiny. At length she was released and the royal finger beckoned the handsome man's companion.

Elizabeth recognised Mary Dudley immediately. Even as a child she had been a friend of the woman who was now Queen. Now married and so named Mary Sidney she had been deep in conversation with her brother. Robert Dudley.

Now there was one who had fulfilled his youthful promise. Strikingly handsome, his dress immaculate without being too precise he had the casual elegance of a courtier born. As his sister departed from the chamber with a pale, nervous-looking Mary Seymour in tow he approached his monarch with a confident spring in his step and a smile that indicated a degree of intimacy.

They were close, that was obvious, but there could be nothing more. After all, Robert Dudley was a married man and had been for a number of years and the Queen would not be so foolish as to set her sights at a courtier. When she married it would be for political reasons. A foreign king, no doubt.

'See that we are not disturbed, Robin.'

She did not command. She merely asked, as of a friend and with a bow

Robert acknowledged her request, kissing her hand. Did the kiss linger a little too long? Was that smile just a little too private? Plots and schemes and manipulations. Without them the Court would not survive and it would be a very dull place indeed.

As soon as they were alone it became obvious that Elizabeth Tudor intended putting some very searching questions to Mistress Fytton. Her loyalty to the Crown had been demonstrated on more than one occasion. She had been maid to Queen Elizabeth's mother, and to Queen Katherine, King Henry's sixth wife. And in that awful affair of Thomas Seymour when she almost met her downfall it had been this woman who had wiped away the tears and promised that all would be well. And again at Woodstock. She wouldn't have travelled to the Court in her old age without good reason. Who was this dark haired child? She had a look of someone. But who?

'It seems, Mistress that you are adept at keeping secrets, and I suspect this pretty child is one of them. Queen Katherine's baby daughter conveniently disappeared after her father's execution. Am I right?'

Elizabeth nodded. 'At the time no one had the slightest interest in a disinherited orphan, but I knew from experience how times change so I removed her from the clutches of unscrupulous men. She's been raised, secluded in the countryside where she could have a carefree childhood where no one knew her, or even cared.'

'And now?'

'During your sister's reign it became necessary to tell the child of her parentage so that she understood why she should keep to her own way of worship. It was a promise I made to her dying mother. But I am getting old and she is growing into a young woman thinking herself too important to remain in the kitchen at Littlecote. She needs someone of greater authority to keep her ambitions in check. I've done my best but the task has become too arduous for my old bones. My best hope was to see her under your jurisdiction where her fanciful ideas can be nipped in the bud.'

The Queen listened thoughtfully. This woman was right. It wouldn't do to have the daughter of Queen Katherine and Thomas Seymour running loose around the Kingdom. Better here, in full view and kept in line.

'You are certain no on has any idea who she is? Absolutely certain?' Elizabeth Fytton nodded. 'Only the girl herself.'

'Then she cannot be named Seymour. She can take your name and no one be any the wiser as you have been away for so long. Mary. Mary Fytton. You never married?'

'No. I was not so fortunate. The man I loved married another.'

'Ah, not the first to do that I fear.'

Was there some hidden meaning there? Robert Dudley, married to Amy Robsart? Elizabeth wished she could read the Queen's mind. She would have been astounded if she could have.

Leaning back, the Queen closed her eyes at the memory. She had been a child when he had first touched her before apologising for his indiscretion. But now, in adulthood his touch burned like fire and so she had allowed him more liberties than perhaps she should have. But his hand on hers had not been enough. She wanted him to touch her face, her neck, her shoulders. She wanted him to touch her everywhere. She revived the memory of the evenings they had spent together, sometimes half the night as well, permitting him to go a little further. And a little further.

Shivers of excitement had radiated through her body from the deep and secret centre of her slim belly. Her room had been warm and safe. A haven from the stresses and strains of learning to govern her country, and yet even then she had still been Queen.

Every part of her had screamed out for him to possess her, right until the very moment she had felt him poised above her, taut-muscled.

No! She couldn't.

Robert's urges could not so easily be kept in check and she heard him gasp, as with relief, and felt him tremble like a child in her arms as his seed gushed warm and sticky across her virgin flesh. Then she had cried. Here was proof that Robert loved her for herself. To him, she was a woman, not a Queen. Emotion like that could not be turned on to order.

As the tremors subsided and died, the man lay tired and spent, his dark head cradled on her shoulder, Elizabeth Tudor had felt an exhilarating surge of power at his obvious vulnerability. His weakness made her strong and for the first time the Queen realised what weapons she possessed in her ability to attract and her inclination to deny. The warm glow of pleasure she felt then was far greater than the fleeting satisfaction that had been Robert's. She had known in that moment that she wanted to be loved for the rest of her life. Loved, but never owned.

'Who was he? The man you loved?' The Queen was curious about this woman who had been about the Court since before her mother, Anne Boleyn had been Queen.

'William Brereton. He was the seventh of his father's children, yet he became the richest. By virtue of his brains and wit he pulled himself up out of nowhere to become a man of wealth and power, envied by many who had begun in better circumstances. On his death it all became the property of the Crown, and so now belongs to you.'

William Brereton had been loved, it was obvious. He had been the centre of this woman's world until his death. Had he been Anne Boleyn's lover? Queen Elizabeth had tried to dismiss the rumours of her mother's wanton ways, but did this woman know the truth? She absently twisted a red-gold curl around her finger.

'Brereton was a clever man to get so far,' the Queen observed. She gave Mistress Fytton a quizzical look. 'What manner of woman am I?'

'Clever, like him, but born to be Queen.' She seemed to stumble over the words and her voice sank to an almost inaudible whisper. 'The gods have blessed you with the power and strength…'

Her eyes had become glazed as she swayed to and fro, the words she spoke describing the pictures in her head in a strangely lilting chant mingling foreign words with those of English. It sounded almost like Welsh to the Queen's practised ear.

'Peace and prosperity such as this land has never known, nay, the world has never known. It was ordained. You were born to be Queen and no one can gainsay the gods in this matter. And no man shall better you.' Her voice rose as she looked her Monarch in the eye. 'No man shall ever be your equal.'

There was compulsion in her words. Compulsion which forced belief.

Even Doctor Dee had not this confidence when he read her horoscope. Some people truly had the Sight and the Queen was forced to believe that this old woman was one of them. Ordained? Yes. The way had miraculously been cleared of all obstacles to bring her before the High Altar and anointed Queen of England in God's presence. God's presence? Or the old gods, speaking through the voice of her mother's maid in the language of the Tudors themselves?

Responsibility of government and commitment to her office, the weight of which she had scarcely felt until that moment, settled like a cloak around her shoulders. As the years passed she knew it would become heavy and burdensome, but she also knew that she would never be able to shrug it off. By whatever mortal means she had been created, the truth would remain with the decaying bodies of Anne Boleyn, William Brereton, King Henry and Fate. Or God., Call it what you will.

As Elizabeth Fytton slowly regained control of her faculties she realised that her audience was over and that she was at liberty to go. She made to curtsey to the Queen but the young woman was having none of it. Taking both her hands the Queen raised her to her feet and Elizabeth looked for the last time into those violet eyes. How she wanted to fling her arms around this lovely girl, this Queen, who should have been her own daughter. In another world. In another time. Where today was fulfilment and tomorrow full of hope.

'Your Majesty,' Elizabeth hesitated before removing her hands from those of the young Queen. 'May I?' Holding up her left hand she slowly removed the emerald ring that had been on her finger since that heavenly day long ago.

'Would your Majesty accept this as a token of my loyalty and love. I wore it in your mother's service and as I have no children I should like to give it into your safe keeping.'

The Queen took the ring in silence and slipped it onto her finger. They both knew that they would never meet again. It was their last goodbye.

The hands holding Elizabeth's were the last touch of his beloved flesh. Such thoughts were treason and she really was too old to stay in such a dangerous place where her tongue might run away with her. It was a mercy she had a safe refuge to return to and a special brew to comfort her in whatever time she had left on this earth, but to know that William's ring was now in the Queen's possession meant more than anything. It was the end of an era and time for her to leave.

Later she took leave of Kitty, now introduced to the Court as Mary Fytton. She had done her best for the child and now it was up to Mary herself. In having saved her from martyrdom in Queen Mary's reign Elizabeth felt she had achieved the impossible and beaten the Devil at his own game. No fires of Hell for Mary and the Queen would see that the Seymour line died out with the girl. But Mary now lived in a position in keeping with her birthright and Katherine Parr could rest easy in her grave.

Elizabeth Fytton bade farewell to the rooms and corridors which had once been her home. Goodbye to feasts and festivals and the hearty laughter of Londoners frothing from the taverns with the sharp smell of their ales, Goodbye to friends and enemies alike but most of all, goodbye to the cutthroat community which called itself the Court.

Elizabeth Fytton was returning to the country and the company of Mary Winchcombe to die. In peace.

Nineteen

DESPITE Elizabeth's wish for nothing more than a peaceful end she found that the Court had not finished with her yet. True to her word, Meg Clifford wasted no time in paying her a visit, and Mary Winchcombe was only too pleased to leave them well alone as they huddled together, whispering in corners, tasting and testing.

They made an incongruous couple, Lady Strange still young and with an unmistakable look of the Tudors about her, and Mistress Fytton, old and wrinkled in a patched gown that had seen better days. With her reputation for necromancy most people were inclined to avoid her, not wishing her to give them the evil eye, causing their cows to die in the night without cause, or the swine to give out dead litters. Or even their babies flux themselves into an early grave. Leave well alone. Leave Mistress Fytton to her own devices.

Meg Clifford's visit was not one of idle curiosity. As she explained, there was a good lady, known to her for many years, who was in sore need of assistance.

'I've known her since we were children but for some time her husband has used her with indifference and has moved her from one relative to another, providing her with no home of her own. She has no children, and is unlikely to have any now.'

'Because her husband has left her?'

Meg sighed. 'I fear so. She has it in her head that her husband is unfaithful, and with good reason. She waits in dread that he will divorce her and I swear this worry has made her ill. She is in constant pain and sometimes prays to God that she will be released from her torment, hoping that perhaps he'll return and love her as he used to.'

'So she needs two separate tinctures. One for bodily pain and one for heart-ache.' Elizabeth nodded sagely.

'I can take stuff to comfort her on my next journey as I fear the news of her husband's affair isn't good. Your former ward will accompany me. We have become good friends these past months.'

Elizabeth was delighted to hear news that Kitty had settled well into the Court's ways and was staying out of trouble.

'She, like half the Court, is totally enamoured of Lord Robert, the Queen's favourite, but she'll have to watch her step with that one or she'll have the Queen to deal with, and that does not bear thinking of.' As his wife knows to her cost, she thought silently to herself.

Elizabeth prepared the evil-smelling oil from the twisted brown root and sealed in well inside a small stone bottle. It would induce sound sleep within a few minutes of being swallowed. Finally she made a love potion, a tisane of certain sweet flowers with purslane to prevent another woman from binding the erring husband.

Lady Strange left Littlecote Manor satisfied that her friend's pains would soon be healed and Elizabeth Fytton settled back into the normal routine of sipping her comfort and reminiscing about the past, with Will and Cissy and her brother Edward. Mother with Mister Christopher, and the things some people got up to in King Henry's Court.

'I remember the day…'

So all her stories started and she told them with such conviction that they had to be believed as she carved herself a cosy niche in the Darrell household, chewing on a crispy onion, or a button of wild garlic if it was Saturday. Always chew garlic on Saturday night! That was her maxim, though no on was able to make head nor tail of the strange habit, Still, it did no harm except make friends something of a rarity on Sundays.

By the time Lady Strange and Mary, the newest of the Queen's ladies, set out for the borders of Berkshire and Oxfordshire bearing gifts of comfort to Cumnor Place, there were rumours flying that had the most hardened gossips gaping. All talk of Lord Robert divorcing had subsided and it had been whispered that the lady would soon be dead in any case.

To substantiate the tale, servants of the Court were crossing their hearts

275

and swearing it was true. Hadn't Anne Dowe of Brentwood heard it with her own ears? Why should she lie? Every servant in the country knew of it, so how could their masters deny it? They nodded knowingly. The Queen was with child!

Dawn on that misty morning found Meg and Mary rising unhurriedly from their slumber to prepare for church, hearing as they did so the other occupants of the guest house on Thames Street begin to stir. Outside, the sleepy town of Abingdon yawned at the sound of the bell and turned over for another five minutes doze. It was Sunday. A day of rest. The two women quietly attended the service at the old church of St Helen, a mere stones-throw from the river, afterwards waiting on the travellers' bench adjoining the alms houses.

The primrose sun, blurred by an early autumn haze had little warmth at that time of day but the sight of a young boy galloping towards them flushed and out of breath, soon had Meg on her feet and smiling. He'd been quick this time, making certain of his reward. All was well. That was the message. The lady would be alone when they arrived.

It was all Meg needed to know. They didn't want it to be known that they might be spying on the lady's husband and when Meg and Mary arrived at the house it was deserted except for Amy, long-suffering wife of Lord Robert Dudley. She had insisted that the servants took a well-deserved holiday, turning them out to visit the fair in town, making sure no-one would hear of her visitors from Court.

Was there any news yet of the divorce? Why were her servants whispering in corners but keeping her behind a wall of silence? It had been so long since she had seen him. Was he well? How did he look?

Meg decided it would be cruel to repeat the ugly rumour that the Queen expected Lord Robert's child. Especially if it turned out to be completely unfounded. Who knew what such news would do to Amy in her delicate state of health.

Mary watched Robert Dudley's pathetic wife. What could he ever have seen in her? She could never have been anything but insignificant. No wonder he had put her out of his bed.

The young girl surveyed the sparsely furnished accommodation and compared it to the luxury in which Lord Robert lived. And all his wife could do was moan to Lady Strange. No matter how she tried, Mary could not visualise this woman being cherished in his heart and mind. Or his arms. She must be a thorn in his side. If only it could be painlessly removed! How relieved he would be. How grateful. The wonder was he hadn't rid himself of her before this.

But of course he would have to be cautious, not wanting to be seen having any connections with Cumnor Place as his wife declined in health. But if someone else were to give the situation a little help. Someone unconnected with either Lord Robert or his wife...

Meg was explaining the doses needed and the results to be expected from the various herbal remedies she had taken such trouble to acquire.

'Take care with the sleeping draught for fear it does more harm than good.'

Amy sniffed the vial cautiously, wrinkling her nose as she replaced the stopper.

'Are you sure it isn't poison?'

'Certain. The old woman who made it takes it herself. Tell her, Mary. Tell her how skilled your old nurse is these matters.'

Mary nodded her head vigorously, telling the tale she had heard so often of how Mistress Fytton had healed King Henry's leg and how she had been so much in demand at the sick-beds of the Court.

Amy had heard of the woman but had never met her. She cried softly, explaining that she was so frightened these days. If only he would send her word. She never heard from him.

Mary watched the performance without pity. The woman was obviously sick in mind as well as body. The trouble was, she could linger on for years. The thought horrified the girl.

'Thank you for coming so far. I shall be a deal happier for your help. In fact I shall prepare my first comfort the minute you have left.'

They were no more than five minutes walk from the house when Mary discovered that she had left a glove behind.

'Oh, and they are new. Walk on slowly whilst I run to fetch it. I shall be back before you know it.'

The house was silent as the grave. Nothing stirred amongst the lengthening shadows of the hallway as Thomas Seymour's daughter slipped into the gloomy wing of what had once been a monastery building. Somewhere on the upper floor she heard a movement.

Amy Dudley had already taken two drops of the tincture and was surprised to feel an almost instant lethargy, a soothing dream-like state come over her.

'Mistress!'

Mary watched craftily as Lord Robert's wife stepped cautiously to the head of the stairs.

'There was one thing Lady Strange forbore to speak of," she paused as Amy lifted her foot to descend. "They say the Queen expects your husband's child.'

There was no need to go on. The woman above her froze, her face deathly white. Then she fainted, hitting the stair only once before landing on the floor at Mary's feet with a dull thud. It was more than the girl had hoped for. Lifting Lady Dudley's head Mary trembled with a mixture of fear and muted elation. The neck was broken. He was now free!

The seriousness of her position suddenly hit her in the menacing silence of the darkening house. How long before the servants returned? She should leave. And quickly.

Laying the dead woman's head back on the floor, Mary turned to leave. No. That wouldn't do. Stooping, she straightened Amy's cap, and noticing the velvet pouch containing the potions, removed it from the still warm fingers. Now there would be nothing in the house to show that there had been any visitors that afternoon.

Mulberry bushes heavily laden with glossy fruit lined the lane winding its way towards the town. The air was thick with the scents of summer and the sun dipped to the horizon spreading the last drop of molten gold across ripe grasses. It was good to be alive. The velvet package disappeared without trace into the thorny tendrils of the hedgerow to be nibbled and gnawed into a luxury lining for some fortunate field-mouse's winter home.

Discussing the latest Court scandal with Mary Winchcombe, Elizabeth had no idea how close she had been to it all. Lord Robert's wife was dead and he was banished to his house at Kew to await the jury's verdict on the cause of Amy's death. Had he been party to it? One thing she knew for certain. Despite the fact that he was now a free man the Queen never had any intention of marrying him no matter how he thrilled her with his touch and captivated her with his attentions. Elizabeth Tudor's head would always rule her heart.

None of that mattered now. For Mistress Fytton the present often faded into the past and on warm days she would sit under the trees beside the River Kennet drowsy after her drop of comfort. Bright images full of colour and sound took her back to times when her legs were not weak, her hands not shaky and her mind was as clear as crystal.

She felt again the newly awakened passions in Will's arms. Total love for a tiny wrinkled scrap of life as she held her daughter for the first time. The glorious freedom as she left the cloisters of St Mary's to set out for London and King Henry's magnificent Court. Youth was a time for looking forward. Old age was spent looking back. The seasons followed each other with monotonous regularity. And still Elizabeth couldn't die.

***

Mary Seymour stared in horror at the tiny shrivelled crone. Claw-like fingers plucked constantly at the worn fabric of her skirts and sleeves as though they still plucked herbs from the garden. The expression was blank. Not one sign remained of the sharp intellect which had been intact the last time they met. She should have realised. Oh, Lordy! The woman must be well past her seventieth year.

In desperation she flung herself down in front of Elizabeth and taking those wizened hands in her own, prayed that the mind was not as feeble as the body in which it now dwelt. This was her last hope. The only place she could hide. The only place where there was anyone who could help her. Save her!

'Mistress Fytton. Oh, please listen.' There was no one in the kitchen but she lowered her voice to a whisper. 'I am desperately in need of help.'

Elizabeth patted her hand absently. Pretty young woman. Reminded her of...? No. It had gone.

'Mistress, it's Kitty. You remember me, don't you?'

She should have kept in touch. But life had been so full. Men had yearned to possess her. Many a verse had been penned extolling the dark beauty of Mary Fytton and her impregnable virtue. If only she could have kept it that way. But everyone knew that the Queen would never marry Lord Robert, or anyone else for that matter and she'd hoped beyond hope that he would see sense after their secret and passionate affair. But no. He'd made it very clear that it was entirely her own problem.

If the Queen were ever to suspect, her life would be over. Others had been banished but she would surely suffer a much worse fate. So she had begged the Queen to let her travel to Littlecote where her old nurse was said to be dying. Her Majesty could not refuse that old woman's dying wish to see her ward one last time before she departed this earth. But to arrive and find that it was as good as true was a disaster.

She squeezed the fragile hands tighter in her agitation and Elizabeth winced in pain. For the first time since Mary had arrived, secretly, under cover of darkness, the former maid to royalty focused on the present.

'Kitty? Is it Kitty?' She tilted her head back and peered short-sightedly at the beautiful woman in the damp, travel-stained clothes,

Mary sent up a prayer of thanks. 'Aye, 'tis Kitty, and in need of your help.'

It was Kitty. Katherine's girl, returned home to see her. Of course she could help. Hadn't Elizabeth Fytton always helped?

'What is it then, child?'

Child! Mary was a sophisticated twenty-seven year old woman who had been totally bemused to find herself in the terrible predicament she had always scorned other silly chits for.

'I am to have a child. But…' she hesitated. 'The Queen must never find out, or it will be the end of me. Others have been banished but I would fare far worse.' How could she explain the twisting trails of fifteen years of intrigue that had finally brought her to this? It was impossible to describe the emotional tangles of a Court presided over by Queen Elizabeth. Subterfuge had been essential for all the ladies in the throes of romantic affairs but her situation was untenable. If the Queen heard the truth of her present plight she knew she would vanish. Without trace.

'And the father of the child? Does he know who your parents were? Is he trying to use you for gain?' That had always been Elizabeth Fyttons worry.

Mary shook her head. 'Mary Fytton. That is the only name I am known by.'

'And his name?' Elizabeth saw a flash of panic in the young woman's eyes.

'My Lord Robert, Earl of Leicester.'

The words trickled into silence on the breath of a whisper. Elizabeth heard and as realisation hit her she sat bolt upright in her chair, the last of her muddled memories overpowered by the enormity of the young woman's tragedy.

'But he and the Queen!'

'Just so,' Mary agreed, sweating with relief. The old woman understood.

'Robert Dudley. That boy always had a way with him.'

Lord Robert was no boy. He was past his fortieth year and heavier than he should have been for good health but he carried it handsomely. His hair was no longer dark but steely grey and when he looked at her in that certain way it dissolved all fears and made hope for a future grow. Mary kept her secret lover to herself but gloating satisfaction had turned to terror as she realised the consequences of their trysts.

Elizabeth Fytton felt an ice-cold tingle spread through her body. Mary Seymour was her father's daughter and no mistake. She looked like him and it seemed she lived like him. Dangerously. By the looks of her it was too late to rid her of the child. She would simply have to bide her time here until it was born,

Mary was appalled. Too late to be rid of it? Why? She had to be rid of it or how could she stay here in William Darrell's house? He would throw her out, or even worse, back to the Court. This child would bring disaster on the lot of them, Mister Darrell included.

'He will be none too pleased with this turn of events,' Elizabeth agreed, 'But the Queen gave you leave to visit me and mad as he is, he would not anger the Queen by refusing you hospitality. I can convince him to become a party to the deception. All he has to do is keep you out of sight and have the child sent to someone across the county. It has been done before and none the wiser. Or have you forgotten your own start in life?'

The trouble was that the two women had forgotten the notorious temper that had almost killed Robert Winchcombe all those years ago, sending him to travel the seven seas. Darrell roared like some wild beast when confronted with Mary and the reason for her untimely arrival.

'You always were a whore' He spat the words in her face, viciously, his spittle sliding thickly down her cheek. 'Your dress and painted face show you have not altered. Shall I shut you in the barn? Leather you to death?'

To Elizabeth's horror he grabbed Mary by the throat, the square strength of his finger bruising the flesh as his face twisted cruelly. Brutally. His eyes blazing as he shook her so forcefully that she could hardly breathe. Blackness swamped her.

'Slut! Wanton! Whore!' With one last squeeze at Mary's neck he let her drop to the floor where she lay in a crumpled heap, gasping painfully and choking in an effort not to vomit.

The murderous attack galvanised Elizabeth into action. Emitting the high-pitched, staccato notes of a crazed banshee she placed herself between his fury and the sobbing young woman. Darrell stared fixedly at the old crone, unable to tear his gaze from the sudden penetrating strength of those cat-like emerald eyes. His limbs felt as heavy as lead and his head as light as a feather. Mesmerised, he watched her lips part to reveal a grim, dark cavern of a mouth, protected at its upper and lower edges by an uneven row of blackened stumps, exposing themselves slowly from shrivelled gums. The worship stones of some ancient evil cult.

With an enormous effort William Darrell gathered his wits together. As the Devil was his witness they would pay for this. No one could do this to him and get away with it. He struck Elizabeth Fytton so hard across her wrinkled old face that her brain rattled in her skull. Then turning on his heel he left, slamming the heavy oak door behind him. Lock it! Leave the two alone together. The witch and the whore. The witch had little life left in her but the young woman was a different matter. From what they had told him, the Queen knew where she was, visiting her old nurse. What the Queen didn't know, and mustn't know, was that there would be a child. Her Majesty did not take kindly to her ladies making fast and loose with her courtiers to produce what she never could, and he himself had no wish to be implicated in what could be construed as treasonable. When it was all over he would see that the whore was safely back a Court without anyone knowing that she had been within a hundred miles of Littlecote.

For several seconds Elizabeth could hear nothing but the ringing echo of some far-off bell. A warning bell. Stars exploded brilliantly to blind her, like a cluster of comets foretelling doom. The whole room spun crazily around as she tried to regain her balance, tottering sideways on rickety legs. Then her vision cleared and in that moment it was as if the shutters of her inner mind were raised, allowing her to see the truth at last. Just before Will Darrell shut the door she heard it. The unmistakable swish of a forked tale. Smelt the nauseating stench of brimstone. The stench of evil!

They were trapped and Elizabeth knew this was the end. She had seen through the disguise and finally recognised the true form of the Master of Littlecote Manor.

In the weeks that followed the conditions in which they were forced to live told on both of them. Elizabeth mumbled constantly to herself and Mary's looks faded rapidly under the strain of the pregnancy, lack of nourishment and terror of what Darrell might do next. He was capable of anything.

The weather could not have been worse. The wind howled and screeched like a thousand fiends around the cornices and chimney pots of Littlecote as jagged barbs of lightning tore the thunderous sky to shreds. Rain lashed hard against the windows, threatening to break the glass and drown the occupants in the flood of the freak spring storms. And Mary's pains began.

At long last the door was unlocked and left open. Fires were built both in the bedchamber and out on the landing where the huge stone fireplace had stood gaunt and empty through the cold winter months. Mary was forced to wear a rough mask to disguise her. No one must know who she was even now. No word must ever reach the all-hearing ears of the Queen.

'Oh, Kitty. Kitty,' Elizabeth moaned to herself over and over again. 'What have I done? Why did I bring you here? I didn't know this was the Devil's domain. What price Tom Seymour's head now?'

They shuffled the feeble woman out of the chamber. She was too weak to help now. Unprotesting, she sat in the chair beside the roaring fire on the square landing listening to the wind and thunder as they all but drowned out Mary's anguished cries for help. At some point in the night a woman, muffled to the eyes, arrived drenched through to the skin. A midwife. It was a midwife, blind-folded so she wouldn't know where the house was. Nor who the woman was she had to attend.

William Darrell stood impassively, back to the fire, feet apart and hands clenched behind his back. Frowning. Waiting. Like a heavy bronze statue. He never looked at the old woman once. She might have been invisible but for the muttering in that strange unfathomable tongue. What happened to her now Darrell neither knew nor cared. He had made up his mind. He knew what he had to do. For his own safety.

Mary was weak and her struggle agonisingly slow. So slow that Elizabeth began to think that the midwife didn't know her job. If only she could help. She would have seen Kitty alright. It was taking too long. Far too long.

Just as she was beginning to give up hope for both mother and child a heart-rending scream cut her to the quick. The midwife had used her sense at last. In the wake of that agony came the child's first cries and in seconds the wet, naked infant was carried out to the master of the house.

'Where are the clothes? There are no garments laid out. No swaddling.' The midwife wrapped the baby in her apron, unsure what to do next.

'Attend your duties. The woman?' He indicated the room she had just left.

'She needs rest and nourishment, but she'll live.'

Elizabeth heard that with relief, and the baby had a healthy pair of lungs in him, so all should be well.

'Give the child to me.'

William Darrell held out his hands and the midwife automatically handed the baby to him. Only when he turned to the scorching flames did either woman realise what was in his mind. Both cried out at once.

'Give it to me!' Elizabeth's frail voice did its best to make itself heard. 'Give it to me!'

The midwife was on her knees pleading with him to let her take the child. She would never tell where she got it. Only let her take it.

'Get back in there!' The words were said solidly between clenched teeth and the poor woman knew there was nothing more she could do.

Elizabeth Fytton held out her stick-thin arms in vain. He didn't even see her.

For a fraction of a second Will Darrell hesitated, holding the new-born boy in the palms of his upturned hands, almost as though he was offering it to the demons still howling and screaming above him in the chimney. The child had to disappear. There was no other solution. He would not lose his liberty and his lands because of a stupid, odious slut.

Elizabeth's frantic cries gurgled in her throat. Inarticulate. She saw the tiny hands grasping at thin air. Making those first baby movements. Seeking the comfort of its mother's arms and breast. Miniature fingers curled and uncurled, tongues of fire behind them staining them red. Red as blood. She had been so wrong. She had failed to hide Thomas Seymour's offspring from the curse she had made and fortified over the years. It was time to give the Devil his due. Time for the final payment. And there was nothing she could do.

285

He was a perfect little boy. And she had killed him. The reward for Thomas Seymour's head was at last being claimed despite her efforts to thwart that demonic malevolence since Kitty had arrived. She had failed in that too. The satanic forces with which she had meddled were beyond her control. She had done it in revenge for her lover but now all the love and all the hate she had ever felt were embodied in that innocent babe. His tender life was a sacrifice to all those futile emotions.

The impact of that small, squirming body sent up a shower of sparks as it landed in the searing flames. Terrifying screams echoed round and round that enclosed space. The agonising sound of exquisite pain. A sound which would live forever in the fabric of that building. Elizabeth clawed the air as helplessly as the child had done, her fingers trying in vain to pluck time backwards, unable to close her eyes or ears to the horror going on before her.

His face immobile, as though set in stone, Will Darrell picked up another log from the stack in the corner and threw it with some force onto the burning pyre. Only the echoes continued to scream in her head. The new log spat and crackled and Elizabeth's hands twitched convulsively for one last time before complete paralysis set in.

Out of the fire rose a figure, indistinct at first, becoming more substantial as she stared.

The years fell away and Megan stood, not old, but young and smiling, holding the hand of a four-year-old boy. Beside her stood a man, his newborn daughter in his arms. Dafydd.

'Y cyfan er mwyn cariad, Elizabeth. It was all in the name of love.'

The vision changed so subtly that Elizabeth hardly noticed. The figure was now slim and lithe. Narrow shoulders and long dark hair. And laughter. Anne Boleyn , relaxed and happy smiled at her, Harry Percy at her side.

'I loved and was loved. Once and forever. It was all in the name of love.'

Elizabeth's sight became mercifully shrouded as she lost all sense of time and reason. Day and night merged. It was all one now. She was lost in swirling grey mists where there is no time.

Then, in the distance, clear as a bell, she heard a child's voice.

'Our Father, Who art in heaven, Hallowed be Thy name.'

Elizabeth remembered. Kitty had learnt it so well.

'Thy Kingdom come, Thy Will be done on earth as it is in heaven.'

There were no soulful Latin verses to frighten her. No more fear of God.

'Forgive us our trespasses. Oh, forgive us our trespasses…'

The grey shroud of mist was clearing and ahead there appeared a steady glow, as though the sun was reflecting on something bright.

'But deliver us from evil. Deliver us from evil. Deliver us from evil…'

It was the sun glinting on glass, the diamond windows of Gawsworth Hall. The air was clear and fresh and dew still clung to the cobbles of the yard as he strode towards her, hands outstretched and that most dazzling of smiles welcoming her home,

'Amen.'

He had never grown old. The dark gold hair was as tousled as that of a street urchin. Wild and untamed. Deep violet eyes shone with the promise of eternal happiness. He was strong. Handsome. And still dressed in the rich blue velvet cut with silver. Her family's colours. The colours of home. He was laughing as though he found the whole thing amusing. Hadn't he promised he would wait? For ever if he had to?

Elizabeth Fytton realised then the pettiness of worldly worries. How insignificant and small. Why had it all seemed so important at the time? What great imagined cause had driven her to hate so much? Driven her to murder? Only now did she see how futile it had been. How they had wasted their lives scurrying round in vicious little circles stabbing each other in the back and trampling so-called enemies underfoot in an effort to what…? Succeed? What, after all was the measure of a man's success? It would be a long time before there was heaven on earth but despite man's folly the door to heaven was as open wide as the black pit of despair into which she had almost fallen. And here, walking steadily towards her was her deliverance.

William Brereton had not forgotten her.

Suddenly she was free. Bonds and shackles fell away as she ran towards his outstretched arms on youthful, nimble limbs, her long auburn hair flying out behind her. No longer old. No longer crushed and beaten by life. The world and all its silly trivialities ceased to exist finally and forever as the strength of his embrace and the sweetness of his kiss carried her effortlessly into their heaven.

Love was all.

Her last, dying breath was a long, contented sigh.

Author's Note

History does not record the fate of Katherine Parr's daughter and it has always been assumed that she died in infancy.

The identity of the woman giving birth to the baby boy, being burnt to death at Littlecote in 1575 is also an unsolved mystery.

On that stormy night William Darrell, known as Mad Will Darrell, sent servants to bring Mother Barnes, a midwife, from Shefford in Berkshire to attend a lady about to have a child. She allowed herself to be blindfolded and taken on horseback to a "fayre house" where the door was opened by a tall, slender gentleman wearing black velvet who took her upstairs to a great chamber in which there was "a chimney, and therein a great fire." She was then brought into another chamber where there was "a bed rychly and gorgeously furnished, the curtains of the said bed being all closed."

Mother Barnes was promised a great reward if she would deliver the baby and make sure the woman lived.

When the boy was born there were no clothes and the midwife took the child out onto the landing where Mad Will Darrell waited and where the child was murdered.

Although Mother Barnes was bribed to keep silent she eventually went to the Magistrate and confessed. Having brought away a fragment of bed hangings and counted the number of stairs she was able identify the house. William Darrell was sent to the Fleet Prison after giving evidence of the murder to his neighbours, Lord Hertford and Sir Henry Knivett,.

He was released by Sir John Popham, later Lord Chief Justice of England and, when Wild Will Darrell was killed in a riding accident on October 1st, 1589, leaving no heirs, his property was bequeathed to that same Sir John Popham!